IMPOSSIBLE DESIRES

"Why do I feel as if you know more than you're telling, Mrs. Truitt?" Stuart asked me. My palms began to sweat, and I quickly swept them through my hair. I was glad of the darkness to hide the sudden coloring in my cheeks. I swallowed, the sound audible in the quiet room.

Stuart's expression changed, and his blue eyes flickered with suspicion in the dim lamplight.

But I couldn't tell this beloved stranger the impossible truth.

I could never allow myself to forget that Stuart Elliott was on the losing side of this Civil War, nor the fact that I had knowledge that could help the Confederacy. I simply wanted to find my missing daughter and return home—home to the twentieth century. My home, with its own host of memories. It was all I had left, and I wanted it back.

I had no desire to get embroiled in this beautiful man's life, to make new memories, to face new heartbreak, I told myself.

I just wanted to go home. . . .

IN THE SHADOW OF THE MOON

KAREN WHITE

LOVE SPELL BOOKS ✦ NEW YORK CITY

*To Tim, Meghan, and Connor—whose presence in
my life means more than I can ever say.*

A LOVE SPELL BOOK®

August 2000

Published by

Dorchester Publishing Co., Inc.
276 Fifth Avenue
New York, NY 10001

Cover art by John Ennis
www.ennisart.com

ISBN 0-505-52395-7

The name "Love Spell" and its logo are trademarks of Dorchester
Publishing Co., Inc.

Printed in the United States of America.

ACKNOWLEDGMENTS

I'd like to thank my ever-faithful critique partners, Susie Crandall and Vicky Harden, for their immense help and encouragement during the writing and re-writing process. Karen Moser for her invaluable assistance in crafting certain scenes (she knows which ones). Lisa Northcutt, Mary Zipp, Donna Michael, June White, and JoEllen Richardson—thank you for being my first fans and crying for more chapters. You all kept me writing.

Thank you to the members of CompuServe's Civil War forum for all your technical help—especially Pappy Harmon, who shared so much of himself and wasn't embarrassed to show me what Civil War soldiers really wore under their uniforms. Julie Anna Williams deserves a big thanks for telling me all I needed to know about nineteenth century unmentionables and outerwear. And to Jeff Beckner, whose knowledge of American history is unparalleled and whose turn of phrase is greatly appreciated.

Thanks also to the wonderful members of CompuServe's Research and Craft forum—especially Ellen Mandell, Janet McConnaughey, and Rosina Lippi-Green. And a huge thanks to Diana Gabaldon, whose writing is an inspiration and whose encouragement and teaching has meant a great deal to me.

IN THE SHADOW OF THE MOON

> *"The law of humanity ought to be composed of the past, the present, and the future, that we bear within us; whoever possesses but one of these terms, has but a fragment of the law of the moral world."*
>
> *Edgar Quinet*

Prologue

The house stood strong and silent, bidding me to come nearer as if it were an old friend needing companionship. The windows stared at me with an odd familiarity, and the feeling of having been there before hit me with a force so strong that I had to stop in the middle of the brick sidewalk. I grabbed my husband's hand and stared.

"I want this house."

Jack turned to me as if to say something but remained silent. He was well acquainted with my particular brand of stubbornness.

Weeds as high as my pregnant swell grew behind the dilapidated picket fence, the roof over the porch sagged desperately, shattered panes looked out of the two dormer windows, and the entire place needed painting. But four stately columns stood proud sentry, and an elegant fan window crowned the massive front door, while white rocking chairs perched invitingly on the sweeping front porch. It was a remarkable house, but there was something else about it that caused me to pause before it—some sort of unexplainable connection I felt to it. I pictured in my mind's eye Southern belles, gallant gentlemen, and well-mannered children from a time gone by, sweeping down the still-graceful steps.

9

"I hate to disappoint you, Laura, but I don't think it's for sale. I don't see a realtor's sign."

I was already pushing open the front gate, its rusty hinges squeaking in protest.

"We'll never know unless we ask." I waddled up the front steps to the porch, grasping the chipped and peeling wood banister.

Due to the imminent expansion of our family, our Atlanta apartment was no longer large enough. We needed a house. Not just brick, mortar, and roof shingles but a home to love and call our own and raise our family in. An older house with creaky floors and impossible-to-heat rooms with high ceilings. This was my house.

In the absence of a doorbell, I grabbed the dull brass knocker and banged a little too loudly. Jack had his back to the door and was surveying the wreckage of the front yard and porch. I didn't need to see his face to know what expression he was wearing.

I waited for several minutes, ignoring the urge to tap my foot. I was about to knock again when the sound of a latch being drawn from inside rattled the heavy door.

The woman opening the door was tall, like me, but her shoulders were slightly stooped. Still, the intensity of her blue eyes seemed to add height and strength to her willowy figure. A halo of white hair framed an attractive oval face. With her smooth, supple skin, she could have been anywhere from sixty to eighty years old. I made a mental note to ask her what skin-care products she used.

Her smile revealed a row of even white teeth. "Oh, my! You're finally here," she said.

I looked at her in confusion. "Have we met?"

She opened the door wider, and I caught a whiff of moth-balls and furniture polish. I inadvertently wrinkled my nose and stifled a cough. My sense of smell had become acutely sensitive since my pregnancy, and even the slightest odor could overwhelm me. I must have staggered a bit, because the woman grabbed my forearm in a surprisingly firm grasp and brought me inside through the receiving hall to a sofa in the front parlor.

"My dear, you must be careful of this heat in your condition." She motioned Jack to take a seat opposite me in a fiddleback chair. Her voice was rich with the warm accent reminiscent of the Deep South.

I should have been embarrassed by the situation—Jack obviously was, as he kept trying to offer apologies to our impromptu hostess—but strangely, I felt very much at ease in this lady's presence and in her house.

The woman disregarded Jack's sputtering and excused herself to get us all some iced tea and refreshments. Jack was raised up north in Connecticut, where, I figured, people didn't just drop in on strangers to have tea with them. I'd never done it before, either, but for some reason, this stranger didn't seem to think we were imposing on her. There was something in the way she looked at me, as if we had met before.

Situated against one wall was an upright piano, its polished surface in marked contrast to the other dusty pieces of furniture in the room. The ivory veneer was missing on the G key above middle C, as if something heavy had dropped on it and chipped it off.

"Laura, what are we doing here?" Jack busily eyed the cracked wall plaster and a water stain on the ceiling. "You can't possibly be thinking of buying this house."

I rose to stand behind him and put my arms around his shoulders. Kissing him on the cheek, I followed his gaze toward a mess of wires hanging from the ceiling. "Jack, you've got to look beneath the surface to see the real beauty here. Look at those dentil moldings on the ceiling, and the hardwood floors. I bet these walls are a foot thick." I moved over to one and tapped it lightly to make my point. I didn't really care. The emotions I was feeling had nothing to do with plumbing and insulation. The sense of home surrounded me, emanating from the walls. The roof could have been falling in, and I still would have wanted to buy this house.

I sat down just as our hostess came back bearing a large

silver tray of tall iced tea glasses and an assortment of cookies and cakes.

She smiled as she handed me a plate and a frosted glass. "I hope you don't mind my serving you leftovers from yesterday's ladies' bridge meeting. The pastries the girls bring are just so delicious, and my maid and I could never eat them all before they spoiled."

I realized I was starving, but my manners finally interceded. I struggled to sit up straight. "We really hate to intrude. We're Laura and Jack Truitt, and we were merely inquiring about the—"

"House," she completed for me. "I knew you were coming. I was told to expect you. I just didn't know when. I've been wanting to sell this place for years now, but I knew I needed to wait for you." She smiled serenely and settled back against a once-elegant but now faded sofa. "When you've got your strength back, I'll be happy to give you the grand tour."

I glanced over at Jack, who had edged to the front of his seat as if preparing to make an escape. I, too, was feeling a bit strange but not in the least wary.

"I don't understand." I shifted in my seat, accidentally knocking a cookie off my plate and onto the threadbare needlepoint carpet.

As sprightly as a teenager, the white-haired lady leapt up and retrieved it. "I bet that sounded odd, didn't it?" she asked. "Perhaps I should introduce myself. I'm Margaret-Ann Cudahy." She paused to wait for a reaction from us. None was forthcoming, as the name meant absolutely nothing to me or, I was sure, to Jack.

"Do you know my mother, Mrs. Cudahy?" I asked, trying to find a common thread. "Her name is Nancy Chrisler."

She shook her head. "No, I don't believe so. The person who told me you were coming was my great-grandmother, and she passed on years ago. She didn't explain it to me fully, since it didn't really concern me, but she said you would understand it all eventually."

Unease brushed the back of my neck, but I was unwilling

to leave. The overwhelming feeling of being home surrounded me, and this woman and her house intrigued me.

"How long has your great-grandmother been dead, Mrs. Cudahy?" I asked, trying to figure out how her relative could have known me.

"Oh, since 1935. I remember it well. It was the middle of the Great Depression, and I was thirteen years old. She died three days after her hundredth birthday."

"But I wasn't born until 1965! This isn't making any sense at all!" I looked at Jack as he sprang from his chair and quickly stood over me.

"I think we need to be going, Laura." Jack grasped both of my hands and tried to haul me off the sofa.

I held his hands but gave a quick shake of my head. I was not through with this conversation or this house.

"No, Jack. Not yet." His eyes searched my face, and then he let go. He kept one hand resting on my shoulder. I reached for it, my fingers brushing his gold wedding band.

I turned my attention to Mrs. Cudahy. "If you don't mind, could we see the house now?"

"Of course, dear." And with that she helped me off the sofa and slipped her arm through mine. Jack followed closely behind.

The house had four rooms on the first floor and four on the second. A later addition had added a fifth smaller bedroom upstairs, making for interesting architecture at the back of the house. The rooms had lofty twelve-foot ceilings and were all interconnected within the house. The one exception was the preacher's room, with its single entrance from the rear porch. The huge receiving hall ran the entire depth of the house, with large doors in the front and back that could be left open to create a breezeway. A staircase rose from each end of the hall, the one in the back, less elaborate than the other, presumably for the use of servants.

"Legend has it that some of General Sherman's troops garrisoned here in Roswell rode their horses right through this front hall, slashing at everything with their sabers." Mrs. Cudahy waved an arm back and forth, slicing the air, illustrating

13

her story. "Most of the other homes in the area were heavily looted, but not this one. No one knows for sure how, but evidently the family living here was forewarned of the invasion and had hidden just about everything of value. Bulloch Hall, down the road, was saved from being torched because both the owner and the Union commander were Masons. However, local historians aren't sure why this house was left intact." Mrs. Cudahy paused to run her hands gently over the fine, peeling wallpaper. "They did destroy most of the outbuildings and crops and confiscated the remaining livestock and slaves. There's a reason Sherman's name isn't brought up in polite company even today," she said with a smile.

"I hear Sherman was one for the pretty ladies," she continued, giggling like a schoolgirl. "It wouldn't surprise me at all if many of the great houses in Georgia survived because of the Southern women who personally convinced Sherman to spare their property." Mrs. Cudahy gave me such a cheeky glance that I giggled, too. I wondered at her story. I had read biographies of Sherman for a college history paper, and I didn't recall any wartime dalliances. But that was merely the written record. Word-of-mouth stories might be equally valid.

Jack and I held hands as Mrs. Cudahy led us through the back door onto the porch. It was cooler there in the shade, with a soft, warm wind caressing our faces. "The house was built around 1840. As you can see, it's situated on a high point to take advantage of the Chattahoochee River breezes." She caressed the smooth wood balustrade, her hands surprisingly unmarred by time.

"Before the War of Northern Aggression, the property had almost three hundred acres, all planted with cotton, and thirty slaves to work the fields and tend to the house. But that's all gone now, except for the springhouse and hennery out back." Mrs. Cudahy looked at me with a wide grin. "Don't suppose you'll be raising chickens, though!" Then, as perfect strangers are wont to do, she patted my swollen belly.

"Looks like y'all have been busy! This house sure misses the sound of babies. It's been a long time since the pitter-patter of little feet went up and down these floors." Her voice trailed away as she led us to the master bedroom. I imagined the sound of children's voices echoing through the rooms, and I thought, yes, this is home.

She preceded us through the doorway, and I stood, paralyzed, at the threshold. I knew this room, as if I had awakened in it many times. A magnificent mahogany half-tester bed with an elaborately carved pediment hung with heavy draperies dominated one side of the room. A marble-topped dressing table with graceful cabriole legs and an ornate mirror stood between the two floor-to-ceiling windows. A splendid armoire towered toward the ceiling at the other end of the chamber. I felt completely at ease and could picture myself at the dressing table, brushing my hair. I must have seen this room before in a magazine.

"This furniture has been in my family for 150 years. All of it was made by Mr. Mallard himself in his shop in New Orleans for this very room. It's never been moved. Probably too big and heavy to go anywhere else," Mrs. Cudahy explained as she walked over to the bed and smoothed the faded yellow spread. She looked up at Jack and gave him a wide smile. "I bet this bed saw a lot of action in its day. Most of my ancestors were conceived on it!"

Jack, who until that moment was not known to be a prude, turned bright pink. He quickly looked at me, and I buried my face in his shoulder, struggling not to laugh out loud.

Mrs. Cudahy smiled gently at Jack. "I'm sorry if I've shocked you. I used to be an opera singer and traveled and lived in all sorts of strange places. I suppose it's rubbed off on me a little." She winked. "Plus, I'm an old lady. I'm supposed to be a bit batty."

Jack cleared his throat. "So, this house has been in your family since it was built?"

"Yes, but I'm the last in the line, I'm afraid. My husband and I never had any children. Though it wasn't for lack of trying." She grinned mischievously at me, and I grinned back.

As she led us back through the house toward the parlor, I noticed finely carved moldings and thick mahogany doors with leaded glass transoms and heavy brass fittings, all beautiful but very worn. I could tell that a massive renovation would be needed to restore the house to its former splendor. Still, the feeling of familiarity I had had when standing in front of the house persisted, and I could clearly picture in advance what I would see when we turned each corner and opened every door. It was disconcerting, since I was sure I had never been in the house before, but it was also comforting in a way, as if this were a reunion between friends.

Once we were back in the parlor, Mrs. Cudahy refilled our glasses and motioned for us to be seated. Jack sat next to me, holding my hand, his thumb rubbing circles over my knuckles.

The nagging questions in my mind wouldn't go away. "Mrs. Cudahy, I would appreciate it if you could explain further how you knew I would be coming. I'm pretty sure we're not related, so I can't understand how any relative of yours would know about me."

Mrs. Cudahy stood. "Perhaps if I gave you something, it would explain things better than I can," she said as she left the room, leaving a scent trail of Tea Rose perfume.

Jack leaned over to me and whispered, his eyebrows wiggling, "She's probably going to get a gun or something. We should leave now before she gets back."

I elbowed him in the ribs. "Very funny, Jack. Don't you feel it? That feeling of rightness, that this is where we should raise our family?"

He looked at me with a raised eyebrow, then smiled, reaching for my other hand.

"Laura, I certainly hope it's not just your pregnancy hormones talking, because if we buy this house, it'll be a long-term commitment."

"Jack, I'm not blind to the condition of the house, but I'm going with my sixth sense here. I really want this house. Please trust me—have I ever steered you wrong?" I squeezed his hands, my eyes searching his.

He opened his mouth to say something but closed it again when Mrs. Cudahy returned and handed me an object wrapped in yellowed newspapers. "I hope this explains some things."

I gingerly unwrapped the layers of paper. Dust motes rose

from the wrinkled bundle and danced in a shaft of light from the parlor window. Inside lay an ornate silver picture frame. I absently rubbed my thumb over the black tarnish. Then I peered closely at the picture, and my breath caught in my throat. It was a sepia-toned likeness of a woman wearing nineteenth-century clothing and, around her neck, what appeared to be an old-fashioned key hanging from a chain. Her straight dark hair was swept up off her face and coiled atop her head. Her large light eyes staring back at me were tilted slightly at the corners, and her nose was a little too pert for conventional beauty. The upturned lips were reminiscent of the Mona Lisa and anything but demure. I had seen this face before many times—every time I looked in a mirror.

"Where did this come from?" I croaked, as I couldn't seem to find my voice.

Jack leaned over my shoulder. "Oh, my God! It's you, Laura, or someone who looks a hell of a lot like you." He tried to pry it from me to get a closer look, but I couldn't let it go.

Mrs. Cudahy moved closer to Jack. "It is a remarkable resemblance. I wish I had something to add, but my great-grandmother only told me that a woman who looked like this would come to purchase the house. I didn't question her very closely, and she died shortly thereafter. She only asked that I save this picture to give to you." She bent down to pick up the scattered pieces of old newspaper and crumpled them into a ball.

I turned the frame over in my shaking hands and gently pried off the back. Perhaps something was written on the reverse side of the photograph. I removed the delicate picture to examine it more closely, but there were no identifying marks. I studied the key around the woman's neck, hoping it would offer some clue. I thought it a strange ornament to be hanging on a necklace, and I wondered about its meaning. But the face of the woman was my own. There were no subtle differences to account for generations of genetic progression. Had I somehow lived before, and in this very house? I had no idea, but

17

odder things had been known to happen to people. Still, I pressed for some sort of logical answer.

"Mrs. Cudahy, perhaps we're related. If you don't mind, I'd like to borrow this picture and ask my mother about it. She can trace our family back to the American Revolution, and if there's a connection, I'm sure she'll find it." I knew I was overlooking her great-grandmother's prediction regarding me, but I had no idea where to look for answers to that gnawing question. Finding a familial connection would be sufficient explanation for me.

A strong kick from the baby pushed all these thoughts to the back of my mind. I must have gasped, because Jack turned to me and placed his hand over mine on my abdomen. He never tired of feeling our child inside me, and a boyish grin erupted on his face.

"See?" I said, grinning back. "The baby wants this house, too."

Jack leaned his forehead to mine and let go a deep sigh. "If that child is as stubborn as his or her mother, I know better than to fight you both."

Mrs. Cudahy stood. "You can keep the picture as long as you like, dear. As for the house, I've been waiting a long time to sell it. I can certainly wait a little longer while you two discuss it. You know where to find me."

We thanked her for her hospitality and walked slowly to the front door. Impulsively, I leaned over and kissed her soft cheek. "Thank you, Mrs. Cudahy. You'll be hearing from us."

I led Jack out into the front yard and looked up at the house, the shadows of its four columns reaching out like arms to embrace us. I kissed him lightly on the lips. "I love you, Jack Truitt."

He kissed me back, his mouth warm and moist. "I love you, too."

A soft river breeze stirred the wilted garden, summoning the scent from the boxwoods and tickling my brain with a remembrance of something I couldn't quite recall. The baby kicked again as the wind jostled the leaves of an old oak tree, sending one spiraling down to me like a distant memory. For a moment I clutched it tightly, and then I held it up again, watching as the wind carried it away.

"When beggars die, there are no comets seen; The heavens themselves blaze forth the death of princes."
William Shakespeare

Chapter One

Our daughter, Annie, was born exactly two weeks after we moved into the house. Although my strange attraction to our new home never faded, and questions remained unanswered, I pushed them aside and threw myself into my new role of mother.

An engaging and guileless little girl, Annie had inherited equal parts from each parent. She had bright green eyes and an odd, crescent-shaped birthmark on the inside of her upper arm from her mother, and fair hair and perfectly shaped ears from her father. But her little personality was all her own. She was everything I could have wanted in a child.

Annie was a gentle baby, which made it easy for us to resume our active lifestyle even when she was still quite young. She went everywhere with us, her fair head poking up over the carrier strapped to one of her parents' backs, and we enjoyed being together, our little family.

Annie was only twenty-three months old when we took her to see her first comet atop Moon Mountain. Sky-watching was a hobby of mine, introduced to me as a child by my Cherokee grandmother, and I was eager to share my passion with my daughter. Genetti's Comet would be sharing the sky with a total lunar eclipse—a rare enough event to warrant mention in the *Atlanta Journal-Constitution*. Moon Mountain wasn't really a mountain but rather a largish hill and the perfect vantage point for observing celestial happenings. According to my grandmother, who was widely known for her eccentricities, it was also a place with strong, unknown powers. She called it a sacred place to the Cherokee, who had ruled this part of the country for centuries.

Jack grumbled only slightly when I roused him that Saturday morning. It was usually his sleeping-in day, but I had made plans for an early start of antique shopping and general family togetherness before the lunar eclipse that night. He leaned over and rubbed his stubbly chin on my bare midriff where my nightgown had ridden up. Resting his head on my abdomen, he gently traced a circle around my navel with one finger. I ran my hands through the thick mane of his hair and sighed softly. He looked up at me with a raised eyebrow.

"Laura, why don't we just skip the shooting star and stay in bed all day?" He raised himself to nuzzle my neck, sending delicious shivers down my spine.

I pressed my head back into the pillow and tapped him gently on the head. "It's not a shooting star—it's a comet and an eclipse. It'll really be spectacular."

"Hmm," he mumbled.

I shifted my head, enjoying his attentions to my earlobe. Slowly, he worked the spaghetti straps of my nightgown off my shoulders and moved his mouth lower. I looked down at his dark blond head, and my body flooded with love and desire for this man. I sighed, and our eyes met.

His moist lips formed a slow grin. "I've got powerful methods of persuasion, you know."

I sat up, pulling off my nightgown completely. "Yes, you do. You certainly do."

We made love slowly, in the comfortable way old lovers do, and when it was over we held each other close and listened to the sounds of morning outside our window.

"Mommy!" came the shout from across the hall.

Reluctantly, I threw off the sheets. "It was nice while it lasted," I said as I slipped out of bed and into my robe. I leaned down to give him a kiss and then hurried to the nursery, where I was being summoned in a tone now approaching hysteria.

Annie clutched the top rail of her crib and had huge tears of distress running down her cheeks. I tripped over the object of her anguish and bent to pick up her stuffed giraffe, an apparent victim of a fall through the crib slats. Her chubby arms stretched up to greet me as I approached. I handed her the giraffe and reached for her.

"Hello, Morning Glory," I whispered as I picked her up and kissed her baby-fine hair. The mingled scents of baby sweat and shampoo wafted up my nose. "Can Mommy have some good-morning butterflies?"

Annie put her face right up to mine and fluttered her eyelashes, tickling my cheek. She then laid her head on my shoulder, a cue for me to sing and waltz. This had been our morning ritual for as long as we both could remember. I sang to the tune of the perennial favorite "You Are My Sunshine," but the words were my own, sung for my own little ray of sun.

"You are my sweet pea, my only sweet pea, you bring me sunshine every day." I sang as I twirled my delighted partner, my bare feet padding gently on the hardwood floor. "From your button nose to your baby toes, I will love you for all time."

As I laid her on the changing table to dress her, Jack came in to give Annie her good-morning kiss. "Maybe we should get your mother to baby-sit tonight. I mean, Annie will probably sleep through the whole thing, anyway."

I finished snapping up the bottom of Annie's one-piece outfit and lifted her. "Oh, Jack, I thought it would be so much fun with the three of us. My dad used to take me when I was her age, and I remember watching the sky with him. It's such a magical thing."

He shrugged. "All right—if it means that much to you." He kissed me quickly on the lips and reached for his daughter.

21

Karen White

I was fascinated by comets, those ghostly apparitions from the past traveling along sweeping pathways through space and time. Historically, comets have often been considered harbingers of doom, having made appearances prior to the assassination of Julius Caesar, the Black Death, the defeat of the Alamo, and the fall of Atlanta to the Yankees in the summer of 1863. Ancient man thought that comets were God's messengers, alerting mankind to what was to come. Despite Mr. Halley's scientific explanation of the origins of comets, I, too, thought there was something more ethereal about those dirty snowballs of ice and dust.

I was especially intrigued because of something my grandmother had told me when I was a girl. As I was leaving her house after a day of learning some Native American folklore and her own brand of astronomy, Grandma had held my arm and whispered in my ear, "Be careful of moonless nights and speeding stars. Though the magic is there, there can be danger, too, and great heartache."

I had no idea what she was talking about, and she refused to elaborate further on subsequent visits. But her prophetic words would always return to me as I climbed Moon Mountain to witness yet another astronomical event.

Double-checking the diaper bag for Annie's hat and sunscreen, I loaded it into the Explorer. As I bent to tie my shoelaces, a bead of perspiration dripped onto my knee. At ten o'clock in the morning it was already sweltering, a typical August day in Georgia.

It had rained during the night—not one of those gentle rains found in northern climes but a powerful combination of window-shaking thunder and daylight-making lightning common to southern coastal states. But the sky above was now cloudless, a blue dome over the baking earth.

By the end of the day, we found ourselves at Moon Mountain. The National Park Service had fashioned a small asphalt parking lot at the foot of the hill, and I was happy to see that there were no other cars. Even at nine o'clock at night, the heat rose from the blacktop. Perspiration prickled down my back as I stooped to get our sleeping Annie out of her car seat.

Exhaustion had finally overtaken her, but I hoped she would wake up in time to see her first comet. Her head lolled to one side, and I carefully cradled it as I lifted her out. I zipped her snugly into the carrier on Jack's back and laid a gentle kiss on her sweaty cheek.

A gravel path cut across the hillside and disappeared around a bend. After checking the car doors, we began our ascent, refraining from talking so we wouldn't disturb Annie. The only sounds besides the crunching of the gravel beneath our feet were the constant whirring of the cicadas and the distant hum of traffic from Highway 9.

Despite the additional twenty pounds on his back, Jack kept a grueling pace. My shirt began to stick to my back and quickly became drenched under the arms. With a hasty glance behind me to ensure that we were alone, I slid off my backpack for a moment to remove my shirt and continue the climb in my bra. Jack raised an eyebrow and shook his head in mock exasperation.

My heart softened as I watched Annie in her little cocoon, one plump hand resting on her father's shoulder and the thumb of her other hand firmly planted in her mouth. During our climb, I could occasionally hear frenzied sucking coming from the bundle on Jack's back, and it made me smile. A burst appendix when I was sixteen had caused adhesions on my reproductive organs. My doctors never really expected me to become pregnant but had used every weapon in their fertility arsenal to prove themselves wrong. She was worth every visit to the fertility clinic, every poke and prod from the doctors, every ounce of terror and despair we had gone through to have her. We had almost lost her to placenta abruption in the delivery room, and only an emergency C-section had saved her life. We longed for another child, but the doctors said the risks would be high, and we weren't yet ready to accept them.

We reached the crest in about thirty minutes. I quickly took off my backpack and rifled through it for Annie's blanket. I spread it on the ground beside a pine tree and gently lifted the still-sleeping Annie down. Tucking her stuffed giraffe under her arm, I felt the smooth rhythm of her breathing. She stirred

23

slightly and raised her ruffle-covered rump in the air. Her thumb found her mouth again, and she settled back down.

I walked toward the edge of the rise, where a coin-operated telescope was mounted, unnecessary to revel in the beauty of the view from our secluded spot. The twinkling skyline of Atlanta lay to the south, and I could pick out the NationsBank tower rising higher than its sister skyscrapers. A halo of light, outlined in the purple tinge of dusk, surrounded the skyline in gentle benediction. Genetti's comet was dimly visible on the horizon.

Jack approached and pressed his now bare chest against my back. I reached behind me to grasp hold of him. His expert hands quickly unsnapped my bra and then slid around to cup my breasts. I laid my head on his shoulder as he planted lingering kisses on my neck.

"You taste salty," he said as his lips traveled down to my shoulder.

I sighed, enjoying the caress of goose bumps as they traveled down my spine. "Jack, not here. Someone might come." Annie grunted in her sleep, and I shifted around in Jack's arms. "Can you hold that thought until later?"

He touched my cheek, his fingers slowly traveling down to my neck. "If I have to." He reached behind me and re-fastened my bra.

"I have something to cool you off." I stepped back and walked toward where we had dumped our gear. "We should drink something so we don't become dehydrated. I learned that in CPR class." I squatted in front of my backpack and pulled out two bottles of water.

We sat next to each other, leaning against a scrubby tree trunk, and drank our water in companionable silence while waiting for night to fall completely. A soft snore came from Annie, and the rhythm of it, along with our earlier exertions, lulled us both into a semi-stupor. Jack's head sagged forward, and I reached to awaken him, only to find myself seemingly paralyzed. I willed my limb to move, but it lay limp and useless at my side. I struggled to keep my eyes open, but it was as if an unseen force was dragging me into a deep, dark slumber. I made an attempt to wiggle my toes, recalling how doing that had brought me out of bad dreams when I was a girl. I was completely immobile. The last thing I remembered was reaching for Annie.

I dreamed I was running through darkness. My legs were leaden weights and would not propel me toward a dim light shining though the murkiness. A pervading sense of loss enveloped me, and I knew escape was neither imminent nor possible. A loud whirring sound buzzed in my ear, and I turned my head from side to side to make it stop.

I woke up to find a cicada screeching loudly next to my head on the tree trunk. I struggled to orient myself, then remembered where I was. It was too dark to see my watch, but the sunlight filtering around the earth's edge had turned the moon a vivid red. A black shadow already hooded a quarter of the moon, causing me to recall the Mayan myth of a jaguar wolfing down the lunar orb.

I reached over to feel for Annie, and my hand found the warm tangle of her hair. I moved my palm to her back to feel her strong, rhythmic breathing and the heat of her body. Jack's outline slumped asleep against our tree trunk, and I decided not to disturb them just yet. I wanted a private moment with the comet. Standing unsteadily and trying to recall how much wine I had had at dinner, I walked to the clearing to get a better view of the eclipse. I caught a strong whiff of gardenias, which surprised me, as I did not remember seeing any in the vicinity.

Genetti's Comet glowed brightly against the darkened sky. Suddenly, a chill swept down my spine, causing the hair on the back of my neck to rise. I shivered and wrapped my arms around myself. It was then that I realized that the insects had ceased their nocturnal chorus. I couldn't hear the traffic anymore. Silence hugged the hilltop, enshrouding us. Then a wind began to blow, whipping my hair about my face, its sound no gentle whooshing but a howl. The strong scent of gardenias assaulted my nose again, and I trembled with an inchoate fear. My head suddenly pounded, and the blood rushed through my ears. In abrupt, overwhelming pain, I fell to my knees.

Annie. Something was wrong, and I had to get to Annie. I

panicked, trying to rise and reach the spot where I had left her. In the dark I stumbled on something and fell to the ground. I cried out Jack's name, but I couldn't hear anything over the din of the wind. I crawled on my hands and knees, crying out their names. Only the wind answered me. My fingers grasped the edge of the blanket where Annie had been sleeping, and I began to sob with relief. Until I realized the blanket was empty. The bile of pure terror crept up my throat, and I threw up violently. I was still gagging when a hand touched my shoulder.

I screamed, then felt the reassuring touch of Jack's embrace and heard the soothing sound of his voice. "Laura, it's me. Are you okay?"

I struggled in his arms. "Jack, do you have Annie? I can't find her!" My voice sounded frantic, and I worked hard to bring it under control.

"No. Isn't she on the blanket?" Jack released me and searched the blanket.

"No, Jack, she's not there! Oh, God! We've got to find her."

The shadow slowly swallowed the moon. I threw my shirt back on, grabbed a flashlight, and went flying down the path in search of my daughter.

Neither we nor the police found any trace of her. Huge search groups swarmed the area for days despite the heat and torrential rains. After a week, they had given up. Nothing was found—no clothes, no blood, no signs of anything. It was as if she had been absorbed into the night. I know the police suspected us, but no evidence ever surfaced to incriminate either one of us, or anyone else. Annie was just . . . gone.

In the days that followed her disappearance, guilt gnawed at my conscience. I had been the one to insist we bring her to Moon Mountain rather than leave her with my mother as Jack had suggested. My grandmother's warning spun around inside my head. Was this what she had meant? Why hadn't I listened? I almost wanted Jack to lash out at me, to blame me. His silence was worse than any accusation could have been.

When the doorbell rang two weeks later, I was in the middle

of mending one of Annie's dresses. The torn seam at the bottom had resulted from her stepping on the hem as she tried to stand up. She kept doing it again and again, thinking it enormously funny. I had joined in, for her silly giggles were hard to resist.

My needle jabbed and plunged into the yellow fabric, closing the seam surely and swiftly, until I realized the doorbell had rung at least three or four times. I laid a hand on Jack's shoulder as I passed him, his eyes blankly staring at a rerun of *Quantum Leap*. The old clock in the hallway chimed the hour, echoing throughout the still house. I opened the door, still clutching Annie's dress.

A woman and a man stood on my front porch, looking uncomfortable in the heat.

The man spoke first. "Mrs. Truitt?"

I stared at them for a moment before finding my voice.

"Yes, I'm Laura Truitt."

"Mrs. Truitt, I'm Detective Peterson from the Atlanta police, and this is my partner, Detective McGraw." He indicated the woman with his chin. "We have some news for you."

He paused. I could hear the sounds from the TV inside and Jack coughing. A car drove by our house, loud music from its radio evaporating as the car got farther away.

"Mrs. Truitt?"

I must have said something.

"Mrs. Truitt, we've found a child's body. We'd like you to come downtown to—"

The yellow dress fell from my hands, puddling on the floor like crumpled sunshine. "Annie?" My voice sounded stronger than I expected.

"The body is unidentified, but it matches the description of your daughter." The woman's voice was kind, and she took a step toward me.

"A body . . . and you want me to . . . you need me to come down . . ."

I looked behind me and into the parlor at Jack. Angry red marks of exhaustion marred the skin under his eyes. His sunstreaked blond hair looked gray against the pallor of his skin,

27

and for the first time since the beginning of our ordeal, I knew that his pain was as great as mine. I recalled how he had wept when Annie was born, and I suddenly wanted to slam the door shut and erase the choked sound of the detective's voice from my memory. I had the impulse to run into Jack's arms and pretend that everything was normal again and that our dear, sweet Annie was upstairs in her crib. But Jack's arms lay powerless and empty beside him on the sofa, his palms turned upward in silent supplication.

Detective Peterson cleared his throat, and I turned back to face him and his partner.

"Mrs. Truitt, we need you to come to the morgue for identification." More firmly, he said, "You should have someone bring you. If . . . well, sometimes, afterward, it's not easy to drive. . . ."

"I'll have my husband with me," I said. "We'll come right now."

After finding out where to go, I shut the door silently, wondering how I would tell Jack. I forced myself to breathe. Then I sat on the stairs and took as many deep breaths as I could.

As the Explorer hurtled south on I-85, the huge and shimmering Atlanta skyline beckoned from the horizon. The giant peach structure rose up on our left, and I thought of how Annie always pointed at it and said "apple" when we passed by. I stole a look at Jack and saw a tear escaping down his cheek and knew he was remembering, too.

Jack and I clung to each other as we walked through the fluorescent-lit halls of Grady Hospital, where the city morgue was located. The unnatural light made the hollows of Jack's face more prominent, and he seemed to age before my eyes.

We walked ahead as a unit, my husband and I, and were led to the two detectives, who waited by a cold metal slab. On it a white sheet covered a small form, its two little feet sticking up barely high enough to tent the fabric.

A coroner's assistant pulled back the top of the sheet, revealing dirty blond hair matted to a delicate forehead, partially obscuring a large, plum-colored bruise. Translucent skin stretched over the small bones of the face, and the dark lashes on the closed eyelids fanned the pale cheeks.

It wasn't Annie.

I broke down then. I don't know if it was from relief that it wasn't our baby or grief for this loss of gentle life. Maybe it was for all the empty years that I knew lay before us.

"Press close bare-bosom'd night—press close magnetic nourishing night!
Night of south winds! Night of the large few stars!
Still nodding night! Mad naked summer night."
Walt Whitman

Chapter Two

The loss of Annie had been the beginning of the unraveling of my life. The end of it came five years later.

Shortly after Annie's disappearance, Jack took up flying. I remember the heated argument we had when he told me how he was going to deal with his heartache.

"Laura, I've signed up for flying lessons." Jack had continued to read the paper as if he had just suggested that he was going to plant a bed of daffodils.

"You're what?" He had never mentioned such a thing to me before.

"One of the partners at the law firm pilots his own plane, and I thought that might be what I needed." He sipped a bit of his coffee and continued to peruse the paper.

"What you need for what? To kill yourself? Or to spend even more time away from home?" I cringed at the shrillness in my voice. I went to him, placed my hands on his shoulders, then knelt before him. I rested my head in his lap, blinking away tears.

"I miss you," I mumbled into the striped wool of his pants. "I need you. Please come back to me." I looked up at him, uncaring that my tears had soaked into his trousers.

He looked at me with shadowed eyes and sighed, pushing his newspaper away. "You're so strong, Laura. You've picked up the pieces of your life and learned to live with your grief. But I'm falling apart inside. When I'm here or at work, all I see are memories. I need to go where I can feel Annie close to me again. Maybe make some new memories." He ground the heels of his hands into his eye sockets harshly, as if to clear his vision of whatever image he couldn't bear to see.

I wanted to argue with him that I wasn't so strong. I had managed to survive solely by compartmentalizing my grief into a tiny box in my heart and allowing myself to peek inside only when there was no one around to witness the devastation.

I stood, kissed him softly on the lips, and left the room, a tight ball of fear growing in my stomach.

Later, as I sat and halfheartedly tinkled the piano keys, Jack sat down and put his arm around me. He apologized but didn't back down.

I could feel the tension in him. I looked at him and said, "Okay, Jack. If this is what you want to do. Just please be careful. I don't think I could stand to lose you, too."

So Jack searched for Annie in the cumulus clouds and soaring winds while I remained earthbound but with my eyes toward the heavens. By the time I got the dreaded late-night phone call, I had already prepared myself as much as one could. I had been down this route before. The voice on the other end of the line mentioned something about engine failure, but I listened with only half an ear. Whether it had been engine failure or a lightning bolt, the end result was the same. I was a widow at the age of twenty-eight.

For almost a year after Jack's death, I strived to remember the feel of his touch on my skin. I lay awake at night in my empty bed, trying to feel his presence beside me, the warmth that would draw me toward him during sleep. But only the thick air of a Georgia summer settled around my ghosts and me. If sleep did come, it brought only dreams that he was there. I would breathe deeply and smell his warm slumbering breath and hear his quiet murmurings in the night. But in the stale morning air, I would open my eyes and know I was alone.

The never-ending search for Annie kept me moving in the halls of the living. And I had my house. It sustained me through that time, seeming to enclose me in an embrace.

I remembered what my grandmother had told me long ago about heartache and moonless nights and speeding stars, and I sensed that the answer lay high above me. So I continued looking, searching, but no answers came.

I found solace in my music. I returned to work full-time as an elementary school music teacher and continued to teach private voice and piano lessons from my home. Instead of finding the constant presence of children depressing, it was what kept me living.

My mother was concerned about me, but she lacked the ability to truly comfort me. I knew she grieved terribly over Annie and, perhaps, blamed me a little for her disappearance. I longed for my grandmother's wisdom, but she had died years before.

I was surprised when my mother made an impromptu visit on an early summer evening in June. Reclining on the watered-silk sofa in the parlor with Henryk Gorecki's *Symphony of Sorrowful Songs* flooding over me from the stereo, I heard a hesitant knock on the front door. There on the porch stood my mother, her tall, elegant form impeccably dressed, as always, her glossy black hair pulled back in a neat chignon, a nervous smile on her lips.

"Hello, Laura. I hope this isn't a bad time."

"Not at all, Mom. Come in. I'll order out for some Chinese if you're hungry," I said, belatedly noting that my own stomach was rumbling.

My mother gave me a wry grin as she stepped through the doorway. "I see you still don't cook, Laura."

"There's no one to cook for, and I can't see going through all that trouble just for me."

She looked a little chagrined, and I regretted being harsh, but I had detected a hint of censure in her voice, and it had reduced me to a chastised adolescent once again.

"I'm sorry. I wasn't criticizing you. Sure, why don't we order take-out? There's a new place that just opened on Holcomb Bridge Road that everybody is raving about."

As I dialed Directory Assistance, my mother took a tissue-wrapped object out of her purse. I gave a little start as I recognized it. Quickly scribbling down the phone number of the restaurant, I hung up and reached for the picture.

"Mom, I'd almost given up on ever getting this back from you," I said as I pulled the picture from its wrappings.

"I'm sorry for keeping it so long. It got misplaced after we moved to the new house, and then I guess I forgot about it with . . . well, with everything that's happened." She smoothed her already perfect hair behind her ears. "I still can't figure out who she is. And it's obviously somebody we're related to." She looked directly at me and failed to suppress a shudder.

I stared at that all-too-familiar face and felt a cold, unseen finger on the back of my neck. Who was she? I moved to put the picture on the hall table but slipped it into a drawer instead.

Later, sitting at the dining room table cluttered with little white cardboard boxes, my mother and I shared a bottle of wine. She had raised her eyebrows at my extensive collection on the wine rack in the kitchen. I wanted to explain that having a glass or two of wine every night was the only way I could shut my eyes and enter oblivion. Otherwise, I would lie awake in my bed and feel the darkness encircle me. I would imagine Annie calling out for me or feel Jack's gentle caress. Torment would be my companion if I did not have the wine to chase away the ghosts. But I didn't want to worry my mother or suffer through a lecture on alcohol dependence, so I offered no explanation.

Dabbing at the corners of her mouth with a napkin, she said, "Laura, I met the nicest man yesterday at my doctor's office. He's new in the practice, very nice-looking, and—"

I held up a hand. "Stop it, Mom. I'm not interested."

"But you haven't even met him!" She started digging in her purse until she came up with a business card and slid it across the polished surface of the table. "Here's his card. I gave him your number, too."

I left the card untouched in the middle of the table. "Then you'd better call him and tell him I'm not interested." I pushed my plate away and took a long sip of wine.

"Laura, isn't it time to restart your life? I know you miss them. But life goes on."

I closed my eyes in an effort to control my temper. "You don't understand, Mom. Unless you've been there, you couldn't possibly understand. Jack and Annie weren't just a man and a child, easily replaced by the next available candidates. I could never love another man the way I loved Jack or love another child the way I loved Annie. So just forget about your matchmaking, Mom. Love only brings me grief, and I'm through with it. Forever."

Her mouth became a thin strip of disapproval, but she said nothing. Still, when she stood to clear the table, she left the business card.

As I began rinsing the dishes to put them in the dishwasher, my mother finally broached the subject she had come over to discuss. She made a big production of scrambling around in the cabinets to find storage containers for the leftover food. As she did so, she said, "Laura, have you been reading the papers lately?" She compared sizes of Tupperware, then leaned to put one back.

"Not really. I haven't had an interest, I suppose."

I turned on the hot water and let it run until I saw steam rise and condense on the window above the sink. Through the haze I saw my mother's reflection. She was looking at me with a perplexed frown, as if she were pondering whether to tell me something. I began to meticulously poke bits of food down the garbage disposal. When my mother said nothing, I glanced up to find her still gazing at me. I shut off the faucet and turned around to face her.

33

"Why? What is it?" I asked.

She began to empty the contents of a white carton into the plastic container. She slammed it down a little too hard on the counter and said, "There's going to be another lunar eclipse in two weeks. The first one in five years."

Something akin to panic began to creep on little bird's feet into the pit of my stomach. "Oh, really?" I tried to keep my voice calm.

"Yes," she continued. "And there will be another comet visible at the same time."

"Genetti's Comet?"

"No, a different one."

I started to tremble and could feel my knees go weak. I hastily sat down at the kitchen table. My mother snapped the container's lid closed and then burped it. She put it in the refrigerator and shut the door with her hip. She leaned back against the fridge and drew in a deep breath as if to gather her strength.

"It'll be almost the same conditions as when Annie disappeared. I was thinking that maybe whoever took her might come back to the same spot again."

An icy hand began to claw at my insides. I knew what she was going to ask me, and I didn't know if I could do it.

"Laura, I'll go with you if you want. But don't you think that if there's even the slightest chance of getting Annie back, we should try it?" My mother's voice pleaded, and her eyes were moist from emotion. I sensed the love she held for my daughter, and I softened toward her.

"Mom, I want her back more than anything. But I just can't imagine that whoever took her five years ago would return her to the same spot simply because there's another eclipse." I averted my eyes so she could not see the fear in them and stood and walked to the sink.

My mother came to stand behind me and caught my gaze in the reflection in the window. "Laura, I know you're afraid. Remember that I was the one who spent the first few days with you after Annie's disappearance. I knew there was something else."

I drew a deep breath to steady my voice. "Mom, that place was evil. I felt as if my soul was being pulled from my body. I don't know if I'd have the will to survive it again." I looked down at my hands; my knuckles had gone white from gripping the edge of the counter.

"Laura, please think about it." Her words held desperation. But I couldn't offer any assurances. She silently picked up her purse and let herself out the front door.

When I heard the latch click into place, I sank down on the floor and stared ahead numbly. I rubbed my eyes with the heels of my hands, trying to think more clearly. Images of my daughter flashed before my eyes, and I felt the pull of longing as fresh as ever. I knew I would give my life for hers or even just to see her again. Whatever it took, I wanted her back.

When I stood again, I felt stronger. And I knew what I had to do.

"Why I came here, I know not; where I shall go it is useless to inquire—in the midst of myriads of the living and the dead worlds, stars, systems, infinity, why should I be anxious about an atom?"

Lord Byron

Chapter Three

I brought no sunscreen or blankets on this trip, only a grim determination to see a task through. I had considered bringing a weapon but pushed that thought aside. I was completely ignorant of guns, and wielding a knife could also prove disastrous. I figured I could pummel someone with my flashlight if need be. I had no idea what to expect. Only my mother's words and an unexplainable force propelled me to Moon Mountain.

Throughout the day and evening, fat gray clouds hung heavy in the sky, leaking out constant drizzle. Not enough to get soaked but enough to be annoying. The tires of my car squished over the wet asphalt as I prepared to park. I was startled to find a beat-up Volkswagen Bug illuminated by my headlights.

Parking my car next to it, I felt my heart skip a beat as I glanced in the windows. But I saw no dolls or coloring books or other signs that a child had recently ridden in the car. I laughed nervously at my imaginings and turned toward the path. Droplets of rain spotted my jeans as I climbed. I looked up at the dimness of the evening sky and pulled the hood of my slicker over my head.

As I approached the top, my heart hammered—but not from exertion. A blanket and a few tall branches had been converted into a makeshift shelter for a teenaged couple. A small campfire illuminated their faces while the pungent aroma of burning wood and leaves wafted over to me. The boy quickly adjusted his shorts and stood, offering a hand to his girlfriend. I smiled awkwardly at them and averted my gaze.

The thick cloud cover blocked any possible view of the eclipse or the comet, but peering at Atlanta through the telescope would give me something to do. I fished through my pocket for a quarter and put it in.

A wave of dizziness engulfed me before I heard the clank of the coin hitting its target. I gripped the telescope to regain my balance and was hit by the sudden smell of gardenias, bringing with it a fresh recollection of the night Annie disappeared. A man's voice and the whinnying of a horse broke the silence. I whirled around to see who it was. The young couple were absorbed with each other as if they had not heard a thing. I saw no one else.

I was about to dismiss it all as the product of my overactive imagination when I distinctly heard the crying of a child. Not the fretful cries of a baby, but the screams of a youngster who fancies himself injured.

I ran to the couple. "Did you hear that?"

They looked at me with irritation. "Hear what?"

Turning around, I clearly heard the voice of a man. "Don't run away from me when I'm talking to you. It's dangerous in those woods."

A young child answered back, "You're not my father, and I don't have to listen to you!"

"Annie!" I shouted, thinking that maybe the owners of those voices would know where she was.

The couple quickly rolled up their blanket, scooped up mud to throw on their campfire, and scurried for the path leading down to the parking lot.

The pinpricks of a headache began to work themselves up from the base of my neck. Looking up, I saw a partial moon through an opening in the cloud cover, a shadow taking a bite out of the edge. The murky sky obscured any view of the comet, but I knew it was up there, trailing its mark through the sky, just as another comet had done five years previously.

The earth seemed to tilt at an odd angle, and I lost my balance. It had to be an earthquake. They weren't totally unheard of in Georgia, I assured myself. My limbs trembled uncontrollably, so I lay down, curling up in a fetal position. I heard the voices again, closer this time, and the smell of gardenias overwhelmed me as I lost consciousness.

The feel of a rough, wet tongue lapping my cheek woke me. Opening my eyes, I found a strange-looking dog of questionable parentage gazing down at me. It was undoubtedly the ugliest mutt I had ever seen but certainly the friendliest if his pleasure at waking me was any indication.

I sat up quickly and was rewarded with dizziness and spots before my eyes. I put my hands on either side of my head to keep it steady. The dog climbed into my lap and lay down, his tail thumping against the ground.

Absently patting the dog, I looked around. The scenery was new but uncannily familiar. I realized I must have staggered down the hill in my confusion. The gloomy cloud cover of night had blossomed into a sky of glaring blue, and the ground around me appeared bone-dry. Wanting to see how much time had passed, I lifted my arm but was dismayed to find my watch gone. It had been a gift from Jack, and I felt another stab of loss.

Seeing no sign of the asphalt parking lot, I determined that I had managed to roam to the other side of the hill in some kind of delirious state, because I couldn't remember anything. I stood, pushing the dog gently off my lap. The ground appeared to pitch violently, so I sat down again. I searched unsuccessfully for my purse in the overgrown vegetation and then shrugged out of my slicker as the sweltering sun bore down on me. When the earth stopped spinning, I stood again slowly to make my way back to the parking lot.

There were no marked paths, forcing me to walk very slowly. I had to continually brush aside green stalks and sharp grasses, cutting my hands in the process. I paused to rest and wipe the sweat from my face. It then occurred to me that, except for the insistent humming of insects, it was totally silent. No planes flying overhead, no traffic on the highway.

Something pounding through the underbrush on my right shattered the silence. My mouth went dry as I recalled that panthers could still be found in the wild in this part of the state.

I turned as a small boy, aged seven or eight, emerged, hurtling through the underbrush and running smack into my middle. I staggered backward. He looked up at me with wild brown eyes and pointed behind him.

"It's a catamount! Help—he's gonna get me!"

I had no need to ask what a catamount was, as the object of the boy's terror slowly sauntered out of the thicket, its body low to the ground as it moved toward its prey. Instinctively, I shoved the boy behind me. As if to make its intentions clear, the large cat darted its tongue out and flattened its ears. The feral eyes glinted in the sunlight, and I wondered if it could smell my fear. Something moved in my peripheral vision, but I dared not look. A deep growling began in the depths of the cat's belly, and I turned and threw my arms over the boy. He trembled, his sweaty arms sticking to my own. I bent my head, prepared for the gouging of claws through the thin cotton of my blouse. The beast hissed and sprang from the ground. I squeezed the boy tightly, his small bones sharp under my hands, anticipating sharp teeth in my flesh. The crack of a rifle shot at close range split the air.

The feline dropped like a lead weight, hitting my shoulder and knocking us to the ground. Tasting dirt, I turned my head and spat. I scrambled on my hands and knees away from the cat, dragging the boy with me.

About ten feet away, I stopped. Clutching me wildly, the boy sobbed incoherently. I gathered him in my arms and made soothing sounds while keeping a wary eye on the panther for any signs of movement. The acrid odor of gunpowder stung my nostrils.

A shadow fell on us, making us both look up. The boy scrambled to his feet and tried to unobtrusively wipe the tears off his cheeks with the backs of his sleeves. His clothing gave me a start. I couldn't remember the last time I had seen a boy his age in anything but jeans and a T-shirt, but this child wore a white cotton blouse with loose knee breeches and suspenders.

The dog bolted out of the bushes and leapt on the boy with a joyful yapping. I made a move to stand to greet our rescuer but instead felt two firm hands grab me by the arms and hoist me up. I found myself looking up into eyes that reminded me of the Caribbean. I had a flash of recognition for a moment, and then it was gone. The man was about my age, or perhaps a little older, but I was sure I would have remembered him had I met him before. He was looking at me just as closely, his gaze almost intimate. I lowered my eyes.

"Thank you," I managed. "You . . . you saved my life." His hands trembled on my arms, and I realized I was shaking.

"Are you all right?" His look of concern warmed me, and I was ready to say yes until I felt the pain in my shoulder from where the cat had landed on me. I winced.

He released me gently. "I think you need to see a doctor. Do you live around here? I'll take you home."

I blushed when I realized that he was staring at my jeans.

39

"You're not from around here, are you?" He averted his eyes, then looked at my face.

"I live in Roswell. My car isn't far from here. I'm sure I could drive home if you would just help me find it." I brushed dirt and grass off my pants and shirt and then noticed that the man hadn't moved or spoken.

"There are no railroad cars around here, ma'am." He looked at me as if I were speaking a foreign language. "But it would be my pleasure to escort you back to Roswell. That's where we're going, too."

Confused, I opened my mouth to reply, when I noticed his peculiar costume. He wore a long-sleeved white cotton shirt, the pullover variety with three wooden buttons closed up to the neck. His pants were light brown, almost yellow, and held up with suspenders. And then I noticed his rifle. It was huge, almost five feet long, and looked exactly like an antique Civil War Enfield rifle that my history-buff father had hanging in his study.

"Is there a battle reenactment going on?" I asked, hoping that his explanation would soothe the worries I felt tickling the back of my brain.

"No, ma'am. Only battles going on 'round here are the real thing." He looked closely at me with a furrowed brow. "Did you hit your head when you fell?"

I had begun to wonder the same thing and reached up with both hands to feel for bumps on my skull. No such luck.

"No. I don't think so. But I heard a child's voice. I . . . I thought it might be my daughter."

"Your daughter?" He searched the immediate area with his eyes, a look of growing concern on his face. "Willie and I haven't seen anybody at all since we left the house this morning." He took a step closer. "Will you be all right if I leave you here with Willie while I go look for your little girl?"

I shook my head. "No. That won't be necessary. Annie, my daughter, she's . . . she's been gone for five years now. I guess it was only wishful thinking when I heard that voice. It was probably Willie's." I looked away from his intense gaze, feeling once again the crushing weight of sorrow and afraid I might end up crying in front of a perfect stranger.

"I'm sorry."

I looked at him and knew that he was.

"Please, just get me back to Roswell. I'll be fine."

He nodded slowly, then turned his attention to the boy, who stood as still as a tree trunk and looked as if he wanted to blend into the scenery. The tall, lean man limped as he walked, his pants sporting several patches.

"Willie, you are in for the biggest whipping of your life. You could have gotten yourself killed." The man limped over to the fallen animal and nudged it with the butt of his rifle. "This here cat would have had you for supper if I hadn't arrived in time. Sort of what your mother would do to me if I let anything happen to you."

"You're not my pa. I don't have to do anything you say." Despite his defiant words, the boy's lower lip trembled. He stuck out his chin and added, "Anyway, Pa says you're a traitor and should be in prison. I'm not listening to no traitor."

The man paled and looked as if he had been struck. He knelt in front of Willie, keeping his left leg straight out to the side. He grasped the boy by the shoulders and said, "Did he really say that?"

Willie stood still, examining his feet, but I could see his jaw trembling. "Yes. And he said that I needed to protect Ma from any secesh claptrap you might be scooping out." The boy's voice was barely audible, and a tear hit the toe of his shoe.

Despite his reaction to the boy's words, the man gathered the child in his arms and hugged him. "No matter what's between your pa and me, it's not going to change the fact that you're my nephew, and I love you as if you were my own son." He stood and added, "And that means that in your pa's absence, it's my duty to protect you as a father would. I'm sorry, Willie, but I'm going to have to give you the switch when we get home."

The boy stood there meekly, a few stifled sobs racking his small body. My heart went out to him. I went over and put my arm around his bony shoulders.

41

The man looked at me with dark blue eyes. "I'm sorry, ma'am, to involve you in our little family dispute. Please allow me to introduce myself. I'm Mr. Stuart Elliott of Phoenix Hall, Roswell, and this is my nephew, William Elliott, Junior."

I smiled at his gallant bow and introduced myself, mimicking his formal tone. "I'm Mrs. Laura Truitt. I live on Mimosa Boulevard in Roswell."

He gave me a quizzical look. "Where is Mimosa Boulevard? I've lived in Roswell all my life, and I've never heard of it."

My confusion, the heat, and buzzing flies made me snap. "Well, that makes us even, I guess. I've lived in Roswell for seven years, and I've never heard of Phoenix Hall."

He raised his eyebrows. "I think you've suffered a bit of a shock." He gave a shrill whistle, and the ugly mutt came bounding out from behind a tree. "Charlie, get Endy."

I watched in amazement as the dog ran into the thicket and then emerged with the reins of a horse in his mouth, the horse itself bringing up the rear. It was a huge animal with big eyes and a slobbery mouth. The thing sneezed as it approached, spraying us all with God knows what and showing me a mouthful of teeth. Two rabbits hung by their feet on a length of twine stretched across the back of the beast. I had obviously interrupted a hunting expedition.

Stuart grabbed hold of the reins and firmly patted the jet-black flank of the horse. "Mrs. Truitt, would you mind sharing Endy with Willie?"

I looked the man straight in the eye. I had to look up several inches, as he was a good deal taller than my own five-feet-seven. "There is no way I'm getting on that horse. Besides, you're limping. You ride that thing—I'll walk." I took a few steps backward to put as much distance between myself and Endy as I could—and fell over a fallen branch, landing soundly on my backside.

Stuart stifled a laugh, but Willie had no such compunction and laughed outright.

"That's the last time I save you from a vicious animal," I snapped at Willie.

That sobered him up sufficiently. Stuart reached down to

me for the second time that day and hoisted me up. "You sure are a stubborn woman. But I am not going to ride a horse while a lady walks. Wouldn't do for my reputation as a gentleman at all."

Instead of releasing me, he put one arm under my legs and picked me up like a baby. His touch seemed somehow familiar, and I studied his face intently, aware of his own close scrutiny. Neither one of us said anything as he swung me up onto the horse's back. Too petrified to move, I clung to the saddle horn. He reached behind the saddle and pulled out a long gray coat with black collar facings and handed it to me.

"You might also want to wear this so as not to shock the gentle citizens of Roswell."

I stared at the coat as if it were a snake he had asked me to wrap around my neck. I longed for the slicker I had inadvertently left behind.

"It is at least ninety degrees out here, and if you think I'm going to wear a wool coat, much less release my grip on this saddle to put it on, you've got another thing coming." Sweat saturated my cotton blouse, making it cling to my chest. His eyes widened as they rested on my shirt a little too long, and I hunched forward, having contracted a sudden case of modesty.

"Mrs. Truitt, I really must insist. I don't want to be grist for the Roswell rumor mill, and I'm sure you don't, either. It just wouldn't look right for me to bring you into town wearing, well . . ." He looked me up and down as if trying to decide what to call my outfit. "Well, whatever it is that you're wearing."

Still feeling a bit dazed and confused and not in the mood to argue, I took the coat and threw it over my shoulders. He lifted Willie up onto the saddle behind me, shouldered his rifle, and began to lead the way, pulling the reins.

The terrain seemed vaguely familiar, but we never came near enough to the highway for me to get my bearings. I assumed we were sticking to horse trails. After about an hour, we approached a large wooden gate. A hint of recognition pressed on my memory as we passed through the gate onto a long dirt drive. Somehow I knew what I would see before I saw the house looming up in the distance. A buzzing sound ran through my head as we approached it and the front door swung open. A petite but very pregnant woman wearing a long, full dress waddled down the steps toward us. From her fingertips, a squeaking mouse dangled by its tail.

"Stuart! What's happened?"

I had come home. The one thing I was sure of was that this was my house. I didn't know who these people were or why they were in my house, but I had my suspicions. The thought of it all made me very light-headed. I looked at the little creature suspended by its tail, and suddenly I felt that time had me suspended, too, helpless in a world I knew and didn't know. Feeling my head swim, my eyes transfixed on the swinging rodent, I promptly slid off the horse in a dead faint.

"The obscurest epoch is to-day."
                                    Robert Louis Stevenson

Chapter Four

I opened my eyes and found myself staring at close range at a rough cotton shirt. I moved my head and realized I was being carried up the stairs. Stuart stumbled, and my arms shot around his neck. I remembered his limp and attempted to get down.

"You shouldn't be carrying me—I can walk. Please put me down."

Ignoring my request, he crossed the upstairs hallway, entered one of the bedrooms, and laid me gently on a small spindle bed. My hands remained fastened behind his neck as my head reached the pillow, and our gazes locked. I had definitely seen those eyes before, but the wisp of memory floated beyond my grasp.

His breath felt warm on my cheek, and I blushed, realizing I was still holding onto him and keeping his face close to mine. Slowly, I let my arms fall to my sides.

"I didn't imagine a woman who could face down a catamount without a scream would faint at the sight of a mouse." A wry grin touched his face, but I could see relief there, too.

"I didn't faint." I ignored his raised eyebrows. "I've never fainted in my whole life, and I have no intention of starting now."

I looked around me to get my bearings. I recognized Annie's room, but the small bed and stark white walls now replaced the crib and pale pink wallpaper. I sat up with a start as I suddenly realized where I was. I scurried off the mattress and ran past Stuart and out of the room to the balcony. The sight that greeted me confirmed my suspicions. Not an electrical pole in sight, nor any of the familiar streets and buildings that had surrounded my house. The urban blight of strip malls creeping their way up Alpharetta Highway had been replaced by a red clay road shaded by trees. But there was no doubt in my mind that this was my house.

The sound of children's laughter and a dog barking brought my attention to the backyard, where a little girl wearing high-topped black boots chased a boy I recognized as Willie. Stuart approached to stand beside me.

"If you'll excuse me, ma'am. My sister-in-law will be up in a moment."

With a brief nod, he headed down the stairs, not completely hiding a grimace of pain as he bent his leg to descend the steps.

I looked back at Willie and the little girl. It was obvious the boy had forgotten all about the promise of a whipping from his uncle.

Heavy footsteps climbed the wood stairs, and I turned to see the pregnant woman who had been holding the mouse. She carried a small box and a stack of clean linens. The mem-

45

ory of my fainting at our first meeting made me flush, but her gentle smile quickly put me at ease.

"I brought some of my herbs to make you feel better, but I can see you don't need them." She stopped at the top of the steps, breathing deeply. "I'm sorry to have startled you with that little creature. It's only that I had just caught him when I heard Stuart ride up." Her voice was soft and fell easily on my ears as I recognized the gentle inflections of a true Southern accent. It reminded me of my mother's voice, and a twinge of nostalgia made me suddenly wish for her.

Her brow furrowed as she took in my outfit. Taking my arm, she gently guided me back to my room.

"I'm not afraid of a mouse. I've just had a heck of a day, and I think I finally succumbed to the exhaustion." I allowed myself to be led back to the bed and sat down.

She bent her head closer to study the sleeve of my blouse. "I've never seen such a weave—it's truly amazing. Where did you find such a thing?"

I couldn't think of a thing to say, so I mutely stared at her.

Changing the subject, she said, "Stuart said he found you at Moon Mountain. Do you live around there?"

My mind seemed to be working at half-speed, and all I could think of was that I had somehow accomplished the impossible: I had traveled through time. I forced myself to answer. "No, I live in Roswell. At least, I think I do."

Her delicate brows knitted together as she studied me before speaking again. "Why don't you rest some, and then we'll talk." I decided the woman was probably in her early twenties, although her manner made her seem much older. Her light brown hair was pulled off her face into a bun that couldn't quite conceal the curls that popped out around her forehead.

"Yes. I'd like that, if you don't mind." I wasn't tired, but I needed some time to devise a plan. I couldn't tell these people that I had come from another century. I would wind up in an asylum for sure. I wasn't even sure myself that I didn't belong in one.

"I'll send Sukie up in a little while with a tray and some things for you to wear." She studied my face closely. "You look pale, but you don't seem to have a fever," she said, placing the back of her hand to my forehead. "You're exhausted. Rest will be just the thing you need."

She glided out of the room and shut the door softly behind her.

I lay down on the bed and stared up at the ceiling. A breeze blew in the tall windows, stirring the white-lace curtains and moving the hot air around the small room. I needed to use the bathroom and was halfway to the door before I remembered that the hall bath had not been installed until 1921. I went back to the bed and looked under it. I reached to pull out the chamber pot and then decided it could wait. I was in no hurry to discover the inconveniences of the nineteenth century.

The faint ticking of a clock in the hallway lulled me into a doze. I dreamed of Annie—not as an infant but as the young girl of seven she would now be. She was talking to me, but I couldn't make out what she was saying. She handed me a flower, and I bent to smell it and realized that it was a gardenia. I awoke suddenly with the potent aroma still in my nostrils. I got off the bed and followed the scent to the window. Leaning out slightly, I discovered an entire row of gardenias growing below, their pristine petals luminescent in the late-afternoon sun.

A soft rapping on the door preceded a middle-aged black woman entering, balancing a tray piled with food.

"Good evening, ma'am. Miz Julia figured you might be starving by now."

She set the tray on a small table and turned to stare at me as I walked toward it.

In her deeply accented speech, she asked, "What kind of clothes is that? I never seed a lady wear such a thing. Now I see why Miz Julia wants some clothes brought up to you. I be right back."

The rich fragrance of the food reminded me that I hadn't eaten since breakfast. Despite the turmoil going on in my head regarding my apparent trip through time, my appetite, almost absent since Annie's disappearance, had come back with a vengeance. I smiled to myself at the thought of Scarlett

O'Hara's mammy admonishing her to eat like a bird because gentlemen didn't like ladies with big appetites. Luckily, I didn't have to worry about squeezing into a corset.

I was just polishing off the last slice of ham when Sukie returned. Her arms were overloaded with flounces and fabrics and what appeared to be enough clothes to dress me for a month. She dumped the whole pile on the bed.

"My, you sure was hungry. I never seed a lady eat as much as a field hand before."

I guiltily laid aside my knife and fork. "It was delicious. Thank you for bringing it."

"Miz Julia asked me to help you get dressed. This here should fit you." She pointed to the pile on the bed, and while I disrobed, she sorted through the clothing and laid it out in an orderly fashion.

First came the chemise and calf-length cotton drawers. I was a little disconcerted to find that the drawers were split in the middle from the front to the back and only attached at the waistband. After viewing the piles of clothing that would go on top, I quickly figured out that the split drawers would show their usefulness when it came to utilizing the chamber pot.

The chemise and drawers were very comfortable, and I would have been fine wearing just those all day, but I knew there was more to come. A pair of white-cotton, knee-length stockings with ribbon garters followed. When Sukie next held up what I recognized to be a corset, I adamantly refused.

"No way am I wearing that thing. I won't be able to breathe. Put the rest of the stuff over me, and we'll just forget about the corset."

Sukie's eyes widened in surprise. "But, ma'am, all ladies wear corsets!"

I took the offending garment from her hand to examine it. My fingers kneaded the unbending whalebone stays, and I quickly thrust it back at her. "I really would prefer not to."

She shook her head slowly but complied with my wishes.

The next part of the ensemble was almost as bad as the corset. It resembled a cage with a framework of flexible metal hoops joined by vertical bands of fabric tape. I stepped into it, and Sukie tied it at my waist. On top of this came two white cotton petticoats. I was heavily perspiring by this time, and I longed for a tank top and shorts.

Finally, a simple long-sleeved cotton blouse with a matching skirt in a light green floral pattern was put on me, and Sukie deftly buttoned up the front. I felt completely confined and amazed at how heavy the whole ensemble was. But at least I was done. Or so I thought.

Sukie looked at my straight, shoulder-length hair and shook her head. But, after what seemed like an hour of her brushing and pinning my hair, she had arranged it in a neat coil at the back of my head, a severe part bisecting my scalp. Nodding with approval, she stood back to get a better view. "You have beautiful hair, almost as dark as mine. And that dress match your eyes. Don't know why you'd want to wear them men clothes."

While adding two decorative combs to my new hairstyle, she caught my reflection in the mirror. "Mister Stuart says he found you up by Moon Mountain. What you be doin' up there?"

Something flickered in her eyes as I looked at her. "I was searching for my daughter, but I couldn't find her. I . . . lost her on Moon Mountain when she was just a baby, and I hoped . . ." My voice drifted off, and I stared at her reflection again.

"She died?"

I shook my head. "I don't know. She just . . . disappeared."

She quickly reached for something around her neck. It appeared to be a small, red-flannel bag attached to a thin cord. She touched it briefly and then tucked it back into her dress. "Moon Mountain's a mighty strange place. I know only one other lady who would go up there by herself," she said, patting the lump inside her bodice.

"That's really all I remember. I—I think I hit my head. I'm sure it will all come back to me eventually."

She nodded and smiled approvingly at my new hairstyle. "That looks nice. I'll tell Miz Julia you're dressed."

I gave up trying to sit down on the bed and just leaned

49

against it, awaiting the mistress of the house. I looked at my wrist, forgetting again that my watch was gone, but figuring a half-hour must have passed. I finally straightened and opened my door.

Craning my neck out of the doorway, I looked around the hallway. As far as I could tell, I was alone in the house. All the sounds of people going about their daily business seemed to be coming from outside. My surroundings greatly unsettled me. I was familiar with them—yet they were different. The hardwood banister beneath my hands was the same, as was some of the furniture. But the knickknacks and wall hangings all belonged to another family, making me a stranger in my own home. I looked closely at some needlepoint on the wall. It was an elaborate sampler with all the letters of the alphabet in an uneven line and a Bible verse at the bottom. FOR WHAT IS YOUR LIFE? IT IS EVEN A VAPOR, THAT APPEARETH FOR A LITTLE TIME, AND THEN VANISHETH AWAY. The bottom right contained the stitcher's signature: *Margaret Elliott, May 14, 1814, aged twelve years.*

I descended the stairs cautiously, the voluminous skirts hampering my every footfall. I should have practiced walking and sitting in the privacy of my own room before venturing out, as my skirts threatened to throw me headfirst down the stairs. I couldn't see my feet, so I hovered precariously over each step as I felt my way down. In the main hallway below, a cool breeze flowed through the passageway and alleviated a little of the mugginess that clung to my skin. I thought of the central air conditioning that Jack and I had installed and longed for the cold blast from a vent and an ice cold Diet Coke from the fridge.

Ghost-like, I flitted through the rooms, examining every detail. There was no kitchen, and that puzzled me at first until I remembered that in olden days it would have been separated from the main house to protect the house from fire. In the front parlor the upright piano stood in the same spot that I remembered. The dark wood was polished to a gleam, and the G key above middle C still had its ivory veneer top, a piece that was missing in my own time. The smooth keys beckoned me, and I itched to feel them under my fingers, to touch something hard, solid, and real.

After quite a lot of maneuvering, I arranged myself on the bench by tucking all my skirts under me and began to play Debussy's *Claire de Lune*. I was soon lost in the magic of the music, and my surroundings faded from my sight, to be replaced by images of my grandmother whispering her warning to me and, surprisingly, an image of Stuart Elliott. I colored at the latter. I had never fainted in my life, and it irked me to think that he might have thought that I was some damsel in distress who needed rescuing. I had survived on my own for over a year, and I had certainly outgrown the need for Prince Charming.

As the last note died, soft applause sounded behind me. Startled, I swung around on the bench and neatly clipped the edge of the music stand with my elbow. My injured shoulder ached at the movement, and I winced as the stand crashed down on the keyboard. The sheet music fluttered to the floor and scattered. I unceremoniously scooted off the bench, my skirts held high, to face my audience of one and found myself staring into the mirth-filled blue eyes of Stuart Elliott.

"You could have given me a heart attack! Do you normally sneak up on people with the intent to scare the living daylights out of them?"

Without waiting for a reply, I bent down to start picking up the music, and my large skirts tipped the piano bench so that it came crashing down on the hardwood floor. Stuart picked up the bench and then leaned over to help me with the music. His thick black hair fell over his forehead, and he impatiently brushed it away.

"What's this?" he asked. He was holding what looked like a piece of ivory. I looked up at the keyboard and found to my dismay that the ivory veneer on the G key was missing. A small tremor went up my spine as well as a foreboding sense of déjà vu. Since I was the one who had done the damage, did this mean I had always been destined to come back to this time? Well, I now knew what had happened to the piano key, but I was mortified that I had done it.

My voice shook as I reached for the ivory. "I am so sorry. I'm not usually so clumsy." I looked up into his face again and saw him struggling not to laugh. I not-too-gently thrust the ivory back into his hand. "Only when people sneak up and startle me!"

"Pardon me, Mrs. Truitt. I stepped into the house to tell my sister-in-law the doctor was riding up, and I heard the piano-forte. I'm sorry I startled you."

He didn't look the least bit sorry, as his mouth kept twitching into a smirk. I started to say something else when I heard a throat being cleared.

The tall, thin man standing in the doorway looked down his slightly beaked nose at Stuart and me on our hands and knees, scrabbling around the floor picking up music. He appeared not to be amused in the slightest. I wasn't sure about the habits of dress of the times, but the collar of his shirt could not have been stiffer; head movement seemed nearly impossible. His eyes were a soft, liquid brown, and they regarded me with a cool condescension. He had elaborate sideburns that made me think of Elvis Presley, and I grinned involuntarily. His soft chin wagged back and forth as he stared at my silly grin, and that made me grin even more.

Stuart must have guessed that the appearance of this visitor was the object of my merriment and rose to intervene before I began to laugh outright.

"Dr. Charles Watkins, allow me to introduce Mrs. Laura Truitt."

The young doctor bowed stiffly and murmured, "My pleasure, ma'am."

The appearance of the mistress of the house interrupted the pleasantries, her light-brown curls escaping from her bun and framing her oval face.

"Hello, Charles. I see you've already met our guest, although I don't believe that she and I have been properly introduced."

Julia must have been working outside, because her face was beaded with perspiration, but her manner was calm and collected as she approached me with outstretched hands. With a warm smile she said, "I'm Julia Elliott. Welcome to Phoenix Hall."

"I'm Laura Truitt, and thank you so much for taking me in."

Julia turned to the doctor and explained, "Mrs. Truitt saved my Willie's life today when he was chased by a wildcat. She hurt her shoulder, and I'd like you to take a look at it to ensure nothing was broken."

"Oh, really, that's not necessary. It's fine now, just a little bruised. I have full range of motion in it." I demonstrated this by moving my arm like a windmill and involuntarily grimaced as pain shot through me.

The doctor frowned and walked toward me. "Yes, I see, but Mrs. Elliott would like me to examine it anyway."

I unbuttoned the top button of my blouse but stopped before I unfastened the second one as the doctor's face turned the color of a cherry tomato.

"I would not dream of impinging upon your modesty, Mrs. Truitt. I will do my examination through your clothes."

With a slight cough, Stuart excused himself and Julia from the room, closing the door behind them.

The physician motioned for me to sit on the uprighted piano bench. Remembering how lethal my uncontrollable skirts were, I ignored his suggestion and instead lowered myself into a handsome horsehair wing chair.

He placed his left hand firmly on my back while he palpated my shoulder with his other hand. He stared at a spot over my head to avoid eye contact with me during his ministrations.

"Mrs. Truitt, why aren't you wearing a corset? Do you have some sort of breathing affliction?"

"No, Doctor, I don't, but I would if I forced myself into one of those contraptions."

He stopped in his manipulations of my arm and dropped the limb as if he couldn't bear to touch it any longer. "I see," he said in a tone indicating that he did not. "A follower of Catharine Beecher. The notion that corsets unduly constrict a woman and deform her body is balderdash." He stepped back and closed his black bag. "Nothing seems to be broken, just bruised. I suggest restricting your movement of the shoulder, and it should be better in a few days."

"Thank you." I wanted to contradict his opinion on corsets but kept my mouth closed.

"Where are you from, Mrs. Truitt? Your voice has the inflections of the South, but your mannerisms are more reminiscent of the North."

His question caught me off guard, so I blurted out the first thing that came to mind.

"To be honest, I think I hit my head or something, because I don't seem to remember much. I remember my name and that I'm a widow but not much else." I had watched enough soap operas in my day to know that amnesia was a good explanation for just about anything.

"Oh, really?" His expression told me he didn't believe a word.

His examination apparently over, he walked to the door and opened it. Julia appeared in the doorway, an expression of concern on her face. "Is everything all right? No broken bones?"

The doctor's stern features softened as he looked at Julia Elliott. "No. Physically, she seems to be fine."

Julia smiled. "Wonderful. Now, Charles, would you like some coffee? And I insist that you stay for supper."

"Why, yes, thank you, Julia."

Stuart reappeared, and the two men found seats while Julia went to see about the coffee. I remained where I was to avoid any further embarrassment.

Stuart turned to me. "Mrs. Truitt, when I met you, you said something about a Mimosa Boulevard here in Roswell."

I set about straightening my skirts to cover my long pause as my mind raced about for an explanation. "Yes, I do remember. I live on Mimosa Boulevard. I thought it was in Roswell, but you told me there's no such street."

"No, there's not," interjected the doctor. "Your case is very interesting, Mrs. Truitt. I know a woman's mental health is weak at best and, when put under the least bit of strain, tends to suffer greatly. I'm sure after a period of bed rest your memory will return." He stressed the word *memory*, making it sound as if it wasn't my memory but something more akin to my character that was the problem.

I opened my mouth to make some retort about the insufferability of male chauvinists but closed it quickly. I needed their help, and offending them would not advance my cause.

Softly, Stuart said, "You also mentioned something about your daughter."

I nodded and looked at the doctor hopefully. If a child had been found deserted on the mountain, surely she would have been brought to a doctor for medical attention. "Yes, she was only a baby when she was lost on Moon Mountain." I paused, wondering if the five years that had passed in my own time would be the same in this time. "Perhaps . . . perhaps you treated, or heard of, a child found on the hill?"

He tucked his chin into his neck and shook his head vigorously. "No. Never. And how does a mother misplace a child?"

My eyes stung, and I ducked my head, but not before I saw Stuart reach over and grab the doctor's arm.

Julia returned, followed by Sukie, who was carrying a large tea tray. I looked closely at the tray, recognizing it as the one Mrs. Cudahy had used to serve Jack and me iced tea and cookies on the first day I saw this house. Despite the heat, I shivered, remembering something Mrs. Cudahy had said about how the family's treasures had been saved during the War. Something about being forewarned.

Julia poured and handed everyone a cup. I noticed her hands as she bent to her task; they were small and well tended but somehow capable-looking, too. Finished, she sat down on the sofa next to my chair.

I brought the cup to my lips and noticed a peculiar aroma. I took one sip and was rewarded with a taste so bitter and so awful that I literally wanted to spit out the vile stuff. I could feel three pairs of eyes on me, and I made my throat swallow.

"What kind of coffee is this?" I asked politely. "It doesn't taste like any I've ever had before."

"Actually, it's made from a recipe that Stuart brought back

from the army. It's parched and roasted acorns with a little bit of bacon fat. It's not so bad once you get used to it." Julia smiled feebly. "Thanks to the Yankee blockade, we haven't seen a real coffee bean since sixty-one."

"Well, wherever you're from, it would appear that you've been drinking real coffee." The doctor stared openly at me, as if I were Abe Lincoln himself sitting in that parlor. "Perhaps William's sent you down here to spy on us."

Julia's cup slammed into her saucer. "Charles, I demand an apology."

Charles looked chagrinned at her reprimand but continued to eye me warily. "My apologies, Julia, if I have offended you. But she hasn't denied it."

"Who's William?" I asked, feeling nervous at the mention of the word *spy*. As if I needed these sorts of accusations to further complicate matters. Spying during wartime was no light matter.

Julia turned to me. "He's my husband—Willie's father and Stuart's brother."

I turned to the doctor. "I promise you that I've never met William Elliott. And I'm certainly no spy." I took another sip of the foul brew, wondering why Julia's husband would spy on his own family.

Julia's mention of a year prompted me to ask, "What is today's date?"

The doctor paused briefly before replying, "June second."

The thought had barely crossed my mind before I voiced it. "Was there a lunar eclipse seen with a comet last night?"

The room grew silent, save for the ticking of the hall clock. Dr. Watkins narrowed his eyes at me. "Yes, there was. Why do you ask?"

I ignored his question, my mind already racing in another direction. "What year is it?"

The doctor didn't try to hide his exasperation. "Eighteen sixty-three."

My mind spun back to all the history I had learned from my father, an avid Civil War buff, and I remembered the biographies of General William T. Sherman I had read in college, but at the moment I could recall nothing about the year 1863.

"Please—help me refresh my memory. What's happening in the country right now?"

"Our General Lee has finally taken the initiative and is attempting to bring the war into Lincoln's backyard. I imagine he'll be crossing the Potomac any day now and heading north toward Harrisburg, Pennsylvania, smack dab in the middle of Yankee territory. I wish I could be with the troops, but I know this town needs a physician more than General Lee needs one more soldier." The doctor crossed one skinny leg over the other and settled back in his chair.

Keeping his stiff leg out in front of him, Stuart balanced his coffee cup on his other knee and turned to look at Dr. Watkins. "You're right, Charles. It's also convenient that you had to pull your two front teeth—the ones a soldier needs to tear open a cartridge in the heat of battle—and replace them with weak imitations. Unfortunately, that will also keep a man off the battlefield."

The doctor stiffened. "If you weren't such an old friend, Stuart, I'd call you out for that. You know as well as I do that those teeth were rotten and that I am needed here anyway."

"I'm sure you are," Stuart said as he took another sip of the rancid brew and grimaced.

The mention of Pennsylvania and Lee's initiative pricked my memory. "Gettysburg," I murmured. The one piece of trivia that stuck in my mind was that following the battle, Lee's train of wounded stretched for more than fourteen miles.

"What do you mean by Gettysburg?" The doctor looked at me with irritation, his left hand waving my comment aside. "No, Mrs. Truitt, General Lee is going to the state capital of Harrisburg—and will hopefully do to the citizens there what Grant's army is doing to those poor suffering people in Vicksburg."

I knew nothing of Harrisburg, but the Battle of Gettysburg, and its bloody aftermath, would be etched on the minds of the American people for centuries to come. Not wanting to get into an argument and perhaps reveal more than I should, I let his remarks go without comment.

I looked at Stuart, who had evidently been a soldier in this conflict. Although I did not really know him, I was comforted by the knowledge that his disability would mean one fewer bullet-ridden body to be left lying on the field of battle in a war whose outcome was to me a foregone conclusion.

Stuart stood and limped to the window. "Julia, Mrs. Truitt seems to have suffered a blow to her head and can't remember much about herself. I would like to offer her our hospitality until her memory returns or we find out who she is."

"Of course. You may stay as long as you like. I am beholden to you for what you did for my Willie." She placed a warm hand on my arm.

"Thank you both. I'll do my best to help you with the house and children, Julia. And I'll find some way to repay you for your kindness."

"You already have. Don't think any more about it." Julia squeezed my arm gently.

"I'd also like to ask your friends and neighbors if they know anything about a baby being found on Moon Mountain. I . . . I don't know where else to look."

Julia's hand on my arm tightened, and I winced. Her face blanched, and she clutched her rounded belly with the other hand.

"Julia? Is your baby coming?" My voice seemed higher than usual.

She nodded. My first impulse was to rush to a phone to let the hospital know we were on our way. But this was 1863; there were no phones, nor hospitals with high-tech birthing rooms and epidurals. A woman was left to her own devices.

"Where is your husband?"

"I have no idea where William is. He's off fighting with the Yankees out West. I haven't heard from him since last September when he was here on furlough. I don't think I'd want him here right now, anyway," she said, pointing her chin in the direction of the men.

"What can I do?" I asked, trying to push the panic out of my voice. I knew next to nothing about natural childbirth, but

I did know the presence of another woman would be comforting.

"Just help me walk. It's not my first baby, so it shouldn't take too long. And somebody go get Sukie."

I put my arm around her shoulder and gently led her to the stairs.

She stopped and shook her head. "No, not in my bedroom. The birthing room has been prepared down here."

Before we could proceed, Julia gasped, and a small puddle pooled at her feet. She looked back at the two men standing in the parlor doorway, and her cheeks burned red.

Feeling her discomfort, I said, "Don't pay any attention to them. They know that if child-bearing were left to men, it would be the end of the race."

I caught a scowl on the doctor's face but a quick smile from Stuart as I led Julia to the little birthing room at the back of the house.

"In sorrow thou shalt bring forth children; and thy desire shall be to thy husband, and he shall rule over thee."
Genesis 3:16

Chapter Five

The birthing room, which would eventually be replaced by a modern kitchen, was sparsely furnished but clean. There were no beeping monitors, no running water, and no television to wile away the time. I had been left alone with Julia, and it dawned on me that I had somehow been elected to be the birthing coach. I assumed that being a woman was my best qualification. But my own childbirth experience in 1985 bore no resemblance to the episode unfolding before me.

Sukie came in with a clean cotton nightgown and helped me dress her mistress. Julia was so petite and her burden so large, I was concerned until I remembered that this was her third child. If she had already survived twice before, she stood a greater chance.

"Julia, is there a midwife here I can fetch for you?"

She squeezed her eyes shut and shook her head. "No, our midwife died last year. But Dr. Watkins is here."

Her words offered no consolation. As if on cue, there was a light tapping on the door, and the doctor strode in. He walked over to Julia and picked up her hand. The gentleness with which he touched her surprised me. The look of devotion was plain on his face, revealing the extent of his feelings for the patient. I was quite certain his feelings weren't returned.

"Julia, I'll need to examine you now to see where the baby is positioned."

A small groan escaped Julia's clenched lips as another spasm swept through her. She struggled under the sheet, her covered mound roiling as if it were a ship on a stormy sea.

Dr. Watkins looked up at me expectantly. "Madam, I will require your assistance. Please hold up the sheet for me."

Things were happening so fast. Just the day before, I had been in my car, listening to the radio in 1993. And now I was standing in a room in 1863 and being asked to help deliver a baby. I stood staring at the doctor, unsure how to respond.

"Is there a problem with your hearing? Haven't you been present at a birth?"

I nodded. "Just once—but I was the one giving birth."

"Surely, then, you can hold up this sheet."

I stumbled forward and grasped the sheet while the doctor began his examination. I immediately had a flashback to my own birth experience, complete with doctors and nurses garbed in sterilized gowns and masks and rubber gloves. Everything had been coated in a reassuring antiseptic smell. I knew that modern technology was out of reach, but I knew enough about the basics to realize that Dr. Watkins didn't understand the first thing about germs.

"Excuse me, Dr. Watkins. Don't you need to wash your hands?"

He regarded me with complete disdain. "Madam, I am the physician here. If you would like to assist me, I will accept that. But please leave the doctoring to me."

I bristled under his dismissive attitude. I was tired, cranky, and thoroughly confused with the situation I now found myself in. My temper sparked. "I'm sorry, Doctor, but your unsanitary methods are not acceptable. Haven't you ever heard of germs? God only knows where your hands have been, and not sanitizing them could kill both Julia and her child." I remembered that "childbed fever" had been one of the leading causes of death among women in the nineteenth century, and now I knew why. I didn't really know the woman in the bed, but there was some kind of bond between us. Whether or not it was a bonding of two mothers was immaterial. But it was very important to me that she survive this birth.

I bent over the form writhing in the bed and laid a hand on her arm. "Julia, I know I can help you here. Please ask Dr. Watkins to follow my instructions. It could be a matter of life or death for you and your child."

Julia looked up at me with fear in her eyes. But I also saw trust in them, and a deeper bond was formed.

"Charles, please, listen to Laura. Do it for me and for William's baby."

The doctor put the sheet back down slowly and stood at the other side of the bed. "I'll do this for you, Julia, and for the baby. But not for William. Not anything ever again for William."

"Thank you, Charles." Her voice weakening, Julia stifled a shout as she ground her teeth.

I went to the door and called out Sukie's name. She appeared quickly and listened attentively as I gave her a list of items I thought we would need: clean towels and sheets, alcohol, whatever kind of soap she could find, and lots and lots of boiling water.

My mind raced as I tried to think of what kinds of anesthetics they used to have. I faced the doctor. "Do you have anything to help with the pain?"

He turned on me with harshness in his voice. "Madam, suffering in childbirth is not only dictated by God but is also necessary to induce maternal love. Her mind needs to be unclouded now to realize and appreciate this blessed event. I would say that using anything to lessen the pain would be sacrilegious." Two bright spots of color appeared on his cheekbones, his self-righteousness reminiscent of a TV evangelist.

"Obviously spoken by a man who has never had to suffer through childbirth!" I snapped. "How dare you deny her comfort? If you care anything for this woman, you will give her something now!" I was almost choking on my fury, and I might have actually laid my hands on the man, but Stuart's entrance stopped me.

"You two step out of this room immediately so you can discuss whatever it is without disturbing Julia. I could hear your voices outside on the porch!"

A sudden groan brought everybody's attention toward the bed, where Julia struggled to prop herself up on her elbows. Through gritted teeth, as she staved off yet another labor pain, she managed to gasp, "Stuart, it's all right. Charles knows what he needs to do, and he had better do it pretty soon, because this baby's not waiting much longer." She squeezed her eyes shut and then managed to say, "Now hurry up!" Her burst of strength gave out as she dropped back down to the mattress and another labor pain assaulted her small body. The doctor left the room.

Her spirit made me smile, and I went back to the bed. Dipping a cloth in the washbasin Sukie had placed on the nightstand, I wiped Julia's forehead.

"You're an original 'steel magnolia,' aren't you?"

She smiled weakly, and I turned to Sukie, who had returned with the requested items. "Can you stay with her for a few minutes while I talk to Mr. Elliot and the doctor?" She nodded, and I grabbed Stuart's elbow and led him out the door.

The doctor spoke first. "Mrs. Truitt, you are probably unaware that the South is surrounded by a Yankee blockade. Even if I wanted to give Julia some laudanum, I couldn't. We haven't seen laudanum or morphine in a long, long time."

"Is there nothing we can do to help her pain?"

The doctor shook his head. "No. I'm afraid not. But it is her third birth, and they do get easier."

I raised an eyebrow. "And you would know." The doctor didn't look at all offended. "I've got to get back to Julia. Go wash your hands, Dr. Watkins—and don't forget to scrub under the fingernails."

The doctor glared at me as he turned to go.

Stuart turned to face me. "What, exactly, is a 'steel magnolia'?"

"I'll explain later. I need you to occupy the children—make sure they're not scared."

He nodded, and I returned to Julia's side to begin my vigil. Sukie washed Julia and placed towels under her hips. I washed my hands up to the elbows in preparation and sat down to wait and wondered what I was supposed to do when it was time for the baby to be born.

The sun dipped low on the horizon, sending a bright sliver of yellow light through the window. Every once in a while Julia would moan, but she never cried out. I finally turned to her and said, "Julia, it's okay to scream. We all know it hurts—there's nothing to be ashamed of."

But still she lay quietly, her drenched face a mask of pain. The grandfather clock in the hall ticked on, marking the minutes of Julia's labor, its solemn ticking interspersed occasionally by the groans of childbirth.

As the clock struck nine, the doctor reported that Julia was ready to deliver. I could see the baby's head crowning and knew that it wouldn't be much longer. Julia screamed, and I put my hand in hers, and she began to bear down. The bones in my hand ached from the pressure, but I hardly noticed as the baby's shoulders appeared and were gently turned and guided out by Dr. Watkins.

The baby was laid on top of Julia as the doctor cut and tied the umbilical cord. Wet membranes covered the child, but the startling blue skin underneath shone through clearly. Sukie handed the doctor a cloth, which he used to wipe the child. Dr. Watkins looked strangely agitated and started to gently slap the baby on the bottom. It was then I realized the baby wasn't crying. The doctor tried a few more things to revive the child, but the baby lay still and blue, ethereal and peaceful. Solemnly, the doctor shook his head and handed the still form to Sukie, who wrapped the small boy in a blanket.

"Charles? What is it? Why isn't the baby crying?" Julia's feeble voice called out. I moved back to her side and reached for her hand.

I stared, dumbfounded. This couldn't be happening. All that pain and effort for nothing? The doctor directed Sukie to press on Julia's abdomen to deliver the placenta and then took the baby from her. "I'm sorry, Julia. Your son has been born dead. There is nothing I can do."

Her sob brought me out of my stupor. As the doctor started to walk from the room, I remembered the infant-and-child CPR class I had taken when Annie was born.

I quickly walked to the doctor. "Dr. Watkins, please let me have the baby. I think I can help." I reached for the swaddled baby, but the doctor eluded my grasp.

"Woman, the child is dead. He has been delivered unto God, and we cannot reach him. Cease your squawking right now so this family can mourn their loss."

Out of desperation, I tugged at the blanket. "God damn it! Give me the baby!"

Startled, he relinquished his grasp. I took the limp bundle from his arms and laid the baby down on the floor, kneeling by his side. Checking his airway for any obstruction but finding none, I tried not to think how much this child resembled the little girl in the morgue, with the translucent skin and dark eyelashes. I put his head in a neutral position with one of my hands on his brow and the other hand under his chin. Placing my mouth over his nose and mouth, I gave two slow breaths, watching his tiny abdomen rise and fall. I checked for a pulse in his upper arm and couldn't find one. With my two fingers on the child's breastbone, I methodically began to do cycles of chest compressions and mouth-to-mouth breathing, periodically checking for a pulse. My knees ached from kneeling on the hardwood floor, and my fingers felt as if they would break, but I continued. I was aware of other people in the room, but I focused on my task. I was about ready to collapse with exhaustion when a feeble pulse beat in the baby's arm. I put my face down and felt warm air coming out of the baby's mouth. Quickly, I picked him up and shook him gently, causing a startled cry to come out of him. In my relief, I fell back, slid down against the wall, and sat there, cradling the child. My shoulder ached from my efforts, but it didn't matter. The child was alive.

Two hands reached out to take the baby from me, and I resisted until I realized it was Stuart. He took the child to Julia, who seemed dazed.

I couldn't move. I didn't know whether it was from the physical exertion of the last few hours or the sudden realization of the unwanted power I had over these people. I had just altered history. This child would not have survived if I had not been there to save him. Would this event change the course of history's path? I didn't know. And I was too tired to care.

At that moment, a large, dark-skinned man, his black hair streaked with gray and hanging down past his shoulders, pushed open the door and walked in. In his broad hands he carried a delicately carved wooden cradle, which he placed at the side of Julia's bed. At his heels followed the dog, Charlie. I looked at Charlie, and his features somehow seemed familiar to me. I glanced up at the doctor and immediately saw the resemblance: the droopy brown eyes, the soft chin, the perpetual expression of consternation. Someone had obviously given the doctor a namesake. Looking between the two, I burst out laughing and continued to howl until the tears ran down my face.

*"The illimitable, silent, never-resting thing called Time,
calling, rushing on, swift, silent, like an all-embracing
ocean tide . . ."*

Thomas Carlyle

Chapter Six

Wailing pierced the silence, and I shot straight up in darkness.
Disoriented, I leapt out of bed, only to crash against the chest
of drawers. Picking myself up, I gradually remembered where
I was and what the noise was all about. I groped my way to
the door and pulled it open.

After the birth of Julia's baby, I had gone up to my room
and collapsed into sleep, unaware of the time. I had no idea
how long I had slept, but it was still dark outside. Trailing my
hand on the wall, I followed the shrieking and crossed the
upstairs hallway to the master bedroom. Tapping gently on the
door, I walked in. This room never ceased to startle me, as
the furniture and its placement were identical to the way it
was in my own time. The candle on the bedside table cradled
the two occupants of the bed in a soft, glowing light.

Julia leaned against the headboard, her head propped on a
pillow, and the baby nestled in the crook of her arm, mouth
open wide and still bawling. Her dark, wavy hair spilled over
the white pillow like a spiderweb. Her eyes were sunken with
exhaustion, the lids heavy.

I leaned over and gently lifted the baby from her arms. "Let
me take him for a little bit while you get your sleep."

"Thank you, Laura." Her eyes were already closing as I
blew out the candle.

The full moon outside shone through the hall windows,

bathing everything in its gentle radiance. I made my way down the stairs and entered the front parlor.

I stood by the window, absorbed into the tranquillity of the moonlight-flooded room. The baby fretted, so I took him off my shoulder and cradled him in the curve of my arm. He focused on the great orb filling the sky, and he gurgled, raising a fist as if to grab a moonbeam and bring it back to earth. I leaned down to kiss his cheek and saw the moonlight reflected in his eyes.

Oh, moon, where else do you shine tonight? Is my Annie looking at you now, as I am, and wondering where her mother is?

I began to sing softly, swaying the child in my arms. Without thinking, the words flowed automatically from my lips. "You are my sweet pea, my only sweet pea. You bring me sunshine every day."

A splash of moisture landed on baby Robbie's chin, and I realized I was crying. A door opened, and an arc of light appeared on the wall next to us. It grew larger in circumference until the room seemed swallowed by it. At the sound of approaching footsteps, I faced the window again, hoping not to draw attention to myself.

Someone coughed quietly behind me. I pivoted and saw Stuart. He was still dressed, but his dark hair was tousled, as if he had been running his fingers through it. Instinctively, I put out my free hand to smooth it, then quickly withdrew it.

He set down the lamp he carried and reached for the baby, who was quietly chewing on a fist. I had neglected to put on a wrap over my nightgown and was painfully aware of my undressed state.

"Did you hurt yourself?" he asked.

"Pardon me?"

"I thought a herd of cows was trampling you in your room, from the sound of it."

"Oh, that," I said, rubbing a bruised elbow. "No, I just decided a midnight waltz with my chest of drawers would be a good idea." I smiled. "What are you doing up so late?"

Patting the baby's back, he whispered, "I've been going

over the plantation books. They're in a bit of a mess. I'm afraid my brother didn't have much interest in record keeping." He swayed with the baby snuggled onto his shoulder, as if he had done it many times before.

He stopped abruptly, narrowing his eyes as he stared at me. "You've been crying." His face echoed his concern. "Why? Have you remembered something?"

I wiped my remaining tears away with the sleeve of my nightgown. "No. It's just . . . the moonlight. It always makes me think of Annie." I walked closer to the window and pressed my forehead against the cold glass, my breathing making circular patterns and obliterating my reflection. "She disappeared when she was almost two. She'd be seven now. I don't even know if I would recognize her if I did find her."

"How did she disappear?" he asked quietly, still swaying with the drowsy baby on his shoulder, soft sucking sounds filling the room.

I took a deep breath. "My husband and I took her up to Moon Mountain to view a comet during an eclipse. When it was over, Annie was just . . . gone. She was sleeping, you see, so I had placed her on a blanket, where I thought she would be safe. . . ." My voice broke, and I stopped.

He rested his free hand on my shoulder, offering comfort. His touch burned through the fabric of my nightgown, and I had the bizarre impulse to lay my head on his hand.

"Don't blame yourself. No matter how good a mother you are, things often happen that are out of your control."

I turned to face him. The baby was finally asleep, and Stuart had stopped swaying. He looked at me intently, his blue eyes mirroring the gleam of the lamplight.

"Thank you for trying to help. And I know you're right. If only I had a grave to visit or some knowledge of what happened to her, I'd feel better. But I—I have no closure."

His brow furrowed. "Closure? What's that?"

I smiled at my careless use of twentieth-century psychobabble. "It just means that my grieving has no end. I'm not sure if I should be mourning Annie or searching for her."

He nodded silently, and I was struck, not for the first time, by how handsome he was. Not with the fair, evenly chiseled good looks that made women turn and stare at Jack, but in a dark, powerful way that made my eyes seek him out when we were in the same room together.

"Do you think Annie might be in Roswell?" His words brought me out of my examination, and I flushed when I realized I had been staring at him.

"I really don't know. It's been five years. She could be anywhere. Or she could be . . ." I couldn't bring myself to finish the sentence.

"If she's here, I'm sure we'll find her. But I will tell you that it's a small community. If anybody here or in the neighboring towns had found a child on the mountain, we likely would have heard about it. I don't remember anything, but Julia might. We can ask her in the morning." He shifted the baby on his shoulder. "And then we need to find out where you belong."

I was glad of the darkness to hide the sudden coloring in my cheeks. I swallowed, the sound audible in the quiet room. His expression changed, and his eyes flickered briefly in the dim lamplight. "Why do I feel as if you know more than you're telling, Mrs. Truitt?"

My palms started to sweat, and I quickly swept them through my hair. I couldn't tell him the truth. I could never allow myself to forget he was on the losing side of this conflict, nor the fact that I had knowledge that could help the Confederacy. I wanted to find my daughter and return home— my home with its own host of memories. That was all I had left, and I wanted it back. I had no desire to get embroiled in these people's lives. I just wanted to go home.

I shook my head slightly, not meeting his eyes. "I don't know. But I appreciate your opening your home to me. I promise to be gone and out of your hair as soon as I can find a way home—or at least find where home is." I reached for the baby, and Stuart placed him gently in my arms. "Thank you. You have a way with babies, I think." I smiled. "Good night, then."

Before I got to the bottom of the stairway, I turned around

with a question. "Who was that Indian man who brought the cradle the night Robbie was born?"

Stuart limped over to me. "That was Zeke Proudfoot, my grandfather. He lives in a small cabin in the woods behind the house and only comes up here on special occasions."

I nodded, then glanced down at his leg; he was rubbing the knee joint. "Where were you wounded?"

"In the leg," he said, a smile creeping across his face.

I grinned back. "Obviously. But which battle?"

"At Champion's Hill—back in May." He straightened and took a deep breath. "I'm lucky to still have my leg. Those army sawbones just want to chop everything off. But Zeke rode out to bring me back and have Charles take care of me. They saved my leg, and probably my life, too. I guess we're lucky to have Charles—just look what he did for Julia today."

I bristled at that last remark and said under my breath, "Yeah. And Oz didn't give anything to the Tin Man that he didn't already have."

Stuart looked up at me with a quizzical expression, and I explained briefly, "Remind me to tell you a great story when you have time. The main character and I have a lot in common."

"In what way?" he asked, his mouth tilting upward. "Are you both 'steel magnolias'?"

"No." I smiled back. "Actually, she and I just realize that we aren't in Kansas anymore."

He looked perplexed. "I'll look forward to hearing that one."

I put my foot on the bottom stair and commented, "I hope I get to meet Mr. Proudfoot."

"Mrs. Truitt, I'd be happy to take you out to his cabin to meet him. He might be able to help you with your memory. He's sort of a medicine man—though not like Charles."

I paused on the bottom step. "I'd like that. Maybe tomorrow then." As an afterthought, I added, "Please call me Laura."

He paused briefly before replying, the hall clock ticking in the silence. "I don't think that would be proper."

Continuing my ascent, I said over my shoulder, "I promise I won't be offended."

Halfway up the stairs, I heard him call out softly, "Good night, Laura."

I stopped, grinning to myself, and called out, "Good night, Stuart." I reached the hallway and went to tuck little Robbie into his cradle. And then I lay down in my bed, falling asleep before my head hit the pillow.

I awoke the following morning to the rolling sound of thunder and the beating of rain against my windows. Sukie was already in my room, drawing back the curtains and laying out clothes for me on the fainting couch. I smiled every time I thought about a "fainting couch." As if anyone around here had time to faint. The smell of hot food wafted to me from the tray resting on the dressing table.

"Good morning, ma'am," Sukie said as she poured fresh water into the pitcher.

"What time is it?" I asked, rubbing the sleep out of my eyes.

"It's after eleven, Miz Laura."

I bolted straight out of bed in a panic. "Oh, no! I told Julia that I would help her with the children, and all I've done is lie in bed all morning!"

"Don't fret, Miz Laura. Miz Julia told me to let you sleep, seeing as how you was up with the baby last night."

"How long has she been up?"

"Since before six. Miz Julia has lots to do, with all them slaves having gone off with Mister William."

"Stuart's brother took slaves? Whatever for?"

Sukie gave a derisive snort. "Who knows what that boy's thinking? He said that President Lincoln had freed the slaves, and it was breaking the law to keep them. So, when he left to go back and fight with the Yankees last September, he took a whole pile of them. The ones that were too old or just didn't want to leave stayed here."

"But this is his home! Didn't he think of how hard it would be for Julia to manage?"

71

"Mister William don't usually think of anyone but himself." As if to herself, she added, "Hard to believe that he and Mister Stuart are brothers."

"Sukie, if you don't mind my asking, why didn't you go?"

"Oh, no, Miz Laura. This is my home and the only family I know." She fluffed the pillows and arranged them on the bed.

I stood there contemplating what Sukie had just said as she handed me clean undergarments. I was still pretty shy about having somebody help me dress, so I turned my back to take off my nightgown and slip on my underclothes while she busied herself making the bed.

As soon as I was finished dressing, Sukie attempted to make my hair presentable.

She held a lock of it between two dark fingers. "Why did you cut it? Were you sick? Such a shame—it's so pretty and thick." She led me to the dressing table. The breakfast tray was directly under my nose now, and my stomach let out a growl. I recognized grits and hastily stuck my finger in them for a taste.

I could see Sukie's reflection in the mirror shaking her head in disapproval. Whether it was over the shortness of my hair or my appalling table manners, I didn't know. But I felt as if my mother was judging me, and I made a mental note to begin scrutinizing my words and actions.

After eating, I went downstairs to seek out Julia and offer her whatever assistance I could. Seeing as how I didn't garden, cook, or sew, I knew that child-care would be my best bet.

I heard the sound of an ax striking wood and followed it out the back door. The rain had stopped, and the air was thick with moisture and the heady scent of saturated dirt and flower petals. Standing on the back porch, I paused to admire the view. Instead of the lofty pine trees separating my backyard from the highway, long rows of cotton plants and other crops that I didn't recognize stretched as far as my eyes could see. The dark shapes of five or six people leaning over hoes and several mules working in the fields stood out in bold relief. Stuart watched me approach as he stood near a large pile of wood and rubbed his wounded leg. His skin had an olive cast, making his blue eyes stand out under his dark hair.

"Good morning, Laura," he said, with the touch of a smile on his lips.

"Good morning, Stuart." I stopped a few feet in front of him. "What are you planning on doing with all that cotton?" I indicated the furrowed field behind him. "I would think the market's a bit slow these days."

He raised an eyebrow, as if he wasn't used to such questions coming from a woman. "The Roswell mills will take most of it, and I'm hoping to sell the rest to a blockade runner bound for England." His gaze scrutinized me as he spoke.

"What are you staring at?" I asked, feeling a touch self-conscious at his appraising look.

"To be honest, I was just wondering to myself whether it would be better for you to go back to wearing your men's clothing, or to find someone besides Julia to borrow clothes from."

Julia was a good size smaller than I was, and I did feel the uncomfortable pull of the dress across my chest, not to mention that the skirt barely brushed the tops of my shoes.

"Wouldn't do for me to burst my buttons in front of your friends, would it?"

Serious now, he replied, "No, it wouldn't. I'll talk to Julia about it."

"Really, there's no need. These will do for now. I don't plan on staying here forever. But I did want to talk to Julia about my daughter."

He leaned on the ax handle, as if to take the weight off his leg. "I asked Julia about your daughter this morning at breakfast. She doesn't recall hearing anything, but she promised to ask around town." He narrowed his eyes. "We also need to see if anybody recognizes you. I know that if I had seen you before, I would remember it."

I looked away, uncomfortable, and unsure what to do next. Searching for Annie here, in this place and this time, might be fruitless. I had no idea how the powers that had brought me here worked. Annie could be anywhere. I just assumed that whatever had happened to me had happened to her, and this was as good a place as any to start looking.

Turning, I saw Julia approach, a large basket brimming over with an assortment of vegetables hanging on her arm. Her face was shaded by a large straw hat, obscuring her expression.

"I'm sorry to have slept so late. I promised to help you, and I'm afraid I haven't done much more than lie in bed. Tell me what I can do."

The back door opened, and Willie and the little girl I had seen on my first day stepped out onto the porch. Charlie yapped excitedly at their heels, his droopy eyes making me grin.

"Hi, Willie. Is this your sister?"

They both stood silently, shuffling their feet, until Julia approached.

"Willie, Sarah, this is Mrs. Truitt. Mrs. Truitt, this is my daughter, Sarah. You've already met Willie."

Willie gave me an exaggerated bow, and Sarah curtsied. Sarah was taller than her brother by a good two inches. Her blond hair was sun-streaked white in places and hung in two heavy braids. A small spattering of freckles decorated the bridge of her nose, and clear green eyes stared levelly at me.

"It's a pleasure to meet you," I responded with a curtsy of my own.

"Mrs. Truitt has kindly offered to help me take care of you and the baby until she is ready to return to her own home. I expect you to treat her as an honored guest."

A loud rumbling in the sky made us crane our necks upward. An ominous black cloud hovered overhead, and I knew it would be only a matter of seconds before the sky opened up.

"Quickly, children, let's go inside before we get soaked. How would you like to hear a story?" I herded the children in through the back door.

"What kind of a story?" they asked in unison.

"Well, it's about a little girl and her dog who get lost, and an evil witch is chasing them. So she makes friends with a lion, a tin man, and a scarecrow who help her find her way home."

"Is this the girl from Kansas?" Stuart asked as he shut the door behind us.

I nodded. "And she's a long, long way from home," I added as we all headed into the front parlor just as rain began pelting the windows.

"Whoso desireth to know what will be hereafter, let him think of what is past, for the world hath ever been in a circular revolution: whatsoever is now, was heretofore; and things past or present, are no other than such as shall be again: Redit orbis in orbem."

Sir Walter Raleigh

Chapter Seven

The summer rainstorm lasted for over an hour, saturating the fields and yard. Muddy puddles of red clay beckoned the children outside, but I restrained them with the promise of another story. Both children had bright minds, and I wanted to ask permission to teach formal lessons. I left the children playing and went in search of Julia. I heard a fretful Robbie, and I followed the sound into the library.

Julia and Stuart were speaking in whispers, so I paused before knocking on the partially closed door.

"Stuart, I don't know how much longer we can survive here. Flour is already forty dollars a barrel, and salt is one hundred and twenty-five dollars a bag. And the dollars we have are worth less and less each day." The wooden cradle creaked as it rocked from side to side. "I hate to think of it, but we might

75

be forced to leave Phoenix Hall. Perhaps my aunt in Valdosta will take us in until this war is over." There was a brief silence while Julia soothed a fretting baby, and then she continued. "I think we can make it through this winter, but if the army keeps on provisioning itself with our food, we'll be hard-pressed to make it through until spring. They've just about cleaned out my root cellar." Julia's voice was filled with resignation.

There was a slight pause before Stuart answered. "Julia, I'm sorry. You're right. Leaving might be the best thing for you and the children. I've been selfish, wanting to somehow hang onto Phoenix Hall at all costs."

A mosquito landed on my forearm, and I squashed it, splattering blood on my pale skin. Stuart continued, his voice heavy. "As long as our dividends from the mills continue, we should be able to manage financially whether or not the plantation is running."

Julia's voice was soft. "I'm sorry, Stuart. I know how much this land means to you. Much more than it ever meant to William."

I heard a soft grunt of agreement from Stuart and the irregular cadence of his boot heels on the wooden floor. "The only things that have ever meant anything to William were things that weren't his."

The creaking cradle stopped. "Oh, Stuart," Julia said quietly. "Surely you've forgiven him—us. I know how much we hurt you, and for that I will always be sorry. But you've been a good brother to both of us, and I only hope you can find it in your heart to one day forgive us."

I imagined Stuart running a hand through his hair, and I felt a little pang of something—something I hadn't felt in years.

"Julia, that's all in the past. It really doesn't matter anymore. You are part of my family now, and it is my duty to take care of you and your children in William's absence."

At the personal turn in their conversation, I started to back away from the door, when I became aware of Sukie standing behind me in the hall. She raised her eyebrows but made no comment. Rather than appear to have been eavesdropping, I knocked on the door and entered.

Gone was the smell of musty books I had become accustomed to. The bookshelves that lined the wall were full, but I could see no torn or moldy bindings.

"I hope I'm not disturbing you."

Julia was seated at the mahogany secretary, her foot methodically pumping the cradle back and forth. She leaned over the baby as I entered and murmured something unintelligible to all but mother and child.

Shaking her head, she looked up at me. "No, not at all. Stuart was just helping me with the books, and I think my head has had about all the facts and figures it can take for the moment. Would you like some coffee?"

"No!" I said a little too vehemently. "I mean, not right now, thank you." My tongue burned even at the thought of that acid brew they called coffee.

Julia smiled. "Well, I do think Sukie is making some of her strawberry tea if you would like some of that."

"Only if it's made with real strawberries. No roasted acorns or shoe leather, please."

"Of course it's made with real strawberries," she said, laughing. "I'll be right back, then." She picked up the baby and walked out of the room, leaving the door wide open.

Stuart stood at the far wall, absently pulling books from the shelves. "Are you finished with the tales of Dorothy?" he asked as he firmly shoved a brown leather-bound volume back into its slot.

"For now, at least. I've got about a dozen more where that came from, so I should be able to keep the children occupied for the next year of rainy days."

He quickly looked at me. "Do you mean to stay that long?"

The four walls of the room suddenly seemed to close in on me. "I . . . I don't know. No. I want to find my daughter and go home. I just don't know how."

He examined me closely, his eyes never wavering. "Is that really why you're here?"

"If you're asking if I have ulterior motives, no, I don't. I apologize for eavesdropping, but when I heard you and Julia

77

talking, I simply tried to determine if I would be intruding. I'm sorry if I'm a burden."

Brushing aside my apology, he said, "Please don't think you're a burden. In fact, I'm beginning to think of you as a godsend."

"A godsend? Don't you mean another mouth to feed?"

He came to stand in front of me. "No, Laura, we really need you here. You're a wonderful help with the children, and I'll feel better when I leave, knowing Julia has you with her." He paused briefly. "There's a quality of strength about you. And quite a bit of mystery."

I lowered my eyes, eager to change the course of our conversation. "When do you think you'll go back to the fighting?" I asked, suddenly realizing that his answer mattered to me.

"As soon as I can walk without my leg paining me too much. My men need me, and I must get back to them as soon as possible."

"Your men? Are you an officer?"

He raised a dark eyebrow. "Yes. I'm a major in the 42nd Georgia Infantry."

I looked past his shoulder and out the window toward the rows and rows of cotton. "Don't you think you're needed here more than on the battlefield?"

He shook his head adamantly. "No." He turned from me and resumed his perusal of the books on the shelves. "To quote our General Lee, 'Do your duty in all things. You cannot do more; you should never wish to do less.' "

He slid a book back and faced me. "I long to resume a peacetime life. But I cannot."

Julia interrupted us as she returned with the tea. While she busied herself with pouring, I surreptitiously studied her. Yes, she was pretty, in a very delicate sort of way. Short and slender, with dark hair contrasting starkly with her white skin. Large hazel eyes added to her air of innocence. I felt a small twinge when I recalled the personal aspect of her conversation with Stuart. Embarrassed by my inappropriate jealousy, I felt myself blushing. Glancing up, I saw Stuart looking at me in surprise. He must have wondered why the act of pouring out tea should be so distressing for me.

As we sipped our refreshment, I broached the subject of giving the children some lessons, and Julia gratefully accepted my offer. In the ensuing silence, I pondered their earlier conversation. Knowing that General Sherman's federal armies would be invading Georgia and heading directly for Roswell in a year's time, I thought Julia's decision to leave town a prudent one. But I remembered something Mrs. Cudahy had told us when Jack and I first saw the house. Someone had been here to meet Sherman's army and save the house from destruction. If I convinced Julia to leave, who would be here to prevent that?

I cleared my throat before speaking. "Julia, I have to tell you that I overheard you and Stuart talking about your financial situation. Since I have inadvertently become another mouth for you to feed, perhaps I can offer some advice."

Julia and Stuart looked at me expectantly. I continued. "If you haven't already converted all your greenbacks to Confederate dollars, don't. Keep as many greenbacks and as much gold as you can. Then, go into the woods and mark a spot and bury all your money and any other valuables that could be carried away. Most of your livestock is already gone—courtesy of the Confederate Army, I assume—but you might want to hide what you've got left in a pen in the woods. The Yankees will surely take anything that's not bolted down."

Julia looked at me in disbelief. "Surely you don't think the Yankees could get this far?"

I took another sip of my tea and nodded. "Oh, yes. Not only do you have the mills here, but you also have a bridge across the Chattahoochee on the way to Atlanta. Trust me—Roswell is circled in red on General Sherman's map."

I was about to say more when Stuart stood abruptly. His teacup slipped to the floor, splattering china and tea in all directions.

"What a cool liar you are, Mrs. Truitt."

Julia stood, too, her usually composed face a mask of anger.

"Stuart! How dare you be so rude to our guest? I insist on an apology."

He stayed where he was, immobile, hard blue eyes—soldier's eyes—scrutinizing me. "I will not. What I will do is turn her in to the proper authorities and have her arrested as a spy."

My hand trembled as I replaced my cup in its saucer, the delicate china clinking wildly. How could I have been so stupid? "Julia, it's okay. I understand why he's upset, and—"

Stuart cut me off. " 'Upset'? You have just given me information that could come only from somebody associated with the Federals. And you're sitting in my parlor drinking tea. Believe you me, I am a good deal more than 'upset.' I have no choice but to turn you in."

Julia strode to him and put a hand on his arm. "No, Stuart. She's trying to help us—regardless of who she is or where she got the information. She has already saved the lives of two of my children. Don't we owe her for that at least?"

Looking at Julia, her delicate features contorted in defiance, I was once again reminded of a flower petal reinforced with steel.

Stuart turned to me, his eyes narrowed. "Why are you here? To spy on the mills to find out if they're supplying the Confederate Army? Wouldn't there be an easier way to do that than making up a story about your lost daughter? What was that for—to gain our sympathy?"

Tears stung behind my eyes, but I dared not show them to him. I stood, my voice trembling. "I *did* come here looking for my daughter. I wish to God I were making that part up. And as for how I know all that, I . . . I don't know. But I do know I'm not here to cause any harm."

Julia came to stand next to me and put an arm around my shoulder. "Please, Stuart. Look at what she has done for us already. How can you think of punishing her? You mustn't turn her in." She straightened her back and lifted her chin. "And if you do, I will go with her."

Dark blue eyes darted from me to Julia. He shook his head, then looked down at his boots, now surrounded by shattered china. His voice deep and slow, he said, "I can't fight you, Julia. I've never been able to, have I?"

Julia's hand tightened on my arm.

He raised his eyes and spoke to Julia, his gaze never leaving my face. "I won't turn her in—but I won't allow her to stay here, either. I want her gone first thing tomorrow morning."

With a nod to Julia, he limped across the floor and left the room. Julia dropped her hand from my arm. "I'll go talk to him. Don't worry, I won't have you thrown out." With a re-assuring glance, she followed Stuart out the door.

I bent to pick up the shards of china, then sat silently in my chair, running over the conversation in my head and wondering what I would do if the Elliotts forced me to leave. Unable to sit still, I began pacing the room. I pulled a book off a shelf and stared at it for a while, the words blurring on the page. Replacing the book, I glanced out the window to see Julia striding purposefully toward the side of the house where I knew her garden was. Her eyebrows were puckered together, and she seemed lost in thought.

Not willing to wait any longer, I decided to seek out Julia or Stuart to learn my fate.

Charlie's barking drew me out the back door. Willie and Sarah were attending to their chores of fetching water and feeding the chickens. They stopped when they saw me approach.

"Did either of you see your Uncle Stuart come this way?"

Sarah looked at me and shrugged. I stopped dead in my tracks. That one movement brought memories of Jack flooding back to me. It must have been one of those things a person does and others don't notice until somebody else mimics the movement, but the resemblance was disturbing. I knelt in front of her, my hands on her shoulders, and stared into her thin face. It had been over five years since I last saw my Annie—a plump little toddler barely able to walk. I searched for that baby in this little girl's face but could not find it. Patting her gently, I let her go.

Willie pointed out toward the cotton field, and I recognized Stuart astride Endy. A tall man stood next to him, and as I walked toward them, I recognized Zeke Proudfoot. As I approached, I stayed to the side of the drainage ditch, not wanting to trample the plants underfoot. Some of the creamy white blossoms had already turned red. Soon they would be sprouting burst bolls stuffed with fluffy white masses of cotton fibers.

Stuart had climbed off his horse and was squatting on his haunches, his long fingers manipulating the leaves of one of the plants. Both men looked at me as I approached, and I had the odd sensation that I had been the object of their conversation.

Stuart stood slowly when I stopped before them, the footprints behind me in the sticky red mud marking my passage. The hens cackled nearby as Willie doled out their meal. Stuart's eyes were cold as he looked at me, and my stomach lurched. The last time I had felt this way was when I had worn my mother's favorite scarf without her permission and ruined it. I looked up at him, prepared to do battle. I didn't know what I would tell him, but it had to be something good to keep me here. I had no place else to go.

He stood slowly, tipping his hat back to glare at me. "Well, Mrs. Truitt. It seems you have an ally in my sister-in-law. I think she's too trusting. But she wants you to stay."

Relief flooded me, but his words cut off my smile.

"Just realize that I won't let you out of my sight. And one wrong move from you, and I will personally escort you to the proper authorities and see you tried as a spy."

I moved closer. Unblinking, I met his blue gaze. "I sure as hell am no Yankee spy."

Zeke walked toward me and placed a hand on the top of my head, his brown eyes softening slightly as he stared into my face. Too stunned by his actions to move, I remained still. "You travel in the shadow," he said softly. It wasn't a question.

"What do you mean?" His eyes were warm, and I felt a familiarity with his presence.

Removing his hand and turning to Stuart, he continued, "She will not harm you. Her heart is good, and her powers are strong. Listen to her and trust her. Salvation will lie in her hands." Without another word, he turned on his heel and began walking toward the woods.

"What does he mean?" I asked, half afraid of the answer.

"I'm not sure. Zeke tends to talk in riddles. But I think he's wrong here. He wants me to trust you, but you're holding something back. I have an odd way of not trusting people who are not honest with me." He paused briefly to call for Endy. "Laura, I can only hope that you will tell me everything in due course." He hoisted himself into the saddle, wincing slightly as he put his wounded leg in the stirrup. "Because I will find out. Sooner or later, I will find out who you are. And if your motives are to cause us harm by spying or by other means, then you will wish you had never come here."

Without another word, he galloped away from the field, Endy's hoofbeats muted by the soft, damp earth.

"I live in Possibility—
A fairer house than Prose—
More numerous of Windows—
Superior—for Doors—."

Emily Dickinson

Chapter Eight

I stood motionless, watching Stuart ride off, feeling more hurt than I cared to admit. I slowly walked back toward the house, my thoughts in turmoil. I hadn't asked to be dropped into their lives, and I certainly didn't want to be there any more than they wanted me to be. I kicked a hapless cotton plant as I walked by. I wanted nothing more at that moment than to find

Annie, if she were even within my reach, and then go home. I certainly didn't want to care about Julia, her family, this house. Or Stuart. I only hoped it wasn't too late.

At the thought of home, I looked up. The sweet aroma from the Osage orange trees drifted in the air. They had been planted when the house was built to discourage flies and rodents. The ancient oak treè with its sprawling limbs was still rooted in the same spot in the backyard, looking a great deal smaller than in my own time. There was even a swing on a lower branch, just as Jack had made for Annie. I slowed my pace. How was I going to find her? I stopped walking completely when I considered my next thought. How was I going to get home?

I felt utterly alone. The children were nowhere to be seen, so I turned the corner of the house in search of Julia. I found her amidst cucumber plants and potatoes, furiously pulling weeds. Not seeing me approach, she appeared startled when I spoke her name.

Shielding her eyes with one hand, she looked at me with a frown. I knelt down beside her on the sodden ground and began pulling weeds, the moist earth crumbling easily off the roots, the smell of freshly turned soil reminding me of an open grave. I wrinkled my nose and turned to Julia.

"I can do this, Julia. You just gave birth two days ago—shouldn't you be resting?"

She wiped at a piece of dirt clinging to her forehead, smearing it across her skin. "I don't mind, really. It keeps my mind off . . . things. Besides, there's so much work to be done."

I sat on my heels, watching her attack the weeds. "I wanted to thank you for what you said to Stuart. I promise you that your trust hasn't been misplaced. I swear I'm not a spy." She yanked up more weeds, throwing them with a vengeance into a pile. I continued, "I've only known you a short time, but I feel as if I really know you—you're almost like a sister to me."

A small smile crossed her face. "I feel it, too. We've certainly been through quite a bit since we met, haven't we? It's terribly selfish of me, but I would like you to stay here forever."

I looked down at my hands. "But this isn't my home. As soon as I find my daughter, assuming she's even here, I'm going to bring her back home."

She paused and looked at me, her hazel eyes suddenly cool. "What if you can't find her? Will you stay?"

"No. My home . . . it's all I've got left of . . . of Jack and Annie. I need to go back." A cooling breeze swept over us. Maybe that was why I was sent here, to get away from the old memories that chased me in the night. But I clung to them, and I needed them back.

Children's laughter carried over to us from around the corner of the house, and we turned to watch Willie chasing Sarah, her blond pigtails flying. I remembered again that shrug she had given that was so much like Jack, and I stared at her fair hair, my mouth suddenly dry.

I swallowed thickly. "Julia, Sarah reminds me of someone I used to know." I hesitated, weighing my words. "Is she your natural daughter?"

Her clear eyes studied me, the breeze stirring the curls around her face. Without a pause, she answered, "Yes, I am Sarah's mother." Her gaze never wavered. "Her birth is recorded in the family Bible, and Dr. Watkins was present at her birth. You can ask him, if you like."

She squeezed my hand. I did believe her. But I would still ask the good doctor.

Silence settled between us as she resumed her chore. Suddenly, without looking at me, she said, "I gather such strength from this garden." She grabbed a handful of dirt and let the thick, muddy clods fall slowly from her fist. "It's not much, but it's the only buffer my family has against starvation." A crooked grin settled on her lips. "Before the war, I never would have dreamed of sticking my hands in dirt. It's amazing what one will do to protect one's family." She looked directly at me. "I don't know if there's *anything* I would stop at to protect them."

A cloud drifted across the sun, creating large pools of shadow. I shivered and rubbed my arms. Was she warning me? Did she really think I was a spy? She gently placed a gloved hand on my forearm and smiled. "Laura, you have already saved the lives of two of my children. I am in your debt, and I will do all I can to help you."

I looked down at her as I stood. "Thank you, Julia. I appreciate that. But I don't know if anybody can help me." I brushed at weeds clinging to my skirts. "If the children are done with their chores, I'll go see about starting their lessons."

Leaving Julia, I trudged to the house, searching for the children, who had mysteriously disappeared. I went inside and noticed a piece of the broken teacup left on the library floor. I picked it up, then moved to the window to see if I could spot Willie and Sarah. I saw them by the kitchen, and, forgetting the broken piece of china, I squeezed my hand into a fist to knock on the window. I cried out, dropping the china, and watched the blood ooze from a thin line bisecting my palm. I stared dumbly at my hand, wondering absently what I should do.

A movement from the doorway made me look up. I turned away from Stuart's scowl and looked back at my hand, my eyes tracing the path of blood as it dripped down my wrist and landed in spots on the dark wood floor.

"What happened?" He strode into the room, lifted my arm, and looked at my cut.

"I cut my hand on your broken teacup." I looked into his eyes to see if my tiny barb had had any effect. "If you just want to close the door, I'll be happy to stay in here and bleed to death."

He frowned, but I allowed him to lead me to a sofa. His voice was brusque. "Sit here for a minute. I'll return shortly with something to wrap that with."

He came back quickly with what looked like sewing scraps. He retrieved a bottle of whiskey from the cabinet and sat down next to me. "This will hurt a bit."

I gave an unladylike snort. "As if that would bother you."

He ignored me as he bent to his task of pulling out a small shard of china from the wound. The feel of his hands on my bare flesh made my blood heat. I looked away, wanting him to let go while at the same time not to stop. He soaked a cloth with whiskey and began to bathe the cut. Waves of pain shot up my arm, but I bit my lip, resisting the urge to cry out.

"Go ahead and scream. I know it hurts."

I kept my face turned away. "I wouldn't give you the satisfaction."

He had stopped cleaning the wound but still held my hand. I turned back to him and found him scrutinizing me. I tried to jerk my hand out of his grasp, but he wouldn't let go. I squirmed, trying to get away from the flush of heat his touch was sending through my body.

"Despite what you might think, I do not relish inflicting pain on you or anybody else. Unless, of course, something I love is being threatened." His hand tightened on mine, but I refused to wince. "I would like to suggest a truce between us. If we're going to be living under the same roof, we will have to learn to be civil toward each other—at least for Julia's sake. But don't be mistaken." His blues eyes narrowed. "I'll still be watching your every move. I will also be accompanying you every time you leave the house. So you'd better get used to my company."

I seethed inside but knew that I had no choice but to agree. "All right, then. A truce. Just promise me one thing." He raised an eyebrow. "When you find out that you're wrong about me, I want an apology."

His eyes widened. "Agreed."

He lifted a piece of material to his mouth and bit it, tearing it in half. "Why are you hiding something from us? You have nothing to fear from us here—unless you really are a Yankee."

I looked down at the bandage he was wrapping around my hand. Denying that I was holding something back would only make his suspicions worse, so I said nothing.

He looked at me, his blue eyes solemn, as if awaiting an answer. Shaking his head, he continued his bandaging.

I had always hated the sight of blood and tried to distract myself by looking at the bookshelves. A single title grabbed my attention. *General History of Nature and Theory of the Heavens* by Immanuel Kant.

"What do you know about astronomy?"

He raised his eyes to my face, his expression curious. "Not a lot." Following my gaze, he saw the book. "Oh, those are Julia's mother's books. Pamela had a feeling Nashville would fall to the Yankees and sent them down here for safekeeping."

I studied his thick brush of dark hair as he bent his head back to his task. "Would it be all right if I borrowed one to read?"

He looked at me, his face unreadable. "I don't see why not. But if you really want to learn about astronomy, you should speak with Zeke. He's known as an expert on such matters."

As he knotted two ends of the bandage together, I asked, "Is Zeke's cabin far?"

"No, not far at all if you ride. It's quite a bit of a walk, though."

"I'd prefer to walk, if you can show me the way."

"You want to go now?"

I nodded. "Yes. So if you could just—"

"You're not going without me—remember? I'll accompany you."

I gave him a patient smile. "I assure you, that's not necessary."

"And I assure you, madam, that it is. I must protect my family."

Rolling my eyes, I stood and brushed past him to reach the back door. Charlie yelped with excitement when he saw Stuart following me and happily trotted at our heels.

Despite the tense moments earlier in the day, my step was lighter. This visit with Zeke could be the first move toward finding Annie and the way home.

The path through the woods was well worn, the damp earth compacted by passing feet and littered with fallen pine needles. A weak sun filtered through the high canopy of pines, sprinkling the ground with pinpricks of light.

I deliberately walked fast, knowing that Stuart's limp would make him trail behind. But when I came to a fork in the path, I stopped, unsure of the direction. While I waited for Stuart to catch up, I lifted the hair off the back of my neck and wiped the sticky sweat with the palm of my hand. I unbuttoned the first two buttons on my dress, welcoming a cool breeze.

Stuart's eyes turned a dark shade of blue as he approached, his gaze lingering at my neck. He pulled at his collar, as if it were too tight. My mouth went dry, and I quickly turned away.

Feeling guilty at making a wounded man walk briskly through the woods, I slowed my pace to his and walked beside him. I searched for a neutral topic of conversation.

"Stuart, I've been wondering."

He looked up at me expectantly, probably curious at my civil tone.

"Where did Charlie get his name?"

A smile cracked his stern face. "So, you've noticed the resemblance between Charlie and Dr. Watkins?" He stopped briefly to rub his leg. "So did Sarah, when she was four. She named the dog Dr. Watkins. We made her change it, but she insisted on Charlie. Luckily, Charles hasn't seemed to notice."

I had suspected Sarah was a smart little girl, and that confirmed it. I laughed at her astuteness. "It's a good thing she didn't think he looked like the rear end of a horse!"

Stuart made a strangling noise in his throat, as if he were choking. When he recovered, he said, "Yes, our Sarah has a very active imagination. She's always making up stories."

I smiled, thinking about the bright-eyed child and wondering where that trait had come from. Certainly not from her mother, who seemed to be a whirlwind of activity but contentedly grounded in reality.

As we approached a clearing, I saw a small log cabin. A covered porch surrounded the small abode on three sides. Zeke sat on it in a rocking chair, nodding at us in greeting. Charlie bounded off, running around Zeke and barking happily. The old man leaned over and stroked the dog's back.

Thinking of Zeke's last words to me and feeling suddenly shy, I allowed Stuart to climb the stairs of the porch first. Then both men turned to look expectantly at me.

I smiled and approached the porch.

Zeke broke the silence. "I see you two have made peace with each other."

Stuart cleared his throat, and I looked down at the ground.

Stuart spoke first. "We've called a truce, yes. No reason we can't be civil to each other."

The old man looked at Stuart, and his lined face crinkled into a smile. He picked up a large jug by the side of his chair and offered it to Stuart. After Stuart took a swig, Zeke offered it to me. "Drink some. It will help the pain in your hand."

I realized, for the first time, that my hand was throbbing. Not wanting to appear rude, I walked up the steps and took the proffered jug.

Liquid fire best describes the contents that coursed down my throat. Stifling the reflex to gag, I swallowed stoically. A small wince escaped me, and I quickly took in three gulps of air. I felt the heat all the way from my throat to my stomach, and my head suddenly felt light. The throbbing in my hand decreased to a dull ache.

My walk was unsteady as I made to return the jug. Stuart wore a look of surprise, but Zeke's face remained impassive. To show them what a real woman I was, I took another swig, almost staggering this time with the effects on my muscle coordination.

"That's enough, Laura," Stuart said with concern as he grabbed the jug and sat down in a rocker.

I took a seat on the top step to steady myself. The rustic setting reminded me of camping, and I began to hum a favorite camp song. It wasn't long until I was singing "Rocky Top" at the top of my lungs. I felt two pairs of eyes on me and stopped abruptly.

Stuart ceased rocking. "So, you sing, too. Where did you learn that?"

I avoided his eyes. "Oh, it's just something I picked up along the way. My grandmother, I think."

"Julia would love for you to teach music to the children. Especially Sarah—she seems to have a gift for it."

I smiled. "That would be more than fine with me. I'll talk to her when we return."

I turned to Zeke. "Stuart tells me you know a lot about astronomy. I was hoping you could answer some questions for me."

He nodded slightly and without a word stood and beckoned me to follow him into the cabin. Stuart stood but made no move to enter. Sparse furnishings accented with bright throw rugs and wall coverings added an unexpected coziness to the room. Despite the heat of the day, a cooling breeze blew through the open doorways. A heavy scent of wood ash hovered in the air.

Bookshelves covered one entire wall. He approached the shelves reverently, letting his fingers glide over the bindings. Pulling out a volume, he carried it over to me and gently placed it in my hands. I glanced down and read *Astronomical Discoveries* and the author's name, *Chalmers*. Opening its pages, I instantly picked out the words *to shoot afar into those regions which are beyond the limits of our astronomy*.

I looked up at Zeke. "I want to go home. Do you know how to help me?"

He looked at me impassively and reached for my arm. Carefully, he rolled up my sleeve to reveal my left forearm and the crescent-shaped birthmark. "The sign of a Shadow Warrior," he said.

I stared at the mark I had had since birth and never even noticed anymore. My Annie had the identical mark on her upper arm. "What does it mean?"

He looked at me with hooded eyes. "It is what will bring you home."

"But how?" I shifted the heavy book impatiently, anxious to hear the secret of finding my way home.

"You will learn—keep your ears and eyes open." He paused to examine a lower shelf, then continued. "I will do what I can. But I don't think you'll need my help. I see the strong light that surrounds you. I sense we have need of your strength now. Perhaps that's why you have been sent to us."

He turned back to the bookshelves. "Stuart tells me he found you near Moon Mountain. That's a very sacred place to the Cherokees, you know. Stories of its magic have been passed down for generations. Stories of distant travelers sent here by the moon." His eyes turned toward my face and stared at me intently, but I didn't flinch. "Some of these travelers were bent on evil and destruction and had to be hunted down and killed by other Shadow Warriors." Goose bumps ran up my spine as I listened to his words, and his eyes continued to bore into mine. "Most of them were."

I swallowed thickly. "Zeke, I'm not sure why I'm here. It was purely accidental. All I want right now is to find my daughter and return home."

"Yes, Stuart told me about your Annie." Turning back to the shelves, he plucked out several more books. "You'll need to read these," he said as he piled three more heavy volumes into my arms. "These will tell you when the moon disappears and its powers are at its strongest. As for the rest, it's up to you."

I could feel my anxiety rising. "I don't know how I got here or why I'm here. I have no idea where Annie is. She could be here or anywhere. This was an accident. I don't belong here, and I'm certainly not needed or wanted. I just want to go home."

Zeke touched my arm. "You have survived many hurts. But your life isn't over yet. Perhaps that's why you're here." Our gazes met. "I had dreams of you before you came. I saw you standing in front of Phoenix Hall, staring at a flying machine in the sky, then watching it fall to pieces on the ground."

My mind spun in circles. "Oh, my God. Then you know."

He shook his head. "No, I don't really. But your secrets are safe with me."

"Thank you," I said, not sure what else I could say. I gathered the books tightly to my chest and stepped out onto the porch to find Stuart. I spied the jug and took another long swig, needing to obliterate my thoughts for a while. I ignored Stuart's raised eyebrow and stepped off the porch, Charlie yapping at my heels, my gait unsteady.

I attempted to walk a straight line when we reached Phoenix Hall and I spotted Julia on the back porch, Dr. Watkins and an unfamiliar lady next to her. I felt the waves of disapproval from the doctor and detected an almost imperceptible head-shaking from the woman.

"Stuart! What happened to Laura?" Julia approached me, her skirts rustling.

My mouth twitched. "I had a little sip." I punctuated my words with a hiccup.

Her brow furrowed as she got a closer look at me. "Let me take you inside and get you to bed. I'll introduce you to the doctor and Miss Eliza Smith another time."

She sent Stuart a severe look, then gently took me by the shoulders and led me inside.

"Let the great world spin forever down the ringing grooves of change."

Lord Tennyson

Chapter Nine

I leaned my tired head against the railing as I sat on the back porch steps. I glanced at the almost-empty basket at my feet with a sigh of accomplishment and stretched. Robbie gurgled happily in his cradle next to me, and I itched to pick him up and revel in his sweet babiness. My relief was short-lived, however, as Sukie approached with another full basket of un-shelled peas.

She plopped herself down next to me, and we resumed our work.

Willie appeared, staggering, around the side of the house, a wooden yoke resting on his shoulders, a large bucket attached to each end.

"Sukie, what's Willie doing?"

She rolled her shoulders back. "He's carrying out all the wood ash from the house. We're going to make lye soap tomorrow." She glanced up at the horizon. "The moon has changed. I never boil my soap on the wane of the moon—it would never thicken."

I sighed. Another chore. I was glad that I could be useful, but I was quickly finding that the running of a nineteenth-century house and plantation was a never-ending process. When was I going to find the time to read the astronomy books? In the three weeks since Zeke had given them to me, I had had the opportunity to open them once, and had promptly fallen asleep. Not that it mattered. I still needed time to find Annie. Then I could worry about getting us home.

After relieving himself of his burden, Willie approached the porch. His face and hands were smeared with soot, but he seemed oblivious to the fact as he reached for the door handle.

"No, sir! Don't you touch nothing! Go get yourself cleaned up first before you go inside." Willie rolled his eyes at Sukie and then stomped back off the porch.

"Oh, and Willie," I called after him. "When you're done washing up, please find your sister, and the two of you go and practice your scales on the piano."

"Yes'm," he mumbled.

His shoulders slumped as he continued walking toward the springhouse, where the cool stream flowed around the property. His mother wanted them to learn music, and I was trying my best. Unfortunately, in the two weeks that I had been teaching them piano, Willie had shown a remarkable inability to get beyond even the rudiments. He was very different from Sarah, who showed quite an aptitude for the instrument despite her young age.

I snapped more peas, my thumbs and forefingers slowly becoming stained green.

"Miz Eliza brought some dresses over for you yesterday." Sukie's head stayed bent over her task.

"Miz Eliza? Who's that?"

"Miz Eliza Smith. She was the lady that was here with the doctor when you came back from Mister Zeke's. She lives with her mother and sisters at Mimosa Hall. Can't say I care too much for her, but at least you'll have something respectable to wear now."

I remembered the rather dour-faced young woman I had seen on the back porch with Julia and Dr. Watkins. I could only imagine what stories the doctor had told her about me and why I needed clothes. I didn't plan on living here indefinitely, so I brushed aside my compromised reputation.

"She needs music lessons, too. She plays the organ at church—what a howling mess!"

I smiled. "She didn't look the type to take kindly to my instruction, Sukie."

"That be true. I don't think she likes you."

I stopped shelling. "What? She and I have never actually met."

"True, but she sure is powerful sweet on Mister Stuart."

The pit of my stomach shifted. "Oh? And what does that have to do with me?"

For the first time, Sukie paused in her task and looked at me. "I think she would see you as a considerable threat to her walking down the aisle with Mister Stuart."

Blushing furiously, I bent my head toward my lap. "I can't imagine why. Besides, I think she'd be more threatened by Julia."

Sukie surprised me with her sudden vehemence. "Don't even think it. What was between Mister Stuart and Miz Julia was over the minute she said 'I do' to Mister William. She's always been faithful to her husband and has suffered quite a bit because of him deciding to join the Yankees. Rumors about who her baby's father was has just about killed her. She's barely stepped off this plantation for almost a year—not even to go to church." She shook her head.

I stared at her, dumbfounded. "You mean there's some doubt?"

"No, ma'am. There's no doubt. Just vicious rumors spread by unkind people. Mister William was here last September. He kept quiet on account of people 'round these parts not liking the color of his uniform. But when Miz Julia showed up expecting a child, people who hadn't seen him started talking. Especially since Mister Stuart come home."

Sukie fell silent as Willie approached us again, his face scrubbed pink. He stomped past us and shouted Sarah's name as the back door slammed. Feet clattered down the wooden stairs, and shortly thereafter the piano scales began.

Sukie stood and brushed off her skirt. "I best go and see about making supper and getting a fresh nappy for this little one." She gave a wary glance at my slow progress, picked up Robbie and his cradle, and went inside. Darkness was still a couple of hours away, but the night sounds had already started. The cicadas and crickets creaked duets, and at least one bullfrog bellowed from the nearby woods. I closed my eyes and leaned against the porch railing, inhaling deeply the rich aroma from the boxwoods that lined the side of the house. It reminded me so much of my own time that I was temporarily transported back. Approaching footsteps made me open my eyes. I was caught off guard by the sight of Stuart standing not two feet away from me, one booted foot resting on the bottom step. I tried to ignore the quickening of my heartbeat.

"Well, if it isn't my prison guard." I hadn't been off the property since my arrival, and I blamed Stuart. I was aching to go with Sukie when she ran errands so I could ask around about Annie, but I needed more time to build Stuart's trust before he would allow me my freedom.

He ignored my comment. "Mind if I join you?" He smelled of sweat, horse, and leather—a combination I found peculiarly enticing.

"Help yourself," I said, indicating the bottomless basket of peas.

He reached over and grabbed a handful. "Our hospitality must be lacking if you're finding your stay here comparable to a prison sentence."

I shook my head. "No, that's not what I meant. Everyone, with one exception, has been more than hospitable. But I'm never going to find Annie if I'm not allowed to go look for her."

His long fingers efficiently broke open the pods and emptied their contents into the basket. They stopped, and I realized I had been staring at them, imagining how they would feel touching my face. I resumed my shelling without looking at him.

"I've been asking around town myself. No one recalls a little girl being found up on Moon Mountain." He paused for a moment. "Nor has anybody every heard of a Laura Truitt." He threw a handful of peas into the basket with more force than was necessary.

Our eyes met, and all was quiet except for the monotonous drone of the insects. Finally, I spoke. "You may choose not to believe me, but I have told you the truth. If you would just give me the benefit of the doubt . . ."

He finished, ". . . then my family and this entire town could suffer the consequences."

"Fine. You believe what you want—but when you realize you're wrong, and it's time for your apology, I'm going to make you grovel."

He bit his lip, as if trying to hide a smile. "I'll be looking forward to that, ma'am."

I gave him an exaggerated sigh and continued the never-ending job of shelling peas. I knew I would never look at a pea the same way again.

We sat in silence, listening to the serenade of the dusk creatures. I felt the heat from his body, drawing me nearer, and I hastily shifted away before I was compelled to touch him.

To break the silence, I asked, "Why are you fighting for the South while your brother fights for the North?"

He narrowed his eyes, as if trying to determine the motivation behind my question.

He continued popping the peas out of their pods. "Georgia is my home. Protecting her is in my blood—as much a part of me as the color of my eyes." He straightened his wounded leg as if to stretch it. "I'm also a firm believer in states' rights. It irks me to no end when the federal government interferes in state government." He put his foot down hard on the step and looked at me. "My brother, I'm afraid, is fighting for the North only because I am not."

"I see," I said, though I didn't. I had no idea sibling rivalry could be this intense.

"What about slavery? Aren't you fighting to uphold it?"

"No." He paused briefly and glanced up at the sky, the stars just beginning to make their appearance. "I hate slavery. I wish Georgia had kept it unlawful to own slaves. But without slavery, our crops couldn't compete in the marketplace with those of slave-holding states." He shifted, as if he, too, were trying to move out of the invisible force field that seemed to draw us together.

"Unfortunately, I see no other way to survive on cash crops. That's why I studied architecture at the Oglethorpe University. I figured I'd leave this plantation for my brother to mismanage while I found a respectable living." He paused in his work and grunted. "Life doesn't seem to turn out as one expects it to, does it?"

Our eyes met, the silence broken only by the cicadas. Quietly, I said, "No. It doesn't."

The moment of intimacy disappeared as Willie plunged out the back door, carrying a chamber pot. Sukie called after him, "Make sure you put that downwind this time, Willie!"

I grinned as Willie trudged along toward the cotton field to dump his burden.

"Laura, I'm accompanying Julia to church next Sunday. You're welcome to join us."

I turned my attention back to Stuart, trying to see through his offer. "Why would you want me to go? Are you afraid I'll do some spying on the hens if you're not here to watch me?"

He looked genuinely hurt. "Not at all. I thought you'd like to mix with some of Roswell's citizens. Maybe somebody will recognize you. That is what you want, isn't it?"

I stared back at him, my gaze level. "Yes. Of course it is."

He scooped peas out of a pod and reached for another. "Well, then, don't look a gift horse in the mouth."

I gave him a derisive snort. "I don't consider my freedom to be a gift from you. But, yes, I'd like to go. I take it that Julia hasn't been out in public much lately either."

The muscles in his jaw worked as he clenched his teeth. "No, she hasn't. And it's making her look as if she has something to hide. I think it's high time she showed her face again."

"I agree. I'll be happy to lend moral support."

Scurrying out of the house, Sukie opened the door of the detached kitchen, allowing the aromas of baking cornbread to waft over to us. My stomach growled in response.

"Hungry again?" Stuart asked as he stood and held out a hand to help me up.

Stacking the full basket inside the finally empty one, I responded unapologetically, "I'm always hungry. I seem to have the appetite of a horse."

"You certainly don't look as if you eat like a horse."

I gave him a sidelong glance to see if he was offering me a compliment or not. He grinned, and I noticed how his gaze took in the fabric of Julia's dress stretching across my chest.

He cleared his throat. "Maybe you should curb your appetite a mite until we can find you clothes that fit a bit better than—"

I didn't give him a chance to finish. I shoved him. To my horror, he fell over my perfectly stacked baskets, losing his balance and taking my precious peas with him. I hesitated for a moment, wondering if I should rescue him or my peas first. Then I heard him laughing.

"Laura, if you want to pick a fight, pick on someone who's not already wounded."

He lay flat on his back, and I leaned over to help him up. He grasped my hands tightly and pulled to hoist himself but instead brought me down on top of him. He grunted as his arms went around me, effectively locking me in place, our lips almost touching.

His breath was warm on my face. "If you're not a Yankee, you should be."

I struggled to get off him, but he held me tighter. "What do you mean?"

A small grin touched his lips, so close to mine. "Because you're more lethal than a bullet."

"Let go of me."

He complied, but as I tried to move off him without touching him more than necessary, my right knee collided with his injured leg, making him groan in pain. I quickly rolled off and knelt beside him.

"I'd like to say I'm sorry, but you have to admit you deserved it. And if you're so afraid I might injure you further, why don't you return to the front lines? You'll be safer there."

His eyes were shadowed as he answered, "I'm beginning to think that myself." He sat up unassisted and then hauled himself to a standing position.

He held out his hand to me. "Come on. It's time for dinner."

Ignoring his hand, I stood by myself. "In a minute. I've got to clean up this mess first."

Without a word, he picked up the overturned basket and began gathering peas.

Following dinner, the children were put to bed, and we three adults retired to the parlor. Julia brought her sewing basket, and her slender fingers pushed the silver needle with lightning speed. By the end of the evening she had completed a pair of pants for one of the remaining field slaves.

I volunteered to mend some of Sarah's stockings. After I'd struggled to thread the needle in the dim candlelight and then ended up ripping out most of my uneven stitches, Julia suggested I play the piano. I opened sheet music for the sad Confederate ballad "Lorena" and began to play.

A gentle sob came from behind me as the last note faded, and I turned to look at Julia, whose head was still bent to her sewing. Stuart put a hand gently on her shoulder. Something twisted inside me, and I turned back to the keyboard.

"How about something more lively?" I asked as I broke into a Scott Joplin medley. I was halfway through the "Maple Leaf Rag" when Sukie entered to announce Dr. Watkins.

"What is that noise?" he demanded. "It sounds like music from a New Orleans brothel."

"And just how would you know what kind of music they play in a New Orleans brothel, sir?" I asked.

The doctor turned an interesting shade of red and glared at me.

Stuart intervened. "Now, Charles, Laura was only trying to lift our spirits—which she did marvelously. Why don't you

100

sit down and tell us what brings you here this evening?"

Placated for the time being, the doctor turned to Julia, took something out of his coat pocket, and handed it to her. "I was at the company store today and took the liberty of getting your mail for you."

We all stared at Julia as she opened the letter and read. Her mending slid to the floor, but she didn't pick it up. "My mother is coming from Nashville for a visit." Lines of worry creased her forehead. "I don't know how safe that would be for her."

Stuart leaned forward in his chair. "She'll be fine. As I recall, Pamela is a formidable force to reckon with. I wouldn't want to be the one to stand in her way, and I pity the person who does." Stuart grinned, but something else in his face made me wonder what his true feelings were regarding Julia's mother. "When should we expect her?"

Julia glanced at the top of the page, and her eyes widened. "Oh, my! This letter was written five weeks ago. She could be here any day now. There's so much to do!" She hastily retrieved her sewing and shoved it back into the basket. "Please excuse me, but I've got to get busy." Anticipating my offer of help, she turned to me and added, "Laura, please stay here and play hostess for the gentlemen." Not waiting for an answer, she left the room.

Turning toward the two men, I said, "I won't be offended if you two want to retire to the library for something stiffer than coffee."

"Thank you, Laura. I think we will. But please continue to play the piano."

The doctor raised an eyebrow. "Only if she'll choose something genteel this time. A lady should never consider anything else."

Stuart sent me a warning look over the doctor's head, and I kept my smile plastered in place. As soon as the doors between the parlor and library were shut, I spun myself around on the piano bench and started banging out another Scott Joplin rag. I hoped it was shaking the starch out of the doctor's stiff white collar.

The Past—the dark unfathom'd retrospect!
The teeming gulf—the sleepers and the shadows!
The past! the infinite greatness of the past!
For what is the present after all but a growth out of the
past?

Walt Whitman

Chapter Ten

The following Sunday, after donning one of Miss Eliza Smith's highly serviceable but barely fashionable dresses, I was ready for church. The muslin gown was a sedate brown, with small green flowers striping the skirt and bodice. A prim white collar and white undersleeves completed the ensemble and made me feel almost Puritan. Sukie coerced me into wearing a corset after explaining that without one, I could cause considerable embarrassment to the Elliotts. My ribs creaked as she pulled the laces tight. After walking two steps without being able to expand my lungs, I readily understood the need of a fainting couch.

After donning the requisite bonnet and kid gloves, I walked downstairs and out of the house, beads of sweat already forming on my forehead.

Stuart stood clutching a wooden cane beside the four-wheeled buggy.

I did a double take, as I had never seen him use a cane. "Stuart, is your leg worse today?"

He made a production of fiddling with the horses' harnesses. "No, the leg's fine. Doing much better, actually."

"Then why do you have a cane? Any young ladies at church you're trying to impress?"

He sent me a withering glance. "Yes, it's for show, but it's not what you think."

Trying to tread lightly on the subject, I asked, "I don't mean to intrude, but is it to make the other citizens of Roswell feel sorry for you so that they won't be so hateful to Julia?"

He stopped his fiddling and looked at me square in the eye. "Since you seem to thrive on directness, I'll be direct with you. Yes, there are some nasty rumors about who Robbie's father is, and I'm hoping that if people see how badly I was incapacitated, they won't think that . . . well . . . that I could have done such a thing."

I could tell how hard it was for him to put those thoughts into words, and I had a strong impulse to hug him, but I refrained. I also hid my smile as I considered a fault in his reasoning. "Stuart, I don't know how much you know about making babies, but a wounded leg wouldn't necessarily interfere in the process."

He stared at me long and hard and opened his mouth as if to say something but closed it instead. Narrowing his eyes, he tossed the cane to the grass by the side of the drive and turned to greet Julia as she and Sukie emerged from the house, Sukie holding Robbie. Willie and Sarah appeared behind them, temporarily clean and presentable for church.

Stuart handed us all up into the buggy. Because of the tight fit, Sarah and Willie each had to use an adult lap for a seat. Sarah chose mine, and I was struck, not for the first time, at how much she resembled somebody I couldn't quite place. I studied Julia's face and Stuart's strong profile, but I could find no connection. I assumed the missing piece would be Sarah's father, William.

Sarah looked like a cherub, but having spent considerable time with her at her piano lessons, I knew better. She was full of mischief but had an innate talent for music. I wondered which parent she had inherited that from and again assumed it had to be the absent William, who was growing to mythic proportions in my head.

This was my first time outside the boundaries of the plantation. Although I had lived in Roswell for seven years, almost nothing I saw on the short ride to the Presbyterian church was familiar. Only the church—the same church where my Annie had been baptized—remained relatively unchanged. An air of surprise greeted us as we entered through the massive front door. Julia kept her back straight, nodding to acquaintances on both sides of the aisle. I was relieved to see people nodding back. Stuart walked behind us, holding Sarah's hand and calling out his good-mornings as we made our journey to the front of the sanctuary and took our seats.

I spent the remainder of the service surreptitiously scanning the congregation, hoping to find a girl who resembled the image I had created of an older Annie. My heart grew heavy with disappointment, and I had to lower my eyes to hide the sting of tears.

Following the service—and some particularly horrendous organ playing by Miss Eliza Smith—we all gathered outside the church. I smiled at the curious glances aimed in my direction and kept myself busy dandling Robbie. Julia stayed close by my side, introducing me to the other churchgoers. Oddly, no one questioned my sudden appearance in the Elliot household.

I raised my eyes and caught Dr. Watkins looking at me. He must have already told these people everything they needed to know about me—and I wondered if it had to do with mental illness. It didn't really matter. I had no intention of staying long enough to care what the townspeople thought of me.

Out of the corner of my eye, I caught sight of Eliza Smith walking toward Stuart. He was talking to Dr. Watkins and an older man with muttonchop whiskers I identified as the Reverend Pratt. Eliza linked her arm possessively through Stuart's and smiled up at him. While no one could ever accuse her of being beautiful, her face was transformed when Stuart smiled back.

I hoped that my own face wasn't as transparent. As much as I wanted to dismiss Stuart Elliott from my thoughts for his distrust of me and my motives, I just couldn't seem to stop the blood rushing to my head every time he spoke my name or looked my way.

Stuart caught my gaze and nodded. Eliza gave me a cold stare and squeezed his arm to capture his attention. Robbie whimpered, and I gladly turned back to the child.

"Pardon me, ma'am, but I seem to have missed out on the introductions."

I looked up into baby-blue eyes, clear and wide but not at all innocent.

"You must be Miz Truitt."

Robbie burbled, and I shifted him in my arms. "Yes, I am."

The man appeared to be in his late twenties, with a thin covering of blond peach fuzz on his chin that might pass for a beard. His dirty fair hair was parted crookedly in the middle and hung down in straggly strands on each side of his narrow face. The stale odor of alcohol permeated his brown wool coat. I took a step back.

He grinned, revealing a jack-o'-lantern smile with several missing teeth. I searched for Julia to rescue me, but she had left my side. The man's slow drawl brought my attention back to him.

"I apologize for my manners. Allow me to present myself." He touched a dirty finger to his forelock. "I'm Matthew Kimball. Mostly known around these parts as just Matt."

Robbie began to fret, and I bounced him up and down in my arms, hoping he would start squalling and I could excuse myself. The man stood too close, his foul breath wafting over me. He reached a mud-encrusted fingernail up to Robbie's soft cheek. I jerked the baby away, and his nail scraped the back of my hand. I suppressed a shudder at his touch.

"It's nice to meet you, Mr. Kimball."

"Matt." He gave me a wide smile.

"Right. Matt." I turned my lips up to approximate a smile. "It's been nice talking to you, but I need to change the baby, and—"

"Where are you from, Miz Truitt?" His intense gaze belied the casualness of his question. "I was wondering if we might, perhaps, have some mutual acquaintances."

I examined him closely, wondering if he had mistaken me for somebody else. "I'm quite sure I wouldn't know any of your friends, Mr., uh, Matt. Why would you think—"

Strong arms pulled Robbie from my grasp. "It's time to go, Laura."

Stuart held Robbie with rigid arms, his face stern as he regarded Matt.

Matt's face blanched slightly. "Now, Stuart, we was only having a little conversation. No harm in that, is there?"

Ignoring Matt, Stuart grabbed my elbow. "Let's go, Laura."

He pulled me away before I had a chance to say anything else. I looked back at Matt and found all traces of politeness gone, a menacing scowl now stamped on his narrow mouth.

I stumbled, but Stuart didn't even slow his step. "Let go of my arm. You're hurting me."

Stuart ignored my protests, as well as the curious stares we were receiving. Finally, he stopped on the fringe of the group and dropped my arm. He bent his head close to mine, his voice low and serious. "Do you know that man?"

"Of course not! I've never laid eyes on him. I don't think he's a person one could easily forget, no matter how addled one's memory is. Why? Who is he?"

Stuart's eyes searched mine, as if trying to decipher a puzzle. Slowly, he straightened. "He used to be a boyhood friend of mine—his father was even a preacher at an old church outside town. But he's a deserter. Claims he's on leave, but it's been more than a year now. There are rumors about his loyalties." He looked closely at me. "Such as how they can be bought by the highest bidder."

Anger flamed in me. "Is that what you think of me? That I could be associated with a person like that? How dare you make such accusations about me—you don't even know me!"

He raised an eyebrow. "No, Laura. I don't know you—but it's not because I haven't asked. You've left me with no choice but to make assumptions."

He was right, but my anger refused to let me acknowledge it in front of him. I turned on my heel—and ran right into Eliza Smith. Her watery eyes were bright with curiosity.

Stuart stepped forward and made the introductions.

She nodded brusquely in my direction, and I imitated her action. "Thank you so much for the clothes," I said. "And your organ playing today was . . . incredible."

Two blotchy spots of red appeared unbecomingly on her cheeks, an apparent blush, and I could feel her thaw a few degrees. "Stuart mentioned that you are also musical, Mrs. Truitt."

"Well, I try. I'm teaching Sarah and Willie the piano. Sarah is especially gifted. Willie tries, but I know he'd rather be outside chasing Charlie."

Robbie let out a loud howl, announcing it was his dinnertime. Stuart made our excuses, then found Julia and the children to return home. I sat across from Stuart in the buggy, our knees almost touching. I studiously ignored him, but I caught his gaze on me more than once.

Sunday as a day of rest was strictly adhered to in the Elliott household, and I was looking forward to immersing myself in Zeke's astronomy books. But it was not to be. As we pulled into the long dirt drive, a mud-splattered coach was being led around the side of the house.

Julia leaned out of the buggy. "It must be my mother!"

I stole a glance at Stuart. He also looked at the coach. I could see the muscles working in his jaw. Something about this visitor made him tense.

As soon as we pulled to a stop, Julia jumped from the buggy, not waiting for assistance, and ran into the house.

I gathered the children and led the way inside.

Julia's voice came from the parlor, and I ushered the children into the room, pausing on the threshold. A diminutive woman with gray streaks threading through her hair turned toward us. I couldn't see any resemblance between this woman and Julia. Her small, dark eyes were cold, and when I first walked into the room, I felt something akin to the frigid wind of death blowing through me.

Her eyes flickered over me before her gaze settled on the children. Sarah's hand tightened in mine, and she buried her face in my skirt. Willie was no less obvious as he took a step backward, as if to put as much distance as possible between himself and the newcomer.

The woman gave Sarah a brittle smile before turning to Willie. "Willie, aren't you going to give your Nana a hug?" Her voice was surprisingly deep for such a petite woman.

Willie reluctantly stepped forward and gave her a perfuntory hug. I expected her to ask for one from Sarah, too, but instead she stepped toward Stuart, who held baby Robbie.

"So this is my new grandson." She reached to take the baby from Stuart. A strong maternal instinct made me want to push her away. I knew I was being irrational, but the feeling that I should keep the children away from her pulled hard at me.

As she jiggled the baby to find a comfortable position to hold him, Robbie began screaming. I quickly reached for him and plucked him out of her arms. Immediately, his cries subsided as I held him snugly on my shoulder.

Giving me the brunt of her harsh gaze, she stood in front of me. Her petite stature in no way diminished the force of her character. I could feel the maelstrom created by her personality in the air she breathed out.

"And who is this?" Although looking straight at me, she directed her question elsewhere.

"Mother, this is Laura Truitt. She is a good friend and is staying with us for a while. I'm eternally grateful to her because she saved Robbie's life." Julia walked over to me and put an arm around my shoulder.

"Oh, really? And just how did she accomplish this?" Her gaze finally left my face as she turned to Julia.

"It was the most peculiar thing. When Robbie was born, he wasn't breathing, so Laura laid him on the floor, pushed on his little chest to make his heart beat, and then breathed the air into his mouth until he started doing it on his own."

Her head snapped back to me, her eyes narrowing slightly as they considered me.

Julia squeezed my shoulders. "She also saved Willie from an attack by a catamount on Moon Mountain. We are very much indebted to her."

The older woman stepped closer to us. "Really. I suppose that I am also in your debt."

I finally found my voice. "No. I'm indebted to the Elliotts for their hospitality. They've opened their home to me."

"Where are my manners?" Julia gushed. "Laura, this is my mother, Mrs. Pamela Broderick."

I was grateful for Julia's intervention. I didn't think I could explain my sudden appearance on Moon Mountain to one more person, for I was sure that would be the older woman's next question. I smiled. "Yes, I assumed that's who you were. It's a pleasure to meet you."

She inclined her head slightly. "Likewise."

"Stuart." She held out both hands to him, which he took, and kissed him on both cheeks. "I'm so glad to see you safe. We are so lucky, you know. Most families in the county have lost a son or father or brother, yet you and William are still in one piece."

Julia interrupted, "Mother, have you news of William?"

"Yes. Did I forget to mention that to you in my letter? He's been assigned to General Sherman's staff. He's been in Nashville these last few months. Hasn't he written?"

Julia's face fell. "No, he hasn't. I haven't heard from him since last September." She pointed her chin at Robbie, who was busy sucking noisily on his fist.

Turning her full attention to Julia, Mrs. Broderick reached for her and cupped her face in her hands. "Daughter, don't fret. There's a war going on, and he's got very important duties to attend to for General Sherman. He would have come with me if he could—you know that."

Julia kept her eyes down, hidden from her mother, and nodded solemnly. Forcing a smile to her face, she looked up at Pamela and added, "You must be exhausted. I had Sukie prepare a room for you, so you have a place to rest if you would like."

"Yes, thank you, that would be nice." She slipped an arm through her daughter's and slowly ascended the stairs. Stuart and a servant followed with a large trunk and several smaller bags.

Feeling the need for fresh air, I left the children with Sukie and stepped out onto the front porch. I breathed deeply, filling my lungs, wondering why that woman seemed to take the oxygen out of a room.

The sound of the door shutting behind me and the jangling of keys told me Julia had joined me. I knew her storeroom keys never left her side—being keeper of the food supply of the plantation was one of the myriad duties of the mistress of the house.

She came to stand next to me, looking directly ahead toward the front drive. "My mother can be a difficult woman to get to know. I hope she didn't offend you."

I sat down in one of the white wooden rocking chairs. "No, I wasn't offended."

Julia sat in the chair next to mine and slowly began to rock, her feet gently slapping the porch floor. "She's from Charleston, so her ways are much more formal than they are here. It's off-putting to people who don't know her well." She turned her head to face me. "Pamela is my stepmother, but she's the only mother I've known. My mother died when I was three. My father died when I was five, so I didn't know him very well. He was born and raised here in Roswell, and this is where he brought Pamela after they were married. She and Stuart's mother were the best of friends. Very different people, though. I guess that's why they got along so well." She continued her rhythmic rocking, her face and eyes focused on the past. Her rocking was contagious, and I copied her back-and-forth motion.

"What's your mother doing in Nashville?" Somehow, knowing that Julia was not Pamela's flesh and blood made it even harder for me to understand the affection she had for a woman who made me so apprehensive.

She looked down at her hands, gently folded in her lap. "My mother enjoys a cosmopolitan lifestyle. She likes to be amongst the politicians and policy makers. She's even invested in several businesses and made her home in Nashville to oversee her interests."

Julia sighed and pulled herself to her feet. "I don't know

what I was thinking, dawdling out here. I've got a thousand things to do before dinner. Would you mind, Laura, picking the pole beans from the bean patch?" Her mind already elsewhere, Julia walked toward the door. Stopping, she turned abruptly. "Could you see if you can hunt down Sarah and have her bring in the eggs from the chicken house? I'm going to have Sukie make some cornbread with the little bit of cornmeal we have left." Without waiting for an answer, Julia sailed through the door, her shoes making a rapid tapping on the floors inside.

I gave one last leisurely rock and then stood. The first halting notes of "Greensleeves" told me in which direction to go to find Sarah. She was seated on the piano bench, her eyes glued to the sheet music in front of her.

She smiled when I walked into the room and hastily scooted over to one side of the bench to make room for me. As soon as I sat down, she started plunking out a new tune I had taught her, "Heart and Soul." I added the treble accompaniment and struggled to keep up with her as she raced faster and faster through the repetitions. We ended up collapsing in laughter.

Julia peeked in wordlessly, one finger raised to her mouth. "Shh. Nana's sleeping."

I looked up guiltily and nodded. "Sarah, your mother wants you to gather eggs. Come on, I'll go with you. And then you can show me what a pole bean is."

We stopped in the detached kitchen first to pick up a basket and then went to the henhouse. A pitiful rooster strutted his way across the backyard, perhaps lamenting the loss of most of his harem. Courtesy of the Confederate Army, the Elliotts were down to three laying hens. Using their few eggs so extravagantly on the cornbread was a rare treat.

I held the basket for Sarah as she reached into each nest. As she laid each egg gently into the basket, she counted them out slowly to me. Five. I hoped it would be enough, as I had my heart, and my ever-grumbling stomach, set on cornbread.

Studying the girl as she stood on tiptoe to reach into another nest, I grew curious. "Sarah, how old are you?"

Concentrating on her task, she replied, "Seven."

"Really? When's your birthday?"

She turned around to look at me, clutching one more egg in her hand. "June. But I can't remember which day. It's written in the Bible. I can't read it yet, but Mama says it's there."

I surreptitiously approached a hen, her plump roundness filling the circular cavity she had made to lay her eggs. I attempted to remove her prize and was rewarded with a nasty peck.

"Ouch! That hurt!" With my hands on my hips, I gave Mother Hen my most threatening look. Her small, glassy eyes continued to dart back and forth, as if I were nothing more than a kernel of corn.

"Let me do that one, Miz Truitt. She tends to get a bit broody."

Sarah approached the offended hen by talking softly to it and then silently, stealthily, slid three eggs out of their warm home, one by one.

As we stepped back into the yard, Stuart approached, an ax in his hand. My eyes widened. "Where are you going with that ax?"

He looked at me in surprise. "Julia wants to serve chicken for dinner." I knew where those neatly wrapped, skinless, boneless chicken breasts came from that I bought at the supermarket, but I had never known the animals personally before consuming them.

He walked past us into the chicken house. The desperate squawkings of the unfortunate victim reached our ears, and Stuart emerged holding up his feathered prize.

"You ladies might not want to watch this."

Not really sure that I was up to witnessing the rudiments of meal preparation, I turned to Sarah. She rolled her eyes at her uncle's words and put down her basket. "I'm not scairt."

"Well, I'm not scared, either, but I don't want to spoil my appetite." Seeing the stubborn jut of her little chin, I knew she couldn't be budged. I resigned myself to learning more about nineteenth-century rural life.

He put the chicken on the ground, holding the struggling body down with one hand. With the forefinger of his other hand, he slowly drew a line in the dirt, from the chicken's beak out to about a foot away. The chicken halted all movement and lay as if hypnotized. The shadow of the ax brought my attention away from the still chicken, and I turned my face away at the last minute. A solid thunking sound told me it was over.

Glancing at Sarah to make sure her young mind hadn't been damaged in any way, I looked back at the scene of the carnage. The headless body of the chicken busily flopped its way through the yard, its wings propelling the corpse and blood squirting in neat arcs.

I grabbed Sarah and backed up so we wouldn't get sprayed. She placed her small hand in mine and said, "Don't be scairt, Miz Truitt. Mama says the blood's good for keeping the bugs away and making the garden grow."

Squeezing her hand, I looked down on her blond head. I felt a strong surge of affection for this child and her sturdy little character.

Stuart scooped up our dinner, which had since run out of steam and flopped over in the yard. "I hope this hasn't affected your appetite, Laura."

"Not a chance. I'm so hungry right now, I could eat it with the feathers still attached."

Sarah looked up at me, wrinkling her nose. "Oooo! Yuck!"

I rumpled her hair. "Oh, Sarah, I was just teasing. I'd at least remove the feathers first. But I might not pause long enough to cook it," I said, winking.

I hugged her shoulders as she grinned up at me. Then my eyes were drawn to a movement from a back bedroom window. A dark shape stepped back out of view while I looked. I didn't see her clearly, but I knew who it was. A cold tremor swept up my spine, and I shivered in the hot summer sun.

*"But at my back I always hear
Time's winged chariot hurrying near."*

Andrew Marvell

Chapter Eleven

The sound of approaching hoofbeats made me glance up. I shielded my eyes with a hand to block the glare of the summer sun and watched Stuart approach astride Endy. The sweat ran in rivulets down my back, making my chemise stick to my skin, and the sight of him made me warmer still. I adjusted the egg basket on my arm and waited for him to approach.

I had gradually settled into my new life on a nineteenth-century plantation. I never stopped looking for Annie, but I knew I had time. According to my own calculations, gleaned from Zeke's astronomy books, the next total lunar eclipse wouldn't occur until September 1, 1864. The possibility of a comet being present, or even needed for my purposes, remained a mystery to me. I could only wait and see—and continue asking everyone I met if they had heard of a lost little girl on Moon Mountain.

The plantation work was hard, but I reveled in the simplicity of it. No background noise of traffic, telephones, or televisions. At the end of each day, I eagerly anticipated the quiet evenings in the parlor spent with Julia and Stuart. Julia's mother joined us most of the time, and we eyed each other warily. There was no overt hostility, but it was clear that Pamela somehow considered me a threat, and she continued to fill me with apprehension. About what, I couldn't say.

I spent the majority of my days with the children, either at

114

lessons or assisting them with their chores. And I was learning as much from them as they were from me.

The approaching hoofbeats became louder as Stuart drew near, slowing Endy's pace and finally stopping in front of me. My greeting died on my lips as I looked up and saw his scowl.

"I just came back from town. Matt Kimball's been asking a lot of questions about you."

"About me? Do you think he knows anything about Annie?"

He shook his head. "No. Those aren't the sorts of questions he's asking. He wants to know where you're from and why you're here. Why do you suppose he's so curious about you?"

I put my free hand on my hip. "Why are you asking me? Why don't you ask Mr. Kimball? I think he'd be better able to judge his own motivations. I told you already, I'd never met the man before." In my agitation, my basket dropped to the ground, the eggs miraculously unscathed. "Damn! What do I have to do to make you trust me?"

He stayed high atop his black stallion, looking like a knight in butternut-stained wool. "You could start by telling me the truth."

A dull wind stirred the dust around us, sending grit into my eyes. I blinked hard. How could I explain to him that I didn't want to get involved in the Elliots' lives anymore than I had to? That my only goal was to return home with my daughter before I became inextricably immersed in this time and with these people? Becoming emotionally attached could only bring me more pain, and I had had enough of that to last me two lifetimes.

I picked up my basket. "I am here to find Annie and bring her home. That's all you need to know. I would never hurt you or your family." My eyes smarted, but I didn't turn away.

Endy snorted loudly in my ear, and I involuntarily stepped back. Stuart caught the movement and reined the horse in tightly. He dismounted, then reached into a saddlebag, bringing forth an apple like a peace offering. His face softened, his eyes almost apologetic.

"Perhaps you can gain Endy's trust. He doesn't need truth, just kind and fair treatment."

I moved closer to Stuart, trying to get away from Endy. "If you're going to kill me, couldn't you just shoot me? It would be a good sight easier than setting your horse on me."

Stuart's voice was soothing, close to my ear, the hairs on my neck rippling from the brush of his breath. "The only reason Endymion would ever hurt you is if you threatened him or something he considered his. Not very far from human nature, is it?"

I shook my head, my anger giving way to fear tinged with curiosity. Aside from our trek down Moon Mountain, I had never been this close to a horse in my life.

"Endymion? What kind of a name is that?" I stared warily at the black beast, its huge right eye examining me as it shook its massive head.

"William named him after the Greek god, Endymion. Are you familiar with the story?"

"I'm afraid not. My Greek mythology is a bit rusty." I continued to eye the big horse, hoping that Stuart had been joking when he suggested I develop some sort of relationship with this animal.

Stuart gave Endy a vigorous scratching behind the ears, making the horse nod with pleasure. "Endymion was the husband of Selene, the goddess of the moon." A grin split his face. "He was quite the talented fellow."

I took a step back from the great nodding head. "Oh, really. How so?"

Polishing the apple on his pants leg, Stuart looked away, as if he shouldn't be telling me. "He fathered fifty daughters by Selene, reportedly all while he was asleep."

I smirked. "You're right. He was pretty talented. Not to mention fertile. I hope your Endymion is equally prolific."

Slowly, Stuart shook his head. "No. The god Endymion's children were all pale like their mother and sleepy like their father. Hopefully, Endy's offspring will be a mite more vigorous."

Stuart gave the beast a resounding pat on the side of the neck, apparently a gesture of affection. He pulled off his hat and wiped the sweat off his forehead with his sleeve, then handed the apple to me.

I stared at the fruit in my hand, nervously twisting the stem off the top. "I hope you don't intend for me to feed him this apple. I'm afraid he'll take my whole arm off if I get too near."

The object of our conversation seemed oblivious to our presence as his thick, brushy tail swooshed back and forth in a vain attempt to rid himself of the nuisance flies that flitted about.

"Endy has never bitten anyone." Stuart looked down at his feet and kicked sand at a small lizard scurrying about in the cool shadow created by the horse. "Not seriously, anyway," he added with a twitch of his lips. "Of course, if you're scared . . ."

"That's not fair! I'm just not used to being around horses. Especially not one as big as that—that Goliath!" I wanted to take him up on his challenge, but the thought of getting near Endy's numerous and probably very sharp teeth or his club-like hooves made me want to crawl away like the coward I was around horses. Even small ones.

"Let me take that." He took the basket, then gently nudged me toward the horse's mouth. His arm went around me, his touch warming my skin under the layers of my dress. His other hand forced my own open, so the apple lay flat on my palm. "You don't want him to think your fingers are little carrots. Wouldn't do to get him liking the taste of human blood."

Darting a quick glance at him, I saw him biting his bottom lip, but he couldn't hide the merriment in his blue eyes.

I stretched my hand out toward the gigantic head, trying to keep my body as far away as possible. The horse seemed to eye me speculatively, determining if I was friend or foe. Then he opened his mouth and took the proffered apple.

I expected to feel the grazing of teeth against the skin of my palm and was surprised with just the gentle touch of soft lips delicately picking up the apple.

The thick jaws worked back and forth, the loud crunching sounding like the crushing of bones. Small bits of apple and a great deal of slobber formed around the horse's mouth, spraying me and the vicinity. Instead of spitting out the core, Endy swallowed the entire thing.

The big head then looked at me, as if waiting for another morsel. Determined not to be the next item on the menu, I looked to Stuart for help and was astounded to feel a velvet-soft muzzle coupled with a few juicy apple bits nuzzling my cheek. Thoroughly disgusted with the messy show of affection, I jumped backward, only to be stopped suddenly by Stuart's body. I almost knocked him over, and he reached around my waist to steady me and pulled softly the reins in his other hand to ease the attentions of my equine suitor.

"See? Look at that. You've made a friend." His arm remained around me, and when I tilted my head I could see the little crinkles at the sides of his eyes as he laughed.

Narrowing my eyes, I asked, "Are you making fun of me?"

"Certainly not. I'm admiring your bravery. And your appeal to males of all species."

I turned to look at him, and he slowly dropped his arm. He stood very close as his smile faded, his gaze never wavering from my face. His eyes darkened, and my pulse quickened.

Without moving back, he reached into his pocket and pulled out a handkerchief. "You've got pieces of apple on your cheek." He cupped my head in one hand to hold it steady while he gently swiped at my face with the soft linen cloth. I closed my eyes, so I wouldn't have to look into his, and tried not to think about how close his lips were to mine.

I opened them again when I realized he had stopped wiping but still held my head in his hands. His gaze was concentrated on my mouth, and my lips parted involuntarily. The horse snorted to remind us of his presence, but neither of us paid him any mind. We did, however, notice the small green projectile that suddenly sailed over our heads. Stuart's battle savvy seemed to take over, and he quickly forced me down to my haunches.

Before I could ask what was going on, Sarah and Willie emerged running from the side of the house, Willie in the lead. Another green missile landed on the ground in front of me. I reached to pick it up, rolling the hard, verdant bud in my palm.

"Damn!" said Stuart, plucking the object from my hand. "Begging your pardon," he added absently, extending a hand to me to help me up.

"What is it?"

"It's a cotton bud. They're not supposed to be stripping my crop before they've bloomed."

Realizing that it was perhaps my negligence that was causing the children to run wild, I grabbed my basket and hastened after them. "Don't worry. I'll talk to them."

As I approached the rear of the chicken house, I narrowly missed being sideswiped by Willie as he dodged another small projectile.

"Willie, what do you think you're doing?" I shouted, picking up the errant missile.

Before he could answer, another torpedo shot through the air. I heard Sarah's giggles before I saw her. She stopped when she spotted me, the avenging adult with arms akimbo.

"Children, stop it! How are we supposed to have a crop if there's nothing left to pick? And Sarah, don't throw things at your brother. You might poke an eye out." Approaching the unrepentant child, I added, "And shouldn't you be practicing your piano?"

With a mumbled, "Yes, ma'am," she walked slowly to the back door, trailing a line of cotton buds on the ground as they dropped from her opened fist. I spotted Willie out of the corner of my eye trying to sneak off into the woods. "And you, too, young man. I'll be in to check on your progress in half an hour."

As Willie followed his sister into the house, I turned my head at the sound of hoofbeats and watched Stuart, tall in the saddle, riding out toward the fields, his well-muscled thighs hugging the horse. Strong hands held the reins, and I turned away, trying not to remember how they had felt when he touched my face.

With no one looking, I unbuttoned the top three buttons of my dress, pulled the fabric away from my damp skin, and blew inside, hoping to create a cooling breeze. I closed my eyes in

119

a vain attempt to shut out the heat, succeeding only in stinging my eyes with the salty sweat on my eyelids.

Suddenly, an image of plunging into Vickery Creek filled my imagination, and I immediately set off to fetch Willie and Sarah.

After depositing the egg basket with Sukie in the kitchen, I walked to the back door of the house. The sound of Sarah's crying greeted me as I stood on the threshold. Hurrying to the parlor, I was horrified by what I saw.

An angry red handprint stained the side of Sarah's face, creeping up her delicate skin like poison ivy. She was crumpled on the floor, but her grandmother held her wrist tight. Willie sat on the piano bench, his shoulders hunched forward as if to make himself as small as possible.

Without thinking, I rushed to Sarah. "How dare you strike a defenseless child?" I accused Pamela. I knelt by Sarah and put my arms around her. She buried her head in my shoulder, muffling her sobs.

Pamela let go of Sarah's arm. "This child must learn to respect her elders. I will not tolerate disrespect from a child." Two bright spots of color appeared on her cheeks. "And how dare you speak that way to me? You both need to be taught some manners."

I glared up at her. "I don't know how you were raised, but I am quite sure that striking a child is a very ineffective way to teach them anything."

Fuming and unable to control the deep flush of anger that rose to her face, she hissed at me, "I don't know who you are or why you're here. But you are out of place interfering with the way I discipline my grandchildren." Her hands shook with fury.

Sensing the children's fear, I attempted to lighten the situation. "I think somebody's grumpy and needs a nap."

Sarah's head snapped up to look at me, her eyes wide with surprise. Her look was echoed in her grandmother's expression.

Pamela bent her face toward mine, her beady eyes narrowed, "Don't think that I don't know what you're up to. And you won't get away with it. Not while I'm around."

She turned on her heel and strode out of the room, almost militant in her stride.

I brushed aside the tinge of fear that had begun to grow inside me and gave Sarah a hug, wiping her tears with the sleeve of my dress. "What did you say to her?"

Sniffling, Sarah explained, "She told me that I had no emotion for the music I was playing on the piano." Pausing to hiccup, she continued, "And I told her she was wrong."

I was unable to see the error in Sarah's reasoning and unsure of how I should approach the situation. Wiping the damp tendrils of hair off her forehead, I whispered conspiratorially, "Well, you were right. But perhaps next time you should just agree with your grandmother. After all, it's apparent that she appreciates music about as much as a rock would."

I was rewarded with a small smile. Then I added, "How about a swim?"

A loud whoop from Willie was a clear answer for both of them.

We headed down the path that led to Zeke's cabin but took a different fork in the trail. I welcomed the cool shade of the tall pines and longed for the coolness of the creek.

The children immediately stripped to their undergarments and stood on the edge, their bare toes wiggling amongst the grass and rocks. At that point, the creek was neither wide nor deep, but it filled our criteria by being wet and cool. With a nod from me, their gleeful cries filled the air as they flung their young bodies into the refreshing wetness.

My first impulse was to strip down to my chemise, but I hesitated. I'm sure the children wouldn't have noticed, but I didn't want to be discovered by someone else standing in the middle of the creek in nothing but a sheer piece of wet cotton. Resignedly, I pulled off my ankle boots and peeled down my stockings. Glancing around to make sure no one was lurking, I hoisted my skirts above the knees, sighing loudly as I waded into the stream.

The children splashed me in their exuberance, but I declined to chastise them. The spattering of water on my face was too refreshing. I eyed the children enviously, their bare arms and legs glinting in the sunlight. Sweat still poured down my face, so I scooped a handful of water and splashed it over my head.

The whinnying of a horse jerked me upright. I dropped my skirts in the water as I hastily turned around. I eyed my soaking hem with dismay and quickly picked up my skirts again as I waded back to the shore. Charlie bolted past me and landed with a loud splash, his wet, furry presence greeted with happy squeals from the children.

I faced Stuart as he gingerly dismounted from Endy. "Not to sound discourteous," I began, "but what are you doing here? Making sure I don't bolt from Phoenix Hall?" I wiped a stray drop off the tip of my nose. "I hate to tell you this, but the only covert activity I'm guilty of is trying to cool off in this creek."

Raising his eyebrows slightly, Stuart replied, "I was paying a visit to Zeke. I haven't seen him since Julia's mother arrived. But I heard all this caterwauling, and I came to see what had gotten caught in a trap." He loosely tethered Endy to a tree and walked over to where I stood dripping.

"I thought the children could use a nice respite from the heat." I picked up the edge of my hem and squeezed it, the water droplets scattering dust as they fell.

"The children, hmm?"

"Oh, all right. I was about to melt. And I'd just about give my left arm to be able to take off these damned clothes and go for a swim."

He looked as if he couldn't decide whether to be shocked or amused. "I see." He sat on a large rock at the edge of the stream and began to remove his boots. "As much as I might enjoy the spectacle, I wouldn't recommend it. You'd scandalize the townfolk."

He was struggling with the boot on his injured leg, so I went over to help him. He held up a hand to stop me. "Laura, that's really not proper."

"Stuart, you need help. Believe me, bare feet have never gotten anybody into trouble."

His eyes widened, but he wordlessly handed me his foot,

and I pulled off the boot. He winced slightly but nodded his thanks and stripped off his socks.

I waved a hand in front of my face. "Well, the sight isn't scandalizing me, but the smell sure is. Is that a secret weapon to kill more Yankees than a bullet could?"

Leaning back, he shook his head and laughed. "You know, Laura, I can always depend on you to say what's on your mind. A rare but admirable trait."

"Thank you. I think." I carefully picked my way back into the water and found a seat on a partially submerged tree trunk.

Sobering slightly, he said, "Why such a mystery, Laura? What is so dangerous that you have to keep it hidden from me?"

I didn't dare look at him. Staring down at the bright, reflecting water, I shrugged. "It's merely self-preservation. You have nothing to fear from me."

A welcome interruption came in the form of Charlie bounding through the water toward me, inviting me to play. Grasping hold of the bottom of my skirt, he began tugging.

"Charlie, stop it! Willie! Sarah! Please come get Charlie and make him leave me alone." I wrinkled my nose at the smell of wet dog as I vainly tried to remove my dress from Charlie's clutches.

I stood, prepared to retreat to the safety of the shore when my foot landed on a deceptively slippery rock. One moment I was standing, the next I was sitting on my backside, immersed to my waist in the water.

Once I had recovered from the shock, I politely refused all offers of help in righting myself. Instead, I lay back in my impromptu bath, allowing the water to wash over my face.

I sat up and shouted, "Oh, that feels wonderful! I wish I had thought of that to begin with!" And then I promptly lay back again, feeling my hair move with the soft current.

Opening my eyes under the water, I was surprised to see a dark wavy figure on the bank. I immediately sat up and was relieved to see Zeke.

"Hi, Zeke!" I called out, waving a hand and acting as if

sitting fully dressed in the middle of a creek was something I did all the time.

He raised a hand in greeting, his face stoic but a corner of his mouth twitching.

I stood and slogged my way to the bank. I did my best to squeeze the excess water out of my hair and dress but felt confident that the burning sun would efficiently do the rest.

I blinked at the two men as water from my hair dripped into my eyes.

Zeke nodded silently at me. Turning to Stuart, he said, "Julia's mother has come. The dark cloud over your house has told me this."

I looked in the direction of the house and saw only clear sky.

"Yes, she's here. And she's brought word of William. It appears he's been assigned to General Sherman's staff. He's in Nashville."

Zeke grunted. "That's not far enough. Does he know you're here, Stuart?"

Stuart shook his head. "No, I don't believe so. We've had no contact with him for almost a year. Unless Julia mentioned it to her mother in a letter and Pamela told him."

Zeke nodded. "Then he knows. You should leave as soon as you can."

His words made me start. I knew Stuart was a soldier and that he would eventually have to leave and go back to war. Still, the reality of it jarred me as did this indication of overt hostility between the two brothers.

Stuart's fists tightened at his sides. "Am I the only one around here who has doubts that the Yankees could ever come this far?"

Zeke looked at Stuart, his eyes steady. "Stuart, you're no fool. And you know as well as I do that a well-supplied Yankee army that easily outnumbers the Confederates can do as they please with little opposition."

Stuart sat down and began pulling on his socks and boots. Brusquely waving aside my offer of help, he yanked them on, obviously causing pain to his injured leg. "Damn this leg! But you're right, Zeke. I need to get back. I'm so useless here."

"Stuart, I wouldn't call holding this family and plantation together 'useless.' " I scrambled for reasons to prevent his departure. The thought of him riding off to battle made my mind spin. Yet I laid no claim to him, nor would I ever. My heart could take no more pain. And falling for a man—a soldier, no less, from another time—would be the straightest road to more heartache.

He hoisted himself up off the grassy bank and brushed off his backside. "That's not what I meant. My men are fighting for their country, laying down their lives, and I'm here, living as if the war isn't even happening."

"Don't be ridiculous. It's not as if you chose to be shot in the leg, for goodness sake. And what good do you think you'd do to your men right now? Would you expect them to carry you into battle because your leg won't let you keep up?"

Stuart and Zeke stared at me with raised eyebrows. Making an effort to lower my voice, I continued, "You're far more useful to us right now than you would be to the Confederacy."

Stuart grunted and quickly stepped forward, almost falling as his leg gave out on him. Zeke caught him. His face flushed red with anger, and he glared at me. "You're a real enigma, aren't you? You don't remember anything about yourself, but you know a good deal about what's best for me. Why do you want me to stay? Do you need a hapless informant who can give you information to pass on? Why, Laura?"

His soft voice cut the humid air with its vehemence. I took a step forward, my hands on my hips. "I was only trying to help. Fine. Go back to your regiment and get killed. I hope a cannonball lands right on your head." I kicked at a pebble and turned away, trying to look as dignified as I could with water dripping from my hair and clothes.

Stuart limped past me without a word and untethered his horse. Ignoring him, I called for the children to come out of the creek before their skin grew as dimpled as raisins.

Drying themselves as much as possible on the linen towels we had brought with us, they then threw their clothes on over their wet underclothes and trudged after Stuart, leaving me to follow. Zeke sent me a look of understanding and nodded good-bye as we passed the fork in the trail that led to his cabin. Taking a different path than the one I had been on previously, we soon came upon the gates of a small cemetery. I opened the gates and entered, hoping Stuart would take the children home and leave me to sort out my thoughts alone.

White headstones dotted the quiet, shady knoll, its grass meticulously cut short. From this vantage point I could see two of the cotton mills of the Roswell Manufacturing Company and a sawmill that lay between the two. All was a picture of the hustle and bustle of productive activity as seen from afar but curiously silent from where I stood amidst the gravestones, a welcomed breeze brushing my face and lifting the wet tendrils of hair off my forehead.

A prominent marble monument towered over the other gravestones, and I walked over to it. It had been erected in memory of the town's founder, Roswell King. I had seen this marker in my own time when I visited what was then known as Founders' Cemetery with my father. Besides being a little whiter, the monument showed little change. I touched it with both hands, an anchor in the sea of time.

I listened to the hum of insects as I strolled through the tiny cemetery, glancing briefly at each rounded headstone. Kneeling down in front of a small stone, I traced my fingers lightly over the carved letters. The marker was for a child who had died at age two years, nine months.

The hot prick of tears stung my eyelids, and I pictured Annie in the cold embrace of a tomb. I remembered her beloved stuffed giraffe and fervently hoped that wherever she was, she had it with her.

I rose and again walked slowly through the cemetery, looking for the grave of a child with no name. I squinted to see the lettering on the small tombstones and felt a chill in my heart at the large number of children who had been buried in the cemetery between the years 1840 and 1841.

Feeling a light touch on my shoulder, I stifled a scream, then realized it was Stuart. Willie and Sarah knew their way home; he had returned for me. Sensing my question before I asked it, he explained, "Scarlet fever epidemic. I don't think there was a family in Roswell that did not lose a child."

I nodded in silence, not yet wanting to speak, my anger toward him still strong. A vague relief passed over me as I realized that whatever dangers Annie might encounter in the nineteenth century, childhood disease would probably not be one of them. As an infant, she had been immunized against diphtheria, measles, polio, and the like. Assuming Annie *was* in the nineteenth century, this was no small comfort.

"Are you thinking of Annie?" His voice was low, concern replacing his anger.

"Yes." I paused for a moment to kneel by another tiny tombstone. "I'm also thinking of the parents of all these other children. There can be no greater pain than the loss of a child." Thoughts of Annie consumed me, and I began to cry. I stood and furiously tried to wipe the tears away, ashamed to have anyone see me fall apart. Stuart tried to put an arm around me, but I pushed him away and headed for the gate.

His footfalls sounded behind me as his hands grabbed me and spun me around. Wordlessly, he gathered me in his arms and held me against him.

It had been so long since I had felt the warmth and compassion of someone's arms around me, and it made me cry harder. The smells of horseflesh, leather, and sweat permeated his shirt, and I found them oddly comforting. His chest was hard and solid but made a remarkable pillow for my head as I soaked his shirt with my tears. Long minutes later, I was cried out, with only soft hiccups remaining. I felt Stuart's hands tilt my face upward. With his thumbs, he wiped the tears off my face. He brought his lips close to mine, then paused for a moment. I closed my eyes and felt his lips gently brush mine.

His words barely audible, he said, "You're not alone anymore. Let me help you." Small clouds of tiny flying insects began to hover about us in the dwindling twilight, but we both ignored the dancing swarm. "But you've got to be honest with me and tell me why you're here."

127

My right hand covered my mouth. What had I done? This was not allowed. "Don't. Please—don't."

He held me closer. "What are you afraid of, Laura?"

I looked down at the ground, where droplets from my dripping hair spattered into the dirt around my skirts. I searched for what truth I could tell him. "Of more loss. I could not survive it."

He tilted my face back up to his. "You're a lot stronger than you think."

My gaze rested on his lips, and I wanted him to kiss me again. I tried to turn away, but his hands held me captive. "No, I'm not. You've misjudged me."

His eyes darkened. "There's something else—I see it in your eyes. What is it? What is it you're not telling me?"

I could do nothing but look at him and then lower my eyes again.

He dropped his hands. "Why do you make me feel as if I'm consorting with the enemy?"

"I'm not your enemy. Please trust me on that."

"I wish I could." Walking past me, he left the cemetery and grabbed Endy's reins. Without looking at me, he said, "I am not a patient man, Laura. I will find out your secret. And if I discover you have been playing with our affections and deceiving us, you will live to regret it."

Tugging on the reins, he walked on ahead of me, leaving a trail of red dust behind.

"Oh, call back yesterday, bid time return."
                                            William Shakespeare

Chapter Twelve

The three red drops on my drawers alerted me to the fact that my body was functioning normally despite the abnormal circumstances of my life. My father, a Civil War buff, had dragged me to the Atlanta History Center about a hundred times, the Cyclorama just as many times, and Civil War battle reenactments more times than I could count. But nothing I had ever learned could have prepared me for the realities of living in the 1860s.

Knowing by instinct that a woman's monthly cycle would be a delicate subject, I had to consider who would be the best person to ask how to deal with it. Stuart was out of the question. Julia would probably be able to give me an answer but only with horrendous embarrassment.

There was a brief tapping on my door, and Sukie entered with a pile of clean linens. My muscles still ached from helping to wash the linens the previous day—lifting, turning, and squeezing constantly—and I was pleased to see the fruits of my labor.

I gave her a bright smile. "Sukie, I need some help."

She paused in the middle of the room. "Yes, ma'am. What can I help you with?"

"Um, I need something to protect my clothing. I'm having my period."

She looked at me closely. Then her eyes brightened as the meaning of what I was saying dawned on her. "Oh! You're

129

having your monthly bleeding." She set the laundry down on
the bed and patted my sleeve. "Don't you worry about a thing,
Miz Laura. I be right back."

And that was the easy part. Figuring out what to do with
the cloth belt and mounds of rags Sukie brought for me was
another. Staring at the strange ensemble, I suddenly realized
where the expression "on the rag" came from. Sighing to myself and saying a quick prayer of thanks that I ovulated spo-
radically and nowhere near twelve times a year, I set about
folding the rags into a thick bundle and inserting the ends in
the loops on the belt. I said another prayer of hope that the
thing would stay in place.

Walking down the stairs, I heard the soft murmur of voices.
Hoping to find Julia to enlist her in teaching me about some
of the plants in her garden, I approached the library. I hesitated
in the hallway when I realized it was Pamela's voice I was
hearing.

"It doesn't matter where I got the information. It's from
Sherman's headquarters and could do the Confederacy a lot
of good." I heard the rustle of petticoats and the tapping of
heels against the wooden floor. "Here, take it. Use it." Her
voice was low, the word *use* coming out with a hiss. "And if
you get caught, I've brought some quinine with me. You could
say it's medicine you're smuggling and nothing else."

Stuart's voice was also low, but I heard enough to understand what the conversation was about. "How can you betray
your own son-in-law? Does Julia know?"

I pictured Pamela waving a hand through the air, dismissing
any inconvenient thoughts. "During wartime, one must forget
one's personal needs and concentrate on the needs of the
Cause. I'm not betraying anyone. I am only doing what I can
for the South."

The cabinet door opened, and I heard the clinking of glass.
I pictured Stuart pouring himself a drink. After a slight pause,
he said, "And if William finds out whose side you're really
on—what then? What will happen to Julia?"

Pamela chuckled softly. "Don't worry about William. I'll

contend with him if the need arises. And, as for Julia, I'm sure you'll take care of her."

I heard Stuart slam down the glass. "That's enough! There is nothing between Julia and me. And if I take that piece of information from you, it will be for the Confederacy and not for some petty cause like thwarting William. Despite our many differences, he is still my brother, and Julia is his wife."

Another pause was followed by Pamela's voice. "There's something else, Stuart. That man, Matt Kimball, approached me yesterday in town. He wanted me to pass on a message to Mrs. Truitt. I thought I would tell you first."

I held my breath to better hear her words.

"What is it?" Stuart's words were clipped.

"He says he has information regarding her daughter."

My heart tightened in my chest, and I barely heard Stuart's voice. "I don't trust him. I'll speak to him myself. Don't tell Laura about it yet. If it's anything, I'll let her know."

Pamela's brittle laughter came through the door. "Is it him you don't trust—or her?"

"Never you mind, Pamela. I'll handle it."

The stamp of his boots heralded his departure from the room, and I quickly ducked into the parlor just in time to see him cross the hallway and head out the front door.

I jumped, startled, at the sound of pecking from the parlor window. I walked slowly toward the sound, peering cautiously through the glass. I stepped back as a large crow, its raven-black startling against the brightness outside, brought its beak against the glass. The staccato taps broke the silence of the room as the bird continued to thrust its beak at the window-pane.

The hairs on the back of my neck stood on end, and I abruptly turned around.

Pamela was staring at the crow, her eyebrows raised and her face a pasty white. Without looking at me, she said, "A crow tapping on one's window is a very bad sign."

"What do you mean?"

She turned toward me, her black eyes as cold as marble.

"It's an omen of death." Without another word, she turned and left the room.

My body shivered uncontrollably, and I hugged my elbows to give me warmth.

For the next several weeks, I waited for Stuart to approach me with information from Matt Kimball. When he didn't, I knew I'd have to take matters into my own hands and seek out Matt myself. I just preferred to do it when Stuart wasn't around to catch me doing what I was sure he would consider covert activity.

The news of General Lee's devastating Confederate loss at Gettysburg in Pennsylvania cast a somber pall over the town, and there were considerably more women dressed in head-to-toe black in church on Sundays. I didn't see Matt Kimball again and wondered how I would ever find a way to approach him.

As we moved into September, the overwhelming heat of summer began to dissipate, and the oncoming autumn was evident in the turning leaves and cooler evenings. Since the day in the cemetery, Stuart had been avoiding me, his attitude cool when we did cross paths. But sometimes as we all sat at the dining table or in the parlor, I would look up and find him watching me, his eyes brooding.

Julia was busy in her garden, harvesting the fall vegetables and planting turnips. She explained to me that the turnips would have a sweeter taste if they were planted in time to experience at least one frost. From the amount she planted, I assumed turnips would have a starring role on our winter dining table.

One evening, I sat on the porch before supper, rubbing my knees, made sore from helping Julia in her garden. The door opened, and Stuart hesitated on the threshold.

"I'm sorry to disturb you. I thought you were Zeke."

I stopped rocking and frowned. "I must try harder to stay out of the sun if you're mistaking me for a man three times my age."

Stuart sent me a smile. "No, you misunderstand. Zeke was

132

supposed to come over for a game of backgammon." He held out the board, a bag of playing pieces clinking in his other hand.

I sat up. "Backgammon? I love that game, but I haven't played in . . . in a very long time."

He walked closer to me. "May I challenge you to a match, then?"

"Only if you're not a sore loser."

He cocked an eyebrow without comment as he slid a small table over and pulled up a chair. "Perhaps we should set stakes for this."

"Stakes?" I smiled nervously.

"If I win, I get something. If you win, then you get something."

Worry grew in the pit of my stomach. "But I have nothing to give."

He leaned close to me, his eyes narrowed. "Oh, but you do." His mouth spread in a smile. "If you lose, you have to answer truthfully any question I ask."

My throat felt thick. "And if I win?"

He settled back in his chair and began setting up the game. "That would be your choice. You could have your freedom to come and go as you please. Or I could kiss you again."

I jumped out of my seat. "Of all the arrogant—"

He grabbed my wrist and stood quickly, his rocking chair bobbing behind him. The sudden feel of his skin against mine made me tremble. I jerked my hand away.

"I'm sorry, Laura. I didn't mean to offend you. Truly. I was jesting. But perhaps I should wait for Zeke after all."

Despite my protest, I wanted to stay. Besides, a glimmer of hope burned inside me. If I could win my freedom, go into town without someone to watch me, I would have a chance to find Matt Kimball.

"No, I'll play. Whoever wins the best of seven."

Zeke never arrived. We began playing, and I quickly discovered we were evenly matched. Soon we were called in for supper, and afterward we moved the set indoors to the parlor. A crisp snap had invaded the air, and Pamela and Julia were wrapped in thick shawls. The clicking of Julia's knitting needles and the popping of the wood in the fireplace punctuated the cozy silences in the conversation lulls. I found myself furtively watching Stuart as he contemplated a move. He had the habit of running his hands through his hair when he was concentrating, rumpling the thick black strands in an oddly attractive way.

Dr. Watkins had taken to calling most evenings now that the cotton harvest was over and Stuart had more free time, and he had perched himself in a chair between Julia and her mother. I watched him as he looked at Julia, his eyes softening like a puppy's, and I knew that his tender feelings for her hadn't altered since Robbie's birth.

I had been almost unbeatable in backgammon when I played my father or Jack, but Stuart was a formidable opponent. I won three games in a row, and then my luck seemed to run out. Unfortunately, I was not a gracious loser. By the middle of the sixth game, he was resoundingly whopping me. I looked in dismay at the large number of my counters still on the board and the piles of his pieces resting on the table.

He tossed the dice onto the board and chuckled slightly at the result. I brought my hand down on the table with a thump, making the pieces jump. "That's not fair!" I shouted in mock dismay as I stared at the double sixes. "If you win this game, it will be from sheer luck!"

I realized that all eyes rested on me, and I complained, "The man gets doubles every time he rolls." The three nodded in my direction before resuming their conversation.

Stuart rapidly picked up two of his counters and began moving them home. He looked up at me, a small smile framing his lips.

"Do you really think that's the best move?" I asked, pretending to study the board.

He shook his head slowly. "That's not going to work on me, Mrs. Truitt."

I gave him a look of false innocence. "Pardon? I'm sure I don't know what you mean."

"Hmm," he murmured, as he threw the dice again. Double fours.

I put both elbows on the table and frowned. "Do you think it's gentlemanly to beat a lady at backgammon?" I asked, aware of my own hypocrisy.

Quietly, he said, "If I didn't think I would win, I never would have agreed to our little wager." He leaned forward, as if to make sure nobody else heard him. "But if you continue with your distractions, you might still win this match."

I saw his gaze directed at the low neckline of my dinner dress, one of two from Julia's wardrobe that had been modified to fit me. I quickly yanked my elbows off the table and sat back as far as my hoop skirt would allow, which was approximately two inches. I felt myself blushing as I hastened to roll the dice. Snake eyes. "Whoopedy-do," I said, unenthusiastically.

"Just don't say you never get doubles," Stuart said, laughing as he rolled again and completed moving his counters off the board. His blue eyes gazed steadily at me, making my blood run thick and heavy through my veins. "One more game, then the winner takes all."

I chewed on my inner cheek, wondering how I would answer the question he was bound to ask me. I looked down at the board and began setting up my pieces one last time.

The wind outside picked up, alerting us to the signs of an early-autumn storm. Dried leaves and other debris were tossed carelessly at the window, mixed with the louder *pat-pat* of raindrops against the glass. The crackling of the fire in the fireplace joined the chorus, and I breathed in deeply the homey smell of the pine logs. I absently fingered the smooth polished wood of a counter in my hand, remembering games I had played with my father and with Jack.

"It's your move," Stuart said, his voice low.

I jumped, startled back into the present, and gave him a weak smile. "Sorry, I was daydreaming."

We began to play in earnest, the dice rolling quickly and the click of the pieces on the board drawing us further into the game. We were neck and neck as we pulled our remaining counters into the home stretch. He had three on the first space, and I had four on the fourth space. All I needed was at least a double four, and I would win. I picked up the dice and brought them slowly to my lips. I blew softly on them, then let them drop. They rolled as if in slow motion before coming to rest. Double fives.

I stared at them in shock. "I won," I whispered.

Stuart sat back in his chair, a bemused expression on his face. "This time. But don't think I'm through trying." He rolled a counter between long fingers. "Name your prize."

The tempting thought of claiming another kiss crossed my mind. "I . . . I want my freedom to come and go as I please."

He nodded slightly. "So be it. Unless you do something to jeopardize our trust."

I bit back a retort and watched as he leaned back in his chair, his eyes narrowed.

Julia spoke up. "What a wicked night. Puts me in mind of another night just like this. The night Willie was born." A dreamy smile touched her lips. "The wind was blowing something fierce, and we thought it might be a hurricane. All the shutters had been nailed shut over the windows, and the house was very dark." Her soft brown eyes grew still, looking at me but past me, seeing another autumn night.

She put a hand lightly on her abdomen, smoothing the fabric of her dress. Her voice sounded as if it were coming from a far-off place, barely audible against the violence of the wind outside. "I felt the baby stretching me so tight that I thought I might burst, and I knew that my time had come. But I wasn't afraid. Zeke had told me that everything would be all right." The firelight flickered over her face, casting a portion of it into shadow but illuminating the other half in a soft, radiant glow. The undulations of light and darkness seemed to mimic the surges of an unborn child in the womb, making me grieve afresh for the emptiness of my own.

Julia blinked, as if seeing me for the first time, and smiled. "And he was right. Willie was born in the early-morning hours, chubby, pink, and bawling.

The mood broke as Julia laughed softly, and the click of her knitting needles began anew.

"You're very blessed, Julia. All three of your children are so beautifully healthy." The words hurt, and I hoped that no one detected my pain. "So, now that I know the story of Willie's birth, and I was there for Robbie's, tell me about Sarah."

Dr. Watkins stood and moved to the window. He crossed his arms over his chest and leaned back. "That was frightening, remember, Julia? It was summer—June, if I remember correctly—and she was a good two months early. So small, we didn't think she'd make it."

Julia kept her head down, the needles clicking vigorously. Then an ear-splitting scream broke the silence. Stuart stood immediately but was held in place by a gesture from Julia.

"Let's see if she quiets down by herself."

I looked around me for some sort of explanation, but all faces were turned to Julia in mute awareness. A minute passed in silence, and my heart was beginning to beat at a normal rate again, when the same horrifying scream began again.

Julia stood abruptly, and her knitting needles, still attached to the stockings she had been working on, slid from her lap. "I'll go," she said, and left the room. Suddenly realizing that it was Sarah who had screamed, I followed Julia upstairs.

Muffled sobs reached me as I crossed the landing. Sarah shared a room with Willie, whose curved form I could make out on the opposite twin bed in the dim light.

Julia sat on the edge of Sarah's bed, her arms around her daughter, murmuring unintelligible words of comfort, her hand gently stroking Sarah's back.

Sarah brought her head up abruptly and pointed toward the window. "Mama, make it go away!" she cried, and then buried her face in her mother's shoulder.

The curtains had been pulled back, revealing nothing but pitch-black darkness. The wind still whipped against the house, but the rain had stopped. I approached the window cautiously and peered out. Nothing could be seen in the yard below, but a small brightening of the night brought my gaze upward. Thin strips of cloud slid quickly across the sky, al-

137

ternately exposing a round, full moon and casting it in shadow. As the bright moonlight flooded the room, Sarah screamed again.

"Close the curtains." It was Julia's voice, as soft as usual but commanding nevertheless. I quickly grabbed the two panels and brought them together.

Julia began to sing quietly, and Sarah's sobs lessened. I felt like an intruder in this maternal scene and softly crept out of the room. As I started to walk down the stairs, Julia left the room, closing the door behind her.

I turned to Julia. "What was Sarah so afraid of? Was it the storm?"

Her face was in shadow, dark and unreadable. "No. She's afraid of the full moon. Has been since she was a baby." She stepped past me and walked down the stairs, her dress rustling as it brushed the steps. A chill covered me in goose bumps, and I shivered.

I didn't follow her. Instead, I went to the library and to the shelf where the family Bible was kept. With shaking hands, I pulled it from its place and opened the front cover. There, the next-to-last entry under a long list of births and deaths: *Sarah Margaret Elliott, born June 16, 1856.* Quietly, I closed the book and pushed it back onto the shelf.

Feeling restless, I crept quietly to the front door and stepped out onto the porch. The storm was passing but leaving trailing shifts of wind in its wake. My skirts billowed out around me, and I slapped my hands down at my sides to keep them from making me airborne. The sound of buggy wheels and the brisk trotting of horse's hooves came from the drive, and I assumed the good doctor had taken his leave moments before I came outside. The cloud cover had thinned, and the bright moonlight streamed down on the yard, reflecting in the puddles and illuminating the scattered debris of twigs and leaves.

I walked slowly toward the edge of the porch and leaned on a column for support. The smell of wet clay and damp barnyard assailed my nose, and I breathed it in deeply, as if to convince myself of the new reality of my life.

A different scent caught my attention, and I turned slowly

to see Stuart at the other end of the porch, drawing on a cigar. He walked toward me, his face hidden in shadow but briefly illuminated by the end of the cigar as he inhaled.

I remained where I was. "I'll leave if you want to be alone," I offered.

He stopped several paces away from me and blew the smoke to the side. "Please don't. I welcome your company."

I laughed. "That's mighty big of you, since I pummeled you at backgammon."

He smiled down at me, but his eyes were serious. "Are you sure you won't change your mind about your prize?"

My gaze traveled down his face and settled on his lips. I blushed when I realized what I was doing, quickly looking down at my feet.

"No. I like the idea of being a free woman again."

He tipped ashes over the railing, and I watched them scatter in the night air. "You won the match, which is why I'll allow you some freedom. But don't think it's because I trust you."

I bit back my anger, suddenly realizing how much I wanted to gain his trust. I grabbed the railing with both hands, my back to Stuart. "If you're standing on a river's edge, looking at the water, do you have to wade in to find out that it's wet?"

He didn't say anything, so I turned to face him. "These people—Julia and the children—do you really think I would do anything to harm them? And this house—it's more of a home to me than you would ever realize."

My voice quavered as I remembered standing in front of the house for the very first time with Jack, feeling the powerful force of being home. I shivered as a gust of cool wind wrapped around me.

Stuart took a step toward me, still unspeaking, his face unreadable. Smoke from his cigar danced up between us like little ghosts, vanishing with the wind's whim. "These are dangerous times, Laura. Things aren't always as they appear to be. People, either. Since this conflict began I've met men and women who will risk anything to promote their cause. I've learned to withhold my trust until my boots are completely submerged in the river. Then I'll believe it's wet."

I threw up my hands. "Fine. Just allow me to write the inscription on your headstone: 'Killed by a bullet he wasn't sure would hurt him.' "

He leaned close enough that I could smell the soap on his skin. I pressed my back against the column, unsure of the light in his eyes. "The only thing that sustains me when I'm in the heat of battle is the picture in my mind of this house and my family—knowing they are safe. But now, you are here, living with us. I don't know who you are, where you're from, or what you want. And you're keeping something from me. You've never denied it. And I have a strange way of not trusting people who aren't truthful with me."

I straightened, my anger brimming like static electricity. "What if . . . what if the truth was so insane, so unspeakable, that you wouldn't even recognize it as the truth?" I slammed a fist on the railing. "I don't even know what the truth is anymore, and I really don't care. I just want to find Annie and go home. I just want to go home with my daughter."

"Where is home? And without your husband and child, what remains there that's so important to you—more important than staying here where people have grown to care for you?"

I didn't realize I was crying until he reached up and brushed a tear from my cheek. Pushing his hand aside, I used my sleeve to wipe my cheeks. "My memories are there. Of Jack and of our perfect life with our little daughter."

Stuart's voice was low and measured. "I've watched my boyhood friends die for this cause. I held the head of my best friend while his brains drained into my haversack. And at the time, all I could think of was my rations being spoiled."

His words startled me into facing him again. He threw down his cigar and ground it out with the heel of his boot.

"Why are you telling me this?"

His eyes were dark pools. "Life goes on, Laura. Memories won't keep you warm on a winter's night." He inhaled deeply. "And I also want you to understand what's at stake. We've sacrificed so much, and I won't give away what's left on a silver platter."

"I won't take anything from you. I just need shelter until I find Annie and a way home."

"It's too late."

My hand clutched his sleeve. "Too late?"

"Too late to leave without taking anything with you. You've already captured hearts, Laura. You couldn't go home without leaving at least one casualty."

Somehow I knew he wasn't talking about Julia or the children. The moonlight lent his face an eerie blue cast, giving him the appearance of a ghost. I felt goose bumps on my arms when I realized that, to me, he was a ghost—at least somebody who had lived in the distant past. He saw my shiver and slipped off his coat, placing it gently on my shoulders. His fingers brushed the bare skin of my neck and seemed to linger longer than necessary.

His eyes were clouded in shadow as he looked down at me. "I may as well tell you this now. Charles has told me that I won't be fit for combat duty for a few months yet, but I have some business to attend to and will be making several short trips before I return to my regiment."

I opened my mouth to mention the conversation I had overheard between him and Pamela but quickly closed it. He would never let me go into town if he realized I knew Matt Kimball wanted to speak with me.

"Will you miss me?" he asked suddenly.

I was glad of the darkness. "Yes, I will. A lot," I answered. With a trembling voice, I added, "There's nobody else here who can play backgammon."

He chuckled lightly as he placed his hands behind my neck and tilted my face toward his. He leaned down and kissed me softly. His lips lingered over mine, and a faint sigh escaped me as I tasted cigar smoke and whiskey.

"This might be considered by my superiors as consorting with the enemy, you know."

I kept my head back in the hope he'd kiss me again. "I'm not your enemy, Stuart."

"This coming from the woman who said she wanted a cannonball to land on my head."

His lips were so close, I shut my eyes. My voice sounded languid in the night air. "I didn't really mean that, you know."

His kiss this time was anything but gentle, his lips bruising mine. Then his mouth traveled to my ear, and he whispered, "Memories can't compete with flesh and blood, can they?"

The front door opened, and we stepped apart. Julia looked at us knowingly, a tight smile on her face, and I was glad again for the darkness to hide the stain of red creeping up my face.

"I was wondering where you two had gone off to. Laura, we were hoping you might play something for us on the piano."

We followed her inside, but she stopped me before I entered the parlor so she could adjust my hair. With a raised eyebrow at Stuart, she swept past us and settled herself on the sofa, waiting demurely as I sat at the piano and began to play.

Much later, as I lay in my lonely bed, I tossed and turned, unable to sleep. The full moon turned the blackness in my room to gray, reminding me of how my life was no longer black and white but instead had fallen between the sharply colored cracks of reality. Finally, in the last stages of wakefulness, when the world tends to blur its edges, I imagined I heard the tap-tapping of a black crow's beak against a windowpane, and my blood chilled with dread.

"Much have I travelled into the realms of gold,
"And many goodly States and Kingdoms seen."
                                                John Keats

Chapter Thirteen

I walked into the henhouse with an air of authority. I had
found that this worked with even the most stubborn chicken.
Let them know you were afraid of their pesky little beaks, and
the result would be something out of an Alfred Hitchcock
movie. Besides, soon I would be going into town alone. Stuart
had left on his trip to deliver whatever Pamela had given him,
and Julia needed me to fetch cloth at the company store for
new pants for Willie. They no longer accepted Confederate
money, and we had to rely on what we could trade.

I thrust my hand under chicken number one, whom I had
dubbed Cher, and snatched away a lone egg, placing it in the
folded up skirt of my dress. Number two just as easily acquiesced, until I got greedy and reached for the second egg. She
responded with a resonant squawk and a well-aimed peck at
my forearm.

Despite her protests, I unceremoniously removed her from
her perch and found yet another egg. I left the henhouse, ignoring the squawks of disapproval and feeling a bit smug.

Hastily depositing the eggs in a basket, I changed clothes
and headed out to the buggy. I had received informal training
on how to maneuver the thing, and I was fine as long as I
didn't have to get too close to the horse. Julia ran out of the
house and handed me an empty basket and a list. She shielded

143

her eyes with one hand as she looked up at me, murmuring good-bye.

She looked so forlorn, I felt the need to reassure her. "Don't worry, Julia. I'm not running off. I'll be back shortly."

She waved a hand at me and stepped back from the buggy. "I know that, Laura. It's just that . . . Oh, never mind."

I slapped the horse's rump with a whip, and we trotted off in the cool afternoon air. I recognized the brick facade of the company store, remembering I had eaten several times at the restaurant that would eventually be housed in the building.

The door was propped open, allowing fresh air inside and lighting the dim interior. Waiting a moment for my eyes to adjust, I soon made out a counter at the end of the room with a man standing behind it.

The thick smell of dust, presumably from the sacks of grain propped against the counter, permeated the room, making me sneeze. Tall glass jars, many of them empty, lined the top of the counter. A little girl walked over to one filled with honeyed popcorn balls and touched it gently, but, at a firm shake of her mother's head, she retreated. I knew how dear sugar had become at this point in the war, and the prices for sweets were exorbitant.

"Good afternoon, ma'am." The tall, lanky shopkeeper had long wisps of sparse hair creeping across his scalp like spider legs. "I'm Mr. Northcutt. Is there anything I can help you with today?"

"Nice to meet you. I'm Laura Truitt. I'm staying at Phoenix Hall." I handed him Julia's list. "Julia Elliott sent me to pick up a few things." I lifted the egg basket. "I've brought eggs."

He settled bifocals on his nose and regarded the list. "I'll get these things together for you."

A woman I remembered vaguely from church leaned across the counter next to me. "Is that coffee on the shelf behind you, Mr. Northcutt?"

"Yes, ma'am. I have five pounds of it. Brought to me yesterday by Samuel Baker, who's on leave on account of his arm. Says he got it off a dead Yankee."

"How much are you asking?"

144

"It's worth about thirty dollars for the pound. Or half a hog."

The woman slowly shook her head. "You tempt me, Mr. Northcutt. But I just can't afford it." She sighed, gave me a brief nod, then left the store.

While Mr. Northcutt gathered the items for Julia, I strolled around the store, examining the mostly empty shelves, my skirts kicking up the sawdust scattered on the floor. I was surprised to see a few tins of corn and other vegetables, thinking canning a more modern innovation.

Metal hooks hung from the rafters, dangling a few batches of tobacco leaves where meat had been hung previously.

My toe struck something hard, and I turned to see a wooden barrel on the floor. Lifting the lid, I caught the biting smell of vinegar wafting up, and I could see dark green pickles floating within. Every available shelf and much of the floor was littered with all sorts of baskets, most empty but some full, and sacks and barrels filled with a few things I recognized, such as eggs and molasses, and many items I didn't. The tempting aroma of baked goods led me to the front of the store again, where an assortment of pies sat suggestively on a low shelf. The Elliott house had not had sweets for some time because of the scarcity of sugar, and my mouth watered as I looked at the flaky edges of the pie crusts.

My heels tapped across the oak floor planks, echoing in the small room. A shadow blocked the light from the doorway, and I turned to see who had entered.

The woman was dressed in black head to toe, the severity of her mourning costume not alleviated by even a single piece of jewelry. A little girl of about seven or eight, also dressed in black, followed her, her eyes never leaving the floor.

Stepping into the shop, the woman raised the black veil that had covered her face. Piercing gray eyes alighted on me for a moment before moving on toward Mr. Northcutt. The woman seemed to be in her early forties, but the signs of strain under her eyes and across her forehead added years to her face. I remembered seeing her at church but had not been introduced. Her only son had been killed at Gettysburg by a Yankee bullet,

145

and for this reason she had snubbed Julia. Despite the hours Julia spent rolling bandages for the Confederates, and all the food stores she had given to the Southern armies, her marriage to a Yankee sympathizer branded her.

My attention was drawn to the little girl now standing facing a shelf holding a doll with a porcelain face and exquisite clothes.

My heart jumped at the sight of the girl's strawberry-blond hair, pulled into a single braid running down her back. It was the shade of Annie's hair, although most children's darkened as they grew older.

One small hand reached up to stroke the lace skirt of the doll, and I noticed the spattering of freckles on her hand and wrist. My heart thumped wildly in my chest, and my mouth went dry as I slowly walked over to stand next to the girl.

She looked at me with wide eyes, withdrawing her hand guiltily. Her large brown eyes answered my question: she was not my Annie. My heart sank in disappointment, but I smiled at her and returned to the front counter to settle the account with Mr. Northcutt.

As he handed me the items, I asked, "Would you by any chance know where I might find Mr. Matt Kimball?"

The shopkeeper looked at me with tight lips, and the bereaved mother sent me a disapproving glance.

"No, I'm afraid not, Mrs. Truitt."

Embarrassed, I thanked him and stepped outside. I was immediately confronted by a blast of wind, sending an icy chill up my skirts. I loaded the baskets into the buggy and was contemplating driving around in the hope I might catch sight of Mr. Kimball, when I spotted the man crossing the town square.

Recognizing that yelling to him wouldn't be appropriate, I watched to see where he was going. He disappeared inside a two-story brick building on the east side of the square. Making sure the reins were tethered properly, I turned and walked in that direction.

I stopped in front of the building, under the painted sign that read AUNT CLAIRE'S ROOMING HOUSE. After all this time,

I might finally have information on Annie. I knocked, and when nobody answered, I turned the knob.

The door swung open into a deserted hallway. Tall, narrow stairs led upward against the wall on the right, and a short corridor stretched out in front of me on the left. A baby cried somewhere above me but was quickly drowned out by a man and woman shouting. Two closed doors, their brown stain faded to gray, fronted the hallway. There were no mailboxes, signs, or anything to tell me who lived in the house. With shaking hands, I knocked on the first door.

I stood in the corridor, listening to the hushed sounds of other people's lives around me and trying to hear any movement behind the door. I knocked again for good measure before moving onto the next door.

Before my fist struck the wood panel, the door flew open. A hatless Matt Kimball stood in the doorway, a darkened room behind him.

I forced a smile. "Hello, Mr. Kimball."

"Laura. And do remember to call me Matt. It's much more . . . friendly." He separated his lips, showing the bottom edges of his teeth in an apparent smile. "What brings you to my door?"

I decided to be blunt, not really wanting to prolong conversation with him. "I understand you have information regarding my daughter."

He nodded. "Ah, yes. I'm surprised it took you this long." He remained in the doorway, making no move to invite me in.

"I . . . I wasn't able to come any sooner." I deliberately shifted my gaze over his shoulder. "May I come in so we can talk?"

He raised his eyebrows, and I knew I had crossed the boundary of propriety. But I didn't care—I needed the information about Annie and would get it any way I could.

With a grin, he moved back. "Why, of course."

The stench of sweat and unwashed sheets hit me, and I immediately regretted my decision to come inside. Resisting the impulse to cover my nose with my hand, I glanced around

147

for a place to sit and was horrified to find the only furnishings consisted of a bed and a chest of drawers. A scrawny black cat sat upon the grimy pillow and acknowledged my presence with a bored yawn. The back of my nose tickled, calling to mind my cat allergy.

I stayed with my back against the closed door and tried to appear calm. Kimball didn't step back but remained directly in front of me, so close I could see specks of food on his collar.

"Mr.—Matt." I swallowed hard, trying not to sneeze or choke on the filthy air. "I heard you had news of my daughter."

A grin slipped over his face. "Yes, your daughter." He leaned toward me with an outstretched arm, bracing his hand on the door behind me.

I didn't flinch but surreptitiously felt behind me for the doorknob. I looked up at him expectantly. "My daughter disappeared on Moon Mountain when she was two, and I haven't seen her since. I heard you might know where I could find her."

He leaned nearer to me, his stale breath washing over me. "And just what did you have in mind as payment?" His gaze shifted to my chest and insolently traveled back to my face.

I had had my doubts about Matt Kimball, but I had never once anticipated this turn of events. "Payment? You want payment for telling me about my own daughter? Believe me, Mr. Kimball, I have no intention of paying you for anything in the manner you are insinuating." I pressed my back against the door, my hand clutching the cold brass knob.

"Why else would a woman come alone to a man's room?"

My fists clenched in rage, and I struck out without thinking. I managed to clobber him on both sides of the head, making him reel backward, more from the shock of a woman hitting him, I'm sure, than from any pain I might have caused. Regardless, it gave me the opportunity to twist the knob and run out into the foyer. He had made it to his doorway by the time I reached the outer door. I yanked it open and ran outside and down the short flight of steps to the pavement. I looked back at the rooming house in time to see the front door slam shut.

My breath came in deep gulps, and I noticed to my dismay that a clump of hair had fallen from my upsweep and now dangled in front of my face. I raised my hands to fix it and at that moment noticed Eliza Smith on the sidewalk, stock still and staring directly at me.

Her pinched face bore an eerie resemblance to an apple that had been on the ground too long. I would have laughed if I weren't so shaken, and if I hadn't realized that whatever she thought she had seen would be quickly reported back to Stuart.

"Eliza, it's not what you think . . ."

But before the words were out of my mouth, she had turned without acknowledging me and walked quickly away, her wide skirts billowing around her like a circus tent.

A gust of wind struck me, and swirls of leaves danced around on the sidewalk. I glanced at the front window of the rooming house and saw the black cat watching me, its feline eyes blinking slowly. I stared back, despair mixed with determination. I wasn't through with Matt Kimball. If he did indeed know something about Annie, I would find out.

I drove back to Phoenix Hall as quickly as I could. I needed to do a great deal of damage-control before Eliza had a chance to wag her tongue. Thankfully, Stuart was away. At least I would have time to get Julia on my side before he returned. I sped through town, and my mind drifted to thoughts of a little girl with strawberry-blond hair and freckles across her nose, and of the daughter who seemed so near but so far away.

The house was deathly silent as I entered. I called for Julia but received no answer. I was about to head out back toward the kitchen when the sound of singing came from the dining room. I dropped the basket on the floor in the hall and went in search of the voice.

Sukie was in the dining room, standing on one of the chairs, attempting to wipe the dust off the crystal chandelier with a feather duster.

"Hello, Sukie. Do you know where I might find Julia?"

She nodded, and pointed with the feather duster. "She be out back in the kitchen, messin' with her herbs."

I thanked her, but before I walked away, I thought of something else. I turned around to make sure we were alone in the room and then walked toward her, keeping my voice low.

"Sukie, I was wondering if you could help me with something."

She peered over a chandelier stem at me. "Sure, Miz Laura. What can I do for you?"

"I need to know how I'm supposed to manage these darned hoops without embarrassing myself. I swear I just about show everything under my skirt every time I sit down."

She raised her eyebrows but nodded as she stepped down and pulled out another chair.

"Here, stand in front of this one." I moved myself into position. "Now, back yourself up slowly. While you're doing that, sneak your hand toward the metal hoop that's at the top of your leg. All right, you're doing real good. Now, pull it up gentle like so that when you sit in the chair you won't sit on it. There! How's that?"

I was amazed that I had managed to sit in the chair without mishap. I smiled my thanks and stood. As she leaned over to pick up my chair and replace it under the table, the string around her neck I had noticed before slipped out of her dress. At the end of the string hung what appeared to be a red flannel bag.

Sukie must have realized what I was looking at, because her fingers immediately flew to the bag. She covered it with her hand as if to protect it.

"What is that?" I stepped toward her.

She took a step backward as I approached. "It's nothing, Miz Laura."

I stopped, confused at her reaction. The sound of footsteps from behind caused me to turn around. Pamela lurked in the doorway, her arms folded in front of her.

"It's a charm necklace, Laura. Sukie has powers, I've been told. That little pouch carries all sorts of things—like frog bones, snakeskin, ashes, of course. Isn't that right, Sukie?"

Sukie stared down at the floor while she hastened to tuck the bag back into her dress.

"It's such foolishness, what these people bring with them from Africa. I really don't understand how Julia can allow it. I've tried to talk to her."

Sukie excused herself and left the room without looking up.

Pamela's dark eyes coolly appraised me. "I would be careful around her. That's a powerful charm around her neck."

I couldn't tell whether she was being serious. "I'll be sure to be careful, then." I hoped my words would placate her, as I had no desire to get into an argument with her regarding superstitions. I had it on good authority that magic could be very real. I made a move to leave.

"Yes. You be careful, Laura. Be very careful. Your hold on the Elliotts is tenuous at best. I would behave myself if I were you."

I stopped and stared at her, waiting for her to say something else. Instead, she swept past me in a rustle of silk and climbed the stairs.

An uneasy feeling settled in my stomach as I wondered if Pamela had somehow already heard about my visit to Matt Kimball. Slowly, I walked out to the kitchen in search of Julia.

Julia had removed her hoops and donned a work dress and was busily crushing something with her mortar and pestle. Without looking up, she greeted me by name.

"Hello, Julia." Eager to get this conversation over with, I blurted, "I'm . . . I'm afraid I've done something that might be deemed . . . inappropriate."

She bent to rub her nose on the shoulder of her dress, as if scratching an itch, and continued her work with the mortar.

I continued. "I met with Matt Kimball in his room at his boarding house."

She stopped, the pestle in midair. "You . . . you did what with Matt Kimball?"

I shook my head quickly. "It's not what you think—he didn't lay a hand on me. I . . . I overheard Stuart telling your mother that Matt Kimball had information on my daughter. But when Stuart never approached me with it, I figured I had to do something on my own. I used the opportunity of shopping today to seek out Mr. Kimball."

Her hand shook slightly, her face now the color of the pestle. "Did he tell you anything?"

"No. He wanted . . . payment."

She laid down the pestle and gripped the table with both hands. "I see. Did anyone see you enter or leave?"

I bit my lip, feeling like a scolded child. "I'm afraid so. Eliza Smith saw me as I was leaving. I'm sure I appeared disheveled—"

Julia interrupted, her expression worried. "Did he . . . hurt you?"

"Not that he didn't try, but no. I guess it was foolish of me to go into his room."

She closed her eyes and shook her head. "And Eliza of all people." She looked at me again. "I understand how desperate you are for information about your daughter, but you must be more careful with your reputation in the future. Don't worry. I'll speak to Eliza and try to undo any damage she might have already caused." She pursed her lips. "My main concern at the moment is how we should tell Stuart. You know he'll be furious."

"Furious enough to have me arrested? To believe I went to see Matt for other, political reasons?"

Julia's voice was quiet. "I doubt he would do that. The man has feelings for you, Laura. You'd have to be blind not to notice." She returned to the mortar, rhythmically crushing its contents in even, circular motions, and slipped a quick glance in my direction. "But I've known him to put duty and obligation over his heart before. I'll see what I can do."

I tried to ignore the flush of heat creeping up my cheeks. "Do we need to tell him at all?"

She nodded without looking at me. "Yes. Most likely he'll know before he returns. Gossip travels swiftly, I'm afraid."

I stepped closer to her, the sharp smell of the crushed herb stinging my nose. "I'm telling you the truth about why I went to see Matt. I wasn't . . . passing on information or anything. I just wanted to make sure you knew that."

Her left hand reached out and settled softly on mine. "I know, Laura. I believe you."

She put the pestle down and began scooping the mortar's contents into a glass jar. Turning to me, she added, "Besides, we need to tell Stuart so he can get the information you need from Matt. As a man, Stuart has means of persuasion not available to us."

Julia reached for some dried herbs hanging upside down from the ceiling. "Matthew Kimball has been a troublemaker for years. I can't help but wonder where he got information about your daughter. I know Stuart will do what he can to find out."

With a large kitchen knife, she chopped off small chunks of the root portion and placed these into the mortar. She picked up the pestle, but I stopped her.

"Julia, let me. Perhaps I might even learn something." She smiled and let me take her place. "How did you ever learn all you know about plants and herbs? I can hardly tell the difference between rosemary and a rose."

Her cheeks pinked with a becoming show of pleasure. "My mother taught me everything I know. She must have started teaching me when I was still in bloomers."

"Hmm," I murmured. "I somehow can't picture your stepmother communing with nature."

"Mama is a wonderful healer. I think she derives pleasure from understanding the powers of plants and potions."

"Yes, I can certainly understand that."

I crushed the dried plant parts with the pestle, quickly grinding them into a powder. The rhythmic thumping was like a soothing mantra, and I could feel the calming effects.

The powder smelled strange, and I took a pinch to bring it to my nose to get a better sniff.

Julia moved so fast, I didn't know what was happening until it was all over. She hit my hand, knocking it out of the way and causing me to tip over the mortar. It somersaulted through the air, throwing out powder in great puffs, and landed on its side with a solid clunk. I stared at her in surprise. She was already kneeling on the kitchen floor, trying to salvage what she could of the powdery white substance.

"I'm sorry. I thought you were about to taste it. It's hellebore root—it's poisonous in large quantities or undiluted."

I bent down next to her and began to scrape up as much of the elusive powder as I could.

"I didn't mean to hit you so hard. I apologize. And I certainly didn't mean to knock this over, either. Hellebore grows in the north Georgia mountains, and I have to wait for a peddler to come around with it. But I think I have enough for the tea I was going to make for one of the field hands. He has a bit of a sore throat."

I stared at her. "You're going to poison him because he has a sore throat?"

"Lord, no, Laura! Using a tiny bit in a tisane has wonderful soothing properties. Anything more, though, would kill a person. And I know the difference."

"Good, then I'll let you make the tea."

I left her to her own devices and went in search of the children. I tried to have a regularly scheduled lesson time for them, but between their chores and the haphazard nature of mine, it usually came down to whenever the three of us weren't doing anything else.

Charlie's barks led me to the side yard, where I found the children busily engaged in a pine cone fight. I herded them into the library, deciding to dispense with a strict lesson and instead have story hour. We stopped abruptly on the threshold, and I felt Sarah's hand tighten in mine. Pamela faced us, and I recognized the astronomy volume in her hands. I remembered Stuart telling me that the books were hers.

"Sorry. We didn't mean to disturb you."

She gave us a brittle smile. "You did not disturb me. I was just choosing a few books to take up to my room and read. But I'm done now."

The children followed me into the room and sat down on either side of me on the green velvet sofa. They sat rigid and silent until Pamela left the room.

"Miss Laura, can you tell us the Dorothy story again?" Sarah's green eyes pleaded.

"Well, I guess that can be arranged. But as soon as I'm

done, we're going to work on writing our letters. Without any complaints. Agreed?"

The blond head and the dark brown one both nodded quickly in agreement.

"But first, can you sing us that song again?" asked Willie.

I knew this was a stalling tactic, but I went along with them. "Sure. Which song did you have in mind?"

"The one Dorothy sings about the rainbow."

"Oh, yes. That's a favorite of mine."

I cleared my throat and began belting out "Somewhere, Over the Rainbow," in my best operatic rendition, sending both children into giggles.

I halted, the words "why, oh, why can't I" dying in my throat when I saw the darkening of the doorway. Pamela had returned.

Her chest rose and fell rapidly, as if she had just run a mile, her face a pasty white. I jumped up and grabbed her arm to bring her to the sofa. The children quickly moved away.

She allowed me to sit her down, but she knocked my hands away as I tried to unbutton the top of her dress. "No, really, I'm all right. I think I just climbed the stairs too quickly." Her eyes were wild but did not leave my face.

"I think we should call the doctor. You're not looking well at all."

"No! I'm fine, really." She leaned her head back against the sofa and closed her eyes.

Slowly, she stood and shakily made her way to the door. As if in afterthought, she turned around and asked, "Laura, that was a beautiful song. Wherever did you hear it?"

I quickly searched my head for a plausible answer. "I . . . I don't remember."

She nodded and slowly walked from the room.

The light from the window suddenly darkened, and I looked outside to see dark swells of clouds rolling in and obscuring the sun. A smattering of raindrops hit the window as the children snuggled up next to me again. It felt so natural to be sitting there with them, in that house made for a family. My

155

thoughts turned to Stuart, as they so often did, and I stared out at the storm, picturing him in it. "Be safe," I whispered, hoping that the wind would carry my thoughts to him, wherever he was.

"Give me insight into today and you may have the antique and future worlds."
Henry Wadsworth Longfellow

Chapter Fourteen

During the cold, blustery evenings of December, Dr. Watkins continued to call and would sometimes bring the paper and read aloud any news of the war. This was how we found out about the fall of Chattanooga and the retreat of General Johnston's Confederate forces to Dalton, Georgia. I knew this was the beginning of the end of the war and that in the spring, Sherman would rout Johnston's army and chase them all the way to Atlanta. I looked at the faces around me, their eyes reflecting the firelight, and wondered what would become of us all when Sherman's army reached us here, as I knew it inevitably would. Pamela met my gaze with fire in her own, her jaw clenched. Then her expression quickly returned to its controlled placidity before she resumed her knitting of badly needed socks for Johnston's ragged army.

Zeke no longer came up to the big house—I suspected Pamela's presence had something to do with this—so I took the children to see him at least once a week. I could let down my reserve when I was with him, and it was refreshing to be out of Pamela's watchful gaze.

On an unusually warm December afternoon, Zeke and I sat

out on his front porch. The children's laughter sounded from nearby in the woods as they played hide-and-seek with Charlie. I snuggled down deeper into my shawl to keep out the chill caused by the dipping sun.

Zeke looked up at the sun and the circle of the moon sharing the sky. "It will be a full moon tonight."

I shivered again, but not from the cold.

His face remained bland, chin tilted upward to view two orbs. "Stuart is safe."

I stared at him. "How do you know? Have you heard from him? Where is he?"

"I know. The rest is not important. But he will return to you."

"To me? Don't you mean to his family and home?"

"No. To you."

I tried to absorb his words.

"Be patient with him, Laura. He understands even less than you do. Try to look past his anger, and help him to trust you. He will need that trust in the months to come."

I sighed. "I'm not staying here, so I don't think it matters. Anyway, I don't know what else I can do to win his trust."

"You'll find a way. You must." He didn't say anything else but continued to rock.

Several nights later, I tossed and turned in my bed, thinking of Zeke's words. The furniture in my room seemed to hover about me like great hulking beasts, the room partially illuminated by the bright moon outside. I was slowly drifting off to sleep when I thought I felt a breath on my neck. I sat up abruptly, my eyes scanning the darkness. A horse whinnied outside.

I sat still until I heard the sound again. Stuart! I got out of bed and grabbed a shawl and silently crept down the stairs and out the front door. The night was still, bathed in the cool glow of the moon. A shadow moved near the barn, and I walked toward it.

At first I thought it was an apparition or a trick of my eyes. But when he started walking toward me, I began to run through the damp grass.

I stopped when I reached him, my breath loud and labored in the still night. I wanted him to reach for me, but he remained where he was, hands at his sides.

"You're back." My voice was weak; I was winded from running.

"So it would appear."

"I thought . . . I hoped you'd be happy to see me."

"Not as happy as I'm sure Matt Kimball was to see you walk across his threshold."

My gut clenched. "I'm sorry. I made a mistake."

He took a step toward me. "No. I'm the one who made the mistake. I trusted you, Laura." He coughed, a dry, wracking cough most likely caused by nights sleeping outside in the rain. "I'm surprised to find you still here."

I looked at him calmly, pushing away my growing anger. "Look, you're being a jerk. Just give me a chance to explain."

He coughed again. "Explain how you and Matt are working together? As if that weren't bad enough, did you have to go to his room? Your reputation in this town—"

"My reputation?" I no longer tried to keep my voice quiet. "Who the hell cares about my reputation? I only went to see him to get information about Annie—information you were supposed to find out about and never did. I overheard you talking with Pamela. Didn't you think it important enough to tell me?"

He moved quickly, placing a hand over my mouth, his other arm reaching around me. He smelled of leather and wood smoke, and I tried desperately not to notice how good it felt to be close to him again.

His voice caressed my ear. "I went to see him about it, but he had left town. Why do you think I took so long to go on my trip? I was waiting for him to return. But I couldn't wait anymore, so I left. I wanted to talk to him myself before I told you. I don't trust the man. He could have just been cooking up a reason to get you to talk to him." He dropped his hand from my mouth. "Assuming, of course, that you were unaware of his motivation."

I pulled away from him. "You're damned straight I was

unaware of his motivation. Do you think I would have willingly put myself in a position to be . . . ogled by that man?"

Stuart gripped both my shoulders, the scratchy wool of my shawl digging through my thin nightgown. "Did he touch you?"

"No. But . . . but if there's no other way to find information about Annie, I might have to . . . to make . . . concessions."

He shook me, none too gently. "Don't ever say that again. Not ever. I don't want you to even glance in Kimball's direction, do you understand? I will deal with him." His hands tightened on my arms. "I will find out why you went to see him, Laura. And I hope, for all our sakes, that he has information about your Annie."

I balled my hands into fists and pushed against his chest. "You don't own me, Stuart Elliott. I will do what I have to do to find my daughter and go home."

He released his grip on me. "So be it. But do realize that there will be consequences if you disobey me again. I've told you before, these are dangerous times."

I bowed my head, staring at my bare feet beneath my nightgown, their whiteness like glowing rocks in a sea of grass. "Yes, they are."

He touched my chin and brought my face up again. "What are you afraid of, Laura? Why can't you let me help you? I could take hearing that you're a Yankee spy. It's the not knowing that's killing me."

I wanted to tell him then, to ease the tension between us. But the less I told him, the thinner the bond between us, and the easier it would be to say good-bye. I shook my head, missing the feel of his touch as he moved his hand away.

His words were curt, abrupt. "Go back to bed, Laura. You'll catch your death out here."

I turned to leave and felt the shawl slip from my shoulders. He bent to pick it up, then moved nearer to drape it on me again. His arms wrapped around me as he settled it over my back, but he didn't move away. His breathing was warm and heavy on my cheek, and I tilted my head to see him clearly in the moonlight.

His lips covered mine before I had a chance to read what was in his eyes. His arms tightened behind me until I felt the buttons of his jacket pressing against my chest. My arms, seemingly of their own accord, went around his neck as I stood on tiptoe for a deeper kiss, feeling the rough stubble of his unshaven chin. The shawl slid again into the grass as Stuart's hands moved over the cotton of my nightgown, molding the curves of my back and hips.

He pulled away suddenly, his eyes wide, a question stalled on my lips.

"Damn it. I'm sorry." He rubbed his hands over his face. "I'm no different than Matt Kimball."

I stared back at him, the blue shadows from the moon accentuating the planes of his face. "Yes, you are." My fingertips brushed the stubble on his chin. "I wanted you to touch me."

His breath grew white in the night air, and I watched it rise toward the sky. "Not as much as I wanted to touch you."

Two worlds separated us, his and mine, and suddenly I was afraid of what might happen should they collide. I felt for a moment as if I held the country's fate in my hands.

A horse whinnied from the barn. I turned away and scooped up my shawl, my fingers fumbling as I attempted to tie the ends in a knot. "Good night, Stuart." I didn't look back.

I started for the house, listening for his words, but he remained silent. Yet I knew his eyes followed me until I entered the house.

Heedless of leaving wet footprints, I ran across the foyer and up the stairs. As I reached my bedroom door, I heard a soft click from somewhere in the house. I knew it wasn't Stuart, or I would have heard him follow me. I silently opened my door and slipped inside. Still chilled by the night air, I left my shawl on and crawled into the cotton sheets, shivering as their coolness touched my bare legs.

I stretched out, hearing my spine pop as I pointed my toes and reached my hands over my head, yawning in the process. My foot hit something in the bottom of the bed, something that hadn't been there before. I reached down and pulled it out from under the covers. I didn't need a candle to see what

160

Thrill to the most sensual, adventure-filled Romances on the market today...

FROM  LOVE SPELL BOOKS

As a home subscriber to the Love Spell Romance Book Club, you'll enjoy the best in today's BRAND-NEW Time Travel, Futuristic, Legendary Lovers, Perfect Heroes and other genre romance fiction. For five years, Love Spell has brought you the award-winning, high-quality authors you know and love to read. Each Love Spell romance will sweep you away to a world of high adventure...and intimate romance. Discover for yourself all the passion and excitement millions of readers thrill to each and every month.

Save $5.00 Each Time You Buy!

Every other month, the Love Spell Romance Book Club brings you four brand-new titles from Love Spell Books. EACH PACKAGE WILL SAVE YOU AT LEAST $5.00 FROM THE BOOKSTORE PRICE! And you'll never miss a new title with our convenient home delivery service.

Here's how we do it: Each package will carry a FREE 10-DAY EXAMINATION privilege. At the end of that time, if you decide to keep your books, simply pay the low invoice price of $17.96, no shipping or handling charges added. HOME DELIVERY IS ALWAYS FREE. With today's top romance novels selling for $5.99 and higher, our price SAVES YOU AT LEAST $5.00 with each shipment.

AND YOUR FIRST TWO-BOOK SHIP-MENT IS TOTALLY FREE!

IT'S A BARGAIN YOU CAN'T BEAT! A SUPER $11.48 Value!

Love Spell ✦ A Division of Dorchester Publishing Co., Inc.

GET YOUR 2 FREE BOOKS NOW—AN $11.48 VALUE!

Mail the Free Book Certificate Today!

TWO FREE BOOKS

Free Books Certificate

YES! I want to subscribe to the Love Spell Romance Book Club. Please send me my 2 FREE BOOKS. Then every other month I'll receive the four newest Love Spell selections to Preview FREE for 10 days. If I decide to keep them, I will pay the Special Member's Only discounted price of just $4.49 each, a total of $17.96. This is a SAVINGS of at least $5.00 off the bookstore price. There are no shipping, handling, or other charges. There is no minimum number of books I must buy and I may cancel the program at any time. In any case, the 2 FREE BOOKS are mine to keep—A BIG $11.48 Value!

Offer valid only in the U.S.A.

Name _____

Address _____

City _____

State _____ *Zip* _____

Telephone _____

Signature _____

If under 18, Parent or Guardian must sign. Terms, prices and conditions subject to change. Subscription subject to acceptance. Leisure Books reserves the right to reject any order or cancel any subscription.

A $11.48 VALUE

Get Two Books Totally
FREE —
An $11.48 Value!

▼ Tear Here and Mail Your FREE Book Card Today! ▼

PLEASE RUSH
MY TWO FREE
BOOKS TO ME
RIGHT AWAY!

Love Spell Romance Book Club
P.O. Box 6613
Edison, NJ 08818-6613

AFFIX
STAMP
HERE

it was. The smooth, pouch-like feel was enough. A pungent herbal odor emanated from the soft cloth, almost nauseating me. I hastily threw it on the floor, eager to get it away from me. What was Sukie's charm bag doing in my bed? I had no idea but would certainly find out in the morning.

I awoke to the feel of someone bouncing on my mattress. From the full daylight flooding my room, I guessed it to be at least mid-morning. Sarah was eagerly jostling me awake and, from the grin on her face, enjoying it immensely. I had no idea what time I had finally fallen asleep, but from the numbness of my head, I hadn't been asleep long. Still, I was embarrassed to have slept so late.

"Miss Laura, Miss Laura! It's time to get up! We're slaughtering Mr. Porker today!"

I glanced at her, dubious of her apparent joy at something I was a bit apprehensive about. I threw back the covers and slowly slid out of bed.

"And Uncle Stuart's home, too. Mama told me to come up here and let you know." I felt my face redden at the thought of Stuart and turned quickly to the washbasin.

Someone had already filled my pitcher, and I hastily splashed my face with the lukewarm water, hoping it would make me more alert. It did not.

"Stop bouncing, Sarah. It's hurting my head."

She stopped and gave me her most endearing smile. "All right, Miss Laura. But if you're not downstairs in two shakes, I'm coming back up to bounce on your bed and make your head hurt again."

I pretended to threaten her with my hairbrush as she raced from the room, her mock squeals descending with her down the stairs.

As soon as Sarah left, Sukie came in. Seeing her, I immediately thought of the pouch I had found in my bed. I hurried to the side of the bed where I had thrown it. The floor was empty.

"Where is it?"

"Where's what, Miz Laura?"

161

I scrutinized her face, but her bland expression hid all thoughts.

"Your charm bag, of course," I said, starting to feel annoyed.

She reached for the string around her neck and pulled out the familiar red pouch. "It's right here. I never take it off except when I sleep."

"Well, it was here last night—in my bed. I threw it on the floor, and now it's gone."

Her hands tightened on the bag. "No, ma'am. I didn't put it in your bed. I found it this morning where I left it last night."

"Then someone must have taken it and returned it. What do you think it means, Sukie?"

Her eyes were darting around the room, looking at everything but me. Feeling nervous, I approached her and grabbed her arm, making her look at me. "What does it mean, Sukie?"

Her warm brown eyes stared levelly at me. "It means you need to be careful."

"Careful? Careful of what?"

"Careful of someone who wants to do you harm."

I was losing patience with this line of conversation. "That's ridiculous! I have a feeling that one of the children must be playing a prank." I waved a hand in dismissal. "I don't want to talk about it anymore. What does one wear to a pig butchering?"

Later, dressed in the simple floral cotton that had become something of a uniform for me, I descended the stairs just in time to see Pamela leaving to go into town. She made these trips at least once a week. She always insisted on going alone and would return humming with an electric energy. I had no doubt that she was deeply involved in espionage. I had even seen her unrolling a piece of paper from her coiled hair once, presumably a secret message. I did wonder who she went to see and if Matt Kimball was involved. Regardless of where she got the information or who her cohorts were, it was clear that Stuart would again be needed to transmit to the Confederate Army whatever information she had gathered.

I found Stuart with two male slaves outside near the pigpen

and was slightly relieved that we weren't alone. Walking into the backyard, I saw one of the black men deliver a stunning blow to the pig's head with the business end of a mallet. A bench had been set up with buckets beneath it to catch the blood, and Stuart and the other man held the animal down on top of it. The pig lay still, allowing Stuart to reach around and neatly slice its throat.

The heavy smell of fresh blood permeated the area as the animal bled to death, the thick gush of fluid in the buckets slowing to a final *drip-drop*. Quickly tying the hind feet together, the two men hoisted the pig up over a kettle of steaming water. I knew this was in preparation for scraping the bristles off the hide before the animal would be disemboweled and halved. No part of the pig would be wasted. From using the bristles for brushes to the small intestines to be stuffed with sausage, every last morsel would be utilized in some way.

Knowing that my Christmas ham and the fresh roast pork for the following day's party was in the process of being made, I had no intention of spoiling my appetite. I wanted to go but remained rooted to the spot. Despite the chill of the day, Stuart removed his jacket, though he kept his shirt on. He sweated in his exertion, and dark tendrils of his hair stuck to his forehead. He swiped his face with his sleeve, leaving spikes of hair framing his face like a crown. I smiled at the effect.

His lean body tensed with the strain of hoisting the carcass, and I admired the firm planes and muscles of his back and arms through his sweat-soaked shirt.

He caught sight of me. "Good morning, Laura."

I swallowed quickly, my throat dry. "Morning."

He straightened, squaring his broad shoulders. "I went to town this morning to see Matt Kimball. His landlady says he's gone north—to Dalton. She doesn't expect him back."

I met his gaze without flinching. "I guess that must mean I gave him information so important he had to rush right off and share it." My voice cracked, but I continued. "And I bet you didn't stop to think that anything he might know about my daughter is gone with him."

Two dark eyebrows shot up. "I'm not giving up on finding

163

him. We are not done with Matt Kimball, you and I." He swiped his face with his forearm; then, with a short nod in my direction, he returned to the business at hand.

Turning from the activity, I made my way to the back of the house. The door crashed open as I reached the steps, and Sarah catapulted into me.

"Whoa, Sarah! Slow down. What's the rush?"

"Sorry, Miss Laura. Mama sent me to find you. She wants you to help her hang the mistletoe and some other decorations for the Christmas party tomorrow."

She made to move past me, but I firmly grabbed hold of her shoulders. "Just a minute, Sarah. I don't think you need to be out back right now."

Sarah looked up at me, her eyes pleading. "But, Miss Laura, Mama's let me watch before. It doesn't scare me one bit. And Uncle Stuart promised I could have the pig bladder."

"The pig's bladder? What on earth for?"

"Me and Willie like to fill it with water and throw it at each other."

"And your mother says it's okay?"

Her head bobbed up and down, her green eyes bright with excitement.

I wasn't her mother, and if Julia approved, I couldn't exactly stand in the way. "All right then. But don't make a nuisance of yourself, and stay out of the men's way."

She turned to go, but I stopped her again.

"By the way, did you or your brother take anything of Sukie's and put it in my bed?"

Her eyes stared at me with clear confusion, and I knew instinctively that she was innocent. "No, Miss Laura, me and Willie would never take anything that didn't belong to us."

I nodded. "Okay. You can go now." Wordlessly, she pounded down the steps.

Julia stood in the hall, a large pile of evergreen boughs and white berries overwhelming the circular table in the middle of the foyer. She offered me a smile as I approached.

"I was thinking you'd be the best person to tell me where to hang some of this mistletoe."

I tried to look guileless. "I suppose I'm as good a choice as any."

She waved a hand. "You can say what you want, Laura, but I happened to see two people out by the barn last night. And it didn't look as if they were watering the horses."

"Oh." I studied the intricate pattern of the wallpaper, not wanting to face her. "I . . . we . . . shouldn't have done that. There's really no future for us together. . . ."

Julia's eyes were warm as they regarded me. "I wanted you to know that I spoke with Stuart this morning. To be honest, I think he's more angry over the fact that Matt tried to touch you than over any information you might have passed on." She picked up a clump of magnolia leaves, their shiny coating glowing dully in the dim foyer light. "But he's giving you the benefit of the doubt until he speaks with Matt." She gave me a meaningful glance. "And he doesn't want you going anywhere on your own again."

I leaned down and gathered a few sprigs of mistletoe. Holding one up over the door, I said, "We can hang this here for when Dr. Watkins arrives and you answer the door."

"Laura! How could you say that about Charles? He's a dear old friend."

"Ha! And you call *me* blind."

She shook her head as she slid a chair to the middle of the hallway. "No, Laura, I'm not blind. I just prefer not to recognize it. That way, he and I can still be good friends."

"Maybe we can get the doctor and Eliza under the mistletoe together."

Julia laughed softly and shook her head. "What did we ever do without you?"

We spent the next hour in contented silence, with only the occasional comment as to the perfect placement of magnolia leaves on the mantels or holly arrangements on the tables. As an afterthought, I hung some of the mistletoe in the library, over the door. I hummed to myself as I did it, trying to remember the last time I had felt any joy at Christmas.

"The universe is wider than our views of it."
                    Henry David Thoreau

Chapter Fifteen

I stared at myself in the mirror, quite pleased at what I saw. Julia had unearthed a gown that had belonged to Stuart's mother, Catherine, and, with Sukie's help, had altered it for me as a surprise. I was touched at their efforts, not to mention the fact that the dress was breathtakingly beautiful. The two women had updated the style to make it fashionable again and made the necessary adjustments so that it would fit. The blood-red velvet accentuated the darkness of my hair, which Sukie had left down with lots of loose curls and tendrils, anchoring only the sides with mother-of-pearl combs. The off-the-shoulder neckline revealed more décolletage than I thought appropriate. I kept trying to hoist the dress up until finally Julia slapped my hand away. I acquiesced to wearing a corset, and Sukie cinched in my waist to a size I'm sure it hadn't been since I was eight. I felt as if I was playing dress-up. And I loved every minute of it.

As Sukie was putting the last touches to my hair, a slight tapping sounded on the door. At my request, the door opened, and Stuart hung back on the threshold, his expression unreadable.

"Have you come for a Christmas truce? Or are you going to just stand there and gawk?"

Sukie quickly grabbed a shawl and threw it over my shoulders while she whispered in my ear, "You don't want to spoil the surprise."

"I suppose you may call this a truce of sorts." Stuart entered the room and placed a small black box on the dressing table in front of me. "These were my mother's, and when Julia told me you would be wearing that dress, I knew you had to have these, too. I remember my mother wearing them together."

Curious, and touched, too, I reached for the box and opened it. Beaded onyx earrings sparkled in a nest of black velvet, the gems glistening and reflecting the candlelight. I picked them up and jiggled them to catch the full effect. I swallowed deeply and searched Stuart's eyes in the reflection of the mirror. "Stuart, these are wonderful. Thank you." I slipped the posts into my pierced ears and shook my head at the mirror, enjoying the slight clicking of the beads.

"Allow me." Sukie stepped back as Stuart leaned over and plucked the matching necklace out of the box and placed it on my neck. The cool beads chilled my throat, but his hands were warm where they rested on my skin while he fastened the necklace. I caught his reflection in the mirror, making me think of a parallel universe. Perhaps Stuart, and these other dear people who now filled my life, had always lived behind the glass, their warm flesh blocked by its coldness and only accessed by the most inexplicable of events.

"You look beautiful, Laura."

"Thank you." I felt a blush start at the base of my throat, and I turned my attention to his clothes, the same ones I had seen him in earlier. "Shouldn't you be getting dressed yourself?"

"Yes, ma'am. I'll see to it right away." Bowing formally, he walked out of the room, almost bumping into Julia on her way in.

"Laura, you look absolutely stunning."

"You're not so bad yourself," I said, admiring her powder-blue silk, its noticeably higher neckline covered with a lace fichu.

Julia caught sight of my earrings and touched one delicately with a fingertip. "These were Catherine's."

"Yes, I know. I hope you don't mind my wearing them."

"Of course not. They're not mine, anyway. They were given

to Stuart—not to William—by their mother before she died. His mother clearly intended that they go to Stuart's wife, not William's."

"Oh," I said, unsure of what that meant. I looked at Julia's expression in the mirror and caught a slight grin.

Sukie excused herself and then reappeared with a tray and two glasses of red wine. "Miz Catherine always said a glass of wine before a party soothed the nerves," she said, handing Julia and me a glass.

I took a sip and immediately felt the warmth traveling through my veins. "This will help my nervousness."

Julia sat on the edge of the bed. "Don't be silly, Laura—you'll be the belle of the ball. Don't allow any mean-spirited people to spoil your fun. You've been through a lot, and I say you deserve to have a little fun."

She drained her glass and reached for my empty one. "And it's time for our guests to arrive. Would you be so kind as to receive with me?"

I nodded and stood on shaky legs. I caught Julia eyeing me with a worried expression. "Maybe you shouldn't have any of my punch. You'll need your wits about you to fight off all the men tonight. Well, maybe not all of them," she added with an uncharacteristic smirk.

I smirked right back at her. "Oh, I think I hear the good doctor downstairs now. I'll make sure to shove you both under that bough of mistletoe in the dining room."

Julia looked genuinely shocked. "You wouldn't dare!"

Seeing my smile, she took my arm in hers and led me out the door.

The murmur of male voices conspicuously stopped as Julia and I appeared at the top of the stairs. Stuart and Dr. Watkins openly stared. I glanced behind me to see what they were looking at, only to have Julia elbow me in the ribs.

We descended slowly, my free hand gripping the banister to steady my wobbly legs. I made a mental note to avoid any further alcoholic beverages for at least another hour. At the bottom of the steps, Stuart took my hand and bent over it, kissing it gently. I felt a small electric shock and a flash of heat.

"Are you all right, Laura? Your face is flushed." His broad grin belied his concern.

"It's just the wine. And the realization that what they say is true."

He quirked a dark eyebrow. "What who says is true?"

"About men in uniform." I was brazenly appraising him now, my boldness engendered by the wine. I had never seen him in full dress uniform, and he was indeed a magnificent sight. His tall, lean form was well suited to the gray knee-length frock coat with black facings and trim. The gilt buttons gleamed in the light of the foyer but did not outshine the resplendence of the braided trim of his rank on the cuffs and collar. Around his slim waist he wore a narrow, red-silk sash under his waistbelt, and his broad shoulders accentuated the masculine line of the coat. My knees felt weak, and I wasn't sure if it was from the wine.

"Must be the jacket," he said, straightening both arms in front of me so I could admire the handiwork. "Julia made it."

I felt a quick pang in my gut, dimming the excitement of the evening for just a moment. Before I could respond, Sukie opened the front door, allowing in a cold blast of air and the first guests. I recognized Eliza Smith, along with her mother and sisters, from the many meetings of the Ladies Aid Society. These meetings consisted mostly of interminable bandage-rolling and listening to idle gossip about other townspeople. I had found no information there about Annie and had just resigned myself to two hours at a time of fending off questions from the well-meaning ladies.

All four women nodded to me. Eliza stared at my neckline, her lips pursed in a show of displeasure. Stuart fussed over her and took her wrap and gallantly kissed her hand. She blushed becomingly with the pleasure of it.

I recognized most of the other guests from the Presbyterian church and from my excursions into town. All were polite to me but slightly aloof, for which I did not blame them. Most of them had lived in Roswell their entire lives, as had their parents. I was an outsider.

Pamela appeared, her eyes raking over my outfit without comment before she turned on her social face and became the gracious hostess with Julia.

The mingled scents of perfume, smoked ham, and fresh pine danced through the rooms, delighting the senses. All the faces reflected a genuine gaiety, obliterating thoughts of war and suffering at least for one evening. Eliza and I took turns at the piano, and I was quite impressed at her repertoire, if not her habit of thumping on the keys. The furniture in the parlor and hall had been pushed against the wall, and several of the guests used the space for dancing.

Stuart claimed me for a waltz and, despite my protests of not knowing how to dance, swept me into his arms. I managed to stay off his toes and follow his lead, most likely due to the fact that he was an accomplished dancer. He waltzed me down the hall and into the library, where a single candle glowed, softly reflecting in the glass of the windows.

"I believe we just passed under some mistletoe," he said, his lips close to my ear.

I pulled away slightly. "I don't think we should . . . do anything about it. I mean, you don't want to be accused of consorting with the enemy or anything."

"Shh," he whispered in my ear. "Truce, remember?"

He bent his head nearer mine, then stopped. "May I kiss you?"

I answered by standing on tiptoe and touching my mouth to his. His lips were warm and full, his tongue pushing my own lips apart. Immediately, my arms went around his neck, and his arms around my back, his fingers splayed wide.

His hands caressed my back through the soft fabric of the dress. "I've been waiting all evening to do this." His lips traveled to the bare skin of my shoulder, causing gooseflesh to ripple up my skin.

"Me, too," I murmured as I tilted my head back farther. "But I was afraid you wouldn't. Now I'm afraid that you'll stop, like you did the last time. And I'm afraid—" I almost said *afraid that you'll mean too much to me,* but I stopped.

His fingers lingered on my neck as his eyes searched mine. "What is this between us, Laura?" He paused for a moment, the music, laughter, and disembodied voices flooding the space between us. "Since the moment I first saw you, it was . . . as if I've always known you. As if there wasn't a time in my existence when I didn't know you."

I remembered the sense of familiarity I had felt when I'd first looked into his eyes on Moon Mountain, and I knew that no matter how I tried to push him away, there was a connection between us. A connection that had nothing to do with linear time.

I thought I heard someone calling my name from outside the room and Eliza's voice saying I was in the library, but I quickly dismissed the distractions from my mind to concentrate on the feel of Stuart's lips on my neck and the thickness of his hair under my fingers.

"Miss Laura!" My head snapped up, and I quickly disengaged myself.

Sarah stood in the threshold, her eyes wide. "Mama needs you. There's something wrong with Robbie."

Adjusting my hair, I followed her out of the room and up the stairs to the master bedroom. Julia sat on the bed, Robbie cradled in her arms. His weak cries sounded like a wounded puppy's, not like his usual lusty wails. His face was flushed slightly, his eyes glazed.

As I approached the bed, she pulled the baby's gown up over his abdomen and lifted a pudgy leg. "Would you please take a look at this, Laura?"

I stared at the round mark on the back of Robbie's thigh. "Did something bite him?"

"I'm not sure. I thought you might know."

I examined the mark more closely, determining that it wasn't a bite because there seemed to be no holes marring the surface of the skin. "Me? Why would you think that?" I sat down next to her on the bed, my hand stroking Robbie's warm cheek. His fretting subsided slightly.

Julia looked at me. "You're so smart, Laura." She lifted a

hand to halt my objections. "No, you don't know much about sewing and gardening, but you always seem to figure out the right thing to do in an emergency."

"Have you called for Charles to come up?"

"Not yet. I called for you first."

"I really think we need a doctor here." Turning to Sarah, who had brought me upstairs, I said, "Go get Dr. Watkins, please. And ask him to bring his bag."

I placed the back of my hand across Robbie's forehead and felt the fever burning his skin.

There was a soft tapping on the door, and the doctor entered, followed by Sarah. With a brief nod to Julia and myself, he took the baby from Julia's arms and laid him on the bed. Robbie started whimpering again as the doctor lifted his gown and prodded his abdomen. Robbie emitted a hoarse howl as the doctor tried to pry open his mouth to examine his throat, and he continued to protest as Dr. Watkins ran his fingers over the glands in Robbie's neck.

Pamela appeared at the door. "Julia, what is wrong?" She glided into the room, her black silk gown swooshing across the floor and trailing the scent of a musky perfume.

Her gaze not leaving the baby, Julia answered her mother. "Robbie has a fever. I want Charles to have a look at him."

Pamela leaned over the doctor while he examined Robbie. "He is flushed. I'll go prepare some wintergreen tea to bring down the fever." She left as suddenly as she had appeared, her heels tapping across the hallway.

Turning the baby over, the doctor paused as he caught sight of the mark on the leg. Stretching the discolored skin between his thumb and forefinger, he bit his lower lip.

"What is it, Charles?" Julia asked, reaching for Robbie.

The doctor scratched his chin and looked at Julia and then me. "It appears to be diphtheria. Little Rosa Dunwody has also come down with it this week."

I knew eight-year-old Rosa and her mother from the Ladies Aid Society meetings. Rosa and Sarah were great friends. But I was even more familiar with the name *diphtheria*.

"Are you sure? Isn't that serious?"

"Yes, I am. But, with good care, we can make him well."
He pulled Robbie's gown back into place. He continued, "The
best way to treat it is give him plenty of rest, keep him comfortable, and try to get his fever down. I suggest a camphor
rub on his chest to help him breathe and for those tending him
to wear a lump of camphor around their necks to ward off the
vapors of the disease." He started to close his bag. "And, most
important, keep him isolated."

He made a nod in my direction and added, "Make sure
everyone who comes in contact with him washes her hands
thoroughly. And that includes all of you here before you return
to the party." Shocked at the doctor's concession to my ob-
session with clean hands when tending the sick, I let his dark-
ages comment about vapor-killing camphor pass unremarked.
But I certainly had no intention of wearing the foul-smelling
stuff.

Julia handed the baby to me. "I'm going to go help my
mother. I'll also find Sukie and have her keep an eye on Robbie because I want you to return to the party and play hostess
for me, Laura."

"Are you sure?" I asked, cradling the baby and feeling his
sweat-soaked gown.

"Laura, this isn't the first child I've ever nursed through a
fever. I just need to give him some of the tea Pamela is preparing to lower his fever and get him settled. I'll be fine."

I thought I caught a glint of something in her eye, but she
gave me a warm, comforting smile. "Really, Laura, Robbie
will be fine. All children get sick. Between Charles, my
mother, and me, we'll have him crawling like a June bug in
no time."

My tongue seemed to thicken in my mouth. In my time
most children were vaccinated against diphtheria. I knew I had
been inoculated, as had Annie. But here, in this time, there
was no such protection. Children were subject to the whims
of virulent diseases that randomly plucked them from their
parents' arms and laid them in small graves.

Turning, Julia opened the door, and a mix of garbled voices
and laughter could be heard from below, climbing the stairs

and pulling me toward it. The doctor followed her out, and the sound of their footsteps descended the stairs. Shortly afterward, Sukie came to take Robbie.

I handed him over just as Sarah, who had remained silent in a corner of the room, approached. "Will he be all right, Miss Laura?"

I laid my hand on her blond head. "Your mama certainly seems to think so. We'll just have to do everything we know how to get him better, and that will include playing quietly when you're inside so you don't wake him up. The doctor says he needs his rest."

She looked down into the little bundle cradled in Sukie's arms and then kissed him.

I pulled the baby away. "No, Sarah! Don't! You could get his germs and get sick, too."

Her eyes widened with fear.

"I'm sorry, Sarah. I didn't mean to shout at you. But I want to keep you healthy." I gave her a hug and propelled her out of the room. "I think it would be best if you stayed away from other people until we know you're not infected. Go ahead and get ready for bed, and I'll come up to say good night." She gave me a somber look and then walked slowly down the hall to her room, her feet dragging in an exaggerated way with each step.

I wasn't yet ready to rejoin the party, so I slipped out the back door and walked toward the fallow cotton fields, the earth cold and brittle in the December winds. Bright stars and a quarter moon brought relief to the inkiness of the night, and I lifted my face to the frigid wind.

"Laura?"

I turned to see Zeke, who had been standing in the shadow of the oak tree.

"Good evening, Zeke. Why aren't you with the party?"

"Too many people for me. I've made an appearance for Julia's sake, and now I think I'll go back home. I need to make a root poultice for Robbie's neck."

But still he stood, not making as if to leave.

He pointed toward the sky. "Can you see the Little Bear?"

I tilted my head back and stared up at the icy black sky. "Do you mean the Little Dipper?" I asked, recognizing one of the constellations I was familiar with.

"Yes. If you let your eyes follow along the handle, you can see the polestar."

"It's the very bright one, isn't it?"

He nodded slightly, still looking upward. "The polestar has been used throughout the centuries by navigators for charting their routes." He was now looking directly at me, as if to convey a meaning to his casual conversation.

"Zeke, are you trying to tell me something?"

"Nothing that you don't already know. Just reminding you to use the skies and your heart to guide you home." Very quietly, he said good night and began to walk toward the woods.

"Good night, Zeke," I called after him. I saw him raise an arm and wave before he was enveloped in darkness. My nose hairs froze as I breathed in the winter air.

My hands felt numb from the cold, so I turned to go back in. I heard the faint notes of the piano tinkling "Dixie." Despite the liveliness of the tune, I felt a deep and abiding sadness. The lives of these people would soon be irrevocably altered. History had already decreed that their way of life would be gone forever, as would many of their sons, brothers, and husbands. But what if I could change that, save one life? I shook my head, focusing on my house and Annie. I had to get back soon before it was too late and I foolishly interfered with fate.

The wind carried scattered voices to my ears, and I listened as if I were hearing them across the passage of time. The back door was opened, and I recognized Stuart's form silhouetted against the light spilling from inside. I could feel his eyes on me, like a beacon on a dark sea, guiding me home. He waited for me as I picked up my skirts and walked toward him.

"And thus the whirligig of time brings in his revenges."
William Shakespeare

Chapter Sixteen

I awoke to the smell of smoke. Jumping out of bed, I ran to the door and was relieved to find it cool to the touch. I cracked it open and stuck my head out to investigate but found no flames, only the pervasive smell of smoke.

I hastily returned to the bed to wake Sarah, who had been moved into my room when Willie, too, had come down with swollen glands and fever. Despite her children's illness, Julia continued to stay infuriatingly calm, though her face now held a pinched, strained look. But it worked, because I did not feel panicked. Robbie didn't seem to be getting any better, but he didn't seem to be getting any worse, either. Dr. Watkins had told us that the disease would climax in about ten days, and then we should see a change.

Every night now, for Sarah's sake, I closed my curtains against the moon, so I stumbled in the dark to the window and threw open the curtains to peer out. I didn't see anything but smelled the heavy scent of smoke in the air.

"Sarah. Get up." She groggily rolled back over into her pillow, and I had to pick her up and get her off the bed so I could remove the blanket. Just in case.

I ushered her out into the hallway. "Fire!" I shouted, deciding to err on the side of caution even if I detected no flames. Julia emerged from the sickroom, the bundled form of Robbie in her arms.

"Can Willie walk?" I asked. She shook her head, so I strode

176

past her and picked up Willie. He had a slight frame, and I estimated he could weigh no more than fifty-five pounds. Light enough to carry, if not for very far.

"Sukie! Stuart!" Shuffling feet sounded from downstairs, and the flickering light of a candle illuminated Sukie as she poked her head up the stairwell. Stuart's door opened from the other end of the hall, and he emerged, hastily buttoning up his shirt. Pamela ran out of her room, her hair unbound and flying wildly about her thin face.

Wisps of smoke now floated haphazardly in the air, infusing everybody with alarm. We all clambered down the stairs, Julia with Robbie in the lead, the baby protesting with thick, croupy coughs.

Sukie ran ahead and opened the front door, allowing the rest of us to take refuge on the front lawn. Leaving Sukie with Julia and the children, I followed Stuart around the side of the house in search of the smoke source.

"Damn!" I heard him swear, and then I echoed him as I saw the kitchen and the adjoining storehouse engulfed in flames. Smoke from the burning wood coated my throat while the heat licked at my face, making me step back. The surprising aroma of bacon cooking filled the air.

Three dark forms ran toward us from the direction of the slave cabins on the other side of the field. Turning abruptly, Stuart said, "Run to the barn and bring every bucket you can find. It's probably too late to save the kitchen, but we might be able to salvage the storehouse."

I ran as fast as I could, ignoring the chill as I stepped away from the heat of the flames, the hem of my nightgown heavy from the moisture on the grass.

The five buckets I found were readily pressed into service as we formed a relay system for bringing water from the creek near the springhouse. Stuart told me to go join Sukie and Julia, but I ignored him, knowing that every arm helping could make the difference between starvation and having enough food to get us by until the spring.

Sparks flew in every direction, and I caught Stuart's worried gaze whenever a stray one shot near the house. My muscles ached from hoisting the heavy buckets filled with water, but we all struggled on, black and white, fighting the common enemy.

A loud splintering sound split the air as the roof of the kitchen crashed down, blowing puffs of flame toward us. We all ran back until I heard Stuart's voice shouting, "The meat box!" He rushed forward, disappearing in a wall of smoke and flame. My heart stuck in my throat as I stared at the spot where he had gone.

Within minutes, he reappeared, dragging the meat box. One of the other men rushed to help him, pulling the precious store of food with them.

Stuart shouted at me over the din to get the other women and children to the relative warmth of the barn, which was far enough away from the flames to pose no danger. Running back to the kitchen, I heard a rumbling sound overhead. All faces turned to the skies in an open appeal and were quickly rewarded with the splattering of icy-cold raindrops.

Stuart's face, awash with light from the flickering flames, wore a huge grin as the clouds released their onslaught, washing the black smudges from his forehead and jaw. A cry of delight went up as the flames diminished, the hissing and popping slowly dying to a low whisper of steam.

I threw my arms around Stuart, our drenched clothes sticking together. I realized how thin my sodden nightgown was as I pressed against him, and I noticed that he did, too, but he did not step back. A bolt of lightning illuminated the sky briefly and was soon followed by more rumbling thunder as sheets of rain fell on us, saturating hair, clothes, buildings, and earth.

Pulling me gently to his side, Stuart turned to the others. "You men go on home. There's nothing else we can do tonight while it's still smoking. We'll see what we can salvage in the morning." Slowly, the other men walked away, back to the dryness and warmth of their cabins. Stuart grabbed my arm and led me to the shelter of the back porch.

Growing worry gnawed at me. "Do you think there will be anything left to salvage?"

His profile was a mere shadow in the dark, but his warm breath licked at my cheek.

He shook his head. "Not much. We had just about everything in that storehouse—salt, syrup, tallowlard, potatoes, turnips—everything. I'm sure it's all gone. Luckily, most of that hog we butchered is still in the smokehouse." He lifted a hand in the darkness and wiped his dripping hair off his forehead. "But I doubt it's enough."

"Enough?" I hated that word. Although there hadn't been any Confederate requisitioning parties to deplete our already low food stores, there never seemed to be enough cornmeal, eggs, flour, meat, or medicine for the sick children. Somebody was always hungry. But when the Yankees came, in less than a year's time, there would be even less.

"Stuart." My voice cracked. "You . . . you need to send them away. Very soon."

His callused fingers rubbed my skin as he cupped my face, his fingertips delicately brushing my temples. "Why? Why are you telling me this?"

A sob escaped my throat. "Because it's true—Roswell isn't safe for them. The Yankees will be here, Stuart—don't ask me how I know, but I do. You need to trust me just this once."

His fingers tightened on my skin, pushing on my skull. "What are you trying to tell me?"

I couldn't see him, but the tense urgency in his words gripped me like claws. I paused, knowing already the choice I had to make. My tears mixed with the rain on my face, and the pressure of his fingers increased. "The Yankees will be here, Stuart—in less than a year. Atlanta will be theirs by September. And then they'll push through Georgia to the sea, destroying everything in their path. They'll be in Savannah by next Christmas. Take Julia and the children south—to Julia's aunt in Valdosta. They'll be safe there until the end of the war."

My hands covered his and forced them away from me. He stood facing me, his eyes glittering in the dim night. "How do you know all this?" He pulled away from me. "Why are you telling me this?"

179

"Don't you know why? I love them, too. Julia, the children, Zeke. Even . . ." I was going to say, *even you, you thick-headed, stubborn man,* but I stopped, not wanting to complicate matters further. Instead, I said, "I want you all out of harm's way. I couldn't live with myself knowing that I did nothing to protect you."

His voice carried softly to me on the night air. "Tell me, then. Who are you, Laura, really? Where do you come from? How do you know these things?"

I shook my head and turned from him. "I've told you enough. I . . . I can't tell you any more. Just let me help you."

The silence between us grew heavy, the hissing of the dying fire filling the emptiness.

I shivered in my damp nightgown, my teeth chattering. Quietly, he said, "Go to bed, Laura. We don't need you catching your death out here."

Without waiting for a reply, he turned and walked off in the direction of the barn.

I was asleep before my head hit the pillow. But I didn't stay asleep long before I heard a little voice beside me. "Miss Laura? Are you awake?"

"Hmmphm."

"Are Robbie and Willie going to die?"

I sat up, wide awake now. For a child so young, Sarah was incredibly perceptive, and I knew better than to try to gloss over the truth. I gave her arm a reassuring pat.

"I don't think so, but I really don't know for sure. They're both very sick right now, but we're doing everything we know to make them get better."

"Oh." She paused for a moment, and I didn't feel her lie back down on the mattress. "I'm not scared of dying, Miss Laura. I already know what it's like."

I remained completely still, willing her to continue. "I know I once had another mama and papa who loved me, but I died, and now I'm here."

I stared at her in the darkness, stunned, but then I recalled Stuart telling me about Sarah's vivid imagination. I patted her shoulder again. "I'm happy you're here with us now."

She lay back down on the pillow, and I tucked the blankets under her chin and kissed her forehead. "Sweet dreams." She turned her head into the pillow, and as I drifted off to sleep, I heard the reassuring rhythm of her breathing beside me.

The following day was Christmas Eve. Despite the war shortages, Julia had done her best to find presents for the children. She had even helped me make a few things, including a pair of socks for Stuart. With paper being such a rare commodity, the socks were tied only with a hair ribbon and hidden under my bed. I recalled the extravagant gifts that Jack and I had exchanged and knew that these socks were more a labor of love than anything I had ever given.

Sarah was already gone when I awoke, and I hastily washed and dressed. The door to the sickroom was open, and I approached it and stuck my head in. Sukie sat in the rocking chair holding Robbie. Willie was sitting up in his bed, his neck swollen, but with a big smile for me. A dry, raspy wheeze came from Robbie as his chest sucked in to get air.

Sukie looked at me, her eyes shadowed. "Miz Julia's gone to get Dr. Watkins. Robbie seems to have taken a turn for the worse over the night."

I laid a hand on his burning cheek. "But Dr. Watkins said that the disease will get worse before it gets better."

She nodded. "Yes, but Miz Julia wanted the doctor here anyway."

"Sukie, why don't you let me hold him for a while." I reached for the swaddled form. A dark-colored liquid oozed from both his ears and his nose, producing an almost overwhelming stench. Sukie handed me a wadded rag, and I wiped his little face. She dipped another rag in the washbasin and laid it on his forehead. Walking over to Willie's bed, she tucked the covers snugly around him and then left the room.

A thin, grayish-white membrane had grown, web-like, over Robbie's tonsils and was getting thicker every day. It interfered with his breathing and swallowing, making it almost impossible for him to suck milk. It was with painstaking care that we were able to feed him a drop of liquid at a time from

181

a spoon, and even that he mostly spat back. Willie had the same thing but, perhaps because of his age, had been able to cope with it better and was managing liquids quite well. Trying to dislodge the membrane only caused it to bleed, and we realized that there was nothing we could do about it until the sickness passed and it expelled itself.

The sharp stench of camphor wafted up to my nose from the hot bundle in my arm. It was supposed to help him breathe, but I don't think it had much effect. I tried to hold him upright, in an attempt to help get air into his lungs, but nothing seemed to make any difference. Every breath was a struggle, and he strained and kicked in his efforts. I held him close and sang to him. It was the only thing I could do, and it seemed to soothe him.

Sarah hovered in the threshold, not daring to enter. It had been a week since Willie and Robbie had become sick, and Sarah still did not show any symptoms of the disease. But that didn't mean she was immune, so she was kept out of the sickroom and away from her brothers. She slid down the doorframe and sat in a heap on the ground, her elbows on her knees and her chin in her hands. She smiled wanly at me, her green eyes uncharacteristically subdued.

I leaned back in the rocker, patting Robbie softly on his back, and began singing my favorite nursery song, one that I had sung to my Annie when she was a baby, and one I had not sung since the night Robbie was born.

"You are my sweet pea, my only sweet pea. You bring me sunshine every day. From your button nose to your baby toes . . ."

A little voice sounded from across the room, clear and compelling, "I will love you for all time."

I stopped rocking, unable to move. Robbie fussed, and I stood on shaky legs. "Sarah, how do you know that song?"

Her clear green eyes, so much like mine, stared back at me. "The mama I had when I lived before used to sing it to me."

My arms shook so much, I was afraid I would drop the baby. I tried to concentrate on holding him steady, but my mind turned furiously, putting all the puzzle pieces into place.

182

"Do you remember what your other mama used to call you?"

"Uh-huh. She called me Annie."

Robbie had fallen into a restless sleep, and I carefully carried him to his cradle and lifted him inside. With shaking legs, I walked over to Annie and crouched in front of her. My hands cupped her cheekbones, solid and real underneath my fingertips. "Annie?" I whispered.

Green eyes, fringed with black lashes, looked at me. "Why are you crying, Miss Laura?"

"Unbutton your dress." I helped her with the small buttons, then peeled the dress off her shoulder to bare her upper arm. I knew what I would see before I gently twisted her arm, but it still shocked me. Her crescent-shaped birthmark was paler than mine but in the same peculiar shape. I thought of the times I had seen Sarah swimming and never noticed it. Most likely because I had never looked for it.

I hugged her tightly, so tightly that she cried out. "I'm sorry, I'm so sorry. I'm just so . . . happy to see you." I hugged her again, more gently this time, feeling her sturdy body in my arms.

The sound of horse hooves and buggy wheels on the front drive reached us. "Julia," I said out loud. The name made me flinch, her betrayal almost more than I could stand.

I looked anew at Julia's face for any signs of duplicity as she and Dr. Watkins entered the room, but all I saw was her concern as she reached for Robbie. She laid him on Sarah's empty bed, and the doctor began his examination. He loosened the bandage that had been covering the skin ulcer on the baby's leg, wrinkling his nose at the foul odor. Eventually, he straightened and closed his black bag.

"Charles, what are you doing? Is there nothing else you can do?" Julia's voice held a frantic note, her fingers clutching at his sleeve.

His whole face dropped as he regarded her. Taking her hands in his, he slowly shook his head. "I'm sorry, Julia. All we can do is wait and pray for a miracle."

Julia bent her head and let go of the doctor. He made a

move as if to embrace her but then stepped back. He picked up his bag. "Rosa Dunwody's parents asked me to come by. I'm afraid she's not doing well, either. I'll be sure to come back here when I'm done."

With a brief nod to me, he left, his boots clattering on the wooden steps, Sarah scrambling down the stairs behind him. Rosa was Sarah's best friend. Children in this time learned about death much too early. I listened as Sarah questioned the doctor, wishing I could call her back but knowing I couldn't protect her from grief.

Julia sat down in the rocking chair and began the incessant rocking that all mothers of sick babies are familiar with. I sometimes even felt myself rocking in my sleep. Her expression softened as she looked at Robbie's pale face. I had seen that look before when she looked at Willie and Sarah. She loved all three of her children. There could never be any doubt about that.

I slowly rolled up my sleeve, then hesitated, unsure if she could handle my revelation. But then I thought of all the times we had spoken of my daughter, and her betrayal stung anew.

I knelt by her rocker, the smell of camphor heavy from the bundle in her arms, and spoke her name. She looked at me, her eyes like dark smudges on the white canvas of her skin, but I showed no mercy. Instead, I held up my arm, the crescent-shaped birthmark like an island on the smooth skin of my forearm.

"My Annie has the same mark. But you know that, don't you? You've seen it before."

She continued rocking but bent her head to Robbie's. His labored breathing slid against my conscience, but I pressed on. My pain was like a piece of fabric caught on a nail, and I kept tugging until something ripped loose.

"Did you think I should go through my life thinking my daughter dead? Did you?"

Tear-stained hazel eyes looked at me. "Did you ever consider that after five long years, maybe Annie had a new family, a happy life? Would you take her away from the only life she remembers?"

My blood stilled in my veins. "She's . . . she's mine . . . my daughter."

Wailing came from downstairs as the back door slammed and little feet ran up the stairs. My daughter rushed into the room, holding her elbow, tears streaming down her cheeks.

"Mama! I fell and hurt myself real bad. It think it might be broken."

I opened my arms to her, but she rushed to Julia's side, burying her face in an available patch of lap. My stomach curled, as if I had been punched. I was just a woman she called Miss Laura. I had been relegated in her memory to a shadowy image singing her lullabies. Julia was the only mother she knew.

I stood, watching Julia comfort both children while also urging Sarah to leave the room because it wasn't safe.

"She can't get diphtheria, Julia. Let her stay." Without waiting for an answer, I left.

Julia stayed in Robbie's room for the rest of the day, and I was glad, not sure what I would say to her. I walked around in a daze, avoiding Stuart, too. I was unsure of his complicity in hiding Sarah's true identity and wasn't yet ready to face him. Not that I needed to avoid him; he was doing a good job of staying away on his own, most likely due to our conversation the previous night.

I skipped the midday meal, having no appetite, and instead ensconced myself in the parlor with a book. I have no idea what the book was, as my eyes kept blurring over the words. Sarah came in at one point, and all I could do was stare at her. She played something on the piano for me, then, after a brief peck on my cheek, she skipped off to visit the sickroom.

I sat down at the piano, my fingers poised over the keys but unable to play. I brought my fists down on the keyboard, creating a cacophony as loud as my grief. Robbie was dying, and my daughter was as gone from me now as if she, too, lay in a grave.

"Julia has asked me to solicit your help in filling the children's Christmas stockings."

Jerking around on the piano bench, I saw Stuart, a grim

smile on his lips. I had forgotten it was Christmas Eve. I re-membered Julia telling Sarah and Willie that although Santa would try his best to run the blockade, he might not be able to bring them very much this year. I pushed my somber thoughts aside to deal with later and stood to join Stuart.

He hammered three tacks into the mantel, and then we got down to the business of playing Santa.

Zeke had carved a wooden doll with jointed limbs for Sarah. Julia and I had made two little dresses for it, and I was quite proud of my handiwork. Stuart had made a stick horse for Willie with a rare piece of tanned leather for a bridle. Robbie's stocking held a stick of plaited molasses, and I tried to think of him enjoying it once he got better. I stepped back and smiled at our efforts, knowing how delighted the children would be. But my smile could not warm my heart. I was wres-tling with my demons and wondering if just knowing that my Annie was alive and happy would be enough for me to go on with my life.

We both turned as we heard a noise from the doorway. Julia stood in the threshold, holding Robbie and looking at me with hollow eyes.

"Is he better?" My breath stuck in my throat, my mouth suddenly dry.

Slowly, she shook her head. "No." Her gaze circled the room, then focused on me again.

The string of popcorn I had been holding fell to the ground, scattering the white puffs on the floor, where they rolled away soundlessly. I walked over to Julia and looked down at Rob-bie. I imagined I heard the beating of wings and a soft brush of feathers on my cheek, and I knew he was gone.

I stroked his still-warm cheek and bent to kiss his forehead. "He looks as if he's sleeping," I whispered, my voice sounding loud in the hushed room.

"He is, Laura." Julia's voice was deceptively strong, until it broke on the last word. "Would you like to say good-bye?"

I nodded, touched that she would release him to me. She kissed the smooth forehead and then handed the bundle to me. I took it, holding it gingerly at first, and then clutching it tightly to my chest. I turned and walked out of the house to the front porch.

I sat in the rocker and rocked, staring up at the unforgiving moon. The inert form in my arms felt lighter than the child I had known, as if his little life force had held all his weight, and with it gone, only bones and flesh remained. The blanket covering Robbie's hair slid off, and I hastily pulled it up before realizing the futility of protecting him from the cold.

The door opened and shut behind me. Then Stuart stood beside me and touched my arm. I flinched and moved away.

"Don't. Please don't."

He stayed close but didn't make another move to touch me. "Julia told me about Sarah. I promise you, Laura, I didn't know." He laid a hand on the baby's head, caressing the delicate skin. "It seems we are both capable of believing the worst about each other."

I rose and walked toward the railing, my footsteps hollow on the wooden floorboards. "I was thinking that maybe it would have been better if I had let Robbie die when he was born. Then you and Julia and the rest would have been saddened, but not as much as now, after we've known him for so long."

Naked branches swayed in the December wind, and I summoned their shadows for a place to hide my heavy heart.

"But then I wondered if it would have been better never to have known Annie than to suffer her loss—and I realized that I would never give up one precious minute of knowing her. No matter what happens, we will always have our memories of Robbie and Annie, and no one can ever take those away from us."

He came to stand behind me, and I felt his lips on my hair.

"Promise me one thing, Stuart. Promise me that if I . . . go away, and . . . Sarah is still here, you will make sure she is taken to Valdosta. Then I'll know she'll be safe."

His hands gripped my shoulders. "I'll keep her safe, Laura. I promise you."

Turning, I buried my face in his chest, cradling the baby between us and feeling the rough wool of his coat against my

187

cheek. His hand stroked my hair, soothing me as if I were a child. Eventually, my tears subsided. He took the baby from me, and I laid a hand on his cheek. "Thank you, Stuart." I again looked at Robbie's serene white face, luminous in the light from the window, his pale lashes closed in restful sleep. I shivered, remembering Jack's face in his coffin, the moment before the lid was closed.

"Did the real Sarah—the one whose birth Julia described— die?" I suddenly guessed.

Stuart nodded. "Yes. Evidently she was born too soon and never seemed to gain any strength. Julia took her to Valdosta and a healing spring there, but even after over a year of treatment, she died. Shortly afterward, before word of Sarah's death was out, Pamela discovered an infant on Moon Mountain—and she bore a striking resemblance to Julia's daughter. Pamela brought the child to Valdosta, and Julia took her in. She knew if she told the townspeople she had found an abandoned child, people might not be kind to the little one—perhaps speculate that she was illegitimate or unwanted." He sighed softly in the cold air, his breath gently rising in the night. "So she buried Sarah quietly and raised your Annie as her own."

He held me for a while, his body warming mine. Releasing me, he said, "It's time to go inside." Pulling out a handkerchief, he wiped my face, then led me back into the house.

I lay awake for most of the night, listening to Willie cough and straining to hear a baby's crying. But the house remained still and hushed, while the insistent ticking of the hall clock continued to mark the time minute by minute, hour by hour.

"Thy fate is the common fate of all;
Into each life some rain must fall."
Henry Wadsworth Longfellow

Chapter Seventeen

The black-clad figures huddled under umbrellas, the hems of skirts and cloaks liberally splashed with red-clay mud. With the war now in its third year, there was no lack of mourning clothes in Roswell.

Despite the heavy downpour, most of the townspeople gathered around the small pine coffin at Founders' Cemetery. Willie, not yet fully recovered, was the only member of our household not present. I stood back from the immediate family, uncertain of my place. Even the dog, Charlie, was there, unusually subdued and sticking close by Sarah. Zeke stood apart from the crowd and as far away from Pamela as he could get. Pamela stayed with Julia, her back rigid, her eyes dry.

Julia turned around, her gaze searching the sea of faces until it alighted on me. Walking past the other mourners, she firmly grabbed my hand and pulled me over to stand next to her, never releasing my hand. The wind blew hard droplets of rain against our faces, and we snuggled deeply into our hooded cloaks, but Julia kept her face level, her expression set like ice, listening to Reverend Pratt's short eulogy. I would have thought she was calm except for her tight grasp on my hand and the slight trembling of her arm.

Stuart and Charles lowered the tiny casket into the dark, muddy hole, the rain thudding against the lid. Sarah wept openly as they began to shovel drenched clay over the box. I

189

reached to comfort her, but she buried her face in her mother's skirts, her tears mixing with the rain. My heart clenched, and I had to look away, the sight of mother and child too painful for me to watch.

As everyone began to file out of the cemetery, I remained behind in the shelter of an oak tree, needing to be alone to gather my thoughts. The pungent aroma of wet leaves and moist earth seeped from the ground. I sat on a cold stone bench under the tree, heedless of the wind whipping my cloak away from my body, welcoming the frigid splash of rain on my face.

If I had been sent to this place and time to find Annie, I had accomplished my goal. But could I, should I, bring her back home? She had a new family now, and new memories. The brief time she had spent with me was all but forgotten. I might do her more harm than good by bringing her with me and forcing her to leave all that she knew and held dear.

The rain stopped, and only the occasional drip from the oak leaves overhead interrupted my thoughts. I heard a footfall behind me and turned to see Stuart taking off his cloak and throwing it over my shoulders. He sat down next to me, making sure our bodies did not touch.

"We were wondering where you were."

"I needed time alone to think."

"About what you're going to do with Sarah?"

I nodded, watching a squirrel skim down a tree and tear through the dead leaves on the ground. "I . . . I don't know what the right thing is. I want desperately to take her back with me, but I don't know if that would be the right thing for her."

He regarded me calmly, his dark blue eyes still and unreadable. "Why leave, Laura? Why not stay here?"

I recalled the pictures and stories of the devastation and starvation of Reconstruction and knew that at the very least I had to save my daughter from that. I would take them all if I could, but I knew that wasn't possible. Besides, by virtue of the time they were born, they were made of stronger stuff than I. They would survive in a world in which I most likely would not.

"Because we would be better off if we left. We don't belong here. This isn't our home."

He stiffened next to me. "The way you pillage and burn, Laura—you must be a Yankee. You've come into our lives, our home—our hearts. And yet you'd leave us without a thought."

His words were so far from the truth that I couldn't think of an answer. Instead, I took his hand and brought the palm up to my lips and kissed it. "I will leave with more regret than you could ever know."

He brought my hands to his own lips and kissed the tops, his fingers resting on the gold wedding band I still wore.

"Memories aren't flesh and blood, Laura."

I bent toward him, seeking out his warmth in the blustery day. "No. But they're safe. They can't hurt me."

Stuart bent and plucked a sodden oak leaf from the ground and began examining the delicate veins. Then he tore the leaf into small pieces and let the wind pick them off his hand, scattering them across the cemetery. "All love does not lead to loss." He picked up another leaf and held it in his open palm.

"It certainly has in my experience. I think I'll cut my losses and retire." I tried to smile but failed miserably.

He leaned over and lightly kissed my forehead, his breath warming my cheeks. "What hasn't killed you has certainly made you stronger. It's made you a lot more resilient than you would like to believe. Sooner or later you will realize that what you had with your husband and Annie is gone, and it's time to move on with your life."

I shook my head gently. "Even if I do, I still can't stay. I am not meant to be here."

His face was close enough that I could see the fine lines at the corners of his eyes. "How do you know this? What is it that pulls you from us?"

I shook my head again. "I just don't belong here."

His fingers tightened on his thighs, then relaxed. We sat in silence for a while until I reached out and touched his arm.

"Do you swear to me that you knew nothing about Annie?

Surely you or her father noticed it wasn't the same child."

He raked his fingers through his hair, the raindrops plastering it to his head. "I was away at the university, and William . . ." He shook his head. "William never looked more than twice at his daughter. Even without the uncanny resemblance, he never would have noticed."

He let go of the leaf, and we watched it drift to the ground, buffeted by the strong breeze. "But I promise you, I never knew the truth until yesterday. And I had no reason to doubt Julia. Please don't think ill of her. She's always loved your Annie as her own."

We continued to sit and listen to the rain drip off the trees and onto the ground covering of leaves. Finally, Stuart spoke. "I have to go away again for a few days. But when I return, I'm moving everyone down to Valdosta."

I reached for his hand and squeezed. "Why are you trusting me on this?"

He cupped my jaw with one hand, his fingers tight. Troubled blue eyes searched my face, brows knitted, as if he was deciding between answers. Finally, he said, "Because of Sarah. You would keep her family safe."

I moved his hand from my face, then let go. "Is that the only reason?"

He turned his gaze from me. "It's enough of a reason."

He stood, grabbing my hand and pulling me up. His cloak fluttered about me like a big black crow flapping its wings. His voice was quiet, the wind pulling the words toward me. "Stay with us, Laura. Make this your home."

I looked down at our feet, his worn boots half hidden by leaves. "I can't. You don't understand . . ."

His voice changed, became pressing, insistent. "Then make me understand. Tell me what you're afraid to tell me."

I forced myself to look at him again, seeing his gray uniform and remembering what it stood for. If he knew who I was, he'd march me directly to General Lee. I knew enough about Stuart's loyalty to know that he wouldn't consider altering history an obstacle. And the longer I stayed in this time, the more I saw myself caring for the Elliotts—especially Stuart. And he was a soldier who would be returning to battle. I could not risk my heart on him. I sighed and slowly shook my head.

He moved away from me abruptly, taking the warmth of his body with him. "Damn you, Laura. Damn you." Turning on his heel, he walked away.

The wind began to blow again, bringing additional rain with it, and I shivered, feeling more cold and desolate than I ever had in my life. I turned my face to the rain and began to walk home, imagining Stuart's cloak was his arms wrapped around me.

With little food in the house, and Willie still sick, the mourners had not lingered. The last buggy was pulling away as I walked up the drive. A form rocked on the front porch, a dark smear against the white paint of the house. As I approached, I recognized Julia. She raised her head and smiled weakly. I sat in another chair and rocked in silence, the floorboards creaking in rhythm.

She surprised me by reaching for my hand. "Thank you for my Robbie, Laura. You saved him when he was born, remember? You gave us six wonderful months with him."

I studied her face, so calm and serene, and felt only deep shame at all the times I had cursed my fate, hated having had a child so I could know what I missed.

I couldn't speak and looked at our hands, clenched together, her capable fingers rubbed red and raw from the constant disinfecting of the sickroom.

"Will you be taking Sarah from us?"

Dropping her hand, I stood and walked toward the railing. "I have to, Julia—she's my daughter. She's all I've got left." I turned back to face her. "Assuming I can find my way home, I won't be leaving until September. You'll have a long time to say good-bye." September 1, 1864, was the next date for a comet and lunar eclipse listed in one of Zeke's astronomical volumes.

"I see." She kept her head down, staring at her hands.

I knelt in front of her. "Julia, I didn't mean for things to happen this way, and I can't thank you enough for all that you have done for my Annie. I will make sure a day doesn't go by without mentioning your name. You will always be her other mother—I won't change that."

She lifted her eyes to mine, hers blurry from the pool of tears. "What about her brother, Willie? And her uncle, Stuart? And her grandfather, Zeke? Who will replace them in her life?"

My hand clutched the arm of her rocker. "I've searched for five years to find my daughter. I must bring her home."

She sniffed once and nodded. "I understand, Laura. But I can't pretend that it's not breaking my heart." She stood to leave.

"I'm sorry." I cursed myself for how inadequate the words were.

As she passed me, she put a hand on my shoulder. "I think we should wait a while to tell her. Robbie has just died, and I think it would be too much."

I nodded and watched her walk inside, the cold breeze drying the tears on my cheeks.

After a while, I followed her, remembering the Christmas gift I had made for Stuart. I wanted to give it to him before he left. I went up the stairs but paused before going into my bedroom at the sound of gagging coming from Willie's room. I rushed in to find Sukie pounding the boy on the back, a breakfast tray on its side in the middle of the bed.

"What's happening, Sukie?"

"He tried to swallow some johnnycake, and he started choking."

I rushed to the side of the bed and put two arms around his middle, preparing to deliver the Heimlich maneuver. But before I could, Willie gave one last cough, and a thick white membrane shot out of his mouth.

Sukie swallowed, probably to keep herself from throwing up, and I did the same. Picking up the cloth napkin, I wrapped the offending tissue in it. "Willie, I think this means you are firmly on the road to recovery. And I doubt you will ever be able to face a johnnycake again."

After seeing Willie retire for a nap, I retrieved Stuart's gift from my room, then went searching for him, half dreading that he had already left without saying good-bye. I found him in the library, facing the window. He turned as I entered, looking overwhelmingly handsome in his uniform. His face remained blank as he regarded me, but his eyes brightened.

I stepped toward him. "Merry Christmas." I handed him the scantily wrapped present.

He took it, but instead of opening it he laid it on the desk. Reaching into his coat, he pulled out a small box and handed it to me. "You go first."

I sat down on the sofa and opened the box. A gold filigree chain lay inside. I held it up, the intricate work reflecting the light in the room. "It's exquisite." Slowly, I lowered the necklace. "But I don't know if I can accept it."

"I apologize if it seems too forward, Laura, but I wanted you to have it—especially now, before I leave."

I looked him in the eye. "Why?"

"You seem so reluctant to take anything of ours, to let us leave our mark on you. You want to banish us from your memories as soon as your back is turned. Perhaps this necklace will make you think of me when you're gone, and remember."

I fingered the chain, the metal cold to the touch. "I won't need a necklace to remember you." I swallowed, forcing myself to keep my voice steady. "I'll never forget you."

He turned suddenly to face the window, his back to me, and ran a hand through his hair, the static electricity making it wild. "You're speaking as if you're already gone."

"No. I have a few months yet, I think. I just thought it was only fair to let everyone know that I won't be here indefinitely."

He walked to me and took the necklace from my fingers. Standing behind me, he placed the gold chain over my neck and fastened the clasp. I closed my eyes to better feel the nearness of him, or the accidental touch of a finger. My head turned toward him, my cheek brushing his hand. The heat of his touch paralyzed me, and I wanted to turn in his arms and kiss him deeply. Slowly, his hands dropped to my shoulders, then deserted me completely.

Shaken, I stood and stepped away. "It's your turn." I indicated the package on the desk.

He left the window and picked up the package. He untied the ribbon and held up the gray wool socks to examine them.

"They're not even square," he said, referring to my first few failed attempts at knitting socks.

"If you're going to be ungrateful, you can just give them back." I stepped forward to grab them out of his hands.

"No, Laura, they're perfect. And thank you. I shall definitely be needing these." He rolled the socks into a ball, examining them as if they were a rare jewel. "I've been told that Sherman's amassing troops in Chattanooga, making preparations for a huge campaign. Like striking south into Georgia." Blue eyes bored into me, but I didn't look away. "I don't know if I should thank you for alerting us beforehand or see you arrested for treason."

I focused on the buttons on his coat. "Just keep your family safe."

He grabbed my shoulders in a tight grip. He clenched his jaw, and, for the first time, I was aware of his sheer strength as his fingers dug into my flesh. "What about me, Laura? Don't you care what happens to me?"

"Oh, Stuart." I touched his cheek, and it trembled under my fingers. "I care more than you know, more than I want to. But there's no sense in it. I can't let myself love you."

His voice shook as he spoke. "It's too late. I knew it the minute I saw you here, when you fainted on the front lawn. You belong here—with us. With me." His kiss was hard, brutal, and I tasted blood in my mouth. It was as if by sealing his words, it would make them true.

I pulled away, my tongue running against my cut lip.

He released his grip, but his strength of will kept me standing. His voice was very low, coming from between clenched teeth. "When all this madness is over, I will come back for you. Wherever you are, I will find you, and you will tell me the truth."

He grabbed his hat off the desk and walked out of the room,

taking my heart with him but leaving the socks I had given him resting on a chair.

I walked out into the hall and almost ran into the black-clad Pamela. Her eyes blazed as she looked at me, her fists clenched at her sides. I had no idea if she had overheard my conversation with Stuart, and I didn't care. I walked past her without speaking, to find Julia. I was desperately in need of companionship.

I found Julia in the dining room, a large basket resting in the middle of the table, its contents spilled out on the polished mahogany surface. She looked up as I entered.

"It was surely an act of Providence that my herb basket wasn't in the kitchen the night of the fire." She picked up a jar to examine it, then put it back on the table. "I had wanted it nearby in—in case Robbie needed something in the night." Her voice caught, but she averted her head, hiding her eyes.

I pulled out a chair and sat down next to her and put a hand on her arm. "Julia, we all miss him. Stop trying to be so strong all the time—it's okay to cry."

She looked at me, her eyes bright, a light smile touching the corner of her lips. "I know, Laura, you're right. But I'm afraid if I start, I'll never stop. And there's so much to do. Stuart said he had mentioned it to you—that we're going to have to take refuge in Valdosta."

I merely nodded.

She went back to perusing the contents of her basket. "For one so smart, you sure can be ignorant." She continued arranging jars, bottles, and pieces of dried herbs back in the basket. "And I can't decide if you're a coward or just plain stubborn."

"What do you mean?"

She placed her hands neatly in her lap and looked at me, her chin tucked slightly, as if preparing to give a scolding. "Laura, life is never easy—especially for us women. We're the ones left behind to pick up the pieces, to make the men whole again or to comfort our children when they ask for their fathers." She lifted a stray piece of hair off her forehead and attempted to tuck it into her bun. "But when life gives us something, and our heart tells us it's something good, we need to grab it with all our strength, regardless of what our head is telling us. What is a life without risk? If the bulbs in my garden didn't risk the cold winter snow, we would never see their glorious blooms in the spring. Stuart loves you, Laura, more than he has ever loved anyone before, I suspect. Open your heart to him. It could bring you great joy."

I felt foolish as the tears started to flow. I wiped at them impatiently. "Julia, you're the one who just lost a baby. I should be comforting you, not the other way around."

She grabbed my hand. "We've all lost something, Laura, and giving comfort is just as good as receiving it." She squeezed my hand before letting go, the warmth in her eyes genuine.

Reaching into her pocket, she pulled out something I immediately recognized, something that made my heart lurch. I reached for the stuffed giraffe, its one eye missing, its fur matted and rubbed off in spots. Annie's giraffe.

I bent my head into its fur, sniffing the musty toy. "Oh, God!" I cried, remembering Jack and baby Annie and the life that we had had, the life that was now gone forever.

Gently, she said, "I thought you would have guessed long before now. Didn't you have any suspicions? She looks so much like you, you know."

I shook my head. "No. Once or twice I couldn't help wondering, but I guess I believed that if you had known anything about my missing daughter, you would have told me. I trusted you like a sister, Julia. I never would have expected you to deceive me. But . . . I do understand why you did it, if that makes it any easier."

She put a hand on my forehead. "You're looking a bit pale. Are you all right?"

I had been nursing a throbbing headache all day, and since my confrontation with Stuart, it had grown progressively worse. "I've just got this dreadful headache. I think I'll go lie down."

"Let me make you a soothing tea, and I'll send it up to you."

"Thank you, Julia." I stood to leave, clutching Annie's giraffe.

Julia held me back. "Stuart's no fool, Laura. And he can be a very determined man once he sets his eyes upon something he wants."

"He didn't get you—he let William take you away from him."

She flushed slightly. "I didn't know you knew that story. But, no, I don't think Stuart ever really wanted me. We would have had a happy marriage—a marriage between friends. But you and Stuart have something else. Something many of us live a lifetime without ever experiencing."

I shook my head, feeling the blood rush through my skull. "I can't think about it right now, Julia. All I really want to do is go home. And I can't do that and have Stuart, too."

She looked at me. "Where *is* home, Laura?"

I gave her a wry grin. "You wouldn't believe me if I told you. But it's closer than you'd think." I rubbed my fingers on my temples to soothe the incessant pounding. "My head is just killing me," I said, wishing desperately for some aspirin.

She nodded and let me go. "I'll send that tea up in just a bit."

I climbed the stairs and heard quiet voices as I passed Sarah and Willie's room, but I resisted the impulse to peek in.

I was sitting at my dressing table, pulling the pins out of my hair, when someone tapped on the door. Sukie entered, holding a cup of tea.

"Miz Julia wanted this brought up to you."

"Thank you, Sukie," I said, warming my hands on the china cup and deeply inhaling the rich aroma.

She left, and I moved to the bed with my cup. The throbbing at my temples soon began to dissipate, and my eyelids grew heavy. I pulled back the covers and lay down.

Vivid dreams hurled themselves at me, full color and overblown, monsters lurking around every corner in the dark. I wondered vaguely if there was something in the tea that had slipped me into a drug-induced dream state. I heard babies crying amidst the overwhelming smell of gardenias. I felt wetness on my cheeks but could not move my arms to wipe it away. Jack emerged from cold darkness and bent to kiss me good-bye, his brittle lips icy against mine. Great balls of smoke hovered around me, twisting around my body and between my limbs, obscuring my vision until Stuart emerged, holding his drawn saber. The wrenching pain in my gut as he stabbed me finally woke me. But the pain was still there. I rolled out of bed and reached my washbasin just in time to vomit. I collapsed on the floor, still retching and sure that I would die from the pain. I tried calling out for Sukie or Julia, but no one heard me. I remember calling feebly for Stuart as I finally succumbed to blissful unconsciousness.

"For I have sworn thee fair, and thought thee bright,
Who art black as hell, as dark as night."
William Shakespeare

Chapter Eighteen

I knew I was going to die. I lay on the floor, unable to move and urgently wishing for death. I stared at the dust balls under the bed and smelled the musty carpet beneath my cheek and made more feeble attempts to call for help. I threw up again and barely had the energy to turn my head. Eventually, I slipped into unconsciousness once more.

A cool washcloth stroked my forehead, and I turned a bleary gaze to the figure hovering beside my bed. Tiny droplets of water trickled down my face as a wet cloth was squeezed over my mouth. My cracked lips opened gratefully as I accepted the nourishment.

I tensed at Julia's voice. "Don't worry, Laura, I'm here. I'll take care of you."

I vaguely remembered the tea that she had sent up to me and her basket of secrets on the dining room table. Flinching from her touch and using what remaining strength I had left, I pushed at her hand. My arm fell useless and flaccid next to me.

"Go away," I croaked through parched lips.

A dark form appeared next to Julia, and I saw black hands take the cloth and dip it in the basin. Julia disappeared from the side of the bed, and I heard Sukie's voice, speaking in a strange tongue I had never heard before. Guttural, oddly soothing clackings reverberated through the room. She opened the pouch around her neck, extracted something from it, and made sprinkling motions over my head. I recalled, in my semi-conscious delirium, that it had been Sukie who had brought the tea. I tried to move away and was startled to find myself paralyzed. I opened my mouth to scream, my lips forming soundless words. My mind and body ached for Stuart, but my lips wouldn't form his name.

"Here, drink this. This should help your stomach." Pamela's glassy eyes hovered in my field of vision. The wrenching pain in my abdomen had not ceased, the agony still knifing through me. I felt her cold fingers on the back of my neck as she held up my head. Opening my mouth, I felt the tepid liquid slip through my lips and spill down my chin.

With as much care as one tending a newborn, she wiped up the spill with a clean cloth, shaking her head and murmuring, "There, there, don't worry. This will all be over soon."

I remembered seeing Julia in her kitchen making medicines and telling me she had learned everything she knew from her mother. Thus Pamela had the power to make me better, and I clung to the slim glimmer of hope and opened my mouth again for more of her healing tea.

"Thank you," I managed.

She pulled up the sleeve of my nightgown, exposing the crescent-shaped birthmark. Her fingers tightened on my arm before she slid the sleeve down again. She moved her face close to mine, and said, "You're very welcome, Laura. Most welcome, indeed."

Her breath brushed my cheek, her face hovering only inches above my own. Her words came to me in an urgent whisper. "Who's Jack, Laura? You keep calling out his name, telling him you're a traveler. What do you mean, Laura? What do you mean?"

Her face leered into mine, and I shrank back into my pillow, until she replaced her leer with a smile. "Don't fret now. We can discuss this when you're better. Let me make you some more tea."

I don't know how long I lay in that bed, moving in and out of consciousness, unaware of what I was saying or to whom I was saying it. I was unable to keep anything down, except Pamela's tea. But the pain never left me, and I had no doubt that I was going to die.

A deep voice from beside the bed brought me out of slumber. "Stuart?" I offered feebly but was dismayed when I recognized Dr. Watkins's voice.

He lifted my wrist and held it gently. I was blinded by my disappointment in not seeing Stuart, and I lay limp as the doctor finished his examination.

"Laura, can you answer some questions for me?"

I could hear him quite clearly but wasn't sure I could answer him. Still, I nodded.

"Do you remember if you ate anything unusual—something that only you ate?"

I nodded. A dark shape stood beside the doctor, but I couldn't see the face clearly.

"Can you tell me what it was?"

He bent his ear close to my mouth, and I tried speaking, my voice raspy. "Tea. From Julia. Sukie . . . brought . . . it."

The shape next to the doctor seemed to materialize closer to me, and I recognized Sukie's voice as she spoke. "No, Dr. Watkins. Miz Pamela gave me the tea to bring up here."

Slow trickles of realization eased their way down my spine.

The doctor straightened and turned to Sukie. "What was in that tea? And has she had any more of it?"

Sukie's agitated voice replied, "I don't know what was in the tea—I didn't make it! And Miz Pamela's been fixing some of her healing teas to make her better. But nothing's working." She wrung her hands, the movement making my stomach roil. "Dr. Watkins, I tried to help her, I did. I even used my magic pouch. She don't know why, and I done deny it, but I put it in her bed before to protect her. But there's an evil power here, one that's much stronger than me."

A fit of uncontrolled trembling possessed my limbs. Surely, I could not survive much more. With my last ounce of energy, I forced out the word, "Stuart."

The doctor's cool hand rested on my forehead. "Are you calling for Stuart, Laura?"

I nodded.

"I'll see what I can do. First, I'm going to get Zeke. He might be the only person who can help you."

He disappeared from the side of my bed, his voice sounding dim. "Sukie, stay with her. Don't let anybody else near her—especially Pamela."

Sukie's warm hands brushed my face, her rhythmic chantings once again soothing me into a deep, dark sleep. I don't know how long I slept, hovering through life, watching the sun's pattern glow and fade on the floral wallpaper. Sukie bathed me and changed my nightgown, and then I slept again.

I opened my eyes, the yellow flame from my bedside lamp creating a hole in the darkness. Voices and heavy footsteps sounded on the stairs outside my room, and then my door was flung open.

"Laura? I'm here. It's Stuart."

I wanted to cry from sheer relief, but I was so dehydrated that nothing came out. With all my strength I lifted a hand to him. He grabbed it and squeezed it tightly.

"Help me," I managed to whisper.

His breath warmed my cheek as he leaned closer. "I will not let you die, Laura. I will not. We're bringing you to Zeke's. Can you move at all?"

I struggled to move my limbs but succeeded only in breaking out in beads of sweat.

"That's all right. I can carry you."

He spoke to another person, but I couldn't make out the face in the shadows.

Strong arms lifted me off the mattress while someone else tucked the blankets around my body. I fleetingly thought that I must look and smell terrible. I turned my head to see Sukie holding the lamp, its flame creating hollows of her eyes as she stared at me. My head collapsed onto the scratchy wool of Stuart's jacket.

The flickering light from the lamp illuminated our way down the steps. I closed my eyes as dizziness assailed me, and I said a quick and fervent prayer that I wouldn't throw up on Stuart.

Biting air hit me as the door opened, but I breathed it in greedily, glad to be rid of the fetid smell of the sickroom. A soft whinnying forced my eyes open. "No," I croaked.

Despite the grimness of his face, I saw Stuart's mouth soften slightly in a smile. "Laura, you and Endy are friends now, remember? He's going to take you to Zeke's as fast as possible."

I nodded, too weak to say any more.

He handed me over to another pair of arms, and I heard the quiet tones of Zeke's voice.

"Is Pamela still here?"

Stuart answered, "Yes, Charles is with her right now, and we will decide what to do with her in the morning. Right now, I only want to get Laura away from here."

Zeke nodded, his long hair brushing my face, then handed me up to Stuart, now sitting astride Endy. Stuart held me tightly with one arm as he gathered the reins in his other hand. All strength now completely gone, I leaned against him and let him hold me.

The moon in the clear sky guided our way through the woods. As I began to drift into unconsciousness again, lulled by the slow rocking of the saddle, I felt the light brush of Stuart's lips against my hair. I gave his hand a quick squeeze before sliding off into sleep.

I vaguely recall being brought into the cabin and bundled

into a warm bed. A roaring fire cast an amber glow throughout, soothing me until I succumbed to darkness once more.

The night began to blend into day, and I found myself existing in a twilight, unable to distinguish between reality and dream. I saw Jack many times, sitting on the edge of the bed, his face cold and pale. He beckoned for me to go with him, but I resisted. Something held me bound to the place where I was, and I could not abandon it.

I held Annie, as a baby, and I spoke to her and sang to her until Jack took her from me and disappeared, leaving me bereft in the twilight once again.

And then I heard a voice, piercing the darkness around my mind, and I reached out to it, seeking deliverance from the overwhelming sense of loss that had settled over me like a blanket.

"Laura!" I heard my name shouted by a voice I recognized as being of the living.

"Stuart," I mouthed, not yet able to make a sound.

"Hold onto me." I felt a strong, callused hand grab mine and squeeze tightly. I seemed to draw strength from it as I turned my head toward the sound of his voice. And then I slept, this time without dreams.

I awoke to the crackling sounds of a fire, the warm orange tones of the blaze illuminating the room. The wall of rounded logs near the bed I was lying in told me that I was in Zeke's cabin. I snuggled deeper under the warm down coverlet, the feeling of being safe, protected, and loved overwhelming me.

A movement next to the bed caught my eye, and I turned my head. Stuart stood from a chair and leaned over me. "Thank God. You're awake."

Another person emerged from the shadows, and I recognized Zeke, holding a cup with steam rising over the edge.

"Yes, she is. Have faith, Stuart. All will be well."

He took Stuart's place by the side of the bed, holding out the cup of tea to me. "If Stuart helps you, do you think you can sit up to drink this?"

My dizziness, although not completely gone, was beginning to fade. And, while I still felt queasy, I also felt the first pangs of hunger. I had no idea how much time had passed since I had last eaten. I nodded.

Stuart grabbed me under each arm and hoisted me gently to a sitting position, then placed the pillow behind my back. The room seemed to spin suddenly as my light-headedness returned. I began to slump and immediately felt Stuart's arm around me again.

"Don't worry, Stuart. She's only weak from lack of nourishment. Charles said that it has been almost a week since Pamela was allowed near her, so most of whatever poison she had been administering is out of Laura's body. We just need to build up her strength."

Zeke brought the cup nearer, and I smelled a strong apple scent. I took a sip, feeling the warmth of the tea slip into my stomach. "Can you drink more?" I nodded and took another sip.

"If you can hold this down, I'll make you some chicken broth."

I managed a weak smile. "Oh, joy."

Stuart's face softened, the creases in his brow disappearing. "I think she's feeling better."

Zeke indicated the chair next to the bed. "Stuart, stay here and help her finish the tea. I need to go out and get more firewood."

A burst of cold air hit me as the door opened and closed. I eagerly took more drinks from the proffered cup and then lay back on the pillows, completely exhausted.

The china clinked as Stuart set the cup and saucer down on the nightstand. I looked into his face and saw the dead seriousness in his eyes. His sharp features were half hidden by a scraggly beard, and the dark circles under his eyes told me it had been days since he had slept.

"You look terrible," I said.

He ran a hand over his stubbly jaw. "I imagine I do. You had me worried sick."

"Oh, so that's it. And I thought you had come back for your socks."

"My socks?"

"Yes. The ones I gave you for Christmas and you left behind."

Smiling, he nodded. "Oh, yes. That was the main reason I returned."

He leaned closer to me, his penetrating eyes inches away from mine, his face serious. "I thought you were going to die, and all I could think of was all that was unresolved between us." He paused briefly, as if unsure what to say next. He seemed to relax a little before saying, "I was determined to keep you alive until you could apologize for being so hardheaded."

Despite my weakness, I struggled to sit up. "Apologize? Me? You must be joking!"

He sat back with a big smile. "Your fighting spirit is back. You must be on the mend."

"You could have just asked me, you know. But I still feel as if I've been hit by a truck."

"A truck?"

Realizing my error, I quickly said, "Oh, just a manner of speaking. It means to be trampled by a large horse."

He regarded me steadily. "You said a lot of interesting things in your delirium."

Feeling a pinprick of uneasiness, I answered, "Oh, really? Like what?"

"You were talking with Jack. I apologize for eavesdropping, but I was out of my mind with worry and couldn't help myself. And you talked a lot about Annie."

"I think I remember that part. Anything else?"

"A lot of it I didn't understand. You mentioned a Mrs. Cudahy a few times, and you kept asking for a Diet Coke."

He looked at me expectantly, but I conveniently smothered a yawn and slumped back down on my pillow. "I'm really tired. Could we talk about this later?"

His eyes narrowed suspiciously, but all he said was, "Of course," and leaned down to kiss my forehead, his beard rubbing my skin.

"Go shave," I muttered as he straightened.

"Yes, ma'am. But we have some serious talking to do when you're feeling up to it."

With my eyes closed, I nodded and snuggled deeper into the pillow.

For the next four days, Zeke nursed me back to health with his teas and simple meals. My appetite returned on the third day, but he wouldn't let me eat anything solid—and he showed an amazing lack of compassion by eating his meals in my vicinity, the tantalizing smell wafting toward me. On the fourth day, in desperation, I climbed out of bed. With unsteady feet, I made my way to the table and snatched a piece of cornbread from his plate.

"Feeling better, Laura?"

Spots swam before my eyes, and he quickly stood and helped me into a chair. "I think I'll feel a lot better as soon as I can eat some decent food!"

The door opened, and Stuart appeared. Zeke threw a blanket over my nightgown, making me smile. Stuart had definitely seen me at my worst, and I don't think the sight of me in a nightgown would have shocked him at all.

I suddenly realized that I hadn't seen Julia or Sukie since I had come to Zeke's cabin. "Where are Julia and Sukie?" I asked, stuffing another bite of cornbread into my mouth.

Zeke and Stuart exchanged glances. Stuart answered, "We weren't sure you wanted to see them. When you were sick, you kept screaming for them to keep away from you. I wanted the chance to talk with you first before bringing you back to the house."

"Oh." I recalled Sukie's face and the powder from her pouch as she sprinkled it over me. "I was wrong. But I think I know now what happened—although I'm not sure why."

Stuart pulled up a chair to the table and sat down. "Are you ready to talk about it now?"

I nodded and swallowed another bite of bread. "I think Pamela tried to poison me."

Stuart held me with a steady gaze. "Zeke and Charles are convinced of it. Why, Laura?"

The cornbread dried into a choking blob in my throat. "I

don't know. I'm aware that she uses you and others to ferry information to the Confederate Army, but I have never done anything to thwart her." I swallowed thickly. "I have no interest in this bloody war. I'm an innocent bystander, I assure you." Dots danced before my eyes again, and I leaned back in the chair. Zeke shook his head at Stuart, staving off any more questions for the time being.

I sat up suddenly. "Where is Pamela now?"

Stuart glanced at Zeke before saying, "She's gone. She left the night we brought you here. Hit poor Charles over the head with her washbasin and made her escape on one of our two remaining carriage horses." He raked a hand through his hair. "What she's done she's done for a reason, Laura. And you are the key. Tell me, why would she want to kill you?"

"I promise you, I really don't know." Angry tears formed in my eyes, and I turned away.

Zeke spoke. "Enough, Stuart. She's been through enough already."

With a screeching of wood on wood, Stuart slid back his chair and stood. "I'll go heat up some water and bring it in for you to wash."

Zeke stood and began clearing the dishes. "And I'm going to go check my traps and see what's for supper today." He set the plates on a low cabinet, pulled on his coat, and added, "I'm also going to pay Julia a visit. Would you like me to bring Sukie here to help you?"

"No, I don't think I need her. I think I'm feeling well enough to return."

"I want you to stay here at least one more day. I want to make sure you are fully recovered. I'm not sure of the evil medicine she used on you. Enjoy your rest. The women will put you to work packing up everything as soon as you cross the threshold."

I knew that leaving Phoenix Hall would signal Stuart's return to the army, so I was in no hurry to go back. And a distant memory tickled my mind—of Mrs. Cudahy mentioning how the big house had somehow been saved from marauding Yankees. Surely, someone would need to be left behind to accomplish this. I hoped that history would take care of itself on this point. I had no real desire to face Sherman's army on my own.

With my stomach full, I felt invigorated and almost whole again—not strong enough to run a marathon, but at least I was regaining my energy.

Stuart returned with buckets of water and began heating them over the fire in the fireplace. "Sorry about the buckets, but Zeke doesn't keep a tub here. He uses the creek to bathe."

"Even in the winter?" The thought made me shiver and long for the convenience of hot water coming through the tap at the twist of a hand.

"All year round. It's not so bad, really, once you get used to it."

"Yes, I'm sure after you lose circulation in all your extremities, you don't feel a thing."

Eager to wash, I shrugged off the blanket Zeke had thrown over my shoulders and began to rummage around for anything resembling soap and a towel.

"Over there," Stuart said, pointing to a rocking chair. "Julia sent them back with me, thinking you might be needing them."

"Yes, we women do seem to think alike. Thanks," I said holding aloft the two items. He stood between the two buckets, his gaze darting about the room, looking at everything but me.

Realizing I was wearing nothing but my white cotton nightgown—and standing before a window, to boot—I immediately understood his discomfiture. I moved the towel in front of me.

"I should be going now. We need more wood." He didn't move.

"Sure. Fine. Thanks for the hot water."

"Oh. Yes. You're most welcome." He picked up his hat from a chair and began backing toward the door. He grabbed his rifle and left with a short nod before shutting the door firmly behind him.

I stripped out of the nightgown as soon as the door closed, shivering as the chilled air touched my flesh. He had placed the buckets in front of the fire, so I knelt and gratefully dipped my hair into one, enjoying the sensation of the hot water on my scalp. I reached for the soap and ran it through my hair. I was glad Zeke didn't have any mirrors in the cabin because it has been some time since I had bathed, and I must have been a sight worthy of a Stephen King novel. After rinsing, I twisted my hair up in a towel turban and continued cleansing myself, dipping a washcloth into the water and squeezing the water over my skin. Droplets snaked their way down my spine, and I closed my eyes, enjoying the sensation. Prickly goose-flesh appeared on my arms, and my nipples hardened. I rubbed my arms harshly, making them red, reveling that I was still alive. Every sense seemed magnified as I continued bathing. The pounding outside of Stuart's ax echoed in the rafters of the cabin. My skin stung from my scrubbing, and I hastily soothed it by squeezing more water over my naked body, relieved to be temporarily free of the confining clothes of the nineteenth century.

Unwilling to put on my soiled nightgown, I took the towel off my head and wrapped it around my body. I took another piece of cornbread that Zeke had left out and sat in the rocker in front of the fire. My proximity to the blazing logs made my skin burn, but I knew that if I backed up even a little, the icy chill of the room would claim me again.

I stared into the fire, trying to conjure Jack's face. I saw blond hair and the color of his eyes, but I could not see the face of the man who had slept next to me for almost eight years.

Instead, deep blue eyes and shaggy dark hair formed in my mind's eye. I saw the fine crinkles at the sides of his eyes as he smiled, and I smelled the pungent aroma of wet wool and horseflesh that hung about him. I hugged my arms around my chest. How could I ever leave Stuart, relegating him to the same world of dim memories as Jack?

Drowsiness settled over me, and I closed my eyes.

Vaguely, I heard a knocking on the door. Without thinking, I sleepily uttered, "Come in."

The door swung open, the frigid air making me bolt upright in the rocker. Stuart appeared on the threshold, his face obstructed by the stack of wood in his arms. He crossed the room and unburdened his load by the hearth. As he straightened, he caught sight of me and stopped, his face stricken.

"I'm sorry," he stammered as he abruptly strode to the open door. "I thought—I'm sure—well, you did say to come in. I'll just leave now."

I wasn't quite sure what I wanted. But I knew I didn't want him to leave. Gripping the towel close to my body, I rushed to the door and shut it. "Please don't go."

Without turning his head, he said, "Laura, I don't know how much strength I've got, but it's not enough to stand this close to you dressed like that and not touch you. I don't believe I can be expected to act like a gentleman if I stay."

Feeling suddenly giddy, I replied, "If you promise not to act like a gentleman, then I promise not to act like a lady."

He looked at me, eyebrows raised. "What are you saying?"

In answer, I stood on tiptoe to kiss him, then stepped back to wait for his reaction.

Without a word, he turned around and latched the door from the inside, focusing his eyes on the rough wood. "I want you, but I don't want to take advantage of you. If you ask me to leave, I will."

I slipped in between him and the door and pulled his face down to mine. "I want you to stay here. I need you." Yellow light from the fireplace warmed the side of his face as he regarded me with darkening eyes. I felt the tension ease out of the thick muscles in his neck.

He closed his eyes for a moment as he touched his forehead to mine. "Oh, Lord. I never thought I'd hear you say that to me."

My teeth chattered in the icy air around the door.

"You're cold."

"Then warm me." My chattering teeth prevented the seductive smile I tried to give him.

Scooping me up in his arms, he walked me over to the bed and laid me down gently. He leaned over me, a hand on either side, and whispered, "Are you sure?"

"Yes." Suddenly nervous, I added, "It's just, well, it's been a while." A quick image of Jack flashed in my mind, then faded as I said good-bye to old memories.

Stuart sat down next to me, his eyes serious. He took one of my hands in his, entwining our fingers. "There have been no promises between us, yet. I feel as if you've been holding onto something that you weren't quite ready to give up. If you're still not ready, I'll understand. But do know this: I want you, Laura. I really do. And not just now. I want you forever."

He kissed me, his lips tentative against mine. He leaned back and slipped off his coat, letting it fall to the floor. His lips parted slightly, and my pulse quickened. I leaned forward to kiss him back, his lips tasting of salt and fresh air.

With shaking fingers, I reached up and slid the suspenders off his shoulders. Keeping one hand clutching the towel close around me, my other hand began undoing the three wooden buttons at the top of his shirt, our gazes locked. I tugged the shirttails out of his waistband and then slid my hand up the wide expanse of his torso. My hand trembled as it glided over his smooth skin, feeling his blood warm at the surface. Goose-flesh rippled under my fingers.

"Your hands are cold."

"Sorry," I said, as I knelt on the bed, facing him. I leaned to kiss him again, but he placed firm hands on my shoulders.

"Just a moment."

I stopped, paralyzed. "Stuart, please don't tell me no again. I don't think I could stand it."

He shook his head. "I don't think I could tell you no even if I wanted to." His gaze scanned the room until it settled on the brown jug on the hearth. He retrieved it and brought it to the bed. "I just need something to calm my nerves."

"Your nerves?" I sat back on the bed. "Do you mean you've never done this before?"

He took a long swig from the jug and then eyed me warily. "Not that I think this is the time to bring up my past experience, but, no, I'm no novice." His glance swept over me, and he reached to smooth the hair behind my ear. "I've just never had anyone heat my blood the way you do."

He removed his shirt and sat again on the edge of the bed.

213

His hand stroked my cheek, his callused fingers rough on my skin. "Shouldn't we be speaking of marriage? I . . . I don't want to dishonor you, Laura."

I removed the towel from my body and put my finger to his lips. "Don't say anything else. This is happening because it is meant to happen and we want it to. We'll think about tomorrow later."

I smelled the whiskey on his breath as his fingers gently traced the line of my collarbone, like a blind man committing me to memory. More firmly, his hands, warm and knowing, spanned my waist. Moving upward, they cupped my breasts.

"Thank you," I said.

His hands stopped. "For what?"

I paused, shy again. "For this—for wanting me. And for making me want you."

He ducked his head, his shoulders shaking.

"Are you laughing at me, Stuart Elliott?"

He looked back up, serious again, a strange light in his eyes. "No, Laura. It's just that you certainly know how to surprise a man. Thanking me, indeed." He leaned over to kiss me and whispered quietly, "Now let me show you how thankful I am."

He stood and untied his waistband from behind, then slid his pants over his slim hips. I stared in open admiration at his lean, muscular body toned from hours in the saddle and the day-to-day work of the plantation. Dark fuzz covered the small hollow in his chest, and I longed to nestle my head there and hear his heart beating beneath me.

I reached out to him, and he lay beside me, only our breaths separating us. I saw the hesitation in his eyes but stilled the question on his lips with a kiss. He moved on top of me, and the solidness of him anchored me here, to this place. His skin scorched me, and I gasped at the unfamiliar feel of him, but his mouth covered mine, blocking out all thought.

He lifted himself on his arms, his breathing heavy. "Roll over."

Dazed, I complied, feeling the soft pillow against my cheek. His breath burned my neck as he lifted my hair with trembling fingers. "I've always wanted to kiss you—here." His lips

214

pressed against the base of my skull. Small bursts of flame traveled down my spine, searing away the last of my resolve to keep my heart protected from this man. "When you wear your hair up, it's all I can do not to touch you. Here." He kissed me under my ear, ignoring the tiny explosions going on under my skin. "And here." His lips traveled lower, to the top of my spine, my resolve now lying in charred ruins along the way.

I turned into his arms, my mouth eagerly seeking his, my palms desperately searching for his solid flesh. I had been brought from near death, and the battle had been fought for this man, for this moment. I bit his neck, tasting the realness of him, and let my head fall back upon the pillow as his mouth moved down to my breasts, kissing and sucking on them, cupping the tender flesh. Goose bumps lifted my skin, stretching it tight across my bones.

His warm breath grazed the hollow between my breasts, his words vibrating against my skin. "I thought I would die from wanting you." He closed his eyes, his dark brows knitted in concentration. He opened them again, his gaze piercing me. "And now I might die from losing you."

I shook my head, afraid to speak lest I cry. I lifted the quilt over us, creating a pocket of warmth, and pulled him to me. I wanted to feel him, belly to belly, flesh to flesh. "Don't talk. Not now." My hands moved down the hard planes of his back and cupped his firm buttocks. His thigh muscles tensed as he shuddered.

His lips claimed mine again, and I opened my mouth to his, feeling myself pushed into the pillow and the mattress, drowning in sensation, drowning in his touching me. His long fingers, callused and rough, moved down between us, slipping inside me, and I moaned, my hips arching toward him.

He stopped, and I opened my eyes in panic, his breath hot on my face. His voice came deep and tremulous in our dark cocoon. "I feel as if I've touched you before, as if my hands and body have loved you forever." His fingers moved again, then stopped, and I gasped, wanting to beg for more or for mercy but not finding the place inside me from where words come.

Sharp teeth bit my earlobe, and I twitched under him. His fingers feathered over my thigh, and I sighed, melting into the pillow.

His face pressed against my hair as his breath wrapped around my neck. "I've known your scent all my life, it seems. Why do you think that is, Laura? Have we always been lovers? Not here, but in some other place?" His hand covered me, moving inside me again and again until I screamed from the wanting of him.

He lifted himself up, his forearm shaking. "Are you sure, Laura?"

I nodded desperately, rubbing my abdomen against his hardness, my intentions clear.

He bent his head, our foreheads touching. "Thank God," he whispered, as he slowly lowered himself into me.

I think I stopped breathing, all my energies spent on the feel of his body against mine, moving inside me, making me shudder with my desperate need of him. He threw the quilt off us, the cool air whipping at my exposed skin.

"I . . . want . . . to see . . . you." Small beads of perspiration covered his forehead, and his eyes remained open, watching me. I spread my thighs farther, feeling a small ball of flame begin to roil and grow inside me. Still he watched, his gaze never straying from my face. I squirmed against him, making him quicken his pace, until the flame grew out of control, bursting within me and leaving me limp and gasping.

My hands slid down the smooth expanse of his back, cupping his buttocks again until I felt them go taut, and Stuart moaned, finally collapsing against me. His blood pulsed under my ear, his skin taut and slick with sweat.

I felt the brush of his lips on my forehead as he rolled over to face me. He pulled back, a puzzled look on his face. He smoothed back a stray bit of hair off my forehead. "You're crying. Have I hurt you?"

I left the tears where they were, my little badges of courage. "No. Oh, no. I'm crying because . . . I don't know why I'm crying." I gave him a crooked smile, and he touched my face again, caressing my cheek. "I think it's out of gratefulness— to you. For resurrecting something inside me that's been dead for so long." I touched my lips to his, tasting the salt of my tears.

"Let me love you, Laura. Let me make you mine."

I remained silent but pulled him into my arms and held him until he fell asleep, his breath as gentle on my skin as a butterfly's landing.

The wind blew fallen leaves across the barren earth outside while battles raged and lives were lost on the other side of our horizon. But inside our warm cocoon, with the flames crackling in the fireplace, we slept away the answers to questions that could never be asked.

> " 'Tis all a Chequer-board of nights and Days
> Where Destiny with Men for Pieces plays;
> Hither and thither moves, and mates and slays,
> And one by one back in the closet lays"
>
> **Omar Khayyam**

Chapter Nineteen

I drowsily opened an eye. From the dim light in the cabin I realized it was late afternoon, the slanting sunlight from the windows reaching silent fingers toward the bed. My head was nestled on Stuart's arm, our legs entangled, his rhythmic breathing the only sound.

My skin tingled from head to toe, and I felt soreness in areas where I had felt nothing for years. I wanted to give a languid stretch and purr like a contented kitten, but instead I remained motionless on the bed, reveling in the slick feel of his bare skin against my own.

I shifted my head slightly to admire his profile—the straight nose, the high, broad cheekbones, the strong chin. In sleep, he was beautiful, reminiscent of a marble effigy I had seen on an old tomb on a visit to England. I shivered. Embers glowed in the fireplace, but I resisted the impulse to leave the comfort and slow, steady heat of Stuart's arms to restart the fire.

A deep rumbling began in Stuart's chest, and I raised my head to see if he had awakened. His eyes remained closed, but his head twitched on the pillow, his eyebrows furrowed. His muscles stiffened under me as he wrestled with demons in his dreams.

He bolted upright in bed, a warrior's cry on his lips, the sound echoing off the rafters. His broad shoulders shone with perspiration as he bent forward, his head in his hands. "Oh, God," he whispered, grinding the heels of his hands into his eye sockets.

I couldn't see the assaults of soldiers in blue and gray, rifles lifted, bodies falling, nor hear the blasts of angry artillery as it blew bits of horses and men across a battlefield. But I could see the tenseness in his back and the desolation in his eyes, and I knew Stuart did see.

He started when I touched him but quickly drew me to him and buried his face in my hair. "Laura." His voice was muffled, but the tone of affirmation in his voice was clear.

I lifted my head to look into his eyes. "I'm here, Stuart." I smoothed the hair back from his forehead and then rested my hands on his neck. His pulse skipped and raced under my fingers, and I knew his battles were still raging. "I'm here," I said again as I leaned forward to kiss his neck. He tasted of warm sleep and salt, and I kissed him again.

He took my head in both hands. "Yes, Laura, now. But will you always be?"

"Isn't now enough?"

The pressure of his hands on my head increased. "No. It's not."

The desperation of his dream filled his eyes, the eyes of a

soldier. They were foreign to me, and I felt a flash of alarm.

"You're hurting me. Please let go."

He began trembling, and the pressure eased as he removed his hands. "I'm sorry, Laura. This war seems to dehumanize us." He looked down at the wrinkled quilt.

"I know." I grabbed his hands and turned them over to kiss each roughened palm. I had felt how gentle his hands could be. Wanting to erase the haunting images in his mind's eye, I held his shoulders and pulled him down on the pillow once more.

His gentleness was gone this time, his lips hard on mine, his body rough and demanding, taking everything I had left to give. He slipped inside me with one thrust, and we reached our release quickly, both of us shaking with the intensity. It left me feeling like a shattered and fallen star, splintering down toward earth, then coming to rest on the barren winter grass.

The last sliver of light disappeared from the floor, leaving only the dim glow of dusk from the windows to illuminate the room. Slipping from under the covers, Stuart walked across the room to rekindle the fire and then returned to the bed with me.

I rubbed a hand against his cheek. "You shaved."

"I was ordered to." His cheek creased as he smiled.

"I didn't order you. I'm much more subtle than that."

"Subtle, hmm? I hadn't noticed."

I elbowed him in the ribs, making him grunt.

"Why hasn't Zeke come back?" My fingers were busy entangling themselves in the black thickness of his hair, brushing it off his forehead.

"He won't be back for a while—he might even spend the night in the woods." Stuart cocked an eyebrow. "He knows. He always knows things that aren't necessarily apparent to others."

"Won't he and the others be scandalized?"

"Not Zeke, and I doubt anyone else would find out. I think the citizens of Roswell are too busy worrying about their next meal to worry about who's going around unchaperoned."

"But it's freezing outside. It's making me feel incredibly guilty."

"Zeke prefers to sleep outside. It's most likely his Indian blood. He once told me that the stars were the eyes of those not yet born. He takes great comfort in sleeping under them."

I smiled, resting my head on his shoulder. "That's beautiful. I'd like to think it was true." I thought of the eyes of my parents, not yet born, watching over me.

I ran a finger over a scar on his chest that I had noticed earlier. It was about the size of a quarter, but it must have been deep, because the skin was purpled and puckered. "What's this?"

His hand rested over mine. "William. He shot me with an arrow when we were boys. It was an accident."

From what I had heard of William, I somehow doubted it had been accidental.

He turned to me and touched his lips to mine. "They're the color of moss, I think."

I looked at him questioningly.

"Your eyes. It will always be your eyes that I'll think about when I'm away from you."

I held a finger to his lips. "Don't. Don't talk about us not being together. I can't stand it."

"Then stay, Laura. Don't go. We could—"

"Shh," I said, and leaned forward to kiss him and silence the next words from his lips. Words that I expected to be my undoing.

A booming sound filled the room, echoing from the nearby woods. Stuart had scrambled from the bed and pulled on his pants by the time I realized it had been the sound of a shotgun.

"Wouldn't that be Zeke hunting?" I was reluctant to move from the comfort of the quilt.

Because he was slipping his shirt over his head, his reply was muffled. "Most likely. But he said he was checking traps. He'd only use his gun if he ran into trouble. I'd best make sure he's all right."

"What kind of trouble?" I wrapped the quilt around me and

walked over to him as he buttoned up his coat and buckled his belt over it.

"If a catamount became interested in Zeke's trap, there might be a fight. Zeke could probably take care of it, but I'd just like to make sure."

He avoided my eyes as he settled his hat on his head. I grabbed his elbow as he reached for the rifle. "There's something you're not telling me."

Pulling a sidearm from its holster, he handed it to me. "Do you know how to use this?"

Reluctant to touch it, I stepped back. "Why would I need that? What's going on?"

He opened the gun, checked it for ammunition, then snapped it shut. "We don't know where Pamela is. But we do know she means you harm."

I had completely put Pamela out of my mind. Obviously, Stuart and Zeke had not. I straightened my spine. "Then you had better show me how to use that thing."

It was the first gun I'd ever held, and I found this Navy Colt to be surprisingly light.

He showed me how to cock the hammer and quickly moved aside as I pointed the gun. "Watch where you aim that. It's got an easy trigger, and, knowing your penchant for accidents, I'd be real careful." His attempt at humor did not dispel the worry from his eyes.

He took the gun from me, released the hammer, and laid it on the table. "I want you to keep the door latched and only open it when you hear our voices. Do you understand?"

I nodded, feeling numb. He wrapped his arms around me. "Don't worry, Laura, it's probably nothing. I just want to make sure."

I reached my arms around his neck, letting the quilt fall, and kissed him solidly.

"We have some more talking to do when I get back." Stooping, he picked up the quilt and handed it to me. "And you might want to get dressed just in case Zeke gets back before I do. Not that I think he'll be surprised, but he is my grandfather."

"Be careful." I couldn't think of anything else to say.

"Yes, ma'am," he said softly as he let himself out the door.
Drops of rain spotted the wood planks of the porch, blown
by a strong wind. I latched the door and stood there briefly,
my hands flat on the hard wood, and whispered a little prayer.

The cabin suddenly seemed vast and empty. I walked over
to the fire to stoke it, making the wood pop and crackle, the
homey scent of pine filling the room. All I could find to wear
was my nightgown, so I slipped it over my head and began
to wait.

The thick silence of the evening woods filled the air with a
palpable heaviness. A discernible feeling of expectation lingered on the darkened windowsills. I peered out into the emptiness and saw only my reflection, my eyes wide. The wind
battered the small cabin, the rain falling more heavily as the
night progressed.

I paced the room until my gaze rested on the full bookshelves. I pulled Victor Hugo's *Les Misèrables*, smiling to
myself as I thought of Zeke reading it.

Propping myself up in the bed, I placed the gun on the
bedside table within easy reach and began to read. My eyelids
grew heavy as the fire burned low, and I quickly fell asleep.

The gray tones of dawn sent a tentative light into the darkened cabin. The fire had long since gone out, explaining the
numbing cold that permeated the room. I sat up abruptly, the
heavy book sliding off my lap. I had no idea how long I had
been asleep.

I crept out of bed. The early light lent a muted quality to
the colors of the room, as if I were still dreaming. But the
sharp poke of the table corner told me I was indeed wide
awake.

Gnawing worry invaded the morning peacefulness. The men
had not returned, and I had no idea what to do next. I walked
to the window, my footsteps sounding oddly muffled. Peering
out, I was met by thick, swirling puffs of fog. I leaned my
forehead against the glass but could see only the hulking shadows of trees near the house.

A shout in the distance made me jump. It had definitely

been a male voice. I sprang to the door, unlatched it, and opened it wide.

The crisp smell of morning and wet pine straw greeted me as I stood on the porch and strained my eyes to see beyond the steps. I took a few hesitant paces before stopping, the hairs on the back of my neck standing at attention, a primordial sign of warning. The soft whinnying of a horse came from nearby. "Stuart?" I called.

I heard a footfall behind me. "Turn slowly, and keep your hands where I can see them."

Despite the frigid morning, sweat ran under my armpits. I turned to face the double barrel of a rifle not two inches from my face. I could not see them through the thick mist, but I felt two dark eyes boring into me.

"Why are you doing this, Pamela? I've never harmed you in any way." I amazed myself with my outward calmness. Inside, my stomach churned with terror.

"I'm afraid I must disagree." She nudged my arm with the barrel. "Let's go inside. We have a little talking to do."

She followed me into the cabin, closing and latching the door behind her. "Sit down."

I allowed myself to drop into the rocker, not taking my eyes off the rifle. I had seen the gun before, in this cabin. I knew it was Zeke's.

"Where's Zeke?" I asked, trying to push down the panic rising in my voice.

Without turning her back to me, Pamela examined every detail of the room, her eyes registering surprise as she took in the well-stocked bookshelves. Her gaze drifted to the tousled bed. "Ah. So you've seduced Stuart. I warned him, but he wouldn't listen. Just like a man. I've found that the best way to deal with a contrary man is to eliminate him—just like Julia's father." She chuckled lightly.

"Where is Zeke?" I repeated, my voice rising.

Pamela hooked a chair leg with her foot and dragged it out from under the table to sit. "Somewhere in the woods." She paused to give me a wide grin. "With a bullet in him. And I hit him in the head with the butt of his rifle for good measure."

"No!" I started to stand up, but the rifle motioned me back. "Is he alive?"

"I don't think so. He wasn't moving when I left him."

"Why would you do such a thing? What has he ever done to you?"

"He helped you, Laura. That makes him my enemy."

My mouth went dry, and I could almost hear my heart thumping. "But I am nothing to you! I don't understand."

"Don't you?" Her look softened slightly as she raised a quizzical smile. "Do you really not know who I am?"

"No, I really don't. But I do know you're crazy. Please let me go find Zeke—I might be able to help him. And what about Stuart?" I clung to the chair like a lifeboat. No matter how much I wanted to get up and run, I knew just as strongly that Pamela would have no problem shooting me before I reached the door. She had already tried to kill me once before.

"He's alive—for now. I think that keeping the two of you alive would be a prudent move on my part. You're far more useful to me living than dead. Right now, anyway."

The woman was certifiably insane.

I tried to reason with her. "Pamela, I think you are a very sick woman. I know you didn't mean to hurt Zeke—or me. Perhaps there are doctors who can help you. Just put down the gun so there are no more accidents."

She stared at me, amazement spreading across her face. "I know who you are. Don't you know who I am?"

Where was Stuart? I glanced at the window, white wisps of fog still stroking the panes. "I know you're an agent for the Confederates, if that's what you mean. But I am not a Yankee spy, as you probably think. To be honest, I don't really think I could choose a side in this conflict." I hoped that keeping her talking could buy me some time until Stuart returned.

The sound that burst from her was like a bark, making me cringe. "I'm not stupid, Laura Truitt. I know you're a traveler."

The blood seemed to evacuate my body, leaving my extremities to tingle with dread. "A traveler?" My voice sounded foreign to my ears.

"When I heard that you had been found on Moon Mountain, I suspected. But I didn't know for sure until I heard you singing that rainbow song. What I don't know is who sent you."

"Who sent me?" My mind reeled. How could she know about the time-traveling?

Her face puckered as she walked closer to me, the rifle barrel prodding me in the chest. "Don't play innocent with me—I will not be toyed with. And I'd just as soon shoot you if you do not cooperate with me."

Realization, as white-hot as lightning, struck me. "Are you a . . . a traveler, too?"

She cackled again. "Of course. From the year of our Lord nineteen hundred and fifty-three to be exact. I'm here on a mission, and you are going to help me succeed."

I remembered her astronomy books, which she had sent down from Tennessee for safekeeping, and her perpetual watchfulness of me. But she was here for a purpose. "Oh, my God," I whispered. "You mean other people know about this?"

Her lipless grin showed small, even white teeth. "Oh, yes." She looked at me with hooded eyes and pulled up the sleeve of her dress. A dark crescent-shaped birthmark marred the whiteness of her forearm. I sucked in my breath. Sarah and I had identical marks.

"How did you get here?" I couldn't move my eyes away from her arm.

"The same way all Shadow Warriors travel. Wrapped in the atmosphere of a comet intensified by a lunar eclipse."

"Shadow Warriors?"

"Yes, dear. Like you and me. And your daughter. I saw her mark when I found her on Moon Mountain. I knew I needed to keep her close by to see who came after her. It was so convenient when Julia's daughter died. Otherwise, I would have had to help her along."

I felt sick. "Surely you wouldn't harm an innocent child."

Her face was serious. "I will do whatever it takes."

I swallowed my fear, eager for answers. "Are there many of us?" I began to shiver. Pamela grabbed the quilt off the bed and tossed it at me. Picking up Stuart's gun from the nightstand, she returned to where I was, pulled out a chair, and sat down opposite me.

Still keeping the gun aimed at me, she began talking. "Not many—usually just one or two every generation. I thought I was the only surviving Shadow Warrior, but now I know I was wrong. I'm a Southern loyalist, and I am here to make sure the South wins. The South will rise again." Her voice shook with vehemence.

I wanted to laugh at the absurdity of it. "You can't be serious. You're only one person—you can't win a war single-handedly."

She leaned back in her chair. "You know, Laura, for a young woman of obvious intelligence, you can certainly be dense at times." Sitting up straight, she continued. "It's like playing the lottery—only you know the numbers beforehand. Besides, I'm not alone. I have a group of loyal followers. And now I have you." She drummed her fingers on the rifle butt. "Now, why are you here?"

I swallowed and took a deep breath, trying to clear my brain. "I really don't know. It was an accident, I think. I was just trying to find my daughter on top of Moon Mountain, and I ended up here." My eyes widened as I considered another possibility. "Do your . . . associates know who you really are?"

"Of course not. Who would believe anything like that? No, they've all been handpicked by me to be slow of brain but quick on the trigger. And a little low on morals. Money talks with these men, and I've got lots of that. I came here prepared."

She laid the rifle behind her chair but kept the handgun trained on my chest.

"Look, Pamela, I am not here for any political purpose, and I refuse to help you do something that will deliberately change the course of history. Aren't you concerned that anything you change now might have repercussions you're not planning on?"

Her eyes sparkled with energy as she leaned forward, elbows resting on her knees. "If I don't intervene, this war will bring the South to her knees, forever tying her to the yoke of

Yankee imperialism. If I succeed, I can relieve the South's suffering by eliminating Reconstruction and lessening the effects of the Great Depression. I will be the South's savior." Her eyes flashed with a fanaticism that chilled my skin.

"I will not help you. Even if the South wins now, it's only a matter of time before the two sides are fighting again. The South cannot win, now or later. It just doesn't have the resources. It's ludicrous."

She leaned forward and hissed, "I'm not asking for your opinion, Laura. And besides . . ." A feral grin crossed her thin face. "If you ever want to see your daughter again, I suggest you listen very closely to what I ask of you."

My heart tightened in my chest. "What? What do you mean? Where's Annie?"

"She's with my associate, Matt Kimball."

"Why is she with Matt?" My fingernails bit into my palms.

She smiled, almost maternally. "Don't you see? Matt is holding Sarah until you do what I ask of you. And if you don't . . ." The smile vanished from her face. "Matt won't think twice about cutting her throat."

I stood, feeling as if I were high on a tight rope. "She's only a child! Oh, God—you can't do this. Tell me where she is!"

She smiled gently at me. "Now, where would be the fun in that?" She pushed the barrel of the gun into my chest and shoved me back into my chair.

"I want you to understand something, Laura. All it will take is a word from me, and you will never see your daughter alive again. But do as I ask, and I will release her to you. It's up to you, my dear."

"Laura!" It was Stuart. He was getting closer, probably at the edge of the woods.

I gripped the seat tighter, willing myself to remain where I was instead of wrapping my hands around Pamela's throat and choking her to death. Only the cold steel barrel of her gun prevented me from moving.

"What do you want me to do?" My voice croaked, my breath vaporizing in the chill air.

"I need you to kill General William Tecumseh Sherman."
She paused, as if waiting for the enormity of her request to
sink in. "We cannot let him take the city of Atlanta. If he is
repulsed and forced to retreat, then the northern war effort will
crash. Our northern neighbors are more sick of this conflict
than we are—it won't take much to make them give up. Without a strong victory here, Lincoln will not be re-elected in the
fall. His opponent, McClellan, will win and sue for peace with
the South. The nation will be torn apart—permanently. The
Confederate States of America will be her own sovereign nation, never to be held in bondage by the Yankee oppressor
again." She tightened her hold on the gun. "I'd do it myself,
but I'm much too valuable."

I shook my head. "You are certifiable. There are a lot of ifs
involved here. . . ."

She brushed my words aside with her hand. "Stuart's getting
closer, Laura. All I have to do is shoot him through the door
with the rifle. What are you going to do?"

I heard Stuart's voice through the door again, coming closer.
"Damn you! I can't—"

She picked the rifle off the floor and trained it on the door.
"You can bury him next to Sarah."

My mind reeled in a sickening kaleidoscope of blood-red
fear. "I'll do it." My voice reverberated throughout the room.

Lowering the rifle, she smiled at me. "Good choice, Laura.
I knew you were smart." She stood, leaving the handgun on
the chair. "Don't tell Stuart about our plan. If you do, I will
find out, and I will kill him and Sarah both. And you must
find an excuse not to go with them to Valdosta. I need you
here." She strode to the door. "Pack a carpetbag with whatever
you'll need for traveling, but keep it hidden. Make sure you
include the red dress you wore at Christmas—General Sherman is sure to find you irresistible in it." She paused, then
added, "Be ready at a moment's notice." She unlatched the
door and let herself out, quickly disappearing into the swirling
mists. The muffled sound of hoofbeats faded in the distance.

Dots danced before my eyes, and I realized I had been holding my breath. Filling my lungs with great gulps of air, I stood
and ran to the door, calling Stuart's name.

"So many worlds, so much to do,
So little done, such things to be."

Lord Tennyson

Chapter Twenty

I flew blindly out the door, only stopping when I realized I
stood in the middle of a wall of fog and could see neither the
cabin nor the woods, although I knew the cabin was somewhere behind me. My breath came hard and fast, my lungs
pressing on my ribs.

"Stuart!" I screamed, feeling the panic rise and struggle to
choke me. Pamela was out there with her gun. "Stuart!" The
swirling haze sucked up my voice, muffling the sound.

A dark form emerged from the mist, and I struck out in an
automatic reflex. A strong hand grabbed hold of my wrist, but
my scream died in my throat when I recognized Stuart.

"Laura, it's me. I've got Zeke—he's been hurt. Let's get
him back to the cabin." A thick shadow hovered over Stuart's
shoulders, and I realized it was his grandfather.

"This way," I said, leading him the way I had come.

Stuart laid Zeke on the bed and pulled a knife from his belt.
Bright crimson spotted Stuart's shirt in an incongruous rose
pattern as the coppery scent of blood lingered in the air.

Stuart cut through Zeke's pants, peeling back the blood-
saturated material. A hole in his right thigh, about the size of
a quarter, oozed red surrounded by black tissue. Congealed
blood spilled down his forehead, making his hair stick to his
skin. A soft groan emerged from Zeke's cracked lips. At least
that meant he was alive. But from the gray pallor of his skin,

I wasn't sure for how much longer. A large loss of blood would lead to shock. He needed a massive infusion of fluid.

I raced to the fireplace and took down the kettle, luckily filled with water. Using a ladle, I began feeding him the fluid his body needed.

"Give me your nightgown." I hardly recognized Stuart's voice.

"What?"

"I need it to stanch the flow of blood." Stuart reached for the hem of my nightgown.

I reached over to the bed and snatched the sheet off of it, leaving the quilt wrinkled at the bottom. "Use this instead." I had already realized that one of us had to run for help, and I certainly didn't want to do it naked.

Stuart and I began ripping at the sheet, aided by his knife.

"It was Pamela, Stuart. I saw her."

Stuart didn't pause, vigorously ripping the fabric and then moving to Zeke's side to apply it with pressure to the gaping wound.

He looked at me, blue eyes blazing. "She was here?"

I paused, not knowing how much I could tell him. "Yes. I heard your shout, so I opened the door, and she was there. She . . . she didn't hurt me. She ran when she heard your voice."

I couldn't look at him, afraid he'd see the lie in my eyes. I went to Zeke and lifted his arm. The skin on his forearm felt clammy and cold. "One of us needs to get help."

"I know." He looked at me closely. "But I have experience with gunshot wounds. And I think it's best that I stay with him." Our eyes met over Zeke's still form. "Endy knows the way blindfolded and can get you to Phoenix Hall quickly."

I swallowed. The thought of riding Endy at a trot in full daylight was harrowing enough. The thought of riding him through the woods in heavy fog at breakneck speed was terrifying. I looked down at Zeke, whose shallow breath barely made his chest rise and the stench of whose blood rose thick in the air. The thought of him dying under my unskilled hands was worse. "All right. I can do it."

He nodded. "You'll be fine." His voice held all the conviction I lacked.

I stayed with Zeke, applying pressure to the wound, while Stuart saddled Endy.

The fog had begun to lift, and it hovered amidst the higher branches of the trees, the murky sun making an effort to penetrate the cloud and illuminate us below.

Stuart wrapped me in his warm coat and strapped his holster and gun around my waist. I knew I had nothing to fear from Pamela but accepted the gun without comment. With a weak grin as he lifted me into the saddle, he said, "Just don't shoot the horse, okay?"

I couldn't make my facial muscles return his grin. "Yeah, sure." I grabbed hold of the pommel. My voice shaking, I said, "Okay. I'm ready."

He gave me the reins, patted the horse on the rump, and shouted, "Go!" The earth slid out from under me as the great beast lurched forward, its speed steadily climbing as he began to cover the distance. All the riding tips and pointers that Stuart had given me during my informal lessons fell by the wayside. The only thing I could think of was holding on for dear life to avoid being thrown off and trampled. The thought of Zeke's pale body on the bed spurred me on, and, with renewed fervor, I kicked the sides of the horse, making him gallop harder.

The outlines of Phoenix Hall appeared, and I leaned over the horse's neck, giving him the lead. The air was sucked out of my lungs, and my fingers were numb from gripping the saddle so tightly.

Endy stopped at the back porch, and I was relieved to see Julia at the door, as I had no idea how to dismount from the horse by myself.

"Julia—Zeke's been shot!" I left out the detail of who had shot him. That would come out soon enough. "He might be dying, and he needs help."

"Where is he?"

"He's at his cabin with Stuart."

231

She stepped forward, grabbing my arm. "Sarah's missing. Do you know where she is?"

"Yes." I swallowed, trying to still the shakiness in my voice. "She's safe for now. We'll talk about it later."

She didn't release her grip. "Did you say anything to her to make her run away?"

"No, Julia. I promised you I wouldn't, and I didn't. We'll talk about it later—we've got to help Zeke now."

Julia turned around to go back up the porch steps, her skirts swirling around her. "I'll get my medicine and take Endy back to the cabin. You go get Charles and bring him there."

Within minutes, we had exchanged places, and I watched her disappear into the woods, her skirts flying around the black flanks of the horse, her long hair streaming unbound behind her.

Charles's house was only about a mile from Phoenix Hall, and I ran all the way. I was out of practice, but the adrenaline pushed me down the dirt lanes and brick road to his house.

A black manservant who was busily trying to erase the sleep from his eyes finally answered my banging on the door.

"Who's there, Linus?" The doctor himself stood on the stair landing, a robe belted over his nightshirt and his face registering shock at my appearance. His eyes took in Stuart's coat thrown over my nightgown and my bare toes peeping out from under the hem.

I pushed open the door and stepped past Linus. "I'm sorry to bother you so early, Dr. Watkins, but we need you. Zeke has been shot."

The disapproving frown disappeared from his face as he sprang into action. "I'll be down in a moment." He paused on the top step, looked at my disheveled appearance once again, and opened his mouth to say something. He closed it, then turned to get dressed.

Knowing the buggy wouldn't fit through the path in the woods, we rode the doctor's horse. I kept tugging my nightgown down over my legs as best I could but eventually gave up, hoping Dr. Watkins had more important things on his mind than my alarming lack of modesty.

232

The cloying aroma of brewing herbs struck me in the face as we entered the cabin. A soft groan came from the bed, and I sighed with relief, knowing Zeke was still alive. Realizing I would only be in the way, I approached the blazing fire, my fingers and toes aching with cold.

"Thank you again, Laura." I started at the soft voice behind me and whipped around to see Julia, her hands caked with blood and droplets spattered on her dress in a macabre pattern.

"For what?"

"For once again coming between my family and disaster."

I waved a hand at her. "Don't be silly. I haven't done anything but be a messenger. I only hope that our efforts aren't in vain."

She sat down next to me in the rocker. Nodding in the direction of the bed, she said, "He's in good hands now. I have faith that Charles can save him."

Julia began to tuck stray ends of hair behind her ears. Then, in a barely audible voice, she said, "It was my stepmother, wasn't it?"

I answered simply, "Yes."

Her shoulders slumped, and she looked down at her lap. "I blame myself, then. I knew she wasn't right in the head. I should have had her committed long ago." Her hands rested in a tight ball in her lap. "But she was the only family I had left, and I just couldn't. I never thought she would do something like this."

I stared into the fire and saw two dark eyes staring back at me over the muzzle of a rifle. "She has Sarah."

"What?" Her eyes widened as the color drained from her face.

I leaned closer, so as not to be overheard. "She's . . . she's blackmailing me. If I do something for her, she'll keep Sarah safe."

Her fingers gripped the chair arms. "Oh, my Lord. What does she want you to do?"

I shook my head. "I can't tell you—it would put all of us in jeopardy. And you can't tell anyone what you know, either—especially not Stuart. She's threatened all of you if I whisper a word. We already know what she's capable of." I glanced at Zeke. "Just trust me, Julia. I will do whatever it takes to get Sarah back. Do you understand?"

She buried her face in her hands, her shoulders shaking from silent sobs. I knelt in front of her chair. "Do you understand, Julia? You're not to tell anyone. You need to trust me."

She nodded, then raised her head, her eyes rimmed with red. "When will this godawful war be over so we can live our lives again? I can't stand it! Nothing is as it should be anymore, and I'm starting to doubt that we can survive it."

I grabbed her with a hand on each shoulder. "Julia, listen to me. This war will end in slightly over a year. You've already made it through almost three years of hardship and worry. I know you can go a little bit more. And I can promise you that you will not lose your house." I wondered if I had said too much, but I couldn't bear to see her give up now.

Her sobs had stopped, and she stared at me. "How do you know these things, Laura? How do you know?"

I glanced at the two men by the bed tending to Zeke and out of earshot. So many precious lives were at stake. I could no longer keep my bizarre secret. "You're going to think I'm crazy, Julia, but I swear it's true. I don't know why or how— all I know is that it really happened, and I'm as sane as I've ever been."

She leaned forward, her swollen eyes open wide. "You're scaring me, Laura! What are you talking about?"

I took a deep breath and in hushed tones blurted out everything before I could change my mind. I didn't leave out any details, as if by including everything, it would seem more believable to us both.

I paused briefly and finished. "I was born in nineteen sixty-five. In other words, I haven't been born yet and won't be for another one hundred and two years." I could now see the whites all around her irises. "Ouch! You're hurting me." Her fingers had become claw-like as they gripped me.

She immediately released her grip. "Sarah, too?" she whispered.

I nodded. "And Pamela. But I don't know how long your

stepmother has been here. She said she was from the nineteen fifties." I felt my shocking secret release a bit of its hold on me, my burden now a bit lighter.

Julia blinked, as if she were trying to focus on something she couldn't quite see. "How is this possible?" she whispered.

"I don't know. All I know is that there's some kind of connection between Moon Mountain and the dual specter of a lunar eclipse and a comet. And this." I showed her my birthmark. She gasped, and I knew she was recognizing it from Sarah's arm. "Besides that, I don't know. But I suspect Pamela does. It was no accident that found her here in this time."

I looked closely at Julia, her face blanched, her eyes dark circles of color in her white face. "Are you okay?" I rose to be able to catch her if she decided to fall out of her chair.

She nodded, but I remained unconvinced. "Really, Laura, I'll be fine. It's just—well, it's a shock." She stood shakily. "But this is the least of our worries right now," she said, indicating the tableau by the bed.

I touched her arm. "I don't know why I'm here—if there's even a reason for it. And I don't know what repercussions it could bring. I've told no one but you. It must remain between us. And I must stay at Phoenix Hall to await Pamela's instructions when you go to Valdosta."

She gave me a weary nod and stood. "Just bring Sarah back safely, Laura. Without her . . ." She looked away, unable to finish her sentence.

Slowly, she returned to the bedside. I stole a glance at the still figure on the bed and felt a sinking sensation in my belly. The sheets were stained a deep crimson, creating a dramatic backdrop to the pale leg lying on top. A white bandage, startling against the blackness of his hair, now covered most of Zeke's forehead. Charles probed into the leg wound with a long metal instrument, while Stuart poured the amber contents of Zeke's beloved jug over the hole, making Zeke's body twitch. I swallowed quickly and turned away. I felt helpless in my inactivity, but I knew there was nothing more I could do.

* * *

235

I awoke to the sound of a log falling in the fireplace. Stuart stood in front of me, prodding at the fire with a poker, his face grim. I sat up with a start, my stomach grumbling. "What time is it?"

His face creased in a slight smile. "Evidently time for you to eat."

I glanced toward the bed. A white bandage had been wrapped around the wounded leg, but there was still no movement from Zeke. "How is he?"

"Better. Charles managed to remove as much of the bullet as he could, and Julia has dressed the wound to prevent it from festering. Now we just wait and see."

"Where are Charles and Julia?"

"They've returned to Phoenix Hall. We're to bring Zeke there later. I don't feel safe leaving him here." I knew we were both thinking of Pamela.

"Stuart." A weak voice sounded from the bed.

Stuart walked over to the bed, with me close behind. Zeke's teeth chattered, his whole body shaking. I pulled up the quilt and tucked it in around him. Zeke had always appeared tall and imposing, but now it was as if his body on the bed was a mere shadow of the man. Instinctively, I laid a hand on his forehead and brushed the hair out of his eyes.

"We've got to get Laura away from here. Pamela . . . it was Pamela."

"Zeke, we know. We're going to bring you back to Phoenix Hall to keep you safe." Stuart poured more water into a ladle and held it to Zeke's lips.

Zeke pushed it away angrily. "No, listen! It's not me she wants—it's Laura. We must . . . get Laura away from here."

He began to raise himself off the bed, but I gently pushed him back. "Zeke, it's okay. Pamela won't hurt me. We reached a truce. We're all safe now."

I felt two sets of eyes on me and could not meet either one.

"What do you mean, Laura? How can we be safe? She's tried to poison you and shot Zeke, and you're trying to tell me that we're safe?" Stuart's voice held a hint of anger, but I managed to meet his eyes.

236

"I need you to trust me again. A lot more than you know is at stake." I held up a hand to his protests. Zeke's eyes had become glazed. "Do you have anything for his pain?"

Distracted momentarily, Stuart answered, "Yes, Julia left some wintergreen tea." He walked toward the fire. "But don't think we're done with this discussion."

Nothing more was said as Endy was saddled and we prepared to vacate the cabin. We rode back to Phoenix Hall near dusk in a somber procession. I sat behind Zeke on Endy's saddle, clutching the older man tightly to prevent him from slipping off. His mind was clouded with pain. He spoke in a tongue I had never heard before—probably Cherokee. I was surprised when Stuart answered him back in the same language; the soothing inflections of his voice told me he offered words of comfort to his grandfather.

While Stuart brought Zeke inside, I raced upstairs to put on some clothes. It felt strange to be in my room again, remembering the last time I had been there, in a haze of poison and near death. I shuddered but entered, the cheeriness of the room pushing back the dark thoughts.

I dressed hurriedly, skipping the corset and hoops but at least remembering three petticoats. My mind raced as I buttoned up the coarse muslin, weighing my options.

When I entered the house, I had noticed all the little things that were missing: pictures from the walls, knickknacks from the tables. I had nearly tripped over a trunk of children's clothes and linens that lay open at the bottom of the steps. It was apparent that Julia was ready to move her household to Valdosta.

Pamela had told me to stay. But I would not endanger Sarah's iife by telling anyone why. I had to think of another reason.

I followed voices into the parlor as I came down the steps. Stuart stood by the window, drinking from a glass. Dr. Watkins stood next to him, his eyes on Julia, who was sitting on the sofa. All heads turned as I entered.

"You're leaving for Valdosta tomorrow." Stuart took a deep swallow from his drink.

I bristled under his authoritative statement. "Excuse me? I beg to differ."

He raised an eyebrow but refrained from commenting.

I turned to Charles. "Surely Zeke shouldn't be moved yet."

"You're right, Mrs. Truitt." He looked at Stuart and shrugged his shoulders. "But the news from up north isn't good. The Yankees are amassing a huge army just north of our border, and Captain Clark of the Roswell Battalion has informed me that they will be making defensive preparations in case of an attack on Roswell. He is advising that women and children leave."

"And it is doubtful my mother will follow us all the way south to Valdosta." Julia's quiet voice was almost lost in the din of the blood pounding in my temples. I had thought of a plan.

"I will stay here with Zeke. When he is well enough to travel, we will follow you."

Stuart and Charles began their protests at once. But Julia's voice drowned them out. "Stop it. Laura is right. It could kill Zeke to move him so far. The Yankees aren't coming tomorrow—she'll be safe for the time being. If she wants to stay, then let her stay."

My gaze met Julia's, and she gave a quick nod.

"But what about Pamela? She tried to kill you and Zeke both!" Stuart ran a hand through his hair, making the ends stick up. I wanted to reach up and smooth it down, but he was busily stomping about the room in his agitation.

"And I could never leave a woman alone here with only a sick old man." He stopped his pacing to stand in front of me. "What kind of a truce did you make with Pamela?"

Charles stepped in. "You can't trust Pamela. Her mind is obviously unhinged. What did she say to you?"

"I can't tell you—I gave her my word." I stared into two sets of eyes, one brown, the other blue, and saw the same expression in them. As if I was some recalcitrant child who needed to be persuaded into something for her own good.

"Look, I'm not some silly girl with a brainless notion. I know what I'm doing, and I know it's for the best for everybody. You'll just have to trust me." I glanced over at Julia, inviting her to voice her support.

"Stuart and Charles, Laura is a determined woman. I trust her and will do as she asks. I'm asking you both to do the same."

I could see Stuart wavering.

Julia stood, imposing despite her small stature. "Would you rather we abandoned the house to looters and put your grandfather at risk?"

The two men looked at us as if we had lost our minds. Stuart scooped his hat off the table and glowered at Julia and me. "I've met mules who were less stubborn than you two women. God help the Yankees if they ever pick a fight with you." Excusing himself, he left the room, Charles following in short order.

Julia gave me a wry grin. "I've got to go check on Zeke. Before I leave tomorrow, I'll have to show you how to change his dressings and how to prepare his medicine." In a rustling of her skirts, she also left the room.

All through the night, the slamming of drawers and trunk lids and the sounds of heavy furniture being dragged across wooden floors shattered the quiet. I was relieved to see the piano remaining; it was too big to be moved anywhere and thus was also safe from Yankees theft.

The following morning, I stood staring out the sidelights of the front door, watching Stuart load one of the wooden farm wagons. Soft footsteps approached behind me, the light fragrance of lavender surrounding me.

"He's almost done," I said. Julia stood beside me and nodded. "What did you tell the men about Sarah?" I asked.

She turned and placed her valise on top of a trunk. "I told them she had been invited by Ruth and Josiah Reed to ride to Valdosta with them and their family. They left yesterday." She took my hand and squeezed it. "Godspeed, Laura. And bring Sarah home safely." Her voice cracked, her eyes pooling with tears.

239

I ignored her reference to *home*, as if the very word wasn't in dispute.

She let go of my hand and reached into a pocket of her cloak. "I want you to have this. It fits the secret compartment in the armoire in my bedroom. It's where I keep all the family records—of births and deaths." Her eyes bored into mine, and I reached for the object she was handing me. I knew which armoire she was speaking of—the same one that would sit in my bedroom more than 130 years into the future. But I had never known it contained a secret compartment.

"I will put personal family letters and documents in it. If you find it necessary to return to your . . . time, you will be able to find out what has become of us all." Her eyes were misty as she dropped a small, heavy object into my hand. I looked down and began to shake. Lying in my open palm was a key. A key identical to the one worn around the neck of the woman in the portrait Mrs. Cudahy had given me. "I have a duplicate key, and I will keep the compartment locked."

I swallowed to ease my suddenly dry throat. "Thank you, Julia. But I hope that I can return this one to you in person." She embraced me tightly, the top of her head resting under my chin and her hair smelling of lavender and wood smoke.

Stuart came in the front door and hoisted the last trunk onto his broad shoulders. He avoided looking in my direction and left again to put the final piece of luggage on the wagon. From the corner of my eye, a gleam of silver caught my attention. Mrs. Cudahy's tray, forgotten on a hall table. Easy pickings for the marauding army. I grabbed it up and ran out of the house, clutching it to my bosom.

"Wait! You forgot this!"

Stuart jumped down from the wagon. "One of the few un-sold pieces of my mother's wedding silver. Thank you." His fingers brushed mine as he took the tray from me.

Our eyes met in the watery reflection of the smooth silver. "I don't suppose I can change your mind about staying," he said.

"No. You can't." I stepped closer to him, placing a hand on his arm. "Do you remember what Zeke told you right after I came here? Something about how you need to trust me, because I would be your salvation? This is the time, Stuart. Regardless of where you think my loyalties lie, you need to believe that I have you and your family's best interests at heart. Staying here with Zeke is something I must do. I'm not helpless, and I certainly don't need a man around to protect me. Don't worry about me—I can take care of myself."

His eyes narrowed into blue slits. "There is an army of about 100,000 men thinking about heading in this direction, and you're telling me not to worry about you. It's all I can do to not tie you up and throw you in the back of this wagon. Maybe all the jostling on the road to Valdosta would knock some sense into you."

I dropped my hand. "I wish we could stop arguing about this. My mind's made up, and I won't budge. Can't we just leave it at that and say a proper good-bye?"

He silently turned away to step back onto the wagon and secure the tray in one of the trunks. I wondered briefly if I would ever see it—or him—again in this century.

I thought again of telling him everything but quickly dismissed the notion from my mind. Sarah's life hung in the balance, as did Stuart's and everybody else's, and there was no doubt in my mind what Pamela would do if she found out I had confided in him. I looked up at his stormy face and knew that no matter what I said, he didn't trust me.

The gray sky overhead held the chill of the air close to the earth, and the heavy cloud cover threatened rain. I wrapped my shawl tightly around me as Willie ambled out of the house, his eyes downcast. Even the horse seemed subdued. I had said good-byes many times in my life but none as painful or as permanent as this one seemed to be.

Julia had gone to the cemetery to say farewell to Robbie one more time. I wanted to reassure her that she would come back to Roswell at the war's end, but all I knew was that her beloved house would survive, not who would come back to claim it.

"Laura."

I turned to see Stuart behind me, an arm outstretched. I took his hand and allowed him to lead me across the winter-brown grass to the side of the house. The deceptively dark green of the boxwoods made it seem like spring, but the drab browns and grays of the rest of the flora reminded me that this was the darkest part of the year.

"No, I'm not going to ask you again. I know your mind is made up. But I can't leave you, in good conscience, without means to protect yourself. I've asked Charles to keep an eye on things here." He stopped walking and turned to me, his blue stare melting something inside me. "And there's something else."

He lifted my left hand, and I felt cold metal on the tip of my third finger. A gold filigree ring with a stone of black jet slid easily over my knuckle, resting next to Jack's plain gold band.

I stared at it, the smooth surface reflecting the clouds overhead. "What is this?"

"My father gave this to my mother when he proposed to her." His eyes studied me, as if measuring my reaction. "I'm giving this to you for protection."

My gaze traveled back down to the ring, dark against the paleness of my skin. "How will this protect me?"

His gaze never wavered. "That would depend on which army you fear more. If you marry me, you would become not only the wife of a Confederate officer, but also the sister-in-law of a Federal officer on General Sherman's staff. You'd be covered on all sides."

I blinked hard. "Are you asking me to marry you?"

"Well, yes."

"To protect me?"

"Yes—among other reasons."

"Like what?"

He paused, scrutinizing me. "I'll tell you everything when you do the same."

I touched the ring with my right hand, shaking my head and choking back tears. "I'm glad that my safety is the main reason. Otherwise, I couldn't say yes in good conscience, knowing that I'll be leaving soon."

His arms went around me, pulling me close. His lips touched mine, gently at first, then hard, pressing into mine and forcing my mouth open. Abruptly, he stopped.

"I'll be back as soon as I can. When I return we'll have Reverend Pratt make it official."

I clutched the ring tightly, trying to hold onto the smallest glimmer of hope. But how could I marry him and then disappear? Could he remarry someday, not knowing what had happened to his wife?

He kissed me again before leading me back to the wagon to say my final farewells. As I knelt one last time in front of Willie, he clutched at my skirt. "Miss Laura, I'm going to miss you so much!" I shut my eyes tight and hugged him to me.

"And I'm going to miss you, too, Willie."

He looked up at me with his tear-streaked face, and I brushed the moisture aside with my fingers before planting a kiss on his freckled nose. I said good-bye one last time and helped him up to the bench seat of the wagon. "Mind your mama now, you hear?"

Stuart mounted Endy, and suddenly there was nothing more to do. They were ready to leave Roswell, and their home, for the duration of the war and perhaps longer. It was time. I forced myself to wave as the wagon pulled out, Endy following closely behind.

"Wait!" I shouted. I ran to catch up with Stuart, my skirts held shockingly high. I reached him all out of breath, and before I could protest, he leaned down and pulled me up on the saddle in front of him.

"Did you forget something?" The side of his mouth quirked up slightly.

"Yes, I did." I swallowed deeply, trying to regain my breath. "I forgot to tell you to be careful." Something flickered in his eyes, his hands tightening on my waist. I threw my arms around him, kissed him soundly, then quickly slid off the horse.

Julia gave me a wan look as the loaded wagon trundled past, and I knew she was thinking of Sarah. I mouthed the words, "I'll bring her back," and she nodded as she passed me. Willie's dark head bobbed beside her, his brown eyes filled with tears. I sucked in my breath and held it, afraid to let it go. Afraid to let them hear me shrieking out my grief at letting them go and my fear of staying behind and not knowing what was to come.

Sukie sat on the other side of Willie, hugging him. A wheel hit a soggy rut, and there was a moment when we thought that their trip would be delayed, but the straining of the horse pulled it out, and they continued down the front drive.

Stuart sat atop Endy, his eyes fixed on me. Finally, as the wagon drove through the front gates, he tipped his hat, turned the horse around, and followed them. I raced after them and stood leaning on the gate, bent over while I sucked in my breath in deep gulps, my gaze anchored to Stuart's back until he disappeared around the bend.

I lifted my muddy skirts and trudged back to the house. I felt the unfamiliar weight on my finger and stopped to examine the ring. The overcast sky clouded the jet, giving it only a murky gleam. I felt the tears coming and knew I couldn't hold them back much longer. But I stared at the house as I got nearer, and with a surge of pride I felt for the first time what compelled Stuart, and so many others like him, to risk their lives for their homes. There had always been a connection between this house and me, ever since I had first seen it with Jack. Phoenix Hall had become my home, and my daughter's, just as the Elliotts had become my family. Perhaps I had been sent here to save them both from destruction. Or maybe I had been sent here to find happiness in my life again. And, maybe still, the two were connected.

A black crow flew overhead, cawing loudly. A feeling of someone walking over my grave settled on me, making my skin tingle with dread, and I thought of Sarah and where she might be. I climbed the porch and entered the house, closing the door soundly behind me.

"Between two worlds life hovers like a star,
'Twixt night and morn, upon the horizon's verge."
                                                    Lord Byron

Chapter Twenty-one

During the remaining cold weeks of January and February, my thoughts were never far from my daughter, and I knew there was nothing that I wouldn't do to bring her back. So I tended Zeke and the garden, watching them both stir in the last embrace of winter, and I waited for Pamela. Every noise in the night and every shadow at the window sent my heart racing.

One warm afternoon, I was rocking on the front porch, enjoying the hint of spring in the air and taking a much-needed break from nursing. Dr. Watkins's familiar buggy appeared at the front gate and ambled its way up the drive. Too tired to stand and greet him, I waved.

Clambering down, Charles lifted his hat to me and joined me on the porch.

"Mind if I sit?"

"No, of course not." I waved a hand in the direction of the chair next to mine.

"How is Zeke?"

"Much better—no headaches for three days now. And he can manage walking with the crutch without my help."

Grunting, he sat back and began to dig in his vest pocket for his pipe and tobacco.

"I'm starting to see something green in the vegetable garden. I—um, might need some help in identifying whatever I'm growing."

Charles nodded and then took a puff from his pipe, slowly letting the smoke leak out of his mouth. The tobacco perfumed the air, and I was suddenly reminded of my father. Without looking at me he said, "Mrs. Truitt, may I call you Laura?" He pinkened under his whiskers.

"I'd like that. But only if I can call you Charles."

The color in his cheeks deepened, and his gaze continued to focus across the front lawn. He nodded. "Yes. Yes, of course."

He began fidgeting with his pipe and cleared his throat three or four times. Not knowing how much of his discomfort I could bear, I asked, "Is there something you'd like to say?"

The stricken look on his face reminded me of Charlie when I had had to pull a large splinter from his rear paw. "Um—ahem, yes, there is, as a matter of fact. Of course. Yes."

I stopped rocking my chair and glanced at him with anticipation. He looked back at me and moved his lips, but no sound was forthcoming. He was beginning to worry me.

"What? Is it about Stuart?"

He stood abruptly, making the back of the rocking chair bang against the front of the house. "Well, yes, in a way, I suppose it is."

I stood next to him, one hand on the railing. "Is he hurt? For God's sake, would you just spit it out before we both grow old and gray?"

He blinked quickly. "I would like to move into the preacher's room. I'd be out of your way, and I could help take care of Zeke."

I narrowed my eyes at him. "What's wrong with your house? The preacher's room is barely big enough for a bed and a Bible. Why on earth would you want to do that? And we both know Zeke is on the mend and I am more than capable of caring for him."

He shifted on his feet, looking down at his boots, seemingly examining every scratch.

"And what has this got to do with Stuart?"

He finally looked at me, his watery brown eyes full of embarrassment. I had to strain my ears to hear him. "Stuart thought that you—um, might need my protection. I told him you wouldn't like it, but he insisted. So here I am."

The echoing honks of geese flying overhead in their V formation brought my gaze heavenward. I turned back to Charles and placed a hand on his forearm, the brown wool of his coat rough under my fingers. "I do resent his insinuation that I can't take care of myself. There is no need for you to move in here. But thank you. Your friendship means a lot."

He pressed his lips together. "I beg your pardon, Mrs. . . . I mean Laura. But for your safety, you should have a male on the premises."

I resisted the impulse to stamp my foot. "I told you and Stuart both, Charles, I am in no danger from Pamela. And the Yankees are still up in Tennessee and no immediate threat. Just because I'm a woman doesn't mean I don't know how to protect myself. And Stuart himself showed me how to use this." I reached into the pocket of my housedress and pulled out the gun Stuart had given me.

Charles stepped back, his eyes widening. "Don't point that at me! It's liable to go off."

"Not very likely, Charles. I'm not an idiot." I turned away from him and started to shove the gun back into my pocket when my ears were split with a sudden explosion. I looked down at the front of my dress and saw a large, smoldering hole decorating the pocket edge.

"Oh, crap."

"Are you all right?" The concern in his voice was genuine, but I was too embarrassed to soften toward him.

"Of course I am. But my dress certainly isn't." I stuck my fingers through the hole and was dismayed at the extent of the damage. My whole fist could have fit through the opening.

Charles straightened. "I'll move my things into the preacher's room this afternoon."

I looked at his determined face and hoped against hope that Pamela wouldn't object to his presence. But I had no doubt that when she was ready to approach me, she would have no trouble avoiding detection by anybody else.

"Fine, Charles. Whatever." I shrugged. "You Southern gentlemen sure are stubborn."

The corners of his mouth turned up slightly. "And so are our women."

I gave him a grudging smile and turned to go into the house. I opened the door and went into the hallway, the sight of a figure at the top of the stairs startling me.

"I heard a gunshot." Zeke held a precarious foothold on the top step, one arm clutching his crutch, the other holding an enormous musket of ancient vintage.

I rushed up the stairs toward him before he could pitch forward and do more damage to his leg or worse. "Zeke, what are you doing on the stairs?" I took the musket out of his hands and grabbed him securely by the arm. "It was only me being stupid. I accidentally fired my gun."

He nodded, making the fine beads of sweat on his forehead run down his face.

"I'm sorry for scaring you." I led him to his room and settled him onto his bed. He leaned his head back, his skin ashen against the stark white of the pillow. His eyes didn't leave my face. "You are in great danger, Laura. My dreams show me a dark shadow hovering behind you. Leave here. Leave while you still can."

I sat down on the edge of the bed and saw the concern in his eyes. "I can't, Zeke. There's . . . there's a problem." Restless, I stood and went to the window, looking out at the gray landscape of naked trees. A few stubborn leaves clung to branches, unwilling to let go. Buds covered the limbs, promising a new spring. I pressed a hand against the window, the glass cool against my palm. I felt I could take Zeke into my confidence, and the strain of keeping my worry about my daughter a secret pulled at me. "Sarah is in great danger. Pamela's taken her and won't release her unless I do something for her."

He grunted softly. "Sarah is well, Laura. I would see in my dreams if she were harmed."

I shook my head. "I want to believe you, but we both know what Pamela is capable of. And she isn't working alone. Matt Kimball and others are involved, too."

His eyes, glazed with pain, regarded me gently. "Sarah is safe. Now, tell me. What is it that Pamela has asked you to do?"

"I can't tell you. It could put you in grave danger. I don't know if I can do what she asks, but I've got to do something. I cannot lose my daughter again."

"Does Stuart know?"

"No. He would also be at risk if he knew. And I'm afraid of what he might do if he did."

I walked over to the bookshelves and pulled out the back-gammon board and began setting it up on the flattened bed-clothes. "I must find Sarah and bring her back soon. According to your books, the next time a comet will appear in conjunction with a total lunar eclipse will be September first, eighteen sixty-four. That gives me seven months. Seven months to sell my soul."

A strong hand grabbed my wrist. "Do what you must, Laura. But remember the legend: the ancient travelers who journeyed with evil spirits were always hunted down and slaughtered. They must not be allowed to walk in this plane."

His grip tightened, and I shuddered. "What would you have me do, Zeke?"

He let go and placed his hand upon my head, just as he had done when we first met. "Sometimes we are called upon to do something greater than ourselves, against forces we might not understand. It is a gift. You will be looked upon as a savior of people—a Shadow Warrior." He pulled my sleeve up over my forearm. The crescent-shaped birthmark looked like a bruise on the pale skin. "See? You have the mark. It is a very rare mark—I've never known of more than three people born within a century to be blessed with it."

Again, I shuddered. I saw his eyes droop and his mouth soften. His hand fell to my arm, and he muttered, "Be careful," before succumbing to sleep.

I settled him, then gathered up the game and left the room. I faltered at the top of the steps, the game board slipping from my grasp and somersaulting down, hitting each stair. The markers danced on the wooden treads, their eventual destination determined by the hand of fate.

I sat down on the top step and rolled my sleeve down. A spark of light caught my attention, and I reached over to a corner of the step. I picked up a marble and rolled it in my hand, feeling the cold smoothness. Fresh grief flowed through me as I recalled Sarah playing with them, lying close to the floor and flicking them with her little fingers toward Willie. I ached for my child with the same intensity I had felt when she went missing on Moon Mountain so many years ago. Her life was in my hands, and I wouldn't fail her again. I stood and began gathering the round markers as I descended the stairs.

The days passed in almost nerve-jangling precision, and still no word from Pamela. I prayed for Sarah, for there was precious little else I could do except wait.

And then, in mid-April, Stuart came back to me. I was in the chicken house, battling with the hens, my skirt held up and full of eggs.

"Hungry again?"

I whipped around at the sound of his voice, letting go of my dress and hearing the muffled thudding of the eggs in the hay. "You're back."

He stood silhouetted against the henhouse doorway, a tall, dark shadow. "Is that the way a bride-to-be greets her groom?"

I walked toward him, a nervous smile teasing my lips. I looked into his eyes and saw my reflection. "You should have called first. My hair's a mess, and I haven't a thing to wear."

He stilled my chattering with his mouth on mine. "Hush, woman, and allow me to give you a proper greeting." He kissed me again, his skin feeling moist and smooth, smelling of soap.

I broke away, laying my hands on his cheeks. "You shaved."

"Yes, ma'am. I know how you feel about beards. And I didn't want to offend your delicate sensibilities."

I snorted. "I didn't know I had any."

His mouth tilted at the corners. "You don't. That's what I find so attractive about you."

Then his expression became serious. "What's wrong,

Laura?" He reached a thumb out to smooth the frown lines above the bridge of my nose.

I blinked, trying to get rid of the sting in my eyes. "I miss Sarah—and the others. And . . . and you, too. I missed you."

He bent to kiss me, his firm body pushing me against the side of the building. I pressed myself against him, showing him how much I had missed him.

Stuart broke away, his breathing heavy. "I'm riding into town tomorrow to talk with Reverend Pratt. I have two more days of leave, and I'd like us to be married before I go."

"For my protection, right?"

A dark eyebrow arched over a blue eye. "Yes. For your protection."

We walked into the peach orchard, where the new buds were just beginning to emerge on the branches above us. Despite the warmth of the day, a chill breeze brushed through the neighboring pines, and I wrapped my shawl closer to me.

"I wish things could be different, Stuart."

I felt him bristle.

"I do, too, Laura. And they could."

I turned away from him, unable to stand the hurt in his eyes. The sky cast deep shades of gold through the trees as the sun set on the distant horizon, like butter melting in a frying pan.

I looked down at my shoes, the cracked brown leather coated with red dust peeping out from under my frayed hem. "I want you to promise me something. If something should happen and we are separated forever, I want you to get on with your life." I held up a hand to still any protest. "Nobody should go through life alone. I've tried it, and I don't recommend it."

I felt his fingers on my shoulders, gently turning me around to face him. A stray breeze lifted the hair off his forehead. "Laura, you always have the choice of going to Valdosta— you'll be safe there. When this war is over, I will come for you there."

"Just promise me." The earnestness in his eyes stopped me from saying more.

Slowly, he nodded. Then I reached for him in the twilight and held him close.

We were married the following afternoon at the Roswell Presbyterian Church—the same church in which my Annie would be baptized in more than 130 years. I stood silently clinging to Stuart's arm, feeling as if I were having an out-of-body experience. Charles was our witness, as was a perturbed Eliza Smith, who also doubled as organist. I shivered throughout the ceremony, wondering if there should be an added clause concerning unexplained spousal disappearances.

Stuart kissed me, his lips warm, thawing the brittle ice of mine. He took my hand and led me down the aisle as Mrs. Stuart Elliot. I halted halfway down and looked at my husband. "Wait. I don't know your middle name."

He stopped next to me, his expression puzzled. "Didn't you hear Reverend Pratt say it?"

I shook my head. "I . . . I wasn't listening. Too nervous, I suppose."

"Are those your teeth chattering?"

"It's either my teeth or my knees. But I really must know—what's your middle name?"

"It's Couper. Why do you want to know?"

I slid my arm through his as we continued down the aisle. "I . . . don't really know. I guess I thought that I couldn't know you well enough to marry if I didn't know your full name."

He stopped to lean down and whisper in my ear. "Laura, I would say that we know each other better than most couples on their wedding day." He gave me a sly wink.

I averted my head with mock prudery. "I'm sure I don't know what you mean."

He chuckled quietly as he led me out into the warm April sunshine.

We spent our wedding night in the room and bed I had shared with Jack in another time. I had at first protested, not wanting to bring an unwanted memory to our marriage bed. But Zeke had insisted, moving to my smaller room, and I couldn't refuse when I saw all the brightly colored blooms strewn over the coverlet, smelling of spring and new beginnings. Stuart and I lay under the half-tester, filling our lungs with the heady aroma of lush petals of violets, azaleas, and roses, the stately mahogany posts bearing witness.

I thought suddenly of Mrs. Cudahy's words—"Most of my ancestors were conceived on this bed"—and a bubble of déjà vu floated through me. I stared into Stuart's eyes, and it occurred to me where I had seen them before. In a tall, elderly woman with glorious skin and eyes the color of the Caribbean. Mrs. Cudahy.

We lay together in the cool night air. I impatiently kicked off the covers, letting them slide into an ungraceful heap on the floor. Stuart's fingers slowly traced circles on my skin. A rough fingertip slid from my collarbone to my navel, pausing on my C-section scar. He hadn't mentioned it the last time we'd been together.

"What's this?"

"It's a scar from . . . from an operation I had."

He bent to kiss it, his lips warm on my bare skin. I sighed. "Did it hurt?"

His lips traveled to my side, reaching my ticklish spot. I squirmed. "I don't remember, Stuart. Did it hurt when you got shot?"

He looked at me, his head cocked to the side. "You certainly have an odd sense of humor, Mrs. Elliott." A warm tongue licked at the curve of my waist, flooding me with liquid heat. "But I like it." He nibbled at my skin, and I clawed at his back—to make him stop or continue, I couldn't tell.

"Don't move." His voice was muffled. I opened my mouth to reply but could only gasp as his breath traveled across my abdomen, blowing warmth over my navel. I squealed, arching like a skittish cat, almost knocking him off the bed.

"I said don't move." His hands slid over my arms, pinning them to the bed.

"I'm ticklish. You have to be . . . oh . . . ." A roughened palm covered my mouth.

"Don't talk. I want to see how strong-willed you really are." His tongue dipped into my navel while bright streaks of light

253

shattered inside my eyelids. Dark hair bristled against my torso, and my skin twitched, but I dared not move. There had been a note of seriousness in his voice, and I dared not disobey.

A stubbled chin brushed my hip, then my inner thigh, blowing away little bits of me inside. I turned my head into the pillow, muffling a moan. Wet kisses traveled slowly down to the bony cleft of my knee, then to the smooth muscle of my calf, heating my blood as it pooled in my core, leaving my limbs limp and heavy. His tongue moved to my other ankle, tasting it, then worked its way up my other thigh, leaving trails of exquisite misery in its wake.

"Please," I sobbed. "Please," I said again, my skin burning under his touch.

My tormentor paused, hovering over me, his breath caressing me between my legs, his eyes burning in the candlelight. "Please what, Laura? Do you want me to stop?" A draft moved the candle, casting his face in dark shadow, hiding the man I knew.

"No, don't stop. Just . . ." I shifted my hands to his shoulders, trying to move him up toward me. "I want you. Now."

He took one of my hands and moved it over my head, his face now over mine. Our hips touched, and I felt his wanting of me, but still he held back.

His voice was hushed but fueled with the urgency of his hunger. "Now you know what it's been like to be me these past few months. The endless needing of you. It's torture, isn't it?" He pulled my other arm over my head and bent toward my lips, biting me gently. ·

I moaned again, squirming under him.

"I've wanted to break you, bend you to my will, so many times—but I cannot. Your strength is what I love most about you, Laura. You're killing me little by little, but I will not take your strength from you. God help me, I won't."

I wrenched my hands from his grasp, sliding them down his back to his hips, pushing him against me, my need too urgent to put into words.

His breath caught. "I *will* leave my mark on you."

My eyes stung as the tears ran heedlessly down the sides of my face. "You have, Stuart. You already have."

I reached my arms around his neck and pulled him down, my core shattering into fragments of sensation as he moved inside me. He rocked me like a baby, his face buried in my hair, and when he reached his release, he cried out my name, and I cradled him, my tears falling in his black hair.

Afterward, while Stuart slept, I stayed awake, watching the distorted shadows dance across the walls. I thought again of Mrs. Cudahy and her words, then drifted off to sleep, dreaming I was floating in a sea of spring blossoms and seeing a pair of startling blue eyes.

"A feeling of sadness and longing
That is not akin to pain,
And resembles sorrow only
As the mist resembles the rain."

Henry Wadsworth Longfellow

Chapter Twenty-two

I awoke before sunrise, the hint of a word whispered in urgency lingering in the cool morning air. Moonlight illuminated the room, etching out vague outlines of the furniture. Stuart slept on his back, his face turned toward me, as soft and innocent as a child. His even breathing told me he had not spoken.

Carefully lifting the covers, I rose from our bed. A flower petal, disturbed by my movement, floated to the ground, its blackness against the wood floor like a drop of blood. I went to the window and looked out.

The dark shadow rose like an obelisk on the lawn, the hidden eyes catching the misty pre-dawn light. My breath caught in the back of my throat. It was time.

I grabbed my carpetbag from under the bed, already packed with a few belongings, including the red dress and the necklace and earrings Stuart had given me. Stopping by the bed, I leaned forward to feel his soft breath on my skin. I closed my eyes, remembering the previous night, then stood. I wished I had time to write him a note, but anything I could have said would have made him come after me.

I blew him a silent kiss, then took the chain he had given me, with Julia's key on it, off the dressing table and slipped it over my head. I quickly shimmied out of my nightgown and threw on a blouse and skirt, skipping most of the underpinnings. I had no idea how we were traveling, but I wanted to be as comfortable as possible.

The front door squeaked as I opened it, and I paused, listening for any stirrings in the silent house. Hearing nothing, I opened it farther and stepped out. Matthew Kimball waited for me on the porch.

His voice hissed in the early morning air. "So, Laura. We meet again. I can't tell you how much I'm looking forward to our little trip together." I could smell his fetid breath from where I stood. "Let's go. We've a train to catch."

"Where's Sarah? And where are we going?" I cursed my voice for wavering.

His teeth appeared gray in the twilight. "Don't you bother your pretty little head about all that. You'll find out soon enough." He offered a hand, but I ignored it, stepping past him.

He left the steps of the porch and began to lead me across the front lawn. We had barely reached the drive before I heard the shout behind me.

"Laura!"

Matt spun around, ripping a gun out of his belt and pointing it at Stuart. "Stop where you are, or I'll kill you."

Stuart made a move to come toward me. I took a step backward. "No, Stuart, don't. He means what he says. Just let me go. I have to do this."

"Do what? What are you doing?" His eyes were hazy with sleep and full of confusion.

I put up a hand to stop him from moving forward. "I'm leaving with Matt. I can't tell you why, but this is something I have to do."

He started walking toward us again, and Matt cocked the gun. Stuart stopped, his face beginning to flush red. "What do you mean? You can't go with him—you're my wife!" He raked a hand through his hair in agitation.

Matt stepped closer, and a veil of fear fell on me. "It's not what you think, but I can't explain. Let me go now, and no-body will get hurt." My eyes burned, and I said the only thing I knew that might ease his hurt. "I love you, Stuart. I wouldn't leave you if I didn't have to."

His eyes widened and clouded over like a storm coming up off the ocean. "You love me? Then how can you go with him?"

He walked toward me, his eyes growing darker until they appeared ebony in the pre-dawn light. "God damn it, Laura. I will not let you leave."

I ran to him to halt his progress. "Stop!" I screamed, suddenly aware of the Navy Colt he had kept hidden behind his leg. If he shot Matt, I would never see Sarah again. "Stop!" I screamed again, pushing his arm up and away from its target. But my voice was drowned by the loud report of a gun. I jerked around toward Matt, his smoking gun lowered at his side and a sneer on his face.

As if in slow motion, I turned back to Stuart. I saw more than pain flash through his eyes. The look of betrayal was like a blow to my gut. Incredulous eyes stared at the blood quickly spreading on his shirt right below the collarbone. His knees buckled, and I reached to catch him but succeeded only in breaking his fall as he crumpled to the dewy grass.

"Stuart—no!" I knelt and touched shaking fingers to his neck, feeling his pulse skitter under my fingertips.

"Leave him."

The cold barrel of a gun pressed into the back of my neck. I ignored it, leaning forward to push on the wound and stop the bleeding that had saturated his shirt and now dripped into the grass. Blood oozed between my fingers, mixing with my tears. "Don't die, Stuart—please don't die. I do love you, I do. God, Stuart, don't you die." His eyes flickered, then closed again.

The pressure from the gun became more insistent. "Leave him, or I will kill you, too. And if you die, there's no more reason to keep Sarah alive."

"But I can't just leave him here. I've got to go get Charles."

As if he had heard his name, Charles appeared at the front door. I stood quickly, my hand firmly on Matt's arm. "Don't shoot—I will go with you willingly now."

Charles ran to Stuart, his eyes full of questions as he stared at my bloody hands. "What happened?"

I shook my head. "Save him, Charles. Please don't let him die."

Before the doctor could respond, Matt pulled on my arm, and we ran together down the drive and out to a buggy waiting on the other side of the gate.

The wheels of the buggy crunched over the dirt road, the pounding of the horse's hooves matching the throbbing in my heart. I stared at the blood on my hands, my tears washing white streaks through the rivers of red. "My God, what have I done?"

I didn't look up when I heard the brittle laughter from my companion. "You just saved Sarah's life." He moved his hand to my lap and squeezed my leg. "Don't you worry about not having a husband no more. I'm available, and I'm kinda partial to widows."

I gagged, moving my head to the side of the buggy just in time. I looked back, like Lot's wife, and half wanted to be turned into a pillar of salt. I saw nothing but the tall oak trees that lined the front drive, their branches sweeping toward the earth, the dew-laden leaves weeping. And on an uppermost branch, a crow rested, its black feathers ominous against the

now cerulean sky. The bird cawed loudly, then descended in
one fell swoop, still cawing, until it disappeared from sight.

The buggy rumbled over the rocky road, jostling my bones. I
clenched my teeth to prevent them from shattering every time
we tumbled in and out of a rut. Bright dogwood blooms heralded spring all around us, the scent of new life heavy in the
air. I would have reveled in the beauty of the day except for
the image penetrating my thoughts—the look of betrayal in
dark blue eyes, and the spreading stain of blood on a white
shirt.

Mid-morning, we approached a mangy-looking pair of
mules pulling a wagon. The gaunt man in front of the rickety
vehicle stared at us without comment, his eyes as empty as
his right sleeve and as sad as the pants leg pinned up at the
hip. The woman next to him barely lifted her head to notice
us, her skin hanging in loose folds, her dress baggy on her
emaciated frame. A baby's weak cries came from the back of
the wagon, and I turned around as we passed them to see seven
children of varying ages, as dirty and hungry-looking as their
parents, thrown in the back like sacks of flour. A little girl
about Sarah's age sat against the side of the wagon clutching
a bundle of rags. A squawking began, and a small hand
thrashed out of the bundle. The girl placed the armload over
her shoulder and looked at me with deep brown eyes, her wan
little face showing no emotion.

Matt stopped the buggy and looked at me. He pointed to
the departing wagon, the dry red dirt swirling in the air between us. "She reminds me of your little girl." He shot a
stream of tobacco juice out of the side of the buggy, not all
of it making it over the edge. He wiped a grimy sleeve across
his mouth, then used the same sleeve to wipe the sweat dripping from his forehead. Brown streaks of tobacco juice marked
his skin, and I turned away, unable to look.

"When do I get to see her? I need to know if she's all right."

He shrugged. "I dunno. But she's safe just as long as you
follow orders." Air pushed through his nostrils in an attempt
at a snicker. "She's real safe—heck, they're keepin' her in an

259

old abandoned church, if that makes you feel any better. It's a nice place, not far from where I was born, as a matter of fact. But I'm just bringing you to Miz Broderick. She'll let you know when you can see your daughter." Leering, he added, "We'll have a bit of time in between to get to know each other better."

I swallowed thickly. "Where are we going?"

"To the train depot in Atlanta. And from there, we're to take the Western and Atlantic railroad to Dalton to see our fine boys in gray, and to a Mrs. Simpson's boarding house. Don't know how Mrs. Broderick plans on getting you to Chattanooga from there, but I'm sure she's got it all worked out." He looked down at my hands. "First we got to find you a stream to wash that blood off your hands. People might start asking questions."

I didn't answer but rested my head on the back of the seat and closed my eyes. But the memory of Stuart kept coming back to me, and my eyes shot open again, my heart filled with dread. I pressed a fist to my heart, his name on my lips as I prayed that Charles had helped him in time.

Failing to save Sarah was not an option. I had already lost too much. I had to approach my task single-mindedly, allowing no other thoughts to crowd my objective.

We reached Atlanta around noon, and Matt had to struggle to steer the buggy through the pandemonium of the city. People bustled about on foot and in every kind of conveyance. The dirt roads had been reduced to muddy ruts, but the hurried pedestrians and wagon drivers carried on as if they were asphalt.

Matt stopped the buggy in front of the train depot. Lines of red dust caked the creases in my dress. I had no mirror, but I knew my face looked equally dirty.

We each grabbed a carpetbag and went in search of the ticket window inside. I gasped at the sack of gold coins Matt pulled from his jacket. He winked at me. "There's plenty more where this came from." I remembered what Pamela had told me about her followers, about how they would do anything for money.

I sat on a bench to wait, and Matt walked down the platform. The hands on the station clock seemed to move in slow motion, each minute seeming more like ten, and an hour like a whole day. The platform grew more and more crowded during the three-hour wait, the din of voices rising as the sounds of a distant train came from down the track.

Matt tugged on my arm. "It's time. Come on."

Matt was now affecting an exaggerated limp, presumably to explain the fact that he wore no uniform. I paused to read a broadside on a pillar. It read:

NOTICE! All able-bodied men between the ages of 20 and 50 are earnestly called upon to join the Southern Army. Rally to the call of your countrymen in the field. One united effort, and those Northern hirelings will soon be driven from our sunny South.

I hurried to catch up, brushing by two soldiers reeking of cheap whiskey, and moved to the steps of the train, where a soldier stood examining traveling papers. He looked at Matt, who nodded; then he looked in the other direction as I mounted the steps and boarded the train. I began to understand the reason for carrying so many gold coins.

As I settled on the seat next to Matt, he stared straight ahead. In a low voice, he said, "Don't sit next to me. Nobody's supposed to know we're traveling together." He then turned toward the window and gazed out in silence.

I stood and grabbed my carpetbag and looked for another seat. The press of bodies in the car made it almost impossible. But, a man across the aisle stood, and before anybody else could spot the vacant seat, I plopped myself into it.

An attractive woman with a little boy and girl sat next to me. She didn't look much older than me, but lines of worry and exhaustion streaked her face. Holding her infant in her arms, it was all she could do to keep the little girl from squeezing past me and toddling down the aisle of the car. I turned and offered to hold the baby boy. With no hesitation and a look of deep gratitude, she handed him to me.

I looked down into enormous blue eyes, and my heart jumped. With those eyes, this boy could be Stuart's child. A child I knew I could never have. He studied my face and stuck a chubby finger at my nose. I laughed, and he laughed back, forging a tender trust.

The mother excused herself and left her seat to retrieve her daughter. After settling herself back down, she said, "Thank you so much. You seem to have a mother's touch."

I smiled back. "So it would seem. He's really adorable."

"Thank you." She tucked the little girl behind one arm and extended her gloved hand to shake. "I'm Elizabeth Crandall. This is my daughter, Alice, and my son, Reed."

"It's a pleasure to meet you. I'm Laura Tru . . . I mean El-liott."

She nodded at the wedding ring on my finger. "Are you going to see your husband?"

I shook my head. "No. He's—uh, he's in Roswell right now. What about you?"

"I hope to. Isaac doesn't know I'm coming—he actually told me that it would be too dangerous. But I know General Johnston will never let the Yankees into Georgia. I hope to reach him so we can celebrate a Confederate victory together." Her confidence sounded forced, and her sad eyes betrayed her true feelings.

I gave her hand a squeeze. "I'm sure he'll be happy to see you and his children."

Reed arched his head back, and I nearly lost my grip. Eliz-abeth let go of Alice to catch him. Seeing her chance, Alice headed straight across the aisle and landed smack in Matt's lap. Matt's head rolled forward groggily as he awoke from his nap, and his eyes focused on the plump toddler. Alice looked up into his face, let out a loud hiccup, and began to scream. I grabbed her and began patting her on the back.

We rode for several hours, chatting about children and re-covering her wayward toddler from other parts of the car. In mid-sentence, I was nearly jerked from my seat by the sudden screeching of the train's brakes. People raced to the windows, straining to see what the problem was. Leaning my head out the window, I spied three soldiers in gray galloping alongside the train. We continued to slow until we came to a complete stop. Two of the men dismounted and entered the engineer's cab.

A man standing next to me, wearing a long duster and a straw hat, stuck his head out the window and shouted to the remaining soldier on horseback. "What's the problem? Why have we stopped?"

The soldier rode up to our window and called back, "We've orders to search for a Yankee spy. She is believed to be on this train."

"Under whose orders? And who is she?"

"Major Stuart Elliott has issued the orders to search the train. The spy's name is Laura Elliott, and she is traveling with a man."

My breath came in deep gasps. Stuart was alive, and I couldn't shout with joy at the news. Instead, I felt my blood flood my skin. I glanced at Elizabeth and found her staring at me, her eyes wide. Then I looked over to where Matt had been sitting. He was gone.

The man in the long coat continued. "Will this take long? I'm headed for Dalton to take a photograph of General Johnston. I don't want to be late."

"Sorry, sir. We're under orders. We will have to detain this train until we can examine every passenger on it."

"Damn," the man said, as he slid off his hat and wiped his forehead. "Begging your pardon," he said to Elizabeth and myself.

The engineer appeared at the door to our car, followed by the two soldiers. I caught Elizabeth's eye, and she gave me an almost imperceptible nod.

"Everybody off the train. We are under orders to have every person on this train interrogated. Everybody off the train."

Children screamed and adults grumbled as we all piled off. Great puffs of smoke climbed over us, and the hot smell of steam and metal filled the air. I spotted Matt standing near the passengers from the first-class compartment. He didn't acknowledge me.

263

The soldiers started with the people from the first car.

"Don't worry," Elizabeth whispered to me. "I'll take care of it. Let's sit."

I sat down, Alice on my lap. Elizabeth sat next to me, cradling a sleeping Reed.

"Why would you risk yourself for me? How do you know I'm not a Yankee spy?"

"Are you?"

"No."

"Well, then. I didn't think so. But you're obviously in trouble and need help. You've been an enormous help to me; let me repay the favor."

"Thank you." I didn't know what she planned, but I knew it couldn't be any worse than the reason I was on the train in the first place.

The man in the long duster approached us. "Pardon me," he said, doffing his hat. I stared at his face, with the dark pointy beard and unkempt brown hair. He looked vaguely familiar. "Would you two ladies like to sit for a photograph?"

The last thing in the world I wanted at that moment was to call attention to myself. But Elizabeth yanked me to my feet and said, "Yes. We would be delighted."

"Forgive my manners, ladies. Allow me to introduce myself. I'm Mr. Matthew Brady, photographer. And if you will allow me and my assistants to fetch and set up my equipment, I would like to capture your images for the sake of history."

I had to forcibly keep my mouth from hanging open. Now I knew why his face seemed familiar. My father had several books of Brady's famous Civil War photographs, one with his picture emblazoned on the front cover.

Elizabeth introduced us, giving me the last name of Crandall, and I stepped forward. "I'm familiar with your work, Mr. Brady. I'd be honored."

While I kept a stealthy eye on Matt for any signal and the soldiers worked their way down the line of passengers, Mr. Brady's two assistants hauled a large trunk out onto the grass and began setting up the equipment. The famous photographer made a fuss about securing a sleeping compartment inside the train for a dark room. One assistant was sent racing back to the train with large sheets of dark cloth.

They set a large wooden box camera atop a tripod and began adjusting it while I kept my eyes on the approaching soldiers.

A soldier began talking with Matt, and he pulled out a white envelope and handed it to the soldier for inspection. The man scanned it briefly, showed it to his companion, and then handed it back before stepping toward the next person in line.

"Ready, ladies, when you are." I turned back to the famous photographer, who had taken off his hat. The children began to fuss, so Elizabeth left my side to see about them. I absently fingered the chain around my neck, feeling the rise and fall of the warm metal in the afternoon sunshine. My hand fell to the key at the bottom of the chain, and I grabbed it to tuck it into my dress. As it slid smoothly down my skin, I froze. The image of a sepia-toned photograph of a woman in nineteenth-century clothing flashed across my memory. The woman, who looked exactly like me, had been wearing a key on a chain.

"Ready? Don't move!" I stood still, not bearing to breath. I stared at the hunched shape under the dark cloth and wanted to laugh. The pieces in this unbelievable puzzle were starting to fall into place. My only hope now was to finish the puzzle without losing any of the pieces. I pulled the necklace back out and placed it in the middle of my bodice. An exact replica of the old picture.

A fly droned past my ear, but I remained still to allow for the long exposure time of the film and thought wistfully of my automatic camera that took pictures with the press of a button.

The soldiers had reached our group just as the shutter clicked. Elizabeth came to stand next to me, a squalling child under each arm. "Here, take one," she said, thrusting Reed at me.

I grabbed him, the odor of baby spit-up and milk filling the air. I looked up as a soldier approached. "Ma'am," he said, tipping his hat.

I looked into somber brown eyes. "Sorry, ma'am, but I have to ask you a few questions."

Reed gurgled and burped in response. Something wet and warm drizzled down my wrist and under my sleeve. "I understand. But please make it quick," I said, holding Reed out in front of me to illustrate my point.

"Yes, ma'am," he said, wrinkling his nose. "What is your name?"

"Laura Crandall," I lied without hesitation.

"Are you traveling alone?"

I glanced at my small companion. "Not exactly."

His weary expression didn't change. "May I see your traveling papers?"

"She's with me." Elizabeth came and stood next to me, a finally quiet Alice perched on her hip.

His gaze took Elizabeth in from head to foot. "And what is your relationship with this woman?"

She looked him in the eye. "She's my sister-in-law. We're going up to Dalton to visit my husband, her brother, who is fighting for our glorious Cause."

She straightened herself to her full height, which was all of about five feet, and stared at him.

"May I see your traveling papers?"

Elizabeth unfurled a piece of paper and gave it to the soldier. He glanced at it quickly and looked back at Elizabeth.

"It doesn't mention a traveling companion."

Elizabeth stared back at the man, unblinking. "No. I'm afraid it was all last minute. This dear woman insisted on accompanying me to help me with my precious children. I just don't know what I would have done without her."

To prove her point, I knelt down, laid the baby on his back, and began to unwrap his diaper. "Elizabeth, do you have a clean nappy? He really needs to be changed." I looked up at the soldier, who was busily looking at everything but us. "Any more questions?" I asked.

"Uh, no, ma'am, no. I think I've heard all I need to know. You're both free to reboard."

Hastily rewrapping Reed in a fresh diaper, I then scooped

him up and followed Elizabeth and Alice back to the train. As I stood on the bottom step, somebody grabbed me from behind. I turned around. Matt stood there, holding my carpetbag. "Let's go."

Elizabeth looked down at me with a sad smile, and I handed Reed to her. "Good-bye, Laura." She studied my face for a moment. "I hope you find what you're looking for."

Our hands touched for a moment before Matt pulled me off the step; then, with one last look at Elizabeth and her children, I ducked and followed Matt under the train to the other side.

I brushed at my skirts, not having had the time to pull them up before being made to crawl on all fours under the train. "Why are we leaving?"

Without answering, Matt pulled on my arm and began running across an empty field toward the cover of woods approximately one hundred yards away. Turning his head toward me, he spat, "Because your damned husband is at the other end of the train."

I yanked my arm from his grasp and stopped. "Stuart's here?"

"God damn it, woman, you're sorely trying my patience. Do you want him to find you? You ain't never going to see your daughter if we don't get away from here real quick-like."

The train blocked my view of everything on the other side of the railcars, effectively blocking their view of us, too.

Matt grabbed my arm again. "Come on—it's only a matter of time before somebody on the train sees us and passes along the information."

With one last look at the train, I lifted my skirts as high as I could and began running to the edge of the woods. As I neared the scrubby pines, I stumbled on a root, sprawling on my stomach, the wind knocked out of me.

The ground rumbled, and I rolled over and stared at the sky in confusion. It wasn't until Matt towered over me and began dragging me into the woods that I realized I was hearing hoofbeats. Dizzily, I scrambled to my feet, half dragged by Matt, and looked back toward the train. I recognized Endy first, and then the man sitting astride him, one arm bandaged immobile against his side, his body heavily over the horse's neck.

Matt shoved me, face forward, into the dense forest, and we began running as fast as we could. We headed toward a small hill, the pines and overgrowth covering it so completely that it looked like the hump of a great beast. When we reached it, he pushed me down to hide behind some bushes and then crouched next to me.

My cheeks stung from the whipping of branches, and small gnats danced around the trickles of blood, but I dared not move.

We crouched in absolute silence for a long while, and my legs had begun to ache, but there was still no sign of Stuart. Mixed with my joy at knowing him to be alive was my fear that if he found me, I would lose my daughter—and maybe him—forever. I closed my eyes and listened but heard no more than the wind through the leaves.

From a distance, the sound of the steam engine starting and moving off vibrated through the earth. The chugging dissipated down unseen tracks, and then there was silence again. Finally Matt shifted. Satisfied that we were alone, he stood, then reached out a hand to me.

A booming sound filled my ears, and Matt seemed to jump, then sprawl backward against the tree behind us. He bounced against the trunk and came to a rest next to me, his hand sliding across my cheek as he fell. I recoiled, seeing the gaping wound in the middle of his chest, white bone visible like a maggot in decaying meat.

I struggled to my feet, my hands held over my head. "Stuart—it's me, Laura. Please don't shoot!"

"I wouldn't shoot my own wife."

Startled, I whipped around, finding him only a few yards away, his hunting rifle now pointed at the ground. I hadn't heard him approach, and I wondered if Zeke had taught him how to move like a Cherokee. Relief and fear flooded me, making my knees shake.

He took a step forward. "But I'd certainly like to wring her neck."

I moved backward, against a slender sapling, alarmed at the

pallor of his skin and the way his eyes darkened as he looked at me.

He took another step forward and stopped. I watched as his eyes rolled up into his head, and his knees buckled as he slid to the ground.

"The wind goeth toward the south, and turneth about unto the north; it whirleth about continually, and the wind returneth again according to his circuits."

Ecclesiastes 1:6

Chapter Twenty-three

I dropped to my knees and bent my ear to his face to feel the reassuring warmth of his breath on my cheek. Realizing he had fainted, I unbuttoned his jacket and the top of his shirt, feeling the bulk of bandaging under the thin cotton. Blood had begun to seep through the bandages, making me aware of how serious his wound was.

"You damned fool," I said to his closed eyes. "You should have stayed at Phoenix Hall, where Charles could care for you properly."

Blue eyes opened briefly. "I am a damned fool—but not for this." His voice sounded strained, as if it took all his effort just to speak. "And I'm not that badly hurt. The bullet passed clean through the flesh to the other side." He took a deep breath, his eyelids fluttering. "I'm ... here to take ... you back with me."

I reached under my skirt and began ripping the cotton ruffle from a petticoat. "I can't go back with you, Stuart." I had to make him understand, and the only way I could was to tell

269

him the truth. I took a deep breath. "Sarah's in great danger. Pamela is holding her hostage unless I help . . ." I could barely say the words. "Unless I help her assassinate General Sherman."

He struggled feebly to sit up, but I pressed him down. Gasping heavily, he squeezed out words between each breath. "I will not . . . allow you . . . to put yourself . . . in danger."

He winced as I struggled to sit him up against the tree. "You don't have a choice. You can barely breathe, much less chase me through the woods."

Narrowed eyes regarded me solemnly. "But my men could."

I'd forgotten all about the other soldiers. My hands stilled. "Don't. Sarah's life is at stake. And I'm the only one who can help her."

I raised his shirt and wrapped my petticoat ruffle around his chest, tightening the pressure on his wound to stanch the flow of blood.

He grabbed my wrist, and our gazes locked. "Damn it, Laura. Why won't you let me help you? You are no longer alone in this world."

I shook my head, fighting the sting of tears in my eyes. "No. If Pamela finds out I've told you, or solicited help, she will kill Sarah. I don't doubt it."

He winced as I pulled him forward to reach around him. "Do you have any idea where Sarah might be?"

With a glance over at Matt's body, I leaned Stuart gently back against the tree. "Only what Matt told me—that she was being held in an old abandoned church. I have no idea where—except Matt did say it was near where he was born."

His forehead was beaded with sweat. "Matt's father was a preacher." He winced, closing his eyes. "It could be that church. It's in Alpharetta—about a day's ride from here."

I sat back on my heels, my heart heavy. "Will your men find you?"

He paused, then nodded. "Endy will show them."

Thunder rumbled overhead as fat drops of rain pelted the leaves and branches, dribbling their way down to where we sat. He lifted his arm, reaching for me, and I leaned forward.

His fingers brushed my cheek, then cupped my jaw, sliding around to the back of my neck. He pulled me toward him, then kissed me deeply, and I lost myself in it. The smell of the rain and wet wool brought me back to awareness, and I pulled back, worried I had hurt him.

His eyes were dark with pain and something else, his words low as he spoke. "I'm half out of my mind with pain, and with anger at you, and still I want you. This wanting of you is sure to kill me if nothing else does."

I gently laid my head on his chest, and his fingers found my hair. "I'm sorry, Stuart. I'm so sorry." I buried my face in his neck, kissing him softly, then raised my head and stood.

He grunted, trying to sit up. "Laura, don't go. I love you. We can find Sarah."

I swallowed my tears, too tired to shed any. "If she's not where you think she is, and I don't show up to see Pamela, they will kill her. And I will not fail my daughter again."

He crumpled back against the tree, and I turned to retrieve my carpetbag, which Matt had dropped as we flew into our hiding spot. It was stuck under one of his legs, and I shuddered as I moved to retrieve it.

I faced Stuart, clutching the red carpetbag. "There's a bag of gold coins in Matt's coat. Take it. You'll need it after the war's over." I ducked my head. "Go home, Stuart. If I know you're being taken care of, that's one less thing I'll have to worry about."

His voice was barely more than a whisper. "Stay, Laura."

Swallowing hard, I shook my head, turned away, then headed up the hill in the dense underbrush.

The rainstorm ended as quickly as it had begun, and I was grateful that I didn't have to slog through mud. I was a poor navigator, despite my four years as a Girl Scout. All I knew was that the train I was on had been headed north to the town of Dalton. So I stayed in the woods but kept close to the edge, where I could follow the bends of the rail tracks. I listened for a while for sounds of pursuit, and when none came, I relaxed a bit. I hoisted my skirts and knotted them as high as I could to make walking easier, only lowering them when the woods gave way to sparsely populated farmland. A road grew out of the fields, and I followed it for a while until a wagon piled high with lumber ambled by. The old man holding the reins showed no surprise at my disheveled appearance when I asked him if the road would take me to Dalton. He nodded solemnly and then offered me a ride. I didn't need any persuasion to accept his offer, and I climbed up onto the running board before he could change his mind. The man did not utter a word, and for a time I thought he had drifted into sleep. I took off my shoes to examine my blisters, starting as the man shouted and slapped the reins at a bumblebee.

He dropped me off at the Dalton train depot, for lack of anywhere else to go. I thanked him, and he rode on, a single hand held up in farewell.

At the ticket window, I asked for directions for Mrs. Simpson's rooming house, the place Matt had told me Pamela was staying. Dreading every step, I headed off for the short walk.

Full dark had settled over the town, the street lamps coloring the clusters of Confederate soldiers a faded yellow. Women, many wearing black, scurried across streets with baskets over their arms or holding on to small children. I wondered if there might be a curfew and quickened my step.

Pamela answered my tapping on the door. When she looked past me into the hallway, I told her simply, "Matt's dead. Confederate soldiers stopped our train and chased us into the woods. He was shot, but I managed to escape."

I kept my voice steady and my gaze firm, never mentioning Stuart. Her eyes flickered over my appearance, and then she held the door wide to allow me in.

"Does anyone know you're here?"

I shook my head slowly.

"Let's hope you're right." She closed the door behind me with a final thud.

I gave myself a sponge bath behind the screen in the room and slipped on a nightgown, pleased to finally rid myself of my torn and tired traveling dress. If it weren't for my growling stomach, I would have been too tired to make it to one of the two single beds.

To remain inconspicuous, we ate our dinner of chicken dumplings, yams, and cornbread in our room. Tight knots clenched my stomach, but I still found my appetite and cleaned my plate, chewing slowly while my mind digested my thoughts.

Pamela's small teeth ground her food, her jawbone jutting out from the colorless skin on her face. As I studied her, my mind skittered in all directions. I thought of Stuart on his way home to Phoenix Hall, where he could completely recover. A part of me wanted him to stay weak for several more months, to keep him out of the war.

We placed our trays outside the door; then Pamela began to dress for bed. As she removed her clothes, I heard the distinct sound of rustling paper. I turned and watched in amazement as she relieved her petticoat of its unusual fullness at the sides and rear by drawing out four newspapers. On her bed she laid out the *Cincinnati Enquirer*, the *New York Daily Times*, and *The Philadelphia Evening Ledger*. I approached the bed and glanced at the dates—all recent editions.

"What are these for?" I asked, thumbing through the Philadelphia paper.

She snatched it out of my hands and stacked them on the floor next to her bed. "They're for our army, of course. To give General Johnston and his staff some insight on the status of Yankee morale and such. Our neighbors to the north are worried about Grant's losses in the east. One more staggering defeat of Federal forces, and I do believe the Yankees will be ready to sue for peace." She grinned widely at me. "The death of Sherman and the resulting loss of morale amongst his men will be the turning point in this war, you mark my words." She chortled with glee as she pulled the bedclothes from the bed. "Mrs. Simpson is a friend of mine and will be sure to deliver these to General Johnston tomorrow."

I watched as she placed a revolver under her pillow and lay down. "Go to sleep, Laura. We've a very busy day ahead."

Pamela turned down the lamp, and as I watched the flickering shadows disappear from the walls, a thought occurred to me. "How will we get to Chattanooga? It's held by the Federals, and I can't imagine them letting us walk right in."

Her voice was sharp in the quiet night air. "We'll have to depend on our own resources and the fact that you are related to an officer on General Sherman's personal staff."

I sat up straight in the bed, my eyes squinting in the dark in Pamela's direction. "What? What are you talking about?"

I could hear the smile in her voice. "Your new brother-in-law, dear. Stuart's older brother. Captain William Elliott, aide-de-camp for General Sherman."

"Oh." I recalled the scar on Stuart's chest and all the things I had heard about William. Knowing William's relationship with his brother and Julia, I was unsure if he could be relied on to be an ally. "And he's supposed to help us get rid of General Sherman?"

"No! And I know you're smart enough not to enlighten him on the matter. He believes me to be a Yankee spy. How else do you think I've been able to get the information to pass on to Stuart? William is merely our passage into the general's company. And then you will take it from there."

I thought of the red-velvet dress with the low neckline I had brought with me. "You're going to have to be more specific than that, Pamela. I haven't a clue how to be a seductress."

"Then you had better start practicing. But I don't think you'll have to do much; men seem to flock to you, regardless." I saw a dark shape against the whiteness of the wall, like a shadow in a nightmare, and realized she was also sitting up in bed, looking directly at me. "I will arrange for you and the general to be alone, to get to know each other. You will suggest a secret rendezvous and your complete discretion. When he meets with you, I want you to blow his head off."

I shuddered. An owl hooted in a tree not far from our window, and I wanted to climb up the tree with him and watch all of this from a safe distance. Instead, I found myself an actress in the middle of this macabre play, with only one way off the stage. Murder. I placed a hand on my heart and felt it fluttering rapidly. I willed it to slow by taking deep breaths.

What if I succeeded in forcing myself to kill General Sherman? Would the war continue longer and the blood of thousands be on my hands? The outcome was immeasurable, unfathomable, and certainly unpredictable. Then I thought of my daughter, scared and alone, her fate an unknown, and knew I didn't have a choice.

I lay back down on the cool cotton sheets and eventually fell asleep in the early hours of the morning.

We left the rooming house before dawn, sneaking down the back stairs and out the door without detection, and headed north through the woods. I shivered in the dark, trying to make out the moonlit shapes in front of me. My long skirts caught on brambles and twigs, so I eventually hoisted them up over my knees, exposing stockings with more holes than fabric. After a couple of hours, I stopped from weariness, prickles of sweat beading my forehead. I dropped my carpetbag and opened my hands, which had been clutching the handle and my skirts, painfully stretching the small bones and muscles. The blood-red sun appeared low in the sky, bleeding light into the dark forest.

"Do you have any idea where you're going, Pamela?"

She stopped about ten yards ahead of me. "Of course. I have studied this terrain for years. Now pick up your bag, and let's keep going. We've a lot of ground to cover."

I stayed where I was, swaying with exhaustion, tiny gnats flitting about my face. "How many miles from Dalton to Chattanooga?"

"About thirty. But don't worry—we will commandeer a horse as soon as we see one."

I grabbed my bag and hurried up behind her. "You want us to steal a horse?"

She didn't answer, and we plowed on. We followed the railroad tracks of the Western & Atlantic, trying to stay out of sight. A few miles west of town, we had to walk on the tracks through a narrow gap in two facing rock walls—what Pamela called Rocky Face Ridge. I said a silent prayer that no trains would come, as there would be no room for us to escape.

275

By mid-morning, we reached a clearing. Pamela motioned me back, and I peered from behind her to see a wooden rail fence enclosing a large pasture. The morning breeze carried the pungent aroma of horse manure. A saddleless horse stood on the far side of the pasture, its head in the tall grass. I looked past the horse to the white farmhouse, where a woman stood next to a woodpile, her ax raised before she drove it into a log. Two little boys ran around barefoot in the dirt, causing the mother to stop her chopping and bark at them, with little effect.

The woman's husband was nowhere in sight—a familiar occurrence in these times. I worried about her vulnerability, perched as she was between two opposing armies. My gaze traveled along the side of the house until I saw her only protection—a long rifle leaning against the brick chimney.

"We can't take this woman's horse," I said. "It looks like it's the only piece of livestock she's got left."

Pamela snorted. "If we don't take it, the Yankee army will. Probably kill it, too, just to prevent the Rebels from getting it. It's well past its prime, but it will do."

"But she's got a gun."

Pamela patted her pocket. "So do we."

I turned to see if she was bluffing but could tell from the glint in her eye that she wasn't.

"Let's walk around to the other side of the fence."

She led me to the edge of the woods before ordering me to crawl. I longed for my jeans. Maneuvering in long skirts on this journey was a nightmare. We reached the other side without incident and stopped by the rail fence, not ten feet from the horse. It eyed us lazily and resumed munching.

"What now?" I whispered.

"Give me your bag."

I complied, not sure what my other options were. She reached inside and pulled out a carrot, one of several we had taken from a root cellar earlier in the morning, and handed it to me.

"Go show this to the horse, and make him come to the fence so we can mount him."

Even though I had learned how to get along with Endy, I still hated horses. Even mild-mannered horses like this one made me jittery. Still, I knew it was hopeless to argue, so I took the carrot and entered the fenced-in area.

The horse showed only mild curiosity as I approached but at least raised his head from the grass. I showed him the orange vegetable, and he began walking toward me. The reverberating thwacks in the distance told me the woman was still chopping wood and hadn't noticed that her only form of transportation was being stolen from right under her nose.

I backed up, the carrot raised in front of me, until I felt the fence at my back. Pamela had climbed to the top rail and easily slid her leg over the back of the horse. I flattened my hand, as Stuart had shown me, and gave the entire carrot to the horse. While he busily munched, I handed up the carpetbags, climbed the fence, and settled in front of Pamela.

It was then I noticed that the chopping sounds had ceased. We both turned in time to see the woman race toward the side of the house and grab the rifle.

I dug my heels into the sides of the horse just as I felt a ripple of air to my right and the resounding report of a gun behind me. The horse lurched forward, nearly toppling both of us off his back, and then began to gallop. Luckily, the horse wore a halter, giving me a grip. I leaned forward over the neck, Pamela clinging tightly to my middle, the carpetbags tucked securely between us. I felt us listing to the right but maintained a tenacious hold as I heard another shot fired from the house. I threw one last look behind me and saw the woman standing in the middle of the pasture, her arms loose at her sides, staring forlornly at us as we disappeared with her horse into the woods.

We slowed our pace once we were within the shadow of the woods. We found a well-worn dirt road through the forest and headed north. Soon after, we heard hoofbeats in front of us. Quickly guiding the horse off the road, we hid amongst the tall trees and underbrush as a detachment of Yankee soldiers rode by, their crisp navy-blue uniforms in marked contrast to the tattered and mismatched uniforms of the Confederate soldiers we had seen in the previous days. As the last soldier passed us, Pamela whispered, "We're almost there. Be prepared to be stopped by the Yankees' advance guard. Don't protest—they will shoot."

We pulled back onto the road and resumed our ambling pace, the old horse frothing slightly at the mouth. I felt sorry for it and tried hard not to shift my weight too much.

I swiped my forehead with my sleeve. "How did you come here—to this time?"

"The same way all of us marked as Shadow Warriors travel. Wrapped in the atmosphere of a comet intensified by a lunar eclipse." The droning of a fly interrupted her, and she swatted it away with her hand. "You see, every comet has a set orbital time period. For instance, Halley's Comet reappears every seventy-six years. It has been doing this since the beginning of time and will continue until the end of time. And a Shadow Warrior, being in the right place and the right time, can be swept up in the tail of the comet and moved within the comet's orbital time period." She took a deep breath. "With practice, one can navigate within any orbital time period."

"What do you mean, 'navigate'?"

I glanced back at her, and she gave me a look with the exaggerated patience of a teacher with a slow student. "If I want to travel back two hundred years, I don't necessarily need to find a comet with a two-hundred-year orbit—just one in which the time period between now and then is divisible into two hundred. Like a fifty-year comet. One would just need to navigate to arrive in the correct time."

"But how does one learn to navigate?" I asked, more confused than ever.

She touched my forehead with a long, pale finger. "You use parts of your mind that are usually ignored." A thin smile appeared on her lips. "But sometimes it happens accidentally. Just like you—and Sarah—with Ginetti's Comet."

The name startled me. "How did you know about Ginetti's Comet?"

She laughed, a dry and brittle sound. "I know the orbits of every comet that's been and will be. And I also know the places where the powers are strongest. Moon Mountain is one of only three."

My heart beat faster. Finding the answers to my questions might allow me to control my own future—assuming I had one. "One of three? How did you learn about this phenomenon? It's not exactly science book material."

She pulled out a handkerchief to wipe her face, then placed it back in her skirt pocket. Taking a deep breath, she continued, "For centuries the Cherokees and other native people around the world have passed down legends. As a history major at Vanderbilt, I became fascinated, almost obsessed. And when I found a picture of an ancient Cherokee carving that matched my birthmark, I knew there had to be some truth to the stories. The legend of the dragons that would mysteriously appear and disappear on Moon Mountain certainly intrigued me. There seemed to be a void or a warp there that would trap ancient, or perhaps future, creatures in this place. But they were always hunted down and killed, as were the people who were caught traveling through time. They were considered an aberration of nature that needed to be destroyed." She shrugged. "The one thing I haven't been able to ascertain is how many of us there are. I suspect the number is quite small—perhaps one or two every generation."

I shifted, her words making me uncomfortable. "Don't you miss your family, your friends? Aren't they worrying about you?"

She snorted. "People disappear every day. Besides, there was no one to miss me. I made sure of that."

I thought of my parents and my friends and wondered if they were still looking for me and how long they would continue searching before they gave up. And then I thought of Stuart, and I knew in my heart that he would search for me forever.

The plodding pace soothed me, each step lulling me closer to sleep until I felt myself fall over the horse's neck. Pamela yanked me up by the back of my dress. It was then I noticed that the sounds around us had changed. The birds had stopped twittering in the trees—even the crickets had stopped their incessant chirping. I looked up through the thick canopy of trees and saw clouds creeping over the sun and casting us in shadow. But there were no storm clouds, nothing to cause the rippling of flesh up my spine.

I stifled a scream as a man in a dark-blue uniform stepped out of the trees in front of us, his rifle pointing at my chest.

"Halt!"

Leaves above us rustled, and I craned my neck to see another soldier roosting on a branch, his weapon trained on a spot near my head. I pulled on the horse's bridle hoping it would stop. A speckled yellow leaf drifted down onto my lap as the sniper scrambled down to stand in front of us. He was at least a head shorter than the other soldier, with light blond fuzz covering his cheeks. He looked no more than nineteen.

The taller soldier walked over to us. "What have we got here, Johnny? A couple of Rebs, if you ask me."

Johnny took off his hat. "They're just women, Corporal." His rifle wavered but remained fixed on us.

Without lowering his gun, the tall corporal asked, "Who are you, and what are you doing here?"

Pamela shifted the carpetbags, which seemed to have made a permanent dent in my back, and reached for her pocket.

"Stop!" The corporal approached the side of the horse and, without apology, stuck his hand in Pamela's pocket. I forced myself to remain calm and reminded myself that Pamela was smart enough to have removed her gun.

My heart sank as he pulled out a folded letter. I stole a glance at Pamela, but her eyes were on the soldier, staring at him expectantly. "Open it."

He did, and then looked back at Pamela, while Johnny reached for the letter. "Are you Mrs. Pamela Broderick?"

She nodded, her eyelids downcast in mock servitude.

He indicated me with his rifle. "And who is this?"

"This is Laura Elliott, William Elliott's sister-in-law."

"And you are Captain Elliott's mother-in-law?"

Again she nodded.

"Is he expecting you?"

She shook her head. "No. But I'm carrying important information for him to pass onto our General Sherman. Once I obtained it, it was too late to notify Captain Elliott—and far too dangerous. The information I'm carrying is much too sensitive to fall into enemy hands."

I peered down at the letter in his hand. I recognized the handwriting from old letters from William that Julia had shown me.

"Why is this young lady with you?" The shorter soldier spoke to Pamela but stared at me.

"I needed her for protection. I'm an old lady—not as strong as I used to be."

The boy raised his eyebrows and looked at me. "Are you armed?"

Pamela answered, "No, but she's a lot stronger than she looks."

I sat quietly on the horse, my hands clenched tightly in front of me.

The older soldier ordered us to dismount, taking a step backward as I reached the ground. His gaze traveled up and down me while he spoke. "Ladies, we will escort you to our sergeant. He will bring you to the Provost Marshal, who will decide if you will see General Sherman." He turned his head slightly and spat a long stream of dark brown juice out of the side of his mouth, wiping the remaining bits clinging to his lip with his sleeve. "And if you aren't who you say you are, Uncle Billy will probably string you up, women or not."

The younger soldier led the way, and we followed him down the path. I saw more shadows in the woods and knew we were being watched by other soldiers on picket duty. Our two guards no longer pointed their rifles at us but still held them where they could easily be aimed and fired. The taller one led the horse by his bridle.

"Why do you call him 'Uncle Billy'?" I asked.

Johnny answered with a shy smile. "That's what we call General Sherman, on account of him being one of us. Real personable. Me and the corporal been with him since Shiloh, and there just ain't a better soldier." He paused for a moment. "But he doesn't much like women, preachers, or newspaper people in his camp, that's for sure. I'd recommend telling him what you need to and then getting out of the way."

For the first time in this odyssey, I was nervous. I remembered pictures I'd seen of the sour-faced Sherman and his reputation in Georgia as being the Nero of the nineteenth century. This was the man I was supposed to seduce? Being shot sounded like a fine alternative.

We walked in silence, our footsteps punctuated by the occasional wet slap of tobacco juice and spittle against dead leaves. We crested a ridge, and I felt a tightening in my chest. Below me lay the South's destruction. White canvas tents filled with men in blue uniforms covered the green slopes and hills. I sighed into the breeze as I eyed the show of strength before me. Soldiers hurried between tents like ants at a picnic, scurrying from one place to another. Horses and artillery crowded the far rise, and I sucked in my breath at this show of force. History said that the pride and patriotism of Johnston's Southern army would be laid low in the deep grass of Georgia's hills, bowed down in the face of the awesome power of lead and the sheer numbers that lay before me. But the ink in the history books was apparently not indelible. It could be changed.

Our procession attracted stares and downright leers as we were led into the encampment. I was acutely aware of my status as a female in a sea of males who were prepared to die. I gathered my skirts closely around me and hugged the carpetbag over my chest.

Campfires dotted the field, and the smells of bacon and coffee made my mouth water. I hadn't eaten a meal since dinner the previous evening.

Our horse had been left on the outskirts of the camp. I wanted to ask someone to take it back to the woman we had stolen it from but realized that perhaps she wouldn't welcome the soldiers on her isolated farm with only her single rifle to protect herself.

It was late afternoon before we found our way into Chattanooga. We had been given horses to ride and escorted from the encampment by four soldiers from 7th Company, Ohio

Sharpshooters. I could feel my hair springing loose from its pins and straggling against my neck. My skirt had a jagged tear up to the knee, exposing my ripped petticoat and holes from my two days of walking through the forest. I was sure dark circles of exhaustion ringed my eyes. Hopefully, my brother-in-law would have pity on us and take us in without question.

We entered a large house at 110 East First Street. I was given to understand that the house had been commandeered from the wealthy Lattner family, who had fled the city when the Yankees first captured it in 1863.

Rich carvings accented the tall ceilings, and crystal chandeliers glittered light into the rooms. Our feet tapped on black-and-white marble floors, heralding our arrival. We were shown into the parlor and left alone to wait for William.

Pamela seated herself on a red velvet sofa and stared at me with level eyes. Desperate for a mirror, I searched the room for anything reflective. I noticed a petticoat mirror at the bottom of the buffet, for the ladies to unobtrusively check to see if their underskirts were visible below their dresses. Being unobtrusive wasn't a current concern, so I knelt on the floor to inspect the damage to my hair and face.

I licked my fingers and began to remove a dirty smudge from my chin and was in the midst of scrubbing it when I heard a throat being cleared. Too deep to be Pamela. I stood, hitting my head on the ledge of the buffet and knocking a dish to the floor, shattering blue-and-white china into tiny pieces.

Rubbing my head, I stood and found myself staring into familiar blue eyes. My heart skipped a beat as I looked at his face, seeing the beloved similarities. The hair was the same, straight and dark and parted to the side. The nose a trifle longer, a bit haughtier. The same strong jawline. But there was something else—a fundamental difference. No light shone behind these eyes. I peered into them and saw only coldness in the icy blue depths.

I forced myself to smile at him. "You must be William."

He looked at Pamela in confusion. "What is going on here?" He looked back at me and let his gaze travel up my costume—

from my mud-encrusted shoes to my dirty face and wayward hair. He narrowed his eyes. "Who are you?"

"I'm Laura Elliott. Your sister-in-law." I couldn't stop myself from staring.

"My sister-in-law?" Without preamble, he grabbed my left hand to examine my ring. "This was my mother's." I saw a slight flush stain his cheeks, as if he were angry.

I could see the effort he made to smile back at me. "Then let me welcome you into our family—Sister." He embraced me, crushing me to his chest. I felt his moist lips linger on my cheek, and I stilled my hand from wiping his kiss off my skin.

I studied his face again and instinctively knew that I could not count on this man to be my ally.

Our attention was turned by a commotion in the foyer and several loud voices reverberating through the hallway. One in particular caught my attention. Deep and clear, with staccato accents, it seemed to be a voice of authority. "Tell those busy-bodies that my trains are for supplies for my army. I have no room—I repeat, no room—for do-gooders and those damned newspaper people."

Footsteps approached the parlor, and I waited expectantly for the owner of the voice to appear. He walked in and stopped abruptly, taking us in with a bold appraisal. The aroma of cigar smoke entered the room with him.

He was tall and very thin, his weathered face lined with deep crevices. His dark red hair, standing up as if at attention, should have made this man a comical character but somehow did not. The stars on his shoulders outshone the stained and sloppy appearance of his dark-blue uniform. There was no doubt who this man was. I had heard him referred to by various names—from Nero to Satan to Georgia's nemesis to, recently, Uncle Billy. This was without a doubt none other than the man who would coin the phrase "War is hell": General William Tecumseh Sherman.

He blinked rapidly at us before turning his attention to William. "Captain Elliott. Who are these women, and why are they here?"

William snapped to attention and began introductions. "General, you've met my wife's mother, Mrs. Pamela Broderick, at a dinner in Nashville at the home of Andrew Johnson. And this is my brother's wife, Mrs. Laura Elliott."

The General peered at me through narrowed eyes and then turned back to William. "Captain, isn't your brother with the Rebel army?"

"Yes, sir. As much as it pains me, he is."

"I see." General Sherman scratched his short beard. "And your sister-in-law. Is she a Rebel, too?"

"That would depend," I interjected, smarting at being treated as if I weren't in the room.

The General raised his eyebrows at me. "I see. And what would that depend on?"

"On who was asking the question."

Pamela stepped forward. "I beg your pardon, sir. Mrs. Elliott and I are both staunch supporters of the Union. We are here to pass on information that might be of some use to you."

I knew the information she was speaking of. Direct from Confederate General Joseph E. Johnston's headquarters in Dalton, she had a list of the entire strength of the Southern armies—down to the last mule. She handed the small stack of papers to him without pause, knowing it would be of little use to him or his army once he was dead.

He took the papers from her and examined them, the crease between his brows deepening. "Where did you get these?"

"I beg your pardon, sir, but I must keep my sources secret. Suffice it to say, the gentleman in question is a member of General Johnston's own staff."

He nodded and folded the papers in half. His hands were calloused and spattered with dark brown freckles. "Very good. I will, of course, verify these figures. But your efforts are greatly appreciated. I hope the two of you will do me the honor of dining with me and my staff this evening."

Not pausing to wait for an answer, Sherman faced me, his eyes flickering over my appearance. "Madam, have you been traveling?"

My knees nearly buckled with fatigue, and my weariness

pushed all thoughts of politeness and the purpose of my visit out of my head. "No. I always look like I've been in a train wreck."

A stunned silence punctuated my remark. I heard the passing of a carriage outside and someone shouting. He raised an eyebrow. "I see. And does your husband approve?"

One knee did buckle, and I tried to estimate how many steps backward I'd have to take to make it to the nearest chair. "I don't think my appearance is a major concern of his, General."

He coughed into his hand, but I could see he was grinning. "Actually, I meant does he approve of your Unionist sympathies?"

"Uh, not exactly."

He rubbed his beard, the rasping sound grating on my nerves. "Are you still on speaking terms?"

"Yes, you could say that." I took another step backward and felt the backs of my knees make contact with the edge of a chair. I dropped into the seat without looking. The cushion vibrated in startled movement and erupted with a loud meow.

I jumped out of the chair. "Shit!" I exclaimed as the black-and-white feline escaped through the doorway. All eyes were on me as the blood rushed to the tips of my ears, and a small gasp came from Pamela.

Ignoring my outburst, General Sherman said, "You must be tired." He turned to William. "Captain, please see that these ladies have a room. Dinner is at eight o'clock." He bowed sharply and left, but not before I saw the grin through his beard.

I plopped back down in the empty chair. William came and stood before me, offering his hand. "My, my. Where did my brother find you?"

Ignoring his hand, I stood. "You wouldn't believe it if I told you."

He threw his head back and laughed—Stuart's laugh. Tears sprang to my eyes. I needed Stuart now. I needed him to tell me I was doing the right thing. I turned my head away.

"What I need now is a room and a bath. Perhaps after that I will be in the mood to chat about Julia and your family, since I'm sure they're your primary concern." It hadn't escaped my notice that he hadn't mentioned Julia's name once.

"Yes, I'd like that." His face registered annoyance as he picked up our bags and indicated with a nod that we precede him through the door. "Ladies."

With a heavy sigh, I followed. Low voices drifted toward me from the library, like murmurs of ghosts from the past. I felt eyes on my back, and I turned to see General Sherman and another officer watching our progress. I inclined my head slightly, then turned back, my feet tapping against the marble floors. The sound made me think of footprints in history. I wondered if my own would be indelible, with thick, deep impressions in the soil, or fade with time, like the yellowed pages of an old history book.

> "Oh Time! the beautifier of the dead,
> Adorner of the ruin, comforter
> And only healer when the heart hath bled;
> . . . Time; the Avenger!"
>
> **Lord Byron**

Chapter Twenty-four

A large beetle crawled across the toe of my satin slipper. Hearing my intake of breath, Pamela turned in time to see the insect scurrying under the puddled draperies. She stooped to pick it up, its shell shiny in the thin light from the lamp, then tightened her fingers around it until it crunched. She stepped to the window and discarded the remains into the garden below.

Wiping her hand on her skirt, she walked back to me, studying my red-velvet dress with a critical eye. She reached up with both hands and tugged at the short sleeves, exposing as much chest and shoulder as the dress would allow without being obscene. My hand twitched, wanting to pull the dress up to my neck, but I was resigned to the fact that I would need to do whatever it took to get Sherman's attention.

Pamela had done a decent job on my hair, and I thought, as I fastened the jet earrings in my ears, that I was more than passable. The smell of cooking drifted up the stairs, making my stomach rumble. Pamela crooked an eyebrow at me. "Perhaps we should go down for a drink before dinner, hmm?"

I turned to face her, my fingers clutching at the fabric of my dress. "I need proof that my daughter is . . . alive."

She gave me a condescending smile. "I'm sorry, dear. But that's just not possible."

"What if I refuse to . . . to cooperate unless I know she's all right?"

Her smile evaporated. "Then she will be killed. Any more questions?"

I stood, frozen, then shook my head and walked toward the door.

She stopped me with a hand on my elbow. "One last thing. When this is all over, you will not implicate me or anybody else. You are acting on your own accord, because of your hatred for the Yankees. This is part of the bargain, Laura. Follow it through, and there will be enough people to risk their lives to save you. And then you will be reunited with your daughter."

I swallowed heavily. "How do we know this will turn out as you plan? This is all very risky, isn't it?"

"No different from life, Laura. We can only do what we can. Now go downstairs. I'll follow you shortly."

Pamela closed the door behind me. The stilted strains of a Beethoven sonata drifted toward me. I followed the music to a room across from the parlor we had been in earlier. I remembered floor-to-ceiling bookshelves from my brief glance inside—books left behind by the previous tenants. I stood tentatively on the threshold, one hand pressed to my collarbone where the blood pounded under my fingertips.

My eyes were immediately drawn to the grand piano in the corner, the highly polished mahogany lustrous in the yellow light. A bone-thin woman sat on the bench, her jaw working as she plunked on the keys in an attempt to recreate Beethoven. I gravitated toward the instrument before I realized there were other people in the room, and they were all watching me. The music stopped abruptly as the woman looked at me, pale gray eyes staring coolly out from under ash-blond hair.

"I don't believe we've been introduced." Her voice was flat and nasal, straight out of a New England town.

William emerged from a cushioned sofa and came to stand beside me, his long fingers, so much like Stuart's, holding a short glass filled with amber liquid.

"Please, allow me. Mrs. Mary Audenreid, my sister-in-law, Mrs. Laura Elliott." I inclined my head slightly in acknowledgment while she sat motionless, her expression cold. She was several years younger than I, but her bearing was that of someone much older.

I saw three other gentlemen by the bookcase on the far wall, and each was introduced in turn. One was Mrs. Audenreid's husband, Captain Joseph Audenreid, the officer I had seen General Sherman speaking with earlier. He was tall and fair, like his wife, but his eyes were warm as they appraised me. The other man on the general's staff was Captain James McCoy, a man whose girth pulled his uniform taut, threatening to send the brass buttons into orbit. He bowed slightly, his graying hair falling forward over his forehead. The grimness of his eyes as he contemplated me belied his physical likeness to St. Nick.

William continued, "And you've already met General Sherman."

I gave him a warm smile and wished fervently for a drink.

"Are you a Rebel, Mrs. Elliot?"

I looked at the woman who had spoken, surprised to hear such a direct question.

Before I could respond, General Sherman stepped forward. "That would depend, now wouldn't it, Mrs. Elliot?" The creases in his face deepened as he regarded me, his amusement apparent.

289

I smiled back tentatively. "Yes. And since it is a Union captain's wife who is asking the question, I would have to say no."

The woman sniffed in response, holding a hanky to her nose. "Honestly, I don't see why we're fighting them. Let them have their miserable climate and torturous months of spring." She sneezed loudly into her hanky.

I loved spring in the South, and I figured something had to be wrong with somebody who thought otherwise. "Oh, yes. Cold, damp springs are much preferable to warm ones full of abundant blooms that may cause a few sneezes. Perhaps you should speak to a few more generals, Mrs. Audenreid. To think that you've had the answer to ending the war all this time and have been keeping it to yourself."

The tomb-like silence was broken by Pamela's entrance. She was dressed all in black, like a crow, and greeted everyone stiffly as introductions were made.

Mrs. Audenreid resumed her playing, this time a barely recognizable Chopin scherzo. A black manservant appeared with sherry for the ladies. I gulped mine quickly to still my nerves.

Mary Audenreid stopped playing. There was a small smattering of applause as she stood to take her glass of sherry. She came to stand next to me, a slight frown on her face. "That was Chopin, Mrs. Elliot. I'm not sure if civilized music has made its way south yet. I'm trying to educate these poor unfortunates with every bit of culture that I can." She took a sip of her sherry, her pink tongue darting out to lick her lips. "Ignorance is to be expected, though, from a people who subjugate others and whip them to within an inch of their lives each and every day."

I glanced over at William, who wore a tight smile on his face. "How very kind of you. Let me speak for all my unwashed brothers and sisters of the South and give you a heartfelt thank-you for all your selfless efforts. It is a wonder, isn't it, that the North would want our participation in this country at all, with us being so backward and evil and all." I let my accent slip into a redneck impersonation, eliciting a laugh from a male behind me.

I welcomed the anger that flushed through me, settling my nerves. And I had never been known to back down from an argument. I set my glass on a table and walked slowly to the piano. "My. So many keys. Would you mind if I tried?"

With a condescending glance, she fluttered a pale hand at me. "Please do. But not too loudly, please."

Pulling out the bench, I sat down and did a few short finger exercises to warm up my hands. Next came a few arpeggios, my hands racing up and down the length of the keyboard. Mary Audenreid's mouth pursed itself into a perfect O. A red flush appeared high on her cheekbones, spreading over her entire face. Enjoying the effect, I continued with the floorshow.

"This is Debussy. He's from France. That's a big country across the Atlantic, where they speak French. Have you heard of it?" I asked wickedly as I played a few bars of *Claire de Lune*.

"This is Mozart. He was from Salzburg—a beautiful city if you don't go during the winter. He died tragically young, but what a gift of music he has given to the world. Not that uneducated people like myself would ever realize it." I played a page of a Mozart sonata, my fingers flying over the keys. Mary Audenreid sat as still as a piece of furniture, her cheeks and nose a bright pink.

"Have you ever heard of Beethoven? His *Für Elise* is a bit overdone, as is his *Pathetique*, but they are two of my favorites," I said as I quickly ran through a sample of each.

I felt all eyes on me, but I was on a roll and couldn't stop. I quickly broke into Scott Joplin's *Heliotrope Bouquet* and pounded out the entire thing in record time. My spontaneous recital ended without applause.

Mary stood and walked slowly to me and stated simply, "You, madam, are common and not fit to be in this room with us."

I skidded the piano bench behind me, mindless of the damage to the highly polished floor, and stopped her with my hand.

"And you, madam, are an insufferable boor. You prance

around with your high ideals about Southerners and their atrocities to their slaves. But I'll have you know that I speak to the slaves with a great deal more respect and kindness than you have just shown me." I said this with great control, enunciating every word.

"Let go of my arm."

I dropped her bony limb and watched her storm out of the room.

My corset stopped me from taking a much-needed deep breath, so I found myself gasping in tiny puffs of air. "I'm sorry," I said, to no one in particular. "I usually have better manners."

Her husband stepped forward, coughing into his hand. "No, she provoked you. Perhaps you'd better understand it if I told you that her brother was killed at Gettysburg by a Confederate bullet."

I studied his face and noticed a scar that started at the jaw and neatly bisected his left cheek. "It explains it, but it certainly doesn't excuse it. My husband was badly wounded by a Yankee bullet, but I can't seem to hate all northerners because of it."

He set his face with a grim look. "Apparently. Or else you wouldn't be here."

I heard a grunt from Captain McCoy. I turned to find him closely examining his boots.

The manservant interrupted by announcing that dinner was served.

William offered me his arm, and I reluctantly placed my hand on it. As he closed his hand over mine, I repressed a shudder, much as I would have done if a large and hairy insect had been crawling up my arm.

We filed into the dining room, and I felt not a little guilty, knowing a family had been evicted from these premises, a family that should have been sitting around the dining table, talking about their day's activities.

I sat on General Sherman's right, with Captain Audenreid to my right. His wife sat in stony silence across from me. Conversation was stilted, owing as much to the fact that I was a Southerner as to the fact that there were women present. At one point, a courier came in, and I could see General Sherman's eyes light with excitement. He ate faster, as I'm sure he was anxious to share the news with his officers. No doubt it had something to do with his imminent plans to move his massive army southward toward Atlanta.

We eagerly turned our attention to the food—the abundance of which was truly amazing in this place and time. An entire side of roast beef occupied the center of the cherry pedestal table. It was surrounded by countless other dishes, including three different kinds of vegetables and all sorts of sauces. Eyebrows were raised at my heaping plate. I shrugged and took another helping of the honey-glazed yams.

Mrs. Audenreid appeared to be enjoying the spread as much as I was. "This is truly the most delicious food I've had since our honeymoon in Paris."

Captain McCoy shifted in his seat and swallowed a mouthful of savory rice. "I shall take credit for that, Mrs. Audenreid. I brought my chef from home. Monsieur Fortin is indeed French."

I eyed the Captain's girth and knew he spoke the truth.

Mary Audenreid continued, "I would truly like to thank him, but I don't speak a word of French. My mother thought it was pretentious, so it was never taught to us."

"I speak French." I smiled at her, an innocent enough expression. "I'll be happy to give you an appropriate phrase to show your gratitude."

She smiled primly. "Really? I'm surprised. But thank you. I would appreciate that."

I hid my grin by giving my attention to the chocolate torte, stabbing my fork into the rich, creamy layers. I washed it down with real coffee, savoring the taste and smell of it.

As we left the table, I approached Mrs. Audenreid and whispered in her ear. She gave me a quizzical look and repeated the phrase back to me quietly. I nodded, assuring her it was perfect. When Monsieur Fortin appeared in the doorway to satisfy himself that all the guests were contented, she said, with an amazingly good French accent, "Monsieur Fortin, *voulez-vous couchez avec moi, ce soir?*"

Pamela began coughing, choking on her last sip of coffee. Somewhere behind me a china cup dropped onto the wooden table, but I was unable to look anywhere else but at the unfortunate chef's face. Mary Audenreid looked around the room, from the beet-red face of the chef to the mortified look on the officers' faces. "What did I say? Was my accent wrong?"

A flash of lightning illuminated the night, followed shortly by a loud crash of thunder. Accepting the interruption as a sign that I should leave, I promptly excused myself and went up to our bedroom before I exploded in mirth. As I ran up the stairs, I heard French spoken with a tone of righteous indignation by Monsieur Fortin and a loud exclamation from Captain McCoy. The last thing I heard before slamming the door behind me was Mary Audenreid shrieking at her husband and a gaggle of male voices speaking in a mixture of French and English.

I threw myself on the bed, burying my face into the pillow, laughing until I cried.

And then I couldn't stop crying. How could I shoot a man in cold blood? How could I not? Images of Annie sustained me—images of her as a baby and then as the little girl she had grown to be. I had made my choice, and there was no turning back. Reluctantly, I sat up, smoothing my hand absently on the drenched pillow. I rolled off the bed and began pacing, waiting for an opportunity to present itself.

For a while, I heard the excited murmur of male voices, and then the house grew still. I stopped my pacing to listen to the wind blow against the house. I pulled the curtain aside and saw only scattered debris on the deserted street. I longed to loosen my corset, but I needed help to do it, and Pamela was nowhere to be seen. Surely she didn't think I'd need our bedroom for a purpose other than sleeping. I rubbed my hands together and was startled to find that they were moist. I wiped them on my skirt and resumed my pacing.

I found myself standing in front of the dressing table, peer-

ing at the reflection of a woman I didn't know anymore. My
skin flushed pink against the glaring red of the gown, my dark
hair an elegant contrast. I took a deep breath and almost
laughed at the show of cleavage I revealed. At least I knew I
had it if I needed it.

A whiff of cigar smoke tickled my nose. General Sherman
must still be downstairs. Without thinking about what I was
doing, I dug Pamela's carpetbag out from under her bed and
thrust my hand inside. My fingers closed around the cold steel
of the revolver. I pulled it out and examined it with an im-
partial eye. I pulled off my stockings, placed the garter around
my calf, and tucked the gun into my garter. I straightened,
smoothing my skirts. Giving the woman in the mirror a backward glance, I left the room and carefully made my way down
the steps.

My skirts trailed behind me on each rise until they pooled
elegantly around me as I reached the bottom. The aroma of
cigar smoke was stronger in the foyer. A triangle of light illuminated the floor outside the partially opened door to the
library. I walked toward it, my steps purposeful, like a hunter
stalking its prey. I heard the scratch of pen against paper as I
gently pushed open the door.

I was relieved to find the general alone. He looked up as I
entered, a new cigar clenched between his teeth. He sat at the
desk, arm poised above a ledger. I could feel the gun rubbing
against my leg. His jacket was unbuttoned, displaying a dirty
white shirt underneath. His red hair stuck up like a porcupine's
quills, as if he had been rubbing his hands through it as he
pondered how to feed his troops off fertile Southern land.

I stopped in front of the desk, not sure how to proceed.
Perhaps I should perch myself on the edge of the desk, but I
knew that with my voluminous skirts and hoop I would cause
considerable damage to the items on the desktop.

"Good evening, madam. Are you looking for French lessons?" A flicker of amusement crossed his face.

I felt my cheeks flame and shook my head. Before speaking,
I retrieved the whiskey decanter from the sideboard and refilled his glass to the top.

He studied the tiny rivulets running down the side of his glass and forming a small puddle on the desk. He leaned back in his chair, quirking one ruddy eyebrow.

"Mrs. Elliot, are you trying to get me drunk?"

I reached for an empty glass and sloshed whiskey into it. "No. I just don't want you to see how drunk I'm going to get." I took a long swallow, then came up for air, gasping.

He stood and came from behind the desk, taking the glass from my hand, his callused fingers touching mine briefly. "Mrs. Elliot, why are you here? You do know I'm a married man."

I felt my cheeks flame red again as the whiskey began to work its magic and swim through my head. His face was a mere foot away, and I stared into gray-blue eyes, intelligent eyes, and not nearly as cold as I would have expected. I think I knew then. I couldn't kill him. Nor could I jeopardize the outcome of the war. I was diminished in the grand scheme of things, and my wants and desires were merely grains of sand on the great beach of history—of no more consequence than an ant facing an army of soldiers.

"I . . . I need your help, and I'm trying to figure out the best way to ask you so that you'll believe me."

He placed the glass on the desk and led me over to the sofa. "Sit," he commanded, his voice soft but stern. I sat, and he looked me over from head to foot before speaking again. "You'll find that the best way to deal with me is to speak plainly. You're an intelligent woman, Mrs. Elliot. Please don't waste my time with social niceties."

I swallowed and eyed him levelly. "There's a plot to assassinate you. And I . . . I'm supposed to pull the trigger."

He stood stock still, his widened eyes the only clue that he had heard what I said. "I see." He raised a hand to scratch his face, the rasping sound loud in the quiet room. "And can I assume you've changed your mind?"

I stood to face him. "You think I'm joking? Look." I leaned over, jerked my skirts up, and pulled the revolver from the garter at my calf. He took a quick step back, nearly tripping in his haste to put distance between himself and the gun.

"Do it, Laura. Now."

I turned to the doorway where Pamela stood, pointing a small silver pistol at me.

Sherman showed no fear as I raised the revolver. I heard a buggy pass by on the wet street outside, voices dying as it drove away. I saw Sarah's face, and Stuart's, and wondered if I had lost everything again.

Calmly, I pivoted, aiming the gun at her shoulder. Before I squeezed the trigger, I heard another blast, and my arm exploded in fire. My hand jerked, and my gun went off, the force knocking it out of my fingers. I was thrown against the bookcase, toppling several volumes down on me as I slid to the floor.

I clutched at my upper arm in a semi-lucid state. General Sherman was leaning over me, his voice frantically calling out for help. I turned my head to find Pamela. I had seen her fall, but I did not know if she was still alive. I inched along the floor toward her placid figure, the pistol still clutched in her hand. Blood and thick clots of tissue oozed from a ragged hole in her neck. It dripped onto the powder-blue rug, saturating it and giving it an eerie shimmer in the lamplight. I remember thinking absently that it would ruin the carpet, and I stretched a hand out to stop the flow. Her eyes twitched, and I realized she was still alive.

The General raced to the door, flung it open, and again shouted for help. I looked back at Pamela. Her lips moved, as if in slow motion. "Sarah's dead." The sound gushed from her mouth, the words bubbling with blood.

The last thing I saw before slipping into unconsciousness were dark, unseeing eyes, as cold as ice and as still as death.

"The Angel of Death has been abroad throughout the land, you may almost hear the beating of his wings."
                                                           John Bright

Chapter Twenty-five

I awoke in shadows, the forms of people around me dark stains against the pale wall. I groaned and tried to sit up, only to be held down by strong hands and the flaming pain in my arm. I thought of Sarah and of Pamela's last words to me, and I stopped struggling.

"Mrs. Elliott?"

I opened my eyes wider in an attempt to focus on the features looming over me. I recognized Captain Audenreid's face as he leaned closer. "The doctor has given you a bit of morphine, so your head will be rather unclear, I'm afraid." A soft pillow cushioned my head, and I realized I was back in the bedroom.

Hands gripped my shoulder, and white bandages were being wrapped around my upper arm. A soft shawl, smelling gently of lavender, was placed over me. Pain snaked its way back into current memory, and I winced.

"You've been shot," he said matter-of-factly.

I grimaced. "Yeah. I know." My lips felt like paper, cracked and stale.

"But you're a very lucky young lady. It was a clean wound—no bone fragments to worry about. It's been cleaned thoroughly, and I expect it to heal without incident. I have found a local physician to continue with your care." He went to the door and whispered something to the person on the other side.

"Why not an army surgeon?" I shifted, trying to ease the pain.

He paused by the side of the bed. "Mrs. Elliott, General Sherman has ordered all troops to move from Chattanooga tomorrow morning. He's been very strict with his orders— we've been stripped to our barest essentials, and no extraneous persons will be allowed. You will need to stay here."

I dug my heels into the mattress, forcing myself to sit up against the headboard and heedless of the pain that radiated through my body. "No! I can't stay here. I need to go home." The word *home* came easily to my lips, softening the ragged edges of my soul. Stuart would be there, to comfort me, to help me. "I have to get back to Roswell. I need . . . I need to find my daughter." I refused to believe that what Pamela said was true. I grabbed at the captain's arm. "Please. I can't stay here."

A shadow emerged from the back of the room, and William came to stand next to the captain. "As your closest male relation, Laura, I cannot allow you to leave."

"The hell you can't! I want to speak to General Sherman." I kicked off the bedclothes, then slid from the bed, the wall of pain pressing on my senses and making me light-headed. I hastily pulled the shawl over my nightgown, then stumbled for the door but was restrained by a light hand on my uninjured arm.

"Mrs. Elliott. Wait. If you want to speak to the general, I'll arrange it for you." Captain Audenreid gave a stern look to my brother-in-law, who stood silent, his lips pursed in anger. "But may I suggest changing your clothes first. I'll send my wife in to help you."

My legs gave out, my bottom landing firmly on the rug. I held up a hand. "I'm all right—just a little light-headed." I brought my knees up and rested my forehead on them. My voice sounded muffled, but I couldn't seem to raise my head to speak. "But I'm afraid that your wife might just finish the job Pamela started."

I heard a smile in his voice. "No, you're wrong. We all know what you did. We're very much in awe of your bravery and are indebted to you for saving the general's life."

I put my head back between my knees, the room beginning to swim before my eyes. "But at what cost?" I whispered. I squeezed my eyes shut to keep the room steady. I wouldn't allow myself to think about it.

Captain Audenreid and William helped me back to the bed, and then the captain excused himself to get his wife.

I lay back on the pillow, exhausted from the physical exertion, and closed my eyes. I felt a tentative touch on my cheek. I lay still, not yet having the energy to open my eyes. The touch grew stronger as the unseen hand stroked my jaw. My eyes flew open. William's face leered into mine, a mere few inches between us.

"You're an exciting woman, Laura. My brother is a fool to let you go so far from home."

I moved my head back as far as it would go, recoiling from his touch.

His hand fell to my neck, and I felt my body go rigid. "Stuart never did know how to control a woman. You need somebody stronger, Laura. Somebody like me—a man who knows how to handle a woman."

I fought back the tears of anger and grief. I would not give him the satisfaction of seeing me cry. "Leave me alone. You disgust me."

He leaned his face closer to mine, his blue eyes sparkling with malice. "Come away with me, Laura. We'll go west— together. Build a new life, away from this war. Let me show you the difference between a real man and a boy." Light, feathery strokes caressed my collarbone. I cringed back into my pillow.

He continued, his voice low and teasing. "Besides, Laura, I doubt you'll be welcome back at Phoenix Hall once Julia discovers what you did to her stepmother. I don't think you have much of a choice." He pressed his lips against mine, and I felt his tongue probe my mouth. I jerked my body away from him, the pain in my arm a flaming ball of heat.

With my last effort, I gathered saliva onto my tongue and spat in his face.

He wiped his jaw with the sleeve of his coat as the door opened and Mary Audenreid entered, a steaming pitcher of water in her hand. William straightened and excused himself without a backward glance. As he left, I realized that he didn't know about Sarah—the girl who called him Papa. I wanted to hurt him with the news, but I was also reluctant to share my grief with him. And perhaps if I didn't talk about it, then it wouldn't be true.

Mary Audenreid stood in front of the closed door, her eyes focused on the steam rising from the pitcher. "Mrs. Elliott, it would appear that I owe you an apology. I was hoping that even if we couldn't be friends, perhaps we could be civil to each other."

I nodded. "If you help make me presentable enough to meet with General Sherman, I'll make you my best friend."

She gave me a hesitant smile and began pouring the water into the washbasin.

She helped me wash and then rigged a dress to fit over my bandages. My head still didn't feel steady, and we needed her husband to help me down the stairs for my meeting with General Sherman. I froze at the threshold of the library, remembering what had transpired in there.

"It's all right, Mrs. Elliott. There's nothing in there to disturb you." Captain Audenreid gave me a gentle push on my back.

I was relieved to see the carpet had been removed, as had every trace of Pamela. I shuddered involuntarily as I moved to stand before the general's desk.

He stood and regarded me with strong eyes, the ever-present cigar smoking in an ashtray on the desk. "Mrs. Elliott. It's good to see you already on the road to recovery from your ordeal." He indicated the chair behind me, and I gratefully collapsed into it. "Tell me what I can do for you."

I leaned an elbow on his desk for support. "I need to get home to Roswell, Georgia. I can't do it on my own, especially since I would have to cross lines of battle. I would like your permission to travel with your troops."

He stared at me as if I hadn't spoken, then picked up his cigar and began pacing the room. "Mrs. Elliott, I'm not sure you understand what you're asking. My troops will be traveling fast and light. We will be engaged in battle—a dangerous situation for anybody, even bystanders. I will have over one hundred thousand men on this campaign—no women. Not even laundresses. I cannot think of a single reason I should permit an injured woman to join us."

Spots began dancing before my eyes again, and I drew in a deep breath. I leaned heavily on the desk as I stared into his eyes and said, "Because you owe me your life."

He paused, blowing a puff of smoke into the still air. He nodded once. "Yes. That I do."

I closed my eyes and put my head on my arms. The general called for Captain Audenreid, and I felt myself being gently lifted from the chair. I held on to the chair for a moment. "General?"

He sighed. "I will have my men prepare space for you on a medical wagon."

I nodded my thanks, then allowed myself to be led away. As we crossed the foyer, the front doors were thrown open, and two blue-clad soldiers struggled in, each clasping the arm of a man wearing a tattered gray uniform. The man's head was slung forward, as if he were barely holding on to consciousness, blood and bruises covering the part of his face I could see. He had been beaten, and badly.

"What is this?" William's voice came from the top of the stairs as he descended.

One of the soldiers saluted, almost losing his grasp on the prisoner, and addressed William. "Begging your pardon, Captain. This man claims to be your brother."

I looked back at the soldier, not completely comprehending until my gaze fell on the prisoner's hands. Though they were bruised and torn and tied together at the wrist with a hemp rope, I recognized the strong, long fingers. Blood rushed to my head. I pulled away from Captain Audenreid's grasp and ran. "Stuart? It's me—it's Laura."

Slowly he lifted his head, like a marionette being pulled by strings. Dried blood and grime caked his face, and one eye was swollen shut. But the eye that did shine out at me was a deep blue, and I knew. I wanted to throw my arms around him but knew of no place I could touch him where it wouldn't hurt.

Instead, I turned to William. "He's badly hurt—and he's got a bullet wound under his shoulder. Can we move him to a room upstairs and send for a doctor?"

Ignoring me, William strode over to Stuart. "So, little brother. We meet again. What brings you here?"

The dry, gravelly voice was almost that of a stranger. "I've . . . brought . . . Sarah."

The strangled sound came from my own throat. As if my wish demanded it, the door opened again, and another soldier entered, pushing my daughter ahead of him. She seemed taller than I remembered, and much thinner, but the light in her green eyes was the same.

I fell to my knees, my strength finally deserting me, and opened my arms to her.

"Papa!" she shrieked, as she rushed by me and flew into William's arms.

She nearly toppled him over in her exuberance, and he quickly put her aside, his face a mask of anger and confusion.

"What in the hell are you doing bringing a child here, Stuart?"

One of Stuart's captors stepped forward. "We found them walking down the road from Dalton, just as plain and easy as you please, as if there weren't no damned war goin' on." He coughed before continuing. "We—uh, didn't give him a chance to talk first—sorry, sir. But later he said he needed to reach you—that he was your brother and this was your daughter."

Stuart's eyes fell on me. "Am I . . . in time?"

I nodded, seeing him through a blur of tears. He had somehow found Sarah, then risked his life to bring her here, to prevent me from fulfilling my bargain with Pamela. My joy at seeing Sarah was clouded by my fear over Stuart's predicament. He was in the enemy's camp.

Softly, I told him. "Pamela's dead."

He nodded in understanding.

"Aunt Laura?" Sarah stood by herself, and I reached for her, and she came to me. My fingers searched out her bony shoulders and thick hair, and I cried with relief at the solid presence of her in my lap. "I missed you, baby—I've missed you." I lifted her face and wiped the hair away from her eyes, studying her face. "Are you all right? Did anybody hurt you?"

She shook her head, her hair whipping around her face. "No." She blinked, then leaned forward to rub her face in my neck. "Is Mama here? I miss her."

Her words were like a blow to my stomach. I patted her back, ignoring the hollow feeling in my chest. "No, sweetheart. But I'll take you home. Your mama will be so happy to see you."

William stepped forward and looked down at me. "Am I to understand that my brother knew about the plot to assassinate General Sherman?"

General Sherman stepped out of the library. "What in the hell is all this commotion?"

William addressed his commander. "I believe we have in custody another member of the group who planned your assassination."

I made to stand, but my foot caught on the bottom of my skirt, and I ended up on the floor at his feet. "No, William! He's your brother—how can you do this?" I hugged Sarah close, not wanting her to witness the scene.

William shot me a cold look. "Are you denying that he knew about it?"

"No, but—"

He cut me off and spoke directly to the two guards. "This man is a prisoner. Take him someplace where he can be held under lock and key."

"No!" I screamed. "He needs immediate medical attention."

I turned to the general, on my last leg of strength. "Please—please don't let them send him away."

His face was closed to me. "I'm sorry, Mrs. Elliott. But until we can ascertain the truth, we need to hold him as a prisoner."

Dots spotted my eyes again, and I heard myself shouting for Stuart. Warm air rushed at me as the door opened. I didn't hear Stuart struggling, but I knew he was gone when the door slammed shut. The light dimmed around me as Sarah's voice called for me. With my last ounce of strength before I passed out, I squeezed her hand.

When I awakened, I was in my bed, and Captain Audenreid sat next to me, a look of concern creasing his face. I sat up, wincing at the pain in my bandaged arm. "Where's Sarah?"

"Don't worry—Mary's with her. She's giving her a bath and a fresh change of clothes—not to mention a hot meal. She'll be fine."

I lay back, my mind not completely at ease. "But what about my husband? He's wounded—he needs medical care." I turned to him. "Please. I beg of you. Can you see to it that he at least gets medical attention?"

He rubbed his jaw, as if needing the movement to make a decision. "I most likely can, Mrs. Elliot. But that's all. He is a Rebel officer, and he will have to face charges."

"But he's innocent." I tried to sit up in bed, but the captain held me back.

"Then he can defend himself on those grounds. In the meantime, I'll see what I can do to get him a doctor."

I nodded, then lay back in the bed, finally succumbing to dreamless sleep.

We left before dawn on the morning of Thursday, May 5, 1864, saying good-bye to Mary Audenreid and the other officers' wives. The throbbing pain in my arm masked any trepidation I should have felt at being the only woman on this march. William ignored us as he rode out in front of the column of men, leaving Captain Audenreid to help get Sarah and me settled. We had originally been placed in the back of a covered medical wagon, but the jostling over the rough terrain was causing me more injury, so I begged to sit up front with the driver.

I didn't know where Stuart had been taken, and nobody would answer my questions. I tried not to think of him in a dark cell somewhere, starving to death. At least I knew his wounds had been tended to, thanks to Captain Audenreid. As I hugged Sarah close to me, I made plans to petition General Sherman for his release. I was out of bargaining chips, but I had to try.

The long column of men stretched out on either side of me in an uninterrupted wave of blue. The dust rising from the ground in their wake wafted over me, and I could feel the grit settle in my hair and clothes.

The soldiers' methodical marching was interspersed occasionally by singing. I recognized some of the songs, and Sarah and I would join in for lack of anything better to do and to take my mind off Stuart. I vacillated between utter joy at having her with me, close enough to touch her and hear her laughter, and the pain in my heart over Stuart. I tried to be angry at him for not returning to Phoenix Hall. But then, that would have meant I wouldn't have Sarah.

Captain Audenreid pulled up on his horse to ride next to the wagon.

"Good morning, Mrs. Elliott," he said, tipping his hat. "And, you, too, Miss Elliott." Sarah giggled, then hid her mouth with a hand as she stared up at the handsome officer. Strands of reddish-blond hair peeked out from under his hat. A single dimple punctuated his smile, and his light gray eyes appraised me openly. The scar on his face did nothing to lessen his handsomeness. It might have even added to his appeal.

Smiling, I nodded in his direction.

"I hope you're not finding this trip too unpleasant."

"No, not at all. It's bringing me home." I had long since lost any feeling in my lower extremities, and I squirmed on the hard wagon seat to bring the blood flow back.

Noticing my discomfort, the officer said, "You might be more comfortable in a saddle. I would be more than happy to find you a horse." The captain smiled affably at me, sitting easily astride his mount.

I had come to the conclusion that one must be born to the saddle to truly be comfortable there.

Sarah squealed with delight. "I want to ride a horse. Can I? Can I?"

I turned to her with worry. "No, Sarah. You might get hurt."

She was already pushing herself to my side of the wagon. "Please, Aunt Laura—please?"

The Captain reassured me. "I'll be careful with her."

I nodded, and he reached down to lift Sarah onto his saddle. He smiled at me. "You're like a mother to her, aren't you?"

Sarah interjected, "But she's just my Aunt Laura. We're going to see my real mama in a few days."

I looked down at my lap, ignoring the sting of tears. "Yes. We'll be home soon." I had explained to Sarah that Julia and her brother were in Valdosta but that I would write to them as soon as I could to let them know we were on our way home. I hadn't yet told Sarah that we would be saying good-bye to them. That would come later.

We continued riding in a companionable silence, moving relatively quickly over the bumpy terrain. I wanted to get down and walk, to get the blood flowing again in my posterior, but was unsure I could keep up with the grueling pace.

I began humming to myself, to keep my mind off the painful thoughts racing around in my head. I started to enjoy the scenery, admiring a southern springtime in full bloom. Suddenly, my humming stopped.

I recognized the area immediately—the small farmhouse tucked inside the clearing with rows of wilted plants stretching out from the house like sunbursts. Clothes still hung on the clothesline outside, dancing a jig with the breeze.

The officer at the head of the column raised a hand, and the lines of soldiers stopped behind him. The driver of my wagon pulled off to the side, allowing me a full view of the farm from the slight rise we were on. Only the soft whinnying of the horses and the jangling of their harness penetrated the silence. I immediately saw the woman's rifle against the side of the house and felt the first ripple of apprehension course through me. She would not have gone far without it.

I strained my ears for the shouts of her little boys but could hear only the clothes snapping on the line.

"Jenkins, Duffy, Lee—you men head down and check things out. This is Rebel territory, so be careful." The officer eyed the withered leaves of newly sprung plants and the wilted stalks in the kitchen garden. "If there are any provisions to be had, take them."

"Wait!" I leapt from the wagon, wincing as I jarred my arm. The officer looked at me and halted his men. "I . . . I know the woman who lives here. She has two small children and might be inside and scared. Perhaps I should go, too."

Captain Audenreid rode up beside me and lifted Sarah back onto the wagon seat. "Only if I accompany you." He dismounted and gave the reins to another soldier. He came with me behind the three infantrymen, their rifles raised in readiness.

With a word to Sarah to stay where she was, we walked through the field and over the dead plants, grinding them into the earth from which they had sprung, and halted outside the porch. A wooden train lay upended on the floorboards, waiting for little fingers to play with it. A mending basket sat expectantly next to the white rocker, a piece of brown thread trailing down the side. The door stood open in invitation.

It was then I noticed the smell. It had been hovering around me like an unpleasant memory, but I had pushed it to the back of my mind. Only as I stood looking at the farmhouse, the breeze teasing my hair, did it hit me in the face. I had smelled that smell before—when I was a child. I had been walking through the woods behind our house with my father on a hot July afternoon. The odor had appeared suddenly, permeating my clothes, hair, and the lining of my nose. It burned with sickening ferocity, and I couldn't escape it. Even after I had heaved my guts out, I couldn't stop gagging. My father had left me, choking on empty air, to investigate and had found a female deer. Its abdomen had been slit, exposing its entrails and creating a veritable feast for all the beasts and insects of the forest. My father had picked me up and brought me home. But I had never forgotten that smell.

I grabbed the front of my skirt and held it against my nostrils. Captain Audenreid motioned the other men back, then pulled his sidearm out of its holster. I walked up the porch steps, close behind the captain. "Hello," I called to the dark space behind the door.

The wind pushed at the wooden door; it sighed quietly, allowing a fresh outpouring of the stench to wash over me. I swallowed thickly as my stomach churned.

"Hello," I called again, walking slowly to the open portal. The captain shoved it gently with his arm. It yawned wide, and we stepped in.

It took my eyes almost a minute to adjust to the darkness. Only two windows illuminated the entire one-room house, creating a murky interior in shades of gray. My eyes squinted in the dimness until they rested on the shape of a double bed.

Swarming flies hovered over me as I approached, the buzzing of the insects growing louder. The two small boys lay on their backs, heads touching and arms folded neatly over still chests. Empty eye sockets stared up at me, and the light reflected off something white and twitching. I leaned forward and saw the maggots swimming in and out of the dark holes. I lifted a hand in an age-old maternal desire to smooth the hair back on a troubled brow. My hand stilled when I noticed what was left of the ear on the child nearest me. A jagged tear ripped the ear in half, dried blood outlining the wound. A pillow lay at the foot of the bed, and I knew instinctively how the children had died. Gingerly, my hand shaking, I put the pillow aside and pulled the quilt over the two bodies, the buzzing of the flies now screaming in my ears. I felt their mother close by, but I wasn't afraid.

I heard heavy breathing behind me and turned to put a hand on the captain's arm. I was surprised to find it trembling.

A loud rustling erupted from a corner of the room. The bushy tail of a fox darted out through the open door, dust rising in its wake. Shots from outside followed its progress.

Captain Audenreid coughed and held a hand up to his face.

I took another step backward, my foot sticking to the floor. I bent to investigate the dark pool, and I saw her hand. Two slits bisected her wrist, and gnaw marks from an animal had nearly severed the hand from the arm. She lay on her side by the hearth, her skirts settled purposefully around her, as if she was posing for a portrait. Her face was mostly gone, but all I could see when I looked at it was the expression of lost hope I had seen as she stood in the middle of her empty pasture.

"Oh, my God," I mumbled, staggering to my feet and stumbling through the door. I walked blindly ahead, away from the soldiers. I needed to be alone. To grieve for this woman and her lost children and for whatever part I might have played in her final desperate act.

Quick footsteps approached me, but I kept walking, breathing in the sweet April air in a futile attempt to eradicate the vile stench of death.

"Mrs. Elliott, stop! We have to move on now."

I continued walking, almost running, calling back over my shoulder, "You go on. I want no more part of your war."

Captain Audenreid quickened his pace, and soon I felt his hand on my shoulder, stopping me. "I'm sorry you had to see that. But that had nothing to do with this war—surely you could see it was a suicide."

I turned on him in fury, knocking his hand off my arm. "How can you say that? Didn't you see? She was alone here on this farm with two small children. Where was her husband? Most likely obliterated by this war." I swallowed back the tears that threatened. I thrust an arm out in the direction of the little house and spat out my words. "Those are just three more victims of this war. You men speak of glory and victory. Tell me this—can you look at the faces in there and tell me that anybody can truly win?"

The tears won and spilled down my face.

I struck out at him with my good arm, and he allowed me to pummel his chest. He pulled me to him and patted my back, murmuring words of comfort until my tears subsided.

Too embarrassed to raise my head, I mumbled into his dark-blue jacket, "Can we at least bury them?"

He paused, weighing Sherman's orders for haste with the scene inside the farmhouse.

I felt him nod. Leaving me where I stood, he walked to the crest of the ridge to speak to the officer there. Orders were given, and two soldiers appeared with shovels, walking toward the little house.

Each sound of shovel hitting dirt felt like a physical blow. I had known loss before but not this devastation of the heart. What final blow to her spirit had driven this woman to such a desperate act?

"She was a good mother, you know." The young soldier digging looked up at me, then resumed his work. I spoke louder. "It would have been much worse to abandon her children to the harshness of war." I closed my eyes tightly, not wanting to see the young mother's look of desperation.

The children were laid on either side of their mother, and I knew I would never be able to smell freshly dug dirt again without thinking of them. There was no minister, so Captain Audenreid said a simple prayer. And then the dirt was sprinkled back into the open grave, obliterating the sun forever from sightless eyes.

I climbed back into the wagon, careful not to wake Sarah, who had fallen asleep. We resumed our march, faster this time to catch up with the rest of the troops. I turned around in the seat and watched the small farm disappear slowly from sight, streams of early-morning sunshine warming the newly-turned earth.

I felt a sharp stab in my lower abdomen, taking my breath away. And then nothing else. I placed a hand on my stomach, feeling its flatness. I had had that sensation only once in my life, when the thought of conceiving a child had seemed just that—a thought. An unobtainable dream. Until I had proof that it wasn't. I smiled with a mother's knowing and looked down at the sleeping face of my firstborn.

311

The wheels of the wagon rolled onward, like the never-ending cycle of life, death, and rebirth. I placed my hand on my abdomen again, willing some sort of sign from the child I knew grew inside. But all was still.

"Cry 'havoc!' and let loose the dogs of war,
that this foul deed shall smell above the earth
with carrion men, groaning for burial."
William Shakespeare

Chapter Twenty-six

We had been brought to Meadowland, an antebellum mansion in Tunnel Hill, about ten miles north of Dalton and the Confederate army. Sherman had made this imposing Greek Revival structure his temporary headquarters, and Sarah and I had been sent to a room and unofficially told to stay out of the way.

She and I talked about her kidnapping, and she seemed to have suffered no long-term ill effects except for an aversion to being left alone. A woman with a child Sarah's age had been sent to care for her, and Sarah regarded the whole thing as a sort of adventure. William had only come to see her once since their reunion, and I told him the truth of my relationship to Sarah. He had reacted to the news with a shrug and a "poor Julia" before casually changing the subject. I still hadn't told Sarah, the reason for my hesitation not clear even to myself.

The sounds of war came from far away, almost as an afterthought. I sat in a rocker on the upstairs balcony, reading aloud to Sarah. I had paused to look at her and was admiring the way the light made her green eyes shift colors when a soft boom vibrated in the air. I stood, the book sliding off my lap. Another boom percolated in the distance as puffs of smoke rose on the horizon and disappeared into the blue morning sky. The soft strains of *The Star Spangled Banner* crept over the trees to tease my ears. The staccato beat of drums reverberated across the hills.

Sarah ran to look over the railing, her eyes alight with excitement. "Are those soldiers?"

I stood paralyzed, my legs shaking and my arm hurting again. I wondered where Stuart was, and if he was safer in a prison than on a battlefield. "Yes, Sarah. Lots of soldiers."

We stayed on the balcony the entire day, my nerves frayed and my imagination running wild. But I couldn't leave the sounds of battle.

Eventually, a private called me to dinner. He brought Sarah down to eat in the kitchen, and I went to the dining room, where I was once again surrounded by Sherman and his staff. This was the first time I had seen the general since Stuart had been taken away, and I vowed not to let the night pass without speaking to him alone.

Midway through the meal, a courier rushed into the dining room and handed the general a telegram. He read it quickly, a large grin splitting his face. "It's from McPherson," he said, referring to General James B. McPherson, commander of the Army of Tennessee. Sherman slammed a fist on the table, making the china and crystal shimmy. "I've got Joe Johnston dead!"

I demurely took another spoonful of soup while the men did a lot of back-slapping and other congratulatory gestures. I glanced up to find William staring at me, one eyebrow raised. I put down my spoon and lowered my gaze.

I couldn't share in any jubilation. I longed for word of Stuart, my fears for him growing with each passing hour. I swallowed my food and bided my time.

I lay awake in my bed for a long time that night, waiting for the last of the guests to depart. Then I slipped from the room with a shawl thrown over my nightgown.

I found the library in the darkened house, only to be disappointed to see it empty. I helped myself to a glass of Scotch, then brought it out to the foyer. I smelled cigar smoke coming from above. Stealthily, I crept back up the stairs to head for the balcony. Pale moonlight shone through the banister slats, creating dark lines marching in formation across the wooden floorboards.

The balcony appeared to be deserted. I leaned over the railing, taking deep breaths of the cool evening air, trying to swallow my disappointment. I knew I could convince General Sherman of Stuart's innocence if I just had the opportunity to speak to him alone. My palms grew moist as I thought of my other plan to convince the general if my words failed to sway him. I stood and started to take a sip of the Scotch but stopped, my lips pursed at the rim of the glass, my other hand resting on my abdomen. I moved my head, the distinctive odor of fresh cigar smoke drifting over to me. From the corner of my eye I saw the unmistakable end of a cigar glowing red in the dark.

"Madam."

The suddenness of the sound caused me to drop the glass, sloshing liquid over my bare feet and bouncing the glass off the balcony. I heard the delicate sound of shattering crystal as it hit the brick steps below.

"You startled me." I bent to wipe the dripping Scotch off my legs.

"Apparently." I heard the smile in the general's voice. "I hope my men talking didn't keep you awake."

I shook my head. "No. Actually, I was waiting for everyone to leave so I could talk with you." I hid a yawn behind my hand. "Besides, I haven't been sleeping well lately. Too many scary thoughts." I straightened, feeling the sticky liquid drying on my bare skin.

"Scary thoughts," he repeated after me. "Well put." He took a long sip from his glass. I heard him swallow in the stillness of the night.

"What did you want to talk to me about?"

I knew he would expect my bluntness. "My husband. He's as responsible for saving your life as I am."

314

"Really?" He brought his glass to his lips and took another sip.

"Pamela Broderick kidnapped my . . . my niece. She threatened to kill her unless I followed through with her plan to murder you. Stuart found little Sarah and brought her to me so I would know I didn't have to go through with it. He risked his life to save me—and you. He doesn't belong in a prison camp."

He paused, and I could hear his deep breathing. "But he's still a Rebel officer, and he was captured. Why should I release him so he can return to his army and fight against me?"

I ground my toes into the floorboard and took a deep breath. "He risked his life to save me. I will do anything to save him. Anything." I let my shawl fall to my elbows, looking at him sharply.

His hand with the cigar froze midway to his mouth. I stepped closer to him, near enough to smell the Scotch on his breath. He appraised me boldly. "Madam, are you making me an . . . offer?"

I forced myself to hold his gaze. "I will do anything you ask in return for the release of my husband."

He took a slow drag on his cigar, his eyes never leaving my face. "You're an attractive woman, Mrs. Elliott. And I'm honored that you hold me in such high regard."

The warm breeze stirred my nightgown around my feet, cooling my flaming skin.

"But I'm afraid I can't accept."

I bit my lip, holding back my anger. "You can't, or you won't?"

Half of his mouth turned up. "Madam, I'm in command of the Military Division of the Mississippi, with over one hundred thousand men. I pull a bit of weight in the ranks."

"Then why? Why won't you help me?"

"I didn't say I wouldn't. If your story is true, which I suspect is the case, then, despite your husband's being a Rebel officer, he's innocent of any crime. I owe you my life, and releasing your husband is the least I can do."

I stamped my foot. "Do you mean you were willing to release him before I even opened my mouth? And yet you let me . . . make a fool of myself?"

He took a slow drag from his cigar. "On the contrary, Mrs. Elliott. I hadn't yet heard a complete accounting of your husband's involvement in the assassination plot." He slowly blew out the cigar smoke. "Besides, you've shown me how much you love your husband. Any man whose wife loves him with such devotion deserves a second chance."

"Oh," I said, for lack of anything better.

"Don't be embarrassed, Mrs. Elliott. War does things to people—it changes us. You were merely doing what you thought you had to do to ensure your husband's safety."

I turned away from him, staring out over the railing and into the night. "I'm not that . . . that type of woman, and I appreciate your understanding. On behalf of my husband and myself, thank you."

We were silent for a few moments before the general spoke again. "I would like to try to convince you to stay here, in safety. It's going to be rougher from here on out, and I think you would be more comfortable staying put."

"No." I shook my head, my loosened hair swinging about my face. "It's very important that I get home. I . . . I'm pretty sure I'm going to have a baby, and I need to get home."

A flash of white appeared above his beard. "Congratulations, Mrs. Elliott. My wife and I have had six children, soon to be joined by number seven." He stopped to stare out at the darkened sky, both hands gripping the railing, the cigar clenched in his teeth, trailing smoke. Quietly he said, "It's almost hard to imagine a new life amidst all this destruction."

I closed my eyes on the darkness, seeing a deserted farmhouse in the middle of a barren field. "War is hell, isn't it, General?" I said, opening my eyes and noticing the bent shoulders on the tall frame silhouetted against the moonlit sky.

"That it is, Mrs. Elliott. That it is." He flicked cigar ash over the railing, then watched the particles filter through the night air.

I turned to leave. "I suppose I should try to get some rest. Good night, General."

He turned his head toward me. "Good night, Mrs. Elliott. I'll see to your husband's release."

"Thank you," I said again, then closed the door behind me. As I stood in the darkened hallway, I heard the tread of feet moving quickly down the stairs and across the foyer. I dismissed an uneasy feeling, then went to my bedroom.

As it turned out, despite his proclamation over dinner the previous night, Sherman did not have Johnston dead. General McPherson had neglected to push his advantage at the little town of Resaca and was now facing a growing Confederate Army. And so we moved south, toward Atlanta, and General Joe Johnston's army. The Southerners were now digging in to defensive positions around Resaca, about ten miles south of Dalton and a mere fifty miles north of Atlanta.

Sarah and I were left with the army wagon train at Snake Creek Gap while the separate divisions took their places around Resaca. The sound of cannon began in the early morning hours of May 14, shaking the earth with their bombardments and creating a heavy cloud of smoke across the valley and over the bald hill that stood as the blind sentry over the battlefield. I began pacing and biting my fingernails. I even tried reading a book to Sarah. But the battle sounds permeated the air around me and could not be escaped.

By the second day of battle, I refused to be a bystander any longer. I had at least one good arm, and I had every intention of putting it to use. I left Sarah in the care of the cook, then trudged along the wagon train, asking for the field hospital. Men pointed and stared, but none tried to stop me.

The smell of burning flesh hit me first. The flaming piles of severed limbs stacked outside the surgeon's tent told me I had reached the right place. Gritting my teeth, I walked inside—and entered hell.

Surgeons in blood-splattered aprons sawed into wounded flesh, oblivious to the screams and moans around them. Two doors, doubtless ripped off nearby farmhouses, served as makeshift operating tables. Scalpels, saws, and horsehair sutures were laid out on a blanket, hastily replenished as they disappeared.

As soon as one limb had been lopped off, the patient was whisked away on his litter and another one brought forward. Using the same bloody saw, the surgeon would again attack a wounded limb, allowing it to plop into a quickly filling basket.

I stood still, being shoved in every direction by the fast-moving people around me, unsure where I could step in and help. Someone grabbed my arm. "Are you a nurse?"

Numbly, I nodded.

"Good. Let's find a way to make you useful."

He brought me to an operating table. "Hold him down," I was instructed. The man speaking had dried blood spattered in his beard and across his forehead. Tiny glasses perched on the bridge of his nose, and his eyes appeared overly large as he regarded me.

Not willing to make excuses for my shoulder, I stood behind the wounded man's head, my hands on his shoulders, and held firmly. The young sergeant stared up at me, panic plain in his eyes. "Ye can't let them take off me leg. It's an imported leg, it is. Straight from Ireland."

The surgeon probed at the open wound with his index finger, studying it intently. A minie ball had shattered part of the bone, spreading pieces of lead, dirt, and torn uniform through the leg. He shook his head.

I looked back down at the patient, trying to keep my voice steady. "You will die if you don't allow the doctor to take it off." He struggled slightly, but I held firm. "Do you have a wife?"

He stopped struggling and nodded. "And six wee ones."

"Well, then, I expect she'd rather see you return from war with one less leg than not at all."

A medic stood by, a towel and bottle of chloroform at the ready. "Will it hurt?" The man's eyes were wide with terror, beads of sweat marking their way down gunpowder-stained cheeks.

"Not as much as childbirth, I shouldn't think."

He looked temporarily shocked, then gave me a weak smile.
"All right, then. Let's get on with it."

I squeezed his shoulder reassuringly as the chloroform-soaked towel was lowered over his nose and mouth.

And so the procession of wounded men and boys continued.
The gut-shot ones were triaged to the rear. They were given
water and pain medication, but there was nothing else to be
done for them. Eventually, they would be taken out behind
the tent to await burial, their stiffening bodies already covered
with flies.

The sun rose high in the sky, making the inside of the tent
an inferno, but we kept working. The fused stench of sweat,
blood, and death filled the confined area, permeating my hands
and clothes, but I wouldn't allow myself to stop. I would hold
hands and talk or give water. I no longer noticed the colors
of uniforms. It simply didn't matter.

By late afternoon, the bombardment of the cannon had subsided, leaving only the moans of the wounded. An orderly
approached me with about ten canteens and instructed me to
go out on the battlefield to help more wounded until they could
be brought in.

I stared numbly out onto the scarred field, the branchless
trees like sentinels guarding the dead. The field sloped down
into a creek choked with felled men, trees, horses, and an
upended flat-bottomed boat. Soldiers in blue and gray lay side
by side along its banks, drinking the dirty water. The canteens
strung around my shoulders bounced and clanged against each
other, the water sloshing inside. Examining the murky depths
of the filthy river, I didn't want to know where the water in
the canteens had come from. I no longer felt the pain of my
wound—the sights and smells around me were too overwhelming.

A thin pall of smoke settled over the ground, the sickly-
sweet smell of sulfur and gunpowder thick in my nostrils. I
coughed, my throat and nose stinging.

Men lay strewn across the battlefield like the discarded toys
of an angry child, elbows and knees bent at odd angles, faces
contorted with expressions of agony. I picked my way across

corpses, looking for a dry mouth croaking the never-ending litany of "water."

I knew it had been a Federal victory, but as I stared out at the broken bodies, I could not feel anything but regret.

I knelt by a soldier, his light-brown hair matted with blood and dirt. "Mama," he whispered, looking directly at me. He looked about sixteen—not even old enough to shave, much less wear a uniform and carry a rifle. I gingerly slid my hand under his neck, lifting his head up to drink from a canteen. The water dribbled into his mouth, leaking down his chin and blackened face.

"Mama," he said again, light-brown eyes staring sightlessly at me.

"Yes," I said, easing myself down to the ground and placing his head in my lap. I stroked the dirty hair, its strands slick between my fingers.

"I'm . . ." He stopped, gasping to fill his lungs. "I'm . . . I'm sorry . . . for . . . leaving."

I paused, not quite knowing what to say. "It's okay. Don't worry any more about it. You're forgiven."

I gave him more water and looked to see if there was anything to be done with his wound. My eyes stopped when they reached his abdomen. His jacket and shirt had been pulled loose and bunched in disarray over his prostrate form. The grass between us was drenched with dark red blood, already humming with tiny insects. His entire side was missing, exposing bone and torn tissue and vital organs. I looked back at his face, now still and peaceful, his vacant eyes reflecting the open sky.

I gently put his head on the ground and closed his eyes with shaking fingers.

I stood and looked out over the sea of gray and blue. A coppery taste settled on my tongue, causing me to gag. I took a swig from a canteen to wash it away, but to no avail. The putrid taste was in the air. I shuddered, realizing it was blood. Collapsing to my knees, I began to retch. I dug my fingers into the dirt and touched my forehead to the grass, breathing in the sweet smell of it. I hadn't eaten since breakfast and could only gag. I wanted to expel the vileness in the air that seemed to saturate my body.

But still the croaks for water continued, bringing me to my feet again. Medics rushed to place the wounded on litters, racing to the tents those who could be helped and leaving those with no hope on the ground where they had fallen.

By dusk, my canteens were empty, and the cries of the wounded had stilled. I saw a large rock by a tree and walked toward it. I stepped on something hard and bent to retrieve whatever it was. It was a small pocket Bible, no bigger than my hand, the binding well worn. It fell open to a page upon which a dried rose lay. I picked up the rose, and it crumbled in my hand, its withered petals scattering in the wind. A single verse had been underlined with thick, black ink, and I read it aloud.

"To everything there is a season, and a time to every purpose under heaven: a time to be born and a time to die; a time to plant, and a time to pluck up that which is planted; a time to kill, and a time to heal. . . ."

I stopped, the words blurring before my eyes. My shoulders sagged, the canteens sliding off into the churned earth. The field was scattered with personal effects of the dead: eyeglasses, letters, and diaries. I couldn't look at them and not see the mothers, wives, and daughters who would be waiting for news. I placed the Bible back on the ground by the tree. The breeze picked up slightly, blowing vanished voices away on the wind.

I looked up at the sound of hoofbeats and recognized Captain Audenreid astride the horse fast approaching me. He tipped his hat as he drew close. "Mrs. Elliot."

I stood quickly, my head light from the effort. I steadied myself on the tree.

The captain dismounted, holding the reins loosely in his hands. "Your husband's sent a courier. He left a missive with General Sherman."

I stared at him mutely, his words not quite registering. "Oh," I said, not quite sure what my next course of action should be.

"I thought you'd be pleased to hear that your husband is no longer a prisoner."

"Yes," I said, suddenly springing into action as I gathered up the empty canteens and raced toward General Sherman's tent, the captain doing his best to keep up with me.

The general was seated in a camp chair outside his tent, holding a piece of paper. William sat next to him in stockinged feet, polishing his boots. They stood as I approached.

"Mrs. Elliot, I have some news for you."

"Yes, I know. Captain Audenreid told me. When can I see him?"

A glance passed between William and the general. "Your brother-in-law and I were just discussing it. We cannot allow you to go into their camp. You're something of a heroine here, and your capture could be used as quite a bargaining point. I would like to suggest a meeting in the middle of the field, on neutral ground."

I stood close to the general, noticing the smattering of freckles on his nose, a marked contrast to the stern expression on his face. "All right. When?"

"I've arranged for tomorrow at dawn. Can you be ready?"

I gave a faint smile. "I'll be there."

Dawn came early. I shivered from cold as I stood to dress, the walls of my tent damp with morning dew. I gasped as I threw cold water, left in my basin from the night before, onto my face.

In my joy at learning Stuart had been released, I hadn't yet thought of what I would say to him. My hand slid to my abdomen, and I patted it with a smile. I knew one thing that was sure to be an icebreaker. I kissed the still-sleeping Sarah, then left my tent. I shivered again, but not from the cold.

I was surprised to see William waiting for me and holding the reins of two horses. He handed one to me, a mock smile on his face.

"It has been decided that I will accompany you, little sister. After all, Stuart is my brother."

I stilled my protest, not wanting a confrontation to spoil my reunion with Stuart.

He assisted me into the saddle, his hand sliding casually down the length of my leg. He then pulled a wooden pole from the ground, a rectangular white flag tied to it, and mounted.

The sky had an ominous red cast to it, and I remembered the saying, "Red sky at morning, sailors take warning." I crouched lower in my saddle, trying to warm myself and stop my teeth from chattering. Campfires flared throughout the field as men bustled about, preparing their breakfast. My stomach churned at the thought of food while at the same time grumbling from hunger. I smiled to myself, acknowledging another sign of impending motherhood.

I didn't have time to be nervous about riding the horse—I was too busy scanning the far side of the field for a familiar figure. We trotted slowly out onto the tortured ground, scarred from the mortars and trampling feet of the previous day. My horse shied away from the decapitated body of another horse, sidestepping quickly, its hooves slipping on the dew-moistened dirt. I held on tightly, following William, who had not paused.

A lone figure emerged from the shadowed woods on the far side. I heard the thin echo of hoofbeats vibrating the ground beneath me. I recognized Endy first, his black coat fuzzy in the morning dimness. Clinging tightly to my reins, I dug my heels into my horse's sides, heedless of William's shouted warning.

The wind stung my eyes, but I refused to close them lest I lose sight of the tall figure in gray atop the large black horse. He, too, broke into a gallop, clods of dirt flying behind him. I reined my horse in tightly, making it rear. I slid off the side, my skirts catching on my saddle and giving any and all spectators a brief and complete show of my undergarments.

I ran as fast as I could, the sound of William's horse close behind me. Stuart had also dismounted, and he stood next to Endy, waiting for me. He started walking, then running as I neared, catching me as I flung myself at him. He swung me

323

around, my skirts flying and his arms wound tightly around my waist. I buried my face in his neck, feeling the unfamiliar fuzz of a new beard.

"Oh, God," I mumbled into his beard, "I would have done anything to be in your arms again."

His voice searched for sure ground. "You're still as beautiful as the first time I saw you." His fingers traced my face, caressing my jaw. "These are the eyes I see each night before I sleep."

I smiled, tilting my head back to look up at him, keeping my uninjured arm around his neck. His face was thinner, and a jagged scar showed through the beard on his jaw. I kissed it first, then kissed him full on the mouth. He responded, his lips hard against mine.

He rested his chin on the top of my head, his arms wrapped tightly around me. "It's your face I'll be searching for when this war is over." He cupped his fingers around my skull, his eyes searching mine, a hint of danger hidden behind the dark blue.

I jerked my head back, my gaze touching his jaw. "I . . . I can't." My hand drifted to my abdomen, and I thought of the child that should be bringing us together but was the one thing that could separate us forever. "I have to go away for a while. But if there's any way in this universe that I can return to you, I promise you, I will." I realized there had been no decision for me to make. The truth had been in my heart for a long time; all I had to do was look and find it.

His hold on me tightened. "You still have secrets, Laura. Haven't I earned your trust by now?" His eyes were cold, but I could feel his craving for me in the touch of his hands. I was nearly breathless in my wanting of him, yet he held me away.

I touched his face, the sensitive place below his ear, the place that made him moan when I touched it with my lips when we were making love. "You've earned my heart and my life, Stuart. I can't keep any more secrets from you."

He stepped back suddenly, his hand touching the revolver in his belt as he looked behind me.

"Hello, little brother. So, we meet again." William put an arm around my shoulders, giving me a squeeze. "We didn't get to talk much last time we saw each other, but I wanted to say that I have found your wife absolutely delightful."

I jerked away from William's hold and stepped toward Stuart. "Go away, William. I have things to discuss with my husband."

He shook his head in an exaggerated way. "I don't think so, sister. You've been privy to too many discussions involving our General Sherman. I don't believe it would be wise of me to allow you to converse any more in private." He smiled broadly. "Besides, I wanted to have a chance to talk to my brother."

Stuart's jaw moved under his cheeks. "I have nothing to say to you, William. I can scarce believe you are actually my brother."

"But I think you might want to hear what I have to say anyway."

Dread filled me as I waited for William to speak.

"Were you not surprised to be released from prison so quickly? And let's not forget your medical care. Did you ever stop to wonder how that was all arranged?"

I suddenly remembered the stealthy footsteps I had heard following my conversation with General Sherman. I turned on William. "Shut up! Everything you say is a twisted lie. Don't listen to him, Stuart—none of it's true."

Stuart slid a glance in my direction. "Just a moment, Laura. I want to hear this."

"She doesn't want you to hear it, Stuart. Or you'll find out what kind of a woman she really is." William turned to me. "Tell him about your conversation with General Sherman. Tell him what you offered the good general in return for Stuart's release." He faced Stuart again. "And it wasn't our mother's jewelry, little brother. Oh, no. Your wife offered him the most precious thing of all."

Stuart moved closer to me and looked into my eyes. "What is he talking about?" Then his eyes widened as comprehension hit him.

325

I looked closely at him, at the beloved lines and soft skin of his neck, wanting to be away from this place with him, all this forgotten. Our gazes clashed, and all sounds seemed to disappear; even the small insects in the grass lay still, waiting for my answer.

"Tell me it isn't true, Laura. Tell me he's lying."

I looked away, then back at his accusing eyes. "It is true I offered myself, but nothing happened. I promise you—nothing happened."

He stepped back. "But you would have."

I squeezed my hands into fists, wanting to strike out at William—and at Stuart. "Yes, God damn it—I would have. I would have sold my soul to the devil to save your life."

Shock registered on his face, and he shook his head as if trying to erase a thought. "Is this the kind of secret you've been holding back from me all this time?"

"No—no! Of course not. Oh, God, Stuart. I love you. I need to tell you everything so you'll understand!"

He walked up so close to me that I could feel his heat. "Then tell me."

I wanted to blurt out everything, to erase the look of hurt on Stuart's face, but William's presence stopped me. He couldn't be trusted with the truth. "I can't now."

Stuart turned and began walking toward Endy. I couldn't let him leave. William held me back by my wounded arm as I tried to go to Stuart.

"Tell him our news, Laura."

I pushed William away and rushed after Stuart, grabbing hold of his jacket. His eyes were bright with anger as he glared at me.

"I'm going to have a baby."

His gaze flickered down me, and then over to where William stood. Then he looked me level in the eyes. "And who's the father?"

I felt as if I had sustained a blow to the stomach. I reached out and slapped him as hard as I could across the face.

He didn't flinch. He simply turned on his heel, mounted Endy, and rode out to the edge of the field, disappearing into the shadows of the woods.

"I have been a stranger in a strange land."

Exodus 2:22

Chapter Twenty-seven

"Hello, Mrs. Elliott. I brought you and your little girl some-thing."

I sat back in the wagon, feeling the heat of the late-June afternoon press down on me. I smoothed a hand over my dress, feeling the slight swelling of my abdomen. Looking at the private walking toward me, I cocked my head.

The soldier pushed a black-and-white cow forward, its large brown eyes lazily browsing the crowd of men who had gath-ered near the wagon train after setting up camp.

I recognized the man as one of Sherman's "bummers," one of the many swarms of soldiers assigned to forage for food. Knowing that these men gleefully stripped the land and its inhabitants of anything valuable and anything edible, I felt guilty as I ate three square meals a day. Still, my pregnancy meant I was hungry constantly, and several of the soldiers, knowing my condition, would make a point of saving the best pickings for me.

Someone shouted from the crowd, "Hell, O'Rory, if I thought you was that lonesome, I would have loaned you some money to come into town with me."

The shouting was met by catcalls and a loud moo from the cow. The soldier faced the growing crowd. "Aw, you all shut up. I thought Mrs. Elliott would like some steak."

"Yeah, O'Rory. And if she don't, I bet you'll take ole Daisy-Mae back to your tent."

Karen White

More ribald laughter and comments followed this remark, and the young man's face grew stern. He turned back to me.

"Please accept this gift, ma'am."

I glanced over the cow, noticing both the full udder and the panicked look in the cow's eyes. I looked back at the soldier. "Well, she certainly does have nice calves."

The group of men exploded in laughter as the man's face turned a deep red. I climbed off the wagon and put a hand on his arm. "I'm sorry. It's a joke I couldn't resist. But I can't accept this cow for slaughter. This is a milk cow. Where did you get it?"

He looked down at his boots, scuffing the dirt with his toe. "From a farm not two miles from here. Stupid Rebs left her all alone in the pasture."

I felt the blood drain from my face. "This cow is full of milk—somebody's been milking her regularly. Probably a mother with young children. I think they need it more than we do."

He stepped between the cow and me, as if to protect his prize. "No, ma'am. They's just Rebs. They deserve to starve to death."

I was a good head taller than he was, and I stepped closer to him to take full advantage of the difference in stature. I leaned over him and said, "Women and children are not your enemies. They're just trying to survive. Imagine if it were your wife and children."

He gave me a defiant look. "I'm not married."

"Then picture your mother or sister and—" My retort was interrupted by the arrival of Captain Audenreid. Since my meeting with Stuart, he had stayed close to my side as much as possible. He never asked about Stuart, and I would not talk about him, but the captain seemed to know that all was not well. I had seen him closely regarding William's dogged pursuit it of me, and he put himself between my brother-in-law and me whenever he could.

He took one look at my blanched face and ordered a camp chair for me. "Are you ill, Mrs. Elliott?" His solicitous look was warming.

I shook my head. "No. It's just that I want this soldier to take the cow back from where he stole it."

The captain was apprised of the situation and ordered the soldier to return the cow.

With much grumbling, the private retreated, the cow faithfully in tow.

I reached out and squeezed the captain's hand in gratitude. He looked at me, startled. "I'm sorry, Captain. I apologize if I was forward. But I wanted to thank you for that."

His face softened as he regarded me in the hot sun. "Remember, I was in that farmhouse, too. I shall never forget it. Nor shall I ever forget you."

I turned away, flustered, not knowing what to say.

"I'm sorry . . . Laura. I didn't mean to cause you discomfort. I . . . I just wanted to let you know that I hold you in high regard. And that you can rely on me to get you home safely."

I looked back at his face, my hand shielding the sun from my eyes. I could see a slight flush under his sunburn. "Thank you, Captain. I shall treasure your friendship."

Smiling warmly at him, I watched him remount and ride away, his hand raised in farewell.

I had traveled with Sherman's massive army through the hot months of May and June as it continually flanked the Confederates and forced them to retreat farther and farther south toward the inevitable confrontation at Atlanta. I kept myself busy in the hospital tents, doling out what mercies I could. I enjoyed the time I had with Sarah, and we spent it becoming better acquainted. I found that her favorite color was blue and that she loved most vegetables but especially corn. I learned the name of her best friend and the way she liked her hair plaited. But I didn't know what it had been like for her when she lost her first tooth, nor what gifts she had received for her last six birthdays. Nor did I know what songs her mother sang to her at bedtime or the words of comfort she listened for when she had nightmares. She still called me Aunt Laura, for I had not yet told her otherwise.

I refused to think about Stuart. If I did, the tightness around my heart would make it almost too hard to breathe. Instead, I made plans. I had been alone before, and I knew I could do it again. Surely I could raise my children on my own. The next conjunction of a lunar eclipse and a comet would be on September first. I would leave the same way I had arrived—borne on the wind of a speeding mass of celestial particles. Stuart could assume whatever he wanted, and I would disappear from his world forever.

By July third, Sherman had entered Marietta, some fifteen miles west of Roswell. I was summoned to Kennesaw House, the town's most fashionable hotel, where Sherman had set up his headquarters.

I left Sarah on a bench outside the office. As I entered the room, the general stood by the window, caught in a fit of coughing. As soon as he finished, I heard the strident wheezing that reminded me of Jack's asthma. To my astonishment, he picked up a cigar from the desk and began puffing on it.

"General, do you think you should be doing that?"

He frowned at me, his brows knitting. "Pardon me?"

"Smoking. It won't help your asthma."

He continued to stare at me and puff on his cigar. "I'll take that under advisement. Sit down, please."

He indicated a seat by the desk, then reached into a drawer, pulled out a letter, and handed it to me. "This is a letter from me granting you and your possessions immunity from Federal authorities." He came around the desk to stand in front of me. "Mrs. Elliott, for your protection, I have sworn to secrecy all who know about what happened to Mrs. Broderick. It might not go well for you if it were known by your fellow Southerners." He smiled warmly at me. "But please don't think it's because I'm not grateful—I am. You did save my life. If there's ever anything that I can do for you, please do not hesitate to call on me." With a sly grin, he added, "And there will be no payment required."

I ignored the flush rushing to my face. "I understand—and thank you for this," I said, indicating the letter. "I know of your men's propensity for burning houses." I shuddered, recalling the smoldering ruins we had passed on our way to Atlanta. All that remained of once-beautiful plantation homes were the chimneys—"Sherman's sentinels" they were called.

"I'm sending you with Brigadier General Kenner Garrard, the Commander of the 2nd Division Cavalry, to Roswell. It has been a real pleasure knowing you, Mrs. Elliott, and I wish you Godspeed."

He moved back behind the desk, and I knew I was being dismissed. I began walking toward the door but hung back, wishing to say one more thing. "General, I have a strong feeling you'll be giving Savannah to President Lincoln as a Christmas present."

He leaned forward with both hands on the desk. "Really? Well, I certainly appreciate your vote of confidence." He began shuffling papers on his desk, and I knew he had lost interest in the topic.

"Good-bye, General. And thank you again." I turned and shut the door behind me.

I almost ran into Captain Audenreid as Sarah and I hurried down the stairway. He was coming up, his hat in his hand, and a small hatbox in his other. "Laura, I'm glad to see you. I hope you don't mind, but I've brought something for Sarah. I thought she could use a bonnet to protect her skin in this hot Georgia sun. I love her freckles, but her mother might not."

Sarah squealed and took the box from the captain with shouted thanks and immediately opened it. She slipped a straw bonnet onto her head and asked me to tie the lilac ribbon under her chin.

I smiled at the effect. "Captain, thank you so much—you shouldn't have. But I'm glad I ran into you. I'm afraid this is good-bye. I'm returning to Roswell today in the company of General Garrard."

He looked genuinely sad as he reached for my hand and bent to kiss it, his mustache tickling my skin. "It has been an immense pleasure, Mrs. Elliott. I shall not easily forget you."

Despite his words, I did not feel uneasy. "Thank you, Captain. Thank you for everything."

He looked at me intensely. "Mrs. Elliott, please be careful. There are those whose intentions toward you aren't completely honorable."

I knew to whom he was referring. "I will. I promise. And you continue to dodge bullets, okay?"

He sent me a sad grin as I reached out and squeezed his hand. "Good-bye," he said softly. He chucked Sarah under the chin. "And you take good care of your aunt, you hear?"

Sarah nodded and gave him a hug.

We turned and walked across the street toward Marietta Square amidst the hustle and bustle of civilians and soldiers.

On Tuesday, July fifth, General Garrard and his forces arrived in an almost deserted Roswell. The Confederates had abandoned the little mill town, burning the bridge across the Chattahoochee as they left. Crossing the river would bring the troops closer to the prize of Atlanta, and I knew the burning of the bridge would be a sore point with General Sherman.

So many of Garrard's men suffered from heatstroke in the broiling Georgia sun, they were falling out of their saddles by the handful. One of the first things General Garrard did was set up hospitals for them on the front lawns of the Dunwody and Pratt houses and also the Presbyterian church where I had been married. Anger rose in me as I saw the ripped-out pews tossed on the front lawn of the church to be used as firewood, but I was helpless to stop the desecration.

I yearned to see my house again. I didn't know what shape Phoenix Hall would be in, but I knew without a doubt it would still be standing.

While the impromptu hospitals were being set up, Sarah and I took the opportunity to join several of the soldiers in picking our fill of blackberries. We seemed to have been forgotten and easily settled ourselves on the side of the road in the middle of town while the soldiers went about the business of setting up camp. I laughed at Sarah, berry juice dripping down her chin. I was busily popping berries into my own mouth when I saw the flames. From the direction they were coming, I realized it was the cotton mill, burned under General Sherman's orders. I knew the Elliotts' main source of income was as stockholders of the Roswell Manufacturing Company, and this would render them destitute.

The flames licked at the sky, large particles exploding the

air. I thought of Phoenix Hall and of how a deserted house would lure looters, and I itched to get there as soon as possible. I assumed Zeke and Charles had long since joined Julia in Valdosta, but a part of me wished they were still there to greet us when we returned home.

I stood and glanced around me to be sure no one watched. Then I took my carpetbag from the back of the wagon and Sarah's hand and began walking the three miles to the house. I had barely crossed the town square when I heard my name being shouted. I turned to face William Elliott.

I hadn't seen him on the trek from Marietta, and I assumed he had stayed with Sherman. Knowing his deviousness, however, I was sure he had managed to come here where he knew I would be. Without a doubt his being in Roswell had nothing to do with his wanting to see his home and family.

I continued walking, barely pausing long enough to shout over my shoulder, "I'm free to go, William. And we really need to get home." I patted the pocket in my dress to assure myself that General Sherman's letter was still there, then turned and resumed walking.

He raced to catch up with us, falling in step beside us. "It's my home, too, Laura, and I've offered the grounds as an encampment area. It certainly wouldn't be proper for you to be staying there with all those men without being chaperoned by a male member of your family. Besides, I wanted to be near my daughter." He ruffled her hair, ignoring her protests.

I stopped to stare at the leer on his face. "That's a bit like the fox watching the chicken coop, wouldn't you think?"

He threw back his head and laughed, the sound grating on my nerves. I continued walking with Sarah, our pace quickening as we neared our destination. My heart fell when I reached the gate. The top hinge was broken, the gate hanging drunkenly by the remaining hinge. The grass grew high around the post, and a tiny green lizard poked its head out from the base. We walked through the gate, noticing the weeds pushing up through the dirt drive. Sarah let go of my hand and began running. I dropped my bag and followed her, grabbing her hand and running with her.

My breath caught in my throat when I saw the chimney rise into view as we crossed the bend in the drive. As the entire house loomed into view, I began to shout. I shouted people's names: Julia, Willie, Sukie, Zeke. But the shutterless house stood silent, its windows vacant.

I barely noticed the peeling paint and missing floorboards on the porch as we climbed the stairs and turned the doorknob. It opened without resistance, and hot, dusty air blew over me. I stepped into the empty hall and stood in the stillness, letting the familiarity settle around me. A slight breeze from the open door danced around me, making the crystal chandelier tinkle a greeting. We had come home.

Sarah darted in and out of rooms, slamming doors and shouting names. I walked around the house more slowly, my fingers making crevasses in the dust heaped atop the furniture. Besides the dust and dirt, everything seemed intact. I collapsed onto the piano bench and ran my fingers across the keys. I wept with joy as I banged out a familiar tune on the off-key piano, my only audience Sarah and the mice and insects that had been inhabiting the house in our absence.

I retrieved my carpetbag from the end of the drive and soon settled down to practical matters. We had no food. The kitchen garden had long since been taken over by weeds, the root cellar stripped clean. We would have to return to camp and beg for our dinner.

At the sound of a horse's hooves, I stepped outside to peer at the sun-speckled lawn, squinting into the brightness to see who approached. I stayed in the shade of the porch until William drew nearer. Clouds of red dust told me more soldiers were on their way.

He doffed his hat as he stopped in front of me. "Laura. How kind of you to offer your home to us, the conquering army. I apologize for imposing on your hospitality at such short notice." He swiped at the sweat dripping off his forehead. "A few of my troops will be camping out in the yard."

Sarah came out and stood next to me, her hand clutching my skirt, tilting her head at the man she called her father as if she no longer recognized him. I leaned against a pillar, my arms crossed in front of me, and watched the soldiers march toward us on the drive. "I don't know what kind of hospitality you're looking for, but you won't find it here. The house is empty of all food, and the garden is dead. Even if there were food"—I couldn't resist a small smile—"I don't cook."

William sent me a brief glance before sliding from his horse. "Not to worry, Laura. We've brought enough provisions, and I'm sure one of the men can do the cooking."

He walked up the steps toward me. I stepped back, giving him a wide berth to walk past us and into my house.

We soon settled into a familiar routine. Happily, mealtime was the only occasion I was forced to endure William's company. The rest of the time I spent in my room or in the library, reading to Sarah. We also took long walks in the woods and checked on Zeke's deserted cabin. I wrote to Julia in Valdosta, letting her know of my return with Sarah, and I waited each day for her reply.

I didn't have the heart to play the piano again, remembering happier times with Stuart. And I made sure my door was bolted every night, knowing that William was in the house and watching me the way a cat would a mouse. Mostly, I bided my time, knowing September quickly approached.

The second week after my return, the nights turned suddenly cool, offering a brief respite from the sticky heat of the day. I threw my windows open wide, allowing the moonlight to illuminate the room, and drifted to sleep listening to the cicadas and other night creatures.

The hand over my mouth startled me, and my eyes flew open to stare at the dark form hovering over me.

"I'll move my hand if you promise me you won't scream, little sister. And if you break your promise, you'll be sorry." His other hand rested on my neck, and he applied enough pressure to make me choke. I silently nodded.

William removed his hand and sat on the side of the bed. He smelled strongly of alcohol, and his hot breath stung my eyes. "Get out of my room! What do you think you're doing?" I backed against the headboard as far as I could go.

He reached out and caressed my cheek. "Now, Laura, it should be obvious what I'm doing. Besides, I'm sure you find me a lot more attractive than General Sherman." I saw a flash of white in the darkness and could picture the leer across his face.

I bent my knees back and kicked him in the chest with both my feet, then lurched for the other side of the mattress. I became entangled in the bedclothes and tumbled to the floor. He leaned toward me. In panic, I scooted away from the bed and felt his hand grab the hem of my nightgown. My feet managed to find the floor, and with a loud tearing sound, I ran for the door.

"You bitch!" he roared, grappling to get to his feet.

I reached the door and pulled. It was locked. I turned around, my hands pressed against the door, and saw him lunge at me. I did the one thing that I remembered from a self-defense course. I raised my knee and rammed it into his crotch.

The effect was immediate. He dropped to his knees, his forehead against the floor. I turned the key and opened the door. Leaning over him, I hissed, "Get out of here. And if you ever try a stunt like that again, I will personally tell General Sherman. I would do it now except for the disgrace you would bring on this family."

He tilted his head up to me, his eyes glittering in the moonlight. "You'll pay for this, Laura. You sanctimonious little whore." He swiped at his mouth with his sleeve, his breathing ragged. "You haven't seen the last of me."

He staggered to his feet and left the room without a backward glance.

I stood in the doorway long after I heard the latch to his door click into place. I slammed my door, then raced to the windows, shutting them tightly one by one.

I didn't see William for several days. I knew that there was a flurry of activity as the Yankees worked diligently to rebuild the burned bridge. I assumed William was thus occupied, and I breathed a sigh of relief. Still, I spent most of my hours in my room or Sarah's, spending as much time with her as I could, as if my mind realized something my heart couldn't yet see. We read a lot, and sometimes I just stared out the window, thinking of Stuart whenever my mind caught me off guard.

On the evening of July fourteenth, I sat in my room after Sarah had gone to bed, watching dusk gather in the sky, one hand resting on my abdomen. Despite being nearly four months pregnant, the rise under my nightgown was hardly noticeable. The sounds from the men encamped around the house changed subtly, and I got up to look out the window. Holding the curtain aside, I peered out at the dozen or so campfires dotting the yard. In the field beyond, a colony of fireflies glowed and dimmed, glowed and dimmed in a primal mating dance. A movement by the side of the house caught my attention. Three uniformed men staggered together, one of them holding a lit torch. Their drunken laughter carried up to me, and it didn't take me long to figure out that they were heading for the smokehouse. The grass was dry and withered, and it wouldn't need much of a spark to burn everything up, including the house.

Grabbing my shawl, I unbolted the door and flung it open. I had reached the top of the steps when the front door flew open, and two men, on horseback, rode into the foyer, sabers raised, slashing at the walls and upholstered furniture. Mrs. Cudahy's voice echoed in my mind, but I brushed the thought away. There were soldiers outside with torches. I ran back to wake Sarah, then grabbed Sherman's letter and raced down the stairs and out the back door.

I left Sarah on the porch with instructions not to move but to scream if anybody came near her, then I flew across the backyard, my bare feet gripping the cool grass as I ran toward the torch. In my haste I had not grabbed a weapon. I was soon to realize my error.

I reached them just as the taller soldier was opening the door to the smokehouse, preparing to toss the torch inside. All three soldiers swayed, apparently in no condition to walk a straight line. Lunging at the soldier, I knocked him out of the way. The torch flew from his hands and landed in the brown grass several feet away.

Wrapping the letter around the chain under my nightgown,

337

I took the shawl in both hands and beat furiously at the torch and the small fire now feeding itself on the dried grass. My arms pumped at a frenzied pace, and I continued to beat the ground until only dust rose to drift out over the field.

Finished with my task, I turned my fury on the three soldiers swaying on their feet and staring at me with disbelief and anger mingled on their faces.

"What in the hell do you think you're doing? You idiots! You could have burned the whole house down—with me and my daughter in it. Combined, you have the brains of a pea!" Having no weapon, I dug my toes into the dirt and kicked it at them.

Stooping to gather up the smoldering torch and take it out of harm's way, I turned around and began to walk back to the house. I felt rather than heard the rush of air behind me.

The impact knocked me facedown in the dirt and temporarily took the breath out of me. Someone was lying on my back, and I could smell his stale whiskey breath while his rough beard stubble chafed my cheek. I felt my assailant get off me and roughly grab hold of my shoulders and flip me over onto my back. My almost-healed wound screamed in pain, but I had no time to think about it. I tried to scramble to my feet, but his hands held me down.

"Look here, boys. See what I got." His hat had fallen off in the scuffle, and sweat dripped down his forehead and cheeks.

His hands groped at my breasts, and I started fighting him in earnest. Drunk or not, the man was too strong for me and was able to pinion my hands above my head with one hand while the other one tried to reach under my skirts. Luckily, his two companions were either too drunk or too stunned at what was happening to join him in his obscene game.

Fighting panic, I struggled with renewed vigor. I opened my mouth to scream, only to have a calloused hand smother any sound. He moved his hand off my body and began to fiddle with the top of his pants. He shifted his weight and raised himself onto his knees. Seeing my chance to knock him off balance, I sat up, shoving at his chest. He fell backward.

No longer captive, I clambered to my feet and began stumbling toward the house. I hadn't gone very far when I heard the distinctive sound of a pistol cocking. I stopped and turned slowly around. He was on his knees and was unsteadily pointing his pistol at me.

"It takes a brave man to shoot an unarmed woman in the back!" I shouted with false bravado as I turned around and began walking toward the house.

An officer on horseback raced around the corner of the house, but I continued walking, not wanting to stop until I had reached the sanctuary of my room with the door bolted securely behind me.

The sound of a gun firing made me jump. I could hear the blood rushing in my head, but I forced myself to remain calm. Without turning around, I shouted over my shoulder. "You missed!" and kept walking.

The officer dismounted and ran toward me, shouting at the soldier to drop the gun. He grabbed my arm as I tried to make my way past him. "What's going on here?" he barked.

I stepped back in astonishment. I knew this face—I had seen it many times in history books. The broad forehead, dark, wavy hair and beard, the affable Scottish looks. General James B. McPherson.

I looked him squarely in the eye. "Three of your gallant soldiers just tried to set fire to my house. Failing at that simple task, they then decided that raping me would be a fun thing to do. Luckily—for me, at least—they failed at both attempts. Now, if you would be so kind as to release me, I would like to go inside. I'd appreciate it if you could keep your men under control while they are on my property."

Other soldiers had run to restrain the man who had attacked me. General McPherson examined my disheveled state, the charred shawl flung over my shoulders. "I'm sorry, ma'am, but these men have been given orders to burn this house and its surrounding buildings. The owners are not only major stockholders in the Roswell Manufacturing Company, supplying the Confederate Army, but they're also known Rebels."

I yanked my arm from his grasp. "No! That can't be! Who gave those orders?"

"I did, ma'am. And I received my information from a reliable source—Captain William Elliott on General Sherman's staff."

I began to shake. How could he do this to his own family? "That son of a bitch," I muttered under my breath.

"I beg your pardon?"

I looked back at him and shook my head. "Never mind. It's not important." My mind began to race, conjuring up possible solutions to this nightmare.

"I will need you to evacuate this house as soon as possible."

"Wait!" I felt my face crease into a wide smile. My hand groped inside my nightgown for the letter. "This is from General Sherman. Read it."

He held the wrinkled letter up in the fading light, scanning the words. He lowered it slowly. "My deepest apologies, Mrs. Elliott. I don't know how this misunderstanding could have happened. I will ensure you are protected. When my troops depart, I will leave a guard."

He handed the letter back to me, and I clutched it to my chest. "Thank you. I'm going inside now. I trust you will see to it that that man who attacked me is duly punished."

"Yes, ma'am. Again, my deepest apologies."

I started walking but turned back, thoughts of lost love heavy on my mind. If my memory of history was correct, this man had less than a week to live. "General McPherson."

He stopped, surprise registering on his face that I should know his name.

I continued. "I have a strong feeling you should write your fiancée soon. Perhaps tonight before you retire." He opened his mouth to say something, his expression quizzical, but was interrupted by shouts behind him from the man who had attacked me and who was now being restrained. I walked to the house without turning back and collected Sarah from the back porch.

The foyer was in a shambles. Feathers from chair cushions floated about the floor like snow. Deep gashes marred the wallpaper, leaving it to sag in places. But the soldiers had gone, and the house had been saved. From the bottom of the stairs, I saw an orange glow in the sky from the upstairs foyer window, and I knew somebody else's house had gone up in flames. Again, I heard Mrs. Cudahy's voice in my head, saying that no one knew why Phoenix Hall had been spared destruction. But now I did.

My legs shook as I climbed the stairs to Sarah's room and put her to bed. She soon fell sound asleep, untouched by the nightmares of the world around her. I stared at her sleeping face, this child who was mine but not mine. This was her home, her time, her people. How could I take her with me? How could I leave her?

I bolted the door and crawled under the covers with Sarah. I listened to her soft breathing and then fell asleep.

Partir, c'est mourir un peu.

French proverb

Chapter Twenty-eight

Less than a week later, the soldiers were gone, creeping ever southward toward the prize of Atlanta. The end was near. General McPherson was true to his word and left a guard and plenty of food to get Sarah and me through the next several months. He also reluctantly mentioned that William had disappeared, probably deserting the army. I hoped that he had fled west and that I would never see him again.

I was out by the well, drawing water, when I heard the unmistakable sound of wagon wheels. I had grown accustomed to this sound, as refugees continued to move out from

Atlanta and seek shelter from the invading army in the Georgia countryside. But this wagon was approaching the house, coming to a halt on the front drive.

Dropping the bucket, I walked quickly to the side of the house to see who my visitors might be and wondering why I hadn't heard the guard.

Turning the corner, I spotted the guard sitting on the front steps, busily munching on hardtack and seemingly oblivious to the wagon that had pulled up.

I opened my mouth to speak when I heard my name. I stopped in disbelief as Julia and Zeke appeared from the other side of the wagon.

"Zeke! Julia!" I ran to them, my arms outstretched.

Sarah bounded out the front door, almost flying as she threw herself into Julia's arms. "Mama!" she shouted. Their heads bent together, and they cried and laughed at the same time. I turned to Zeke, unable to watch the reunion between mother and daughter.

He embraced me, and it felt good to have somebody's arms around me again. I wept on his shoulder as he stroked my hair.

"You are leaving us?"

I nodded, wiping my eyes with my sleeve.

Julia stilled, her arm around Sarah. "Please, Laura. Don't."

I shook my head. "I can't stay Julia. I'm going to have a baby."

Julia gave a shriek of delight and threw her arms around me, catching me off guard. "Zeke told me you had married Stuart. I'm so delighted for you. Now there's even one more reason for you to stay."

Tears, which always seemed near the surface every time I thought of Stuart and of leaving this place, spilled down my face. I looked at Julia. "I have to go back. I won't survive childbirth if I remain. Besides, Stuart doesn't think the baby's his."

Zeke and Julia both wore stunned expressions. "It's a long story, but don't worry, it's just that—a story. Suffice it to say that William planted the seeds of doubt in Stuart's mind."

Julia grabbed my arm. "You've seen William?"

I looked into her warm brown eyes and knew she could handle the truth. "Yes, Julia, I have. And Pamela, too." I saw the panic in her face. I threw my arms around her and Zeke again. "Why don't we go inside and have some coffee—the real stuff—and I'll tell you all about it."

We talked long into the afternoon, until the low rays of the sun faded into dusk. Sarah sat at Julia's feet, never letting go of Julia's skirts, as if she were afraid they would be separated again. Eventually, the child fell asleep, and I was able to speak more freely about what had happened in the months since we had seen each other.

As darkness grew, Zeke lit the lamps while Julia and I prepared dinner. Julia had listened in silence as I told her about Pamela's death. She had not thrown accusations at me, but I still needed her forgiveness.

I broached the subject amidst the clatter of china and silverware. "Julia, I'm sorry for Pamela's death. I didn't mean to kill her. It just happened that way. And I can't say that it wasn't for the best."

She let the remaining silverware in her hand drop onto the mahogany table and walked over to me. "I owe you so much. I'm not one to question your motives. You have shown incredible caring and strength and courage, and I shall always be grateful for that." Her hand swept the hair off my forehead in a maternal gesture. "You rescued Sarah and saved my house—there is nothing to forgive. You did what few of us would have had the courage to do." I felt an inner peace as she reached for my hands and squeezed them. We returned to our chores and didn't speak of it again.

Zeke and Julia stayed with me through the long days of August. Julia and I talked of babies while Zeke whittled or just sat in comfortable silence next to us. I half hoped for word from Stuart, but none came, and I buried my hope deep inside me.

On the last day of the month, I put Sarah to bed, and the three of us sat on the front porch watching the fireflies dance across the lawn. Julia told me that Eliza Smith and many of our Roswell neighbors had also refugeed in Valdosta, making

343

the desertion of their homes a bit easier. Charles had joined the Roswell Battalion and hadn't been heard from since. I told them a little about the twentieth century. Except for washing machines and air conditioners, they weren't too impressed. I somehow agreed with their sentiments. As we talked, my fingers clutched the key around my neck, thinking of things to come.

"Julia, I've been doing a lot of thinking. When this war is over, times will be really tough." I continued rocking, my toes tapping lightly on the floorboards. "I want to try to make things easier for you." I took a deep breath, trying to decide where to start. "First, forget about cotton. Try peanuts instead. You may have to buy some land farther south for a better growing area, but peanuts should make a profitable crop. Peaches, too."

She looked at me as if I had lost my mind. "Peanuts?"

"Yeah, peanuts. You know—goober peas. Haven't you ever heard of peanut butter?"

She shook her head.

"Well, I'll tell you about that later." I slapped at a mosquito on my forearm. "But you also need to find a man in Atlanta by the name of Asa Candler. In about twenty years he's going to get a patent for a non-alcoholic drink that will make him and all his investors millionaires. Invest everything you can afford with him. You won't regret it."

"Asa Candler, peanuts, and peaches," she murmured. "I'll remember that."

"Good," I said, reaching for her hand. "I'll feel better knowing you're all taken care of."

I didn't let go of her hand, nor did I look at her. "I've decided not to take Sarah."

She continued rocking, and I felt her eyes on me. "I know."

I turned to face her. "How did you know?"

With a soft smile, she said, "Because she still calls you Aunt Laura—you've never told her the truth. And besides"—she squeezed my hand tightly—"you love her."

"I do." Tears sprang from my eyes, but I did nothing to

wipe them away. "I can't believe, after all I've been through to find her, that I can't bring her home."

Julia left her chair and knelt before mine. "Come back, then, Laura. Come back after the baby's born. None of us want you to leave."

I shook my head. "But Stuart doesn't want me."

"Yes, Laura, he does. I don't know what went on between you two, but whatever he said to make you believe that he didn't want you was a lie. He must have been hurt or confused, but I know the man loves you." She placed both her hands over mine. "Come back, Laura. We all want you back."

I pulled my hands away, unable to look at her, remembering the hateful words Stuart had said. "No. I can't."

She stood and retreated to her rocker.

I looked out at the red dirt of the drive, committing it all to memory. "Take care of Sarah. Don't let her forget her Aunt Laura."

"I won't ever let her forget you. None of us will."

We continued rocking in silence, until dark descended and the crickets began to cry.

The morning of September first dawned gray and misty. Fat clouds hovered in the sky all day, finally breaking out into huge thunderhead by late afternoon. It had been decided that Zeke would accompany me back to Moon Mountain, so I said my farewells to Julia and Sarah at Phoenix Hall.

"Good-bye, Sarah." I knelt, and she walked into the circle of my arms. I hugged her to me for the last time, transferring to her all my love and hopes for the child I had lost, and found, and then given up. "You keep up your piano practicing, okay? And don't fight so much with your brother."

She sniffled into my shoulder. "All right." She pushed herself away. "I have something for you."

She handed me a sprig of greenery, the silvery-gray leaves almost glowing in the dim light of the day. "It's rosemary— for remembrance. I don't want you to forget me."

I took it from her reverently. "I'll treasure it always—not that I'll need it to remember you." I hugged her again, feeling one more time the solidness of her small body next to mine.

I then hugged Julia, who was dabbing at her eyes with a handkerchief. "What shall I tell Stuart?"

I felt a tremor at my temples. My hurt and anger were still very much alive. "Don't tell him anything. Let him always wonder what happened to me."

"I can't do that, Laura. It would be too cruel. He does love you, you know."

"He couldn't. He so easily believed the worst of me. Just tell him . . . tell him that I've gone back home."

Her fine eyebrows knit together in a frown. "I'll try, Laura. But I think he deserves the truth." She gave me another tight hug. "Don't forget your key. I promise to write everything down and leave it in the secret compartment. I'll let you know about the peanuts, all right?"

"You do that," I said, my voice cracking. With one last good-bye, I turned away and began the long walk to Moon Mountain with Zeke.

Julia called out to me. "Please, Laura, do try to come back. You belong here."

I pretended not to hear and continued walking.

By the time we reached the base of the mountain, the skies had unleashed their fury. Electrical bursts kept the heavens in constant illumination while the thunder rolled ceaselessly. We could see no comet or moon, but I felt the tingling on my skin reminding me of the time before. They were up there, all right, working their magic and pulling at me.

Then, mixed in with the roll of thunder, I heard heavy hoof-beats. I turned my ear toward the sound, then imagined I heard my name shouted. A flash of lightning opened up the sky and the heavens, making all around us as bright as day. I saw Endy, and Stuart astride him. Stuart slipped off the horse and came to me without a word.

We stood in the rain, watching the play of light on each other's face.

I turned from him, but his hand on my arm pulled me back. He had to almost shout to be heard over the din of the storm.

"I was a fool, Laura. William always brings out the worst in me—that's my only excuse."

My skin tingled, and I knew I didn't have much time. "Why are you here?"

He moved closer to me. "To ask your forgiveness." His hand tightened on my arm. "I'm risking being shot as a deserter. The least you can do is forgive me." He reached out to touch my cheek, and I put my hand over his. "I love you Laura—I'll never stop."

I hesitated for a moment, feeling the changing atmosphere around me. There was no more time for anger between us. I fell into his arms, the harsh rain cleansing us, Stuart's lips bruising mine. His hands swept down my sides, then felt the rising mound of my abdomen. The child kicked, and Stuart jerked, his eyes wide with amazement. I brought his lips back down to mine, pushing my body into his, the proof of our union guarded between us. I wanted him then with a fervor I had never known. I wanted him to lie with me on the sodden leaves, to kiss my bare skin in the rain, and move inside me until I screamed from the pleasure of it.

A crash of thunder rolled high above us, and Endy screamed, his front hooves pawing the air. Zeke moved to stand before us. "It's time, Laura."

I smelled gardenias again and quickly reached out to Stuart. He grasped for my hand, but his fingers seemed to pass through mine.

Zeke held up a hand, the rain pouring over him and plastering his long hair to his head, like two wet snakes on either side of his face. He stared straight at me, unblinking. "May the spirits of the ancient Shadow Warriors be with you, Laura, in all your travels."

I opened my lips to speak to Stuart, but the rain flooded my mouth, making me choke. The aura around me became electric, and I could almost see the burned ions splitting the air in front of me. Bubbles of air burst in my head, and I felt myself sink to the rain-soaked earth. Stuart's voice reverberated in my mind, but I could no longer tell where it was coming from.

"Laura—don't go! I love you—please don't go!"

I remember shouting Stuart's name, and then nothing more.

I awoke in a hospital. Not the dirty mayhem of a field hospital in the middle of a Civil War battlefield, but an antiseptic white world of stainless steel and hushed voices.

I blinked suddenly and tried to sit up in the bed.

"John! She's awake!"

I recognized my mother's voice as I focused my eyes on my parents by the side of the bed.

The door swung open, and a nurse rushed in. "Has she come to?"

I stared at her and nodded. She backed her way out of the door, calling for a doctor.

"Laura? Do you know who I am?"

I stared into my mother's familiar face, and I reached for it. "Oh, Mom. Of course."

Her tears drenched my cheek as she gathered me to her. She smelled of Colgate and Youth Dew, and I clung to her silk blouse. "Laura, what happened to you? Where have you been?"

I had no desire to spend countless hours with therapists questioning my sanity. I blurted out the first thing that came to me. "I don't remember."

My mother leaned over me and whispered, "But you're five months pregnant, Laura. Surely you remember something?"

I shook my head, and my father, who had been hovering in the background, came to the other side of the bed.

He held my hand, his palm warm and rough. "Laura, it doesn't matter to us. You're here now, and we'll stand by you. We'll be ready to listen when you're ready to tell us."

I nodded, not sure if they'd ever be ready to hear the truth.

"I had something in my hand—a sprig of rosemary. Where is it?"

My parents glanced at each other, and my mother spoke. "We wondered what that was. We had it put with your personal effects—including an unusual ring we've never seen before. But it must be an antique, because it looks very old."

"It is," I said, and then offered nothing more.

I spent the first week at my parents' house, being coddled and fed. My mother scheduled an appointment with an obstetrician. He must have been coached beforehand because he didn't mention anything about the baby's father. He poked and prodded and pronounced me fit, if a bit undernourished. He sent me home with instructions for my mother to put some weight on my bones.

My parents had held on to Phoenix Hall the fourteen months I was gone, not willing to accept the fact that I might never come back. It still stood, a little bedraggled and with dust covers over the furniture, but glorious in my eyes. Amidst protests from my parents, I quickly moved back into the house that held so many memories for me.

My mother hired a housekeeper, Mrs. Beckner, to cook and clean for me and, I'm sure, report back to her if I wasn't taking care of myself. My father brought in suitcases of maternity clothes they had bought for me and set them inside the foyer. I tentatively walked up the steps and hovered in the doorway.

I took a deep breath and walked in. I examined the polished banister, the gleaming wood floors, the electrified chandelier. I heard the central air shut off and the hall clock steadily marking off the minutes. The piano stood in its same spot in the parlor, the veneer still missing from the G key. I smiled, remembering how it had happened. I half expected to turn and see Stuart standing behind me, his blue eyes smiling. I slammed a hand down on the keys, making my father jump.

"What's wrong, Laura?" He rushed to my side, his hands firmly on my upper arms.

"Nothing, Daddy. Nothing that can be fixed."

He put my head down on his chest and patted my back. "In time, sweetheart. In time."

Mrs. Beckner left at five o'clock, leaving me blissfully alone to enjoy the long shadows creeping along the wood floors. I resisted turning on the electric lights, finding their glare too bright, as if they might illuminate things in the corners I did not wish to see. So I walked slowly through the darkened house, imagining I could hear the brush of long skirts against the wooden floors, and listening for a footfall.

I awakened in the middle of the night with a furious kicking in my womb. I sat up and placed a hand on my swollen belly and felt the roil of tiny limbs pressing at me from inside.

"Mama's here, little one. You're not alone."

My voice seemed to calm the baby, for the kicking ceased. I looked across the moonlit room, gazing at the familiar furniture. It was then that I noticed the strong scent of lavender. I sat up straight in the bed, wondering where the smell was coming from. The windows were all shut, and I could hear the humming of the air conditioner. I slid from the bed to look out onto the front lawn. My throat went dry when I realized there was no moon. The glow was coming from inside my room.

I turned, my back against the window, and heard the distinct sound of rustling skirts. The glow began to shrink and take on the vague form of a person. It undulated with small light bursts until it bore an unmistakable resemblance to a woman wearing an old-fashioned long dress.

"Julia," I said, my voice barely a whisper. The temperature had dropped by at least fifteen degrees, and I began to shiver despite the sweat trickling down my spine.

She stood at the foot of the bed, and I saw her smile. She then turned and, with a glowing hand, pointed to the armoire.

I left the window, no longer afraid, and stood next to her.

"What, Julia? What are you trying to tell me?" The smell of lavender was stronger now, as if I were in a field full of it.

She looked directly at me, then pointed at my chest. My fingers flew to my neck, and I realized the chain holding the key was gone. And I suddenly knew what she was trying to tell me.

"The secret drawer?" I whispered.

She nodded. I reached out to touch her, but my fingers grasped only cold, empty air. The apparition faded into nothingness, and I could almost hear a whispered good-bye as darkness closed in on the room.

I flipped on every light switch in the house as I raced downstairs to the foyer table. I remembered my mother putting my few personal effects in the drawer when I moved back in. With shaking fingers, I pulled open the drawer. Light from the chandelier glinted off the metal key. Gingerly, I picked it up, then clasped it tightly in my palm.

As I began to slide the drawer back into place, the corner of a picture frame caught my attention. I lifted the picture from the drawer and stared at it. It was undoubtedly the picture Mathew Brady had taken of me on my journey to Dalton with Matt. With trembling hands, I shut the drawer and, clutching both the picture and the key, raced back up the stairs.

I threw open the doors of the armoire, sneezing at the faint aroma of cedar mixed with lavender. I knelt in front of the massive piece of furniture, and my fingers, like spiders, crept along the inside wall until I felt the outline of a drawer in the false back.

The overhead light barely reached to the back of the cabinet, and I had to use my sense of touch to open the lock with the key. I grew frustrated, feeling the key slip at the outside of the keyhole. Finally I felt the key slide home. I turned it and heard a click. Pulling on the key, I heard wood slide out. I grabbed the entire drawer and lifted it out into the light.

Old papers, their edges yellowed and ragged with age, were inside the narrow drawer, rolled together to allow them to fit. I spread them on the bed, using various items from my dressing table to hold the pages flat.

Many of the documents appeared to have been removed from ledger books. My eyes widened as I stared at the numbers reflecting dividends from the Coca-Cola Company. The handwriting wasn't Julia's. Instead of her small, flowery style, this was much tighter and bolder. I didn't believe I had seen it before. But I smiled to myself, realizing Julia had heeded my advice and had indeed invested in Asa Candler's fledgling company.

There were more documents pertaining to peach orchards and peanut production and even a recipe for peanut butter. I sat back for a moment to rub my eyes. Julia had obviously prepared this drawer with meticulous care to let me know what

had become of them all. It struck me then that they were all
dead now—even my Annie. I hastily wiped away my tears,
not wanting the wetness to smudge the ink on the pages. The
baby kicked again, and I was once more reminded of the endless cycle of life and death. It was through this child that these
people I loved could live again. I picked up another page,
unscrolled it, and began to read.

August 21, 1867
My Dearest Sister,
   *It has been three years now since we last saw you, and
a day does not go by that we do not think of you or wish
that you were here.*
   *You would be so proud of the children. Willie and
Sarah continue to grow strong and sturdy—due mostly,
I am quite sure, to their great fondness for peanut butter.
Sarah promises to be a great beauty, although most of
the boys here are a bit humbled by her brains and wit.*
   *As you can see by the enclosed papers, we are surviv-
ing, thanks to you. It is still a bit of a struggle, because
nobody has anything, much less any capital to invest in
a new farming venture. Matt Kimball's gold has helped
considerably. But we are managing, and the future of our
new ventures seems most promising.*
   *We have not heard from William. I assume he is either
dead or in the western territories. Either way, I have no
husband, and my children have no father. But I am not
sure if it isn't for the best.*
   *Stuart returned home from the war thin but otherwise
healthy in body—but not in spirit. It is heartbreaking to
see him, Laura. On the night you disappeared, we told
him the truth. I know you didn't want that, but we hadn't
any choice. He wanted to know if you planned to return,
and once we told him no, he stopped asking about you.
But I know you are never far from his thoughts. His eyes
are so sad. Fighting in this war nearly killed him, and I
almost think he wishes it had. He moves about his daily
business, but his heart isn't in it. He loves you desper-*

ately, Laura, and if he could see you but once again, I know that the wonderful spirit of him would return.

Laura, I also told him about the armoire, and he asked if I might include a letter from him. It is contained herewith. I have not read it, as I am sure the private matters between husband and wife should remain private. I hope it somehow heals your heart.

I cannot bear to think that we may never lay eyes on you again. You will forever remain in our hearts. May God go with you, Laura, wherever you may be.

> *With great affection,*
> *Your sister, Julia*

A tear dripped on the bottom right corner, and I hastily brushed it aside with the sleeve of my nightgown. I turned back to the drawer to find Stuart's letter. After sorting through several pages, I saw the familiar handwriting, and my heart leapt. I unrolled it carefully and anchored the corners.

April 28, 1867
Dearest Wife,

How much longer am I expected to live through this torture of not knowing where you are? Julia has told me why you had to leave, but I know that I am solely to blame for your reluctance to return. I begged for your forgiveness on the night you left, and I am begging for it now.

I have no idea how the mechanism of the thing that took you away works, but because you haven't returned to us, I can only assume that you have no desire to see me again—and for this I cannot blame you. You think that I believed the worst of you, but I also knew in my heart that you would never betray me. It was only my stupid pride. And for that, I have lost the most precious thing in the world.

How is our child? I don't even know if I have a son or a daughter. If it is a daughter, I hope she is like you— full of fire and spirit. And if it is a son, I hope he will grow strong and proud and be there to watch over his mother, since his father cannot.

Come home to me, Laura. I will wait for you until the end of time and even beyond, for my love for you is death-less.

With all my love,
Stuart

I lay down on the bed and stared up at the ceiling fan and its ceaseless rotation. The tears rolled down from the corners of my eyes to my ears and hair, saturating the sheets beneath my head. I could never forgive myself if he had gone to his grave believing I had stopped loving him.

I rolled up all the documents and put them back in the drawer. Except for Stuart's letter. I held it close to my chest and fell asleep, clutching it between my arms and our baby.

When I finally awoke the next morning, Mrs. Beckner was knocking on my door with a steaming tray of eggs, bacon, and homemade biscuits. She poked her gray head through the doorway, her expression concerned as I saw her register my puffy eyes and the dark circles beneath them.

"Bad night, was it?" She clucked her tongue like a mother goose. "I remember being pregnant with my last child."

She continued chattering as she bustled about the room, opening curtains and placing my tray in front of me. As I smoothed the blanket down on either side of me, my hand touched something hard and cold. It was the picture frame. I stared at the image for a minute and then reached for the phone to call information.

She was the only Margaret Ann Cudahy listed. Her address was on West Paces Ferry Road in a posh section of Buckhead.

I introduced myself as Laura Truitt, and she recognized my name immediately. She didn't seem in the least surprised that I had called.

"Mrs. Cudahy, I hope you don't find these questions too personal, but I've been trying to do a bit of history on this house and was hoping you might be able to help me."

"I'd love to help you, dear. Ask away." I heard the sound

of opera music playing from a stereo in the background.

"All right. Are you by any chance related to the Elliott family?"

She chuckled into the mouthpiece. "My maiden name was Elliott. Until you, Elliotts have owned Phoenix Hall since it was built."

My hand shook a little as I held the phone. "And your great-grandmother, the one who gave you the picture of the woman who looked like me—what was her name?"

"Oh, these are too easy, Laura. You should find her name very simple to remember, since you have the same first name. Her name was Laura Elliott."

I had to clutch the phone with both hands, I was shaking so hard. "I see," I whispered. "And do you happen to remember your great-grandfather's name?"

"I certainly do. It was Stuart. Stuart Elliott. But I don't remember what his middle name was."

"Couper," I choked into the phone.

"Yes, dear, I do believe that was it. As a matter of fact, were you aware that Stuart and Laura's son is a direct ancestor of our current president?"

I was finding it very difficult to talk. "Mrs. Cudahy, thank you so much for your information. But I'm not feeling well at the moment, and I think I'll need to call you back later."

I dropped the phone and lay on my bed for what seemed like hours, listening to the ceiling fan whir and the incessant beeping of the phone off the hook. The pink elephant that had been sitting in the middle of my room since the day I returned finally stared me in the eye. This was my house, but it wasn't my home. My home was with my husband and the people who loved me. This realization nearly strangled my mind, bringing with it as much anticipation as it did apprehension. My travels through time were not yet over.

"Journeys end in lovers meeting."
William Shakespeare

Epilogue

My son Couper was born on a cold January morning in nine-teen ninety-five. He came into the world kicking and scream-ing, convincing me that he was ready for whatever life would bring him. I knew without looking that he would carry the identical birthmark on his forearm—like his mother and sister. The doctor asked me if I wanted it removed. I shook my head fiercely and told the doctor it was part of my son's heritage and that he would keep it for life.

I spent most of his first two years preparing. I diligently took Couper to the pediatrician for his checkups and vacci-nations and spent a good portion of my afternoons in the li-brary in the astronomy section charting the different comets in their orbital time periods until I found the right one.

I prepared my parents as best I could, telling them that my son and I would be going on a long trip and they should not worry about us. They were instructed to keep Phoenix Hall in good shape in readiness for our return. Just in case.

By the autumn of nineteen ninety-eight, I was ready. I left Sarah's sprig of rosemary on the dressing table in my room for my mother. I carried with me two bottles of children's Tylenol and vitamins and a recent edition of the *Atlanta Journal-Constitution*. But that was all. Everything else I needed was there, waiting for me on the other side of time.

* * *

356

We found Stuart outside the barn, brushing Endy's gleaming dark coat. We stood in the shadow of an old oak tree, our feet crunching on fallen acorns. The horse whinnied in greeting, and I put a finger to my lips. The sound of children's laughter and a dog barking drifted to us on the crisp air, and I closed my eyes for a moment, feeling the tug of the wind on my hair and smelling a wood fire burning in the distance. I shivered with the cold seeping through my cotton sweater and jeans.

Stuart didn't look up but bent over the horse's legs, examining the shoes. The brisk wind made Stuart's hair dance and scattered leaves about our feet. I stared at the mass of dark hair, realizing how much like Couper's it was.

Couper slid down off my back and stood beside me. He looked up at me with piercing blue eyes, and nodded. Slowly, he walked toward Stuart and stood directly behind him. My heart skipped a beat as I saw them together for the first time, father and son. I was struck again by the similarities in their physical appearance.

Stuart picked up a bucket of water and began emptying it into the grass.

"Excuse me." Couper's little face looked up at Stuart as Stuart swung around, splashing his boots and pants with the water.

I stepped back behind the tree, only leaning out enough to see.

Not expecting to find anybody behind him, Stuart nearly tripped over the little boy. He caught himself and looked at the child, his brows knitted tightly. "Who are you?"

"I'm Couper." He peered out from around Stuart's legs. "Is that your horsey?"

Stuart's eyebrows lifted. "Couper?"

"Yeah. Can I pet your horsey?"

Stuart knelt in front of the child, a hand on each shoulder. "Couper, who are you?"

He wouldn't take his eyes off the big black horse. "I told you. I'm Couper. Now can I pet your horsey?"

Stuart lifted him up in his arms and approached Endy. "Be

very gentle. You can pat him right here," he said, indicating the mane blowing in the breeze.

Stuart moved his head back to get a better view of Couper's face. "Couper, where's your mother and father?"

Couper's pudgy fingers were busily entwining themselves in the thick mane of the horse. He tilted his head as if he didn't quite understand the question. "My mommy's over there." He stuck out a sturdy arm in the direction of the oak tree.

I stepped out from my hiding place as Stuart turned, his son in his arms. I saw the color drain from his face, and then he started to shake.

I rushed forward to take Couper, afraid Stuart might drop him. But Stuart shook his head, clutching the child tightly.

"Laura." His voice was barely more than a whisper.

"Hello, Stuart. It's been a while." My voice was barely stronger than his.

His eyes widened, but I saw a ghost of a smile around his pale lips. "Yes, you could certainly say that." He looked at Couper, and his expression changed suddenly. It was as if he were looking in a mirror for the first time. "Are you this handsome young man's mother?"

I gave a small laugh. "Yes, I am. Stuart, I'd like you to meet your son, Stuart Couper Elliott, Junior."

Stuart glanced from me to Couper and back. His face was still handsome, but there were deep creases in his cheeks that hadn't been there before. "I . . . I can't believe this."

I walked closer to him, my eyes searching his. "Believe it. We're here to stay."

He opened his free arm to me, and I walked into his embrace, smelling the autumn air in his clothes and feeling the beloved scratchiness of his cheek.

Couper squealed, his active three-year-old body rebelling at being hugged so tightly. "Hey, stop! You're mushing me!"

Stuart squeezed us even harder as I felt his tears on my head.

The wind picked up momentum, whipping my hair around

my husband and my son and sending the fallen leaves airborne once again in the direction of the beautiful white house. It stood, strong and silent, beckoning me. The sun made shadows of the front columns on the lawn, like arms welcoming me back.

I had come home.

AN ORIGINAL SIN NINA BANGS

Fortune MacDonald listens to women's fantasies on a daily basis as she takes their orders for customized men. In a time when the male species is extinct, she is a valued man-maker. So when she awakes to find herself sharing a bed with the most lifelike, virile man she has ever laid eyes or hands on, she lets her gaze inventory his assets. From his long dark hair, to his knife-edged cheekbones, to his broad shoulders, to his jutting—well, all in the name of research, right?—it doesn't take an expert any time at all to realize that he is the genuine article, a bona fide man. And when Leith Campbell takes her in his arms, she knows real passion for the first time . . . but has she found true love?

___52324-8 $5.99 US/$6.99 CAN

The Sorcerer's Lady

Debra Dier

Victorian debutante Laura Sullivan can't believe her eyes. Aunt Sophie's ancient spell has conjured up the man of Laura's dreams—and deposited a half-naked barbarian in the library of her Boston home. With his bare chest and sheathed broadsword, the golden giant is a tempting study in Viking maleness, but hardly the proper blue blood Laura is supposed to marry. An accomplished sorcerer, Connor has traveled through the ages to reach his soul mate, the bewitching woman who captured his heart. But Beacon Hill isn't ninth-century Ireland, and Connor's powers are useless if he can't convince Laura that love is stronger than magic and that she is destined to become the sorcerer's lady.

___52305-1 $5.50 US/$6.50 CAN

Dorchester Publishing Co., Inc.
P.O. Box 6640
Wayne, PA 19087-8640

Please add $1.75 for shipping and handling for the first book and $.50 for each book thereafter. NY, NYC, and PA residents, please add appropriate sales tax. No cash, stamps, or C.O.D.s. All orders shipped within 6 weeks via postal service book rate. Canadian orders require $2.00 extra postage and must be paid in U.S. dollars through a U.S. banking facility.

Name_____
Address_____
City_____ State_____ Zip_____
I have enclosed $_____ in payment for the checked book(s).
Payment __must__ accompany all orders. ❑ Please send a free catalog.
CHECK OUT OUR WEBSITE! www.dorchesterpub.com

THE OUTLAW VIKING

SANDRA HILL

As tall and striking as the Valkyries of legend, Dr. Rain Jordan is proud of her Norse ancestors despite their warlike ways. But she can't believe her eyes when a blow to the head transports her to a nightmarish battlefield and she has to save the barbarian of her dreams. If Selik isn't careful, the stunning siren is sure to capture his heart and make a warrior of love out of the outlaw Viking.

___52273-X $5.50 US/$6.50 CAN

Dorchester Publishing Co., Inc.
P.O. Box 6640
Wayne, PA 19087-8640

Please add $1.75 for shipping and handling for the first book and $.50 for each book thereafter. NY, NYC, and PA residents, please add appropriate sales tax. No cash, stamps, or C.O.D.s. All orders shipped within 6 weeks via postal service book rate. Canadian orders require $2.00 extra postage and must be paid in U.S. dollars through a U.S. banking facility.

Name_____

Address_____

City_____State_____Zip_____

I have enclosed $_____ in payment for the checked book(s).

Payment <u>must</u> accompany all orders. ❑ Please send a free catalog.

CHECK OUT OUR WEBSITE! www.dorchesterpub.com

SUSAN GRANT
ONCE A PIRATE

Andrew Spencer sails the seas seeking revenge, and there are very few merchants' treasures that he hasn't given a jolly rogering. But on this particular voyage, he finds his task harder than usual. As a brown-eyed beauty is hoisted from the waves, he finds his pirate's soul plundered from without and a fiery need conjured up from within.

The freak storm that causes her plane to go down in the Atlantic sends fighter pilot Carly Callahan's life spinning out of control as well. Pulled from the freezing ocean, she finds herself in the hot embrace of an Adonis. But his eyes are cold and hard, and the man's burning lips swear she is someone else before he claims her as his own. Carly knows she has one chance to go home, but there is so much to see and feel here— and the best is yet to come.

___52364-7 $4.99 US/$5.99 CAN

DESPERADO
SANDRA HILL

Major Helen Prescott has always played by the rules. That's why Rafe Santiago nicknamed her "Prissy" at the military academy years before. Rafe's teasing made her life miserable back then, and with his irresistible good looks, he is the man responsible for her one momentary lapse in self control. When a routine skydive goes awry, the two parachute straight into the 1850 California Gold Rush. Mistaken for a notorious bandit and his infamously sensuous mistress, they find themselves on the wrong side of the law. In a time and place where rules have no meaning, Helen finds Rafe's hard, bronzed body strangely comforting, and his piercing blue eyes leave her all too willing to share his bedroll. Suddenly, his teasing remarks make her feel all woman, and she is ready to throw caution to the wind if she can spend every night in the arms of her very own desperado.

_52182-2 $5.99 US/$6.99 CAN

Linda Jones
On A Wicked Wind

Hurled into the Caribbean and swept back in time, Sabrina Steele finds herself abruptly aroused in the arms of the dashing pirate captain Antonio Rafael de Zamora. There, on his tropical island, Rafael teaches her to crest the waves of passion and sail the seas of ecstasy. But the handsome rogue has a tortured past, and in order to consummate a love that called her through time, the headstrong beauty seeks to uncover the pirate's true buried treasure—his heart.

___52251-9 $5.99 US/$6.99 CAN

Dorchester Publishing Co., Inc.
P.O. Box 6640
Wayne, PA 19087-8640

Please add $1.75 for shipping and handling for the first book and $.50 for each book thereafter. NY, NYC, and PA residents, please add appropriate sales tax. No cash, stamps, or C.O.D.s. All orders shipped within 6 weeks via postal service book rate. Canadian orders require $2.00 extra postage and must be paid in U.S. dollars through a U.S. banking facility.

Name_____
Address_____
City_____State_____Zip_____
I have enclosed $_____ in payment for the checked book(s).
Payment <u>must</u> accompany all orders. ☐ Please send a free catalog.

A Double-Edged Blade

JULIE MOFFETT

Lovely British agent Faith Worthington is sent on a mission to expose a ruthless IRA terrorist. But a bullet to the thigh knocks her back to seventeenth-century Ireland . . . and into the arms of rebel leader Miles O'Bruaidar. Known as the Irish Lion, Miles immediately suspects the modern-day beauty of being a spy. He takes Faith as his hostage, only to discover her feminine wiles are incredibly alluring. But desperate to return to the future, Faith has no time for love—at least not from a mutton-feasting, ale-quaffing brute like Miles. Yet with each passing day—and each fiery kiss—Faith's defenses weaken. Torn between returning to her own time and staying with the charming rogue, Faith knows her heart has been pierced to the quick, but she wonders if their love will always be a double-edged blade.

___52369-8 $5.50 US/$6.50 CAN

Dorchester Publishing Co., Inc.
P.O. Box 6640
Wayne, PA 19087-8640